THE BRIDGE
TO
INFINITY

Bruce Cathie

The Lost Science Series:
The Anti-Gravity Handbook edited by David Hatcher Childress
Anti-Gravity & the World Grid edited by David Hatcher Childress
Anti-Gravity & the Unified Field edited by David Hatcher Childress
The Free-Energy Device Handbook edited by David Hatcher Childress
The Cosmic Conspiracy by Stan Deyo
The Energy Grid by Bruce Cathie
The Bridge To Infinity by Bruce Cathie
The Harmonic Conquest of Space by Bruce Cathie
Vimana Aircraft of Ancient India & Atlantis edited by David H. Childress
Tapping the Zero Point Energy by Moray B. King
The Fantastic Inventions of Nikola Tesla by Nikola Tesla
Man-Made UFOs: 1944-1994 by Robert Vesco & David Hatcher Childress

The Lost Cities Series:
Lost Cities of Atlantis, Ancient Europe & the Mediterranean
Lost Cities of North & Central America
Lost Cities & Ancient Mysteries of South America
Lost Cities of Ancient Lemuria & the Pacific
Lost Cities & Ancient Mysteries of Africa & Arabia
Lost Cities of China, Central Asia & India

The Mystic Traveller Series:
In Secret Mongolia by Henning Haslund (1934)
Men & Gods In Mongolia by Henning Haslund (1935)
In Secret Tibet by Theodore Illion (1937)
Darkness Over Tibet by Theodore Illion (1938)
Danger My Ally by F.A. Mitchell-Hedges (1954)
Mystery Cities of the Maya by Thomas Gann (1925)
In Quest of Lost Worlds by Byron de Prorok (1937)

Write for our free catalog of exciting books and tapes.

THE BRIDGE TO INFINITY

HARMONIC 371244

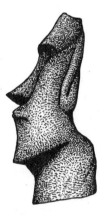

Adventures Unlimited Press
One Adventure Place
Kempton, Illinois

The Bridge To Infinity:
Harmonic 371244
by Bruce Cathie

ISBN 0-932813-05-4

Printed in the United States of America

Adventures Unlimited Press
303 Main Street
Kempton, ILLINOIS 60946 USA
Phone: 815-253-6390
Fax: 815-253-6300

The Lost Science Series:

The Energy Grid by Bruce Cathie
The Bridge To Infinity by Bruce Cathie
The Harmonic Conquest of Space by Bruce Cathie
The Anti-Gravity Handbook edited by David Hatcher Childress
Anti-Gravity & the World Grid edited by David Hatcher Childress
Anti-Gravity & the Unified Field edited by David Hatcher Childress
The Free-Energy Device Handbook edited by David Hatcher Childress
Vimana Aircraft of Ancient India & Atlantis by David H. Childress
UFOs & Anti-Gravity: Piece For A Jig-Saw by Leonard G. Cramp
The Fantastic Inventions of Nikola Tesla by Nikola Tesla
Man-Made UFOs: 1944-1994 by Robert Vesco & David Childress

ACKNOWLEDGEMENTS

For the quotations from published material reproduced in the text and the illustrations in this book I am indebted to the following:

Definitions: Britannica World Standard Dictionary.

Pyramids versus the Space Age, by John Tunstall, The Times, London, July, 1969.

The Pyramid and its Relationship to Biocosmic Energy, by G. Patrick Flanagan.

The Great Pyramid, by D. Davidson and H. Aldersmith, William Rider & Son Ltd. London.

Our Inheritance of the Great Pyramid, by Piazzi Smyth.

The Great Pyramid in Fact and in Theory, by William Kingsland, M.I.E.E.

The Story of the Laser, by John Carroll, The Scientific Book Club, London.

The Beam of Light, by Gaston Burridge, Rosicrucian Digest, March, 1961.

Public Relations Office, Brookhaven National Laboratory, Upton, New York.

Fermi National Accelerator Laboratory, Batavia, Illinois, U.S.A.

European Organization for Nuclear Research, Cern, Geneva, Switzerland.

The Philadelphia Experiment, by Charles Berlitz and William Moore.

The Fire Came By, by John Baxter and Thomas Atkins, MacDonald and Jane's London.

Department of the Environment, London, England.

Planetary Association for Clean Energy, Newsletter, Vol. 3, June 1981.

Science and Mechanics Magazine, U.S.A.

Mr Howard Johnson, Blacksburg Virginia, U.S.A.

United States Patent Office.

Flying Saucers Have Landed, by Desmond Leslie and George Adamski.
Behind the Flying Saucers, by Frank Scully, Rinehard and Winston Inc. N.Y.

Space, Gravity and the Flying Saucer; by Leonard G. Cramp.

The Australasian Post magazine, May 13 1982.

Time Life Books; Imperial Rome, Early Islam.

Rome and Byzantium; by Clive Foss and Paul Magdalino.

Andrew Guthrie; For independent research into the harmonic structure of matter.

George Hunt Williamson, Author of — Other Tongues — Other Flesh
Secret Places of the Lion   Road in the Sky   The Saucers Speak

Also a special thanks to Eric and Margaret Reynolds of "The Apostles of Our Lady of New Zealand" for their help in researching the material on the apparitions of The Virgin Mary, which have occured in many areas around the world.

3

CONTENTS

LIST OF DIAGRAMS

LIST OF TABLES

LIST OF MAPS

LIST OF PHOTO-COPIES

My curiosity has no bounds
I have always wanted to know
the answers to many things
I drove my parents mad
with questions like
what makes the wind blow
the grass grow
How does a seed know
how to make a tree
a flower — or me
Do plants have intelligence
do they feel pain
the heat, the cold, and the rain
Who made the Universe
and what is eternity
Is God out there
or is He really
a part of me
and everything I see.
Do we just live on earth
to die and cease to be
forever.
Or do we have many lives
and travel amongst the stars
constantly experiencing new things
without ever finding out
how it all started
or how it will all end.
Is it our destiny
to take a final voyage
and cross the bridge
to infinity.

Bruce L. Cathie

DEFINITIONS OF TERMS

Harmony and harmonic etc. as defined by the Britannica World Standard Dictionary:

1. HARMONY: A state of order, agreement, or completeness in the relations of things, or of parts of a whole to each other.

2. HARMONIC: Producing, characterised by, or pertaining to, harmony.
(a). Music: Pertaining to a tone whose rate of vibration is an exact multiple of a given primary tone.
(b). Mathematical: Derived from, or originally suggested by, the numerical relations between the vibrations of the musical harmonies, or overtones, of the same fundamental tone: Harmonic functions.
(c). Physics: Any component of a periodic quantity, which is an integral multiple of the fundamental frequency.

In this book I discuss the fundamental harmonies of the vibrational frequencies which form the building-blocks of our immediate universe; and those of the theoretical anti-universe which modern scientists have postulated as existing in mirror-like image of our own. I theorise that the whole of physical reality which is tangible to us is formed from the basic geometric harmonies, or harmonics, of the angular velocities, or wave-forms, of light. From these basic harmonies, or resonating wave-forms, myriad other waves are created which blend in sympathetic resonance, one with the other, thus forming the physical structures.

Einstein stated that the geometric structure of space-time determines the physical processes. I theorise that space and time manifest from the geometric harmonies of the wave-motions of light. The fundamental harmonic of light, in free space, in geometric terms being an angular velocity of 144,000 minutes of arc per grid second, there being 97,200 grid seconds to one revolution of the earth.

When physical matter is manifested in the universe the wave-forms of light from which it is formed are slowed down fractionally in order to release the energy required for the formation process. This is demonstrated by the unified harmonic equations in Chapter One. It was found that to calculate the values of harmonic wave-forms that have sympathetic resonance it was possible to disregard zeros to the right, or left, of whole numbers and extract the values direct from the mathematical tables.

INTRODUCTION

In my earlier books I have stated that all the evidence, pieced together over many years, strongly suggests that modern day scientists have discovered the secrets of anti-gravity; travel in space-time, which makes possible journeys to the most distant stars; the geometric structure of matter and anti-matter; the tapping of energy from the earth itself at almost no cost; transmutation of the elements; disintegration of matter by the use of laser, or light, beams — these can be made selective; almost instant communication between any number of points on the earth's surface, through the earth itself, and a myriad other technical wonders. All this is possible today. In one great surge of progress the whole world could be transformed into a material wonderland with plenty for all.

Now, several years later, my further researches have only helped to strengthen these statements. Small bits of information are beginning to leak out into the public domain, particularly that relating to laser research, but generally the most advanced knowledge held by the scientists is not being released to be used for the welfare of the whole world community. There are many reasons for this which are beyond the scope of this book, but I believe that a comparatively small international group is behind the suppression. They do not wish the knowledge to be made freely available because this would alter the concentration of power, and allow the less fortunate countries to control their own affairs.

I believe that this situation is slowly changing. The public are becoming aware that they are being conned and are starting to demand the truth. Modern communications are making it more difficult to suppress knowledge and the subtle brain-washing techniques used to sway public opinion are not working as well as they did in the past.

The younger generations, with their more idealistic outlook and superior knowledge, are beginning to take over control in the political and scientific fields and hopefully they will learn wisdom as they progress and change the direction of world affairs from the hopeless future facing us today, to a situation more worthy of the human race.

I am optimistic. They will succeed, although the going will be rough at times. The only alternative is oblivion for all of us and I am sure that this lesson is becoming more obvious as time goes by.

This book is a mixture of updated material from my last three books and new information that will help strengthen the earlier theories that were presented, in order to help explain the unified nature of our material and multi-dimensional universe. If a small percentage of my research can be verified as fact by future generations then I will feel that my endeavours have been worthwhile.

Bruce L. Cathie

MATHEMATICS OF THE WORLD GRID

My interest in the increasing UFO activity in the New Zealand area led me to the discovery that the surface of the world was crisscrossed with an intricate network of energy grid lines. I began my research in 1965. The information in this chapter regarding the structure and mathematical values built into the system will consist of material condensed from my first three books plus the findings derived from my recent research up to early 1982.

In a general way I was convinced that UFOs were actively engaged in a survey of the earth for some definite reason. I felt that their visits were not haphazard; they were not just on casual sightseeing tours. Quite a number of investigators around the world had come to the conclusion that the sightings were beginning to form a pattern. At this period, however, this pattern was so complex as to defy any definition, or solution. By the correlation of sightings small sections of track had been identified, and some saucers had been seen moving along these set paths. Some of these had hovered over certain spots at set intervals. But these bits and pieces of tracklines were so scattered around the surface of our planet that it was quite impossible to fit them together into any semblance or order.

I was certain that if an overall pattern could be found and plotted, it might be possible to establish the reason behind UFO activity. I considered that the pattern would be geometric if these things were intelligently controlled, and that if somehow I could find the key to one section then I might solve the rest by duplication and inference.

I had sighted a number of unidentified objects in the sky over a period of several years, and by correlating two of these with other data I was eventually able to construct a grid system which covered the whole world.

One of the sightings was in 1956. I was a DC3 co-pilot crewing a flight from Auckland to Paraparaumu. It was about 6pm, conditions were calm, and there was unlimited visibility. We were just south of Waverley at 7000 feet when I saw this object at an extremely high altitude in the east. I drew the captain's attention to it and together we watched it travel in a curved trajectory from east to west across our track until it disappeared in a flash of light at about 10,000 feet in the area of D'Urville Island. It appeared to travel across New Zealand in the vicinity, or slightly to the north, of Cook Strait, and it was so large that two streaks, similar to vapour trails, were seen to extend from either side of its pale green disc.

When about halfway across the Strait a small object detached itself from the parent body and dropped vertically until it disappeared. It looked almost as if the main disc was at such a high temperature that a globule had dripped from it. I thought about this later and decided that if that were so, the small object would also have a curved trajectory in the direction of the parent body. But this was not so; it detached and dropped *vertically* down at great speed. There could be only one answer for this action: the small body must have been controlled.

10

Calculations at a later date proved this UFO to have been between 1500—2000 feet in diameter. A report in a Nelson newspaper on the following day described an explosion at a high altitude to the north of the city. The shock-wave broke windows in some local glasshouses.

The other sighting occurred on 12 March 1965. This was the best and most interesting of them all, and from then my investigations were pressed on with all speed until they culminated in my present findings.

I had always expected to see UFOs in the sky, and that was where my attention was usually focussed. When I was flying I was alert and ready to analyse any object sighted from the aircraft. I never expected to find a saucer landing at my feet and so far this has never happened. This sighting however, was different from all the others because I observed it lying under thirty feet of water.

I was scheduled to carry out a positioning flight from Whenuapai, Auckland's main airport at the time, to Kaitaia. Departure was at 11am and as no passengers were involved and the weather was perfect, I decided to fly visually to Kaitaia along the west coast. An officer from the operations department was on board and this was a good opportunity to show him some of the rugged country to the north. (I must stress that air-traffic regulations were strictly observed during the flight).

On leaving Whenuapai I climbed to clear the area and when approaching the southern end of the Kaipara Harbour, just north of Helensville, I dropped to a lower altitude to have a better look at anything in the flight path. The tide in the harbour was well out, and the water over the mudflats and estuaries was quite shallow.

I suppose we were about a third of the way across the harbour when I spotted what I took to be a stranded grey-white whale. I veered slightly to port, to fly more directly over the object and to obtain a better look.

I suppose a pilot develops the habit of keeping his emotions to himself. As far as I can remember I gave no indication of surprise, and I said nothing as I looked down. My "whale" was definitely a metal fish. I could see it very clearly, and I quote from the notes I made later.

A. The object was perfectly streamlined and symmetrical in shape.
B. It had no external control surfaces or protrusions.
C. It appeared metallic, and there was a suggestion of a hatch on top, streamlined in shape. It was not quite halfway along the body as measured from the nose.
D. It was resting on the bottom of the estuary and headed towards the south, as suggested from the streamlined shape.
E. The shape was not that of a normal submarine and there was no superstructure.
F. I estimated the length as 100 feet, with a diameter of 15 feet at the widest part.
G. The object rested in no more than 30 feet of clear water. The bottom of the harbour was visible and the craft was sharply defined.

Inquiries made from the navy confirmed that it would not have been possible for a normal submarine to be in this particular position, due to the configuration of the harbour and coastline.

An American scientist checked this spot on the harbour with a depth-sounder in September 1969. He informed me afterwards that a hole had been detected in the harbour bed approximately one eighth of a mile wide and over 100 feet deep, which I consider would indicate some activity had been carried out in this position some five years previously. I published the scientist's report in my second book.

I had a further key to the puzzle in April 1965. My wife saw an advertisement in the local paper seeking members for a UFO organisation called New Zealand Scientific and Space Research. I contacted this organisation and found that a vast amount of information had been very efficiently compiled. Material had been collected from twenty-five different countries over a period of twelve years. I was invited to study the information at leisure.

Amongst this mass of data I discovered the reports of a UFO that had been seen from several different localities in both islands of New Zealand on March 26 1965. People in Napier, New Plymouth, Palmerston North, Wanganui, Feilding and Otaki Forks in the North Island; Nelson Coast Road, Blenheim and Westport (Cape Foulwind) in the South Island, had all reported sightings.

It was decided that I try to plot the track of this UFO. From the considerable amount of information available I found that the maximum variation in the times of sightings from all areas was 15 minutes. Most reports gave the time as 9.45pm. This proved that the object must have been very large and at a high altitude during the greater part of its trajectory.

There was nothing of any great significance or originality in these accounts, and they followed the pattern of many other sightings. However from the mass of detail supplied by so many different people over so wide an area, it was possible to plot the track of the object with reasonable accuracy. I started work on a Mercator's plotting chart, and after several hours of checking one report against the other, and calculating possible elevations and trajectories, I felt I had refined the plot sufficiently to draw in the final track of the object, or objects. The result is shown on map 1.

The track began about seventy nautical miles north of New Plymouth, passed just over to the west of Mt Egmont, and finished at D'Urville Island. When first seen the altitude would have been about 30,000 feet curving down on a flight path to somewhere around 10,000 feet when it disappeared.

Some time after those sightings on 26 March 1965 I had another look at the plot I have made. I could find no flaws in my thinking, but I needed more information. As I was to discover many times later, the clues were quite obvious, but I was not then sufficiently expert in realising their significance. In point of fact this first trackline was to be the starting point of a whole string of discoveries of which I have yet to find an end.

I pored over that plot for a long time before it suddenly occurred to me that the track appeared to be in line with the position where I had sighted the unidentified submarine object, or USO, on 12 March 1965. On extending the line back I found it was in line with the sightings of 26 March. I was positive there had to be a connection — but to prove it was a different matter.

I checked my report files again and found that on 2 March some fishermen just north of the coast of New Plymouth had seen a large object plunge into the sea and disappear. They thought it was an aircraft and reported the incident to the appropriate authorities, but no aircraft or personnel were missing. I checked this position on the map and found that it also fitted the established trackline. Was this connected with the USO of 12 March, and could the two sightings be of the same object, sighted twice in ten days? Could it be working slowly up this track carrying out some project on the sea bed? I tucked this thought away for future reference and carried on with the search.

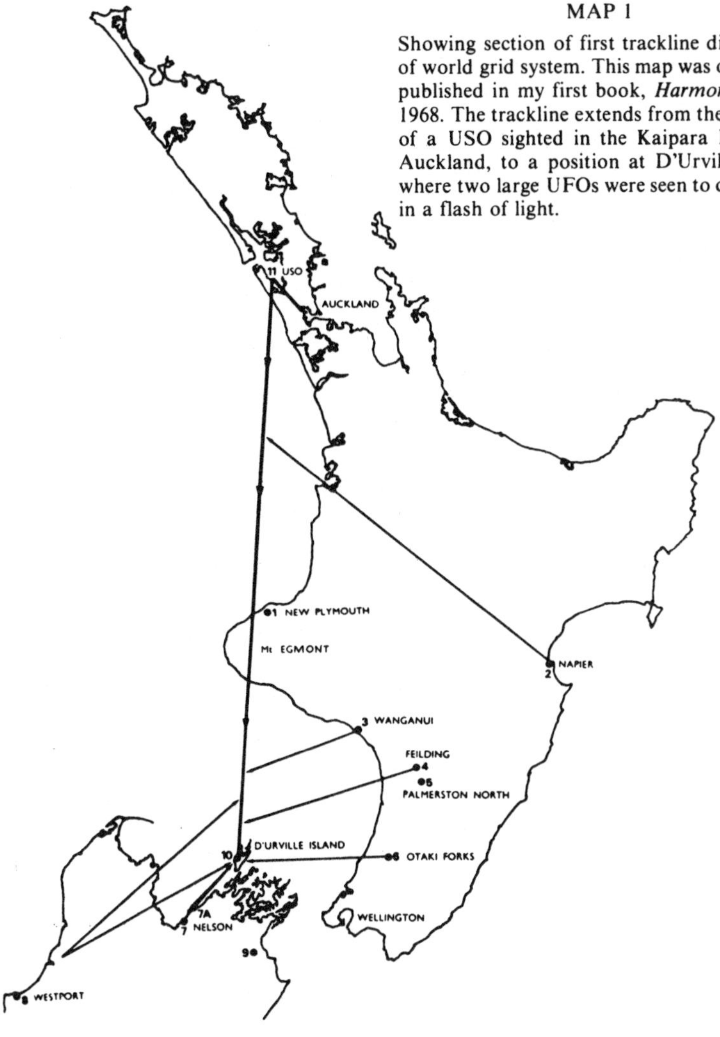

MAP 1

Showing section of first trackline discovered of world grid system. This map was originally published in my first book, *Harmonic 33*, in 1968. The trackline extends from the position of a USO sighted in the Kaipara Harbour, Auckland, to a position at D'Urville Island where two large UFOs were seen to disappear in a flash of light.

13

It was some days later that I remembered the UFO I had seen in 1956. This object was similar and, most significant of all, both objects had apparently travelled at 90° to each other, and finished in the same grand all-illuminating flash in the area of D'Urville Island.

If these objects were *not* controlled, how could anyone explain such coincidences? No two meteors or other natural phenomena could coincidentally carry out similar manoeuvres, travel at 90° to each other, and both decide to end their existence at the same point in space, within nine years of each other. Also, in both cases, objects had been seen to emerge from the parent bodies. Was this irrefutable evidence that they were intelligently controlled vehicles?

I plotted the track of the 1956 UFO on the map at 90° to the north-south line. I realised that I had no definite proof that they were at exactly 90° to each other or that the 1956 track was not a few miles north or south of this position — still, I had to start from somewhere, and I would assume this to be correct unless and until other evidence proved me wrong.

Two track lines at 90° meant little on their own. If I found several at 90°, I might have something — a grid perhaps? These two lines hinted at this, and I believed that if I could solve the system of measurement, then I had two ready made baselines to work from.

Once again I went to the UFO files and found that a Frenchman by the name of Aime Michel had been studying UFOs for a number of years and had found small sections of tracklines in various areas of Europe. Saucers had been seen hovering at various points along these tracklines, and Mr Michel had observed that the average distance between these points was 54.43 kilometres. By itself this was only a small grain of information but, like a starting gun, it set me off again.

Using the Kaipara Harbour as a starting point, I marked off the 54.43 kilometre intervals along the trackline I had found. I was disappointed when I was unsuccessful in obtaining an even distribution of positions to the D'Urville Island disappearing point. I checked and re-checked, but nothing worked out. I slept on the problem, and at some time during the night inspiration turned up the wick; once more the light grew bright.

I remembered that a great number of sightings had occurred around the Blenheim area. Even before the advent of ordinary aircraft in New Zealand, this area had been visited by UFOs. I had read about them in old copies of the local papers, and many recent sightings suggested again that this area had something special about it.

So I dragged out my map and extended the trackline until it cut a 90° coordinate from the town of Blenheim. The distance from this point to the Kaipara position I found to be exactly 300 nautical miles, and one nautical mile is equal to one minute of arc on the earth's surface. Could it be that the rough interval of 54.43 kilometres discovered by Michel was, in fact, an interval of 30 nautical miles when corrected? If so then this interval could be evenly spaced along my trackline ten times. Was this the system of measurement used by the UFO's? There was no proof, of course, but it seemed a reasonable assumption. A minute of arc is a measurement which could be applied to the whole universe.

14

University personnel and others in the academic field attacked me repeatedly over this issue. They maintained that degrees and minutes of arc were arbitrary values set up by the ancient mathematicians and that therefore my calculations were meaningless. I finally found proof of my argument in the works of Pythagoras. As my research progressed I discovered that the harmonic of the speed of light in free space had a value of 144. If this was divided by 2, to find the harmonic of one half cycle, or half-wave, the answer was 72. If this value was then applied to the Pythagoras right-angled 3, 4, 5 triangle and each side was extended in this ratio then the figure had sides of 216, 288 and 360 units. The harmonic proportions thus derived were equal to:

216 = 21600 = the number of minutes of arc in a circle.
360 = 360   = the number of degrees in a circle.
288 = (144 x 2) = 2C, where C = the speed of light harmonic.

It appeared from this that the harmonic of light had a very definite relationship with the geometry of a circle, and that the early mathematicians were fully aware of the fact. This will become clearer as you read through this book.

The fifth interval of 30 nautical miles from the Kaipara position coincided with the position off the coast of New Plymouth where the mysterious object had plunged into the sea. The plotted points of disappearance of the two large UFOs at D'Urville Island did not quite match up with the ninth interval, but this did not worry me unduly as I expected that a small percentage of error must be expected in my original plot. I readjusted this position to the ninth interval, and carried on the search to see how many other sightings I could fit into this pattern.

The results exceeded my expectations. I found that by using units of 30 minutes of arc latitude north-south, and 30 minutes of arc longitude east-west, on my Mercator's map, a grid pattern was formed into which a great number of UFO reports could be fitted. I eventually had a map with sixteen stationary and seventeen moving UFOs plotted on grid intersections and tracklines.

Having satisfied myself that my reasoning and plotting were not false, I considered that I had good proof that New Zealand, possibly other countries, and probably the whole world, were being systematically covered by some type of grid system.

In my first book I demonstrated that the main grid pattern consisted of grid lines spaced at intervals of 30 minutes of arc (latitude and longitude). In my second book I probably confused the issue a bit as I stated that the east-west grid lines were spaced at 24 minutes of arc. This was due to the spacing being measured in nautical miles, or values in minutes of latitude. The actual length of a minute of longitude varies mathematically from one nautical mile at the equator, to zero at the north and south poles.

The value of 30 minutes of arc in terms of longtitude in the New Zealand area happened to be an average of 24 nautical miles, which can be confusing those readers who are not familiar with map scales.

Reference to the grid structure will therefore be stated from now on in minute of arc values only, for latitude and longitude, to minimise confusion.

I subsequently discovered that the grid lattice could be further divided. It is now evident that the grid lines in the main system are spaced at intervals of 7.5 minutes of arc north-south, and east-west. The importance of this will prove itself when compared with the rest of the calculations in this book. There are 21,600 minutes of arc in a circle, and when this is divided by 7.5 we get a value of 2880. The grid lattice therefore is tuned harmonically to twice the speed of light (288), as will be shown in other sections.

It appeared that I had found a section of geometric grid pattern in the New Zealand area. I now had to form some theory of construction for the whole world. I could then possibly fit the New Zealand section into it.

By drawing a series of patterns on a small plastic ball I finally found a system which could be used as a starting point for a global investigation. (The basic pattern is shown in diagram 1).

I was sure I was on the right track, but now I had to super-impose this pattern on the world globe. It was essential that I find a point position somewhere on the earth upon which to orientate the geometrical pattern. I finally came up with an item of news that gave me a very important clue on how to proceed.

On 29 August 1964 the American survey ship *Eltanin* was carrying out a sweep of the sea-bed off the coast of South America. A series of submarine photographs was being taken of the area by means of a camera attached to a long cable. A surprise was in store when these photographs were developed. On one of the points, in marvellous detail, was an aerial-type object sticking up from an otherwise featureless sea-bed.

This object appeared to be metallic and perfectly symmetrical in construction. The array consisted of six main crossbars with small knob-like ends and a small crossbar at the top. Each cross looked to be set at angles of 15° to the others, and the whole system stood about 2 feet in height. The position where this object was found was given as latitude 59°08′ south, longitude 105° west.

As this bit of ironmongery was situated at a depth of 13,500 feet below the surface, I was certain that no human engineers had placed it there.

Scientists may be able to descend to those depths in specially constructed bathyspheres, but I don't think they could work as deeply as that on a precision engineering problem. In view of my earlier sightings in the Kaipara Harbour, I was willing to accept that the aerial-type object had been placed there by an un-identified submarine object, or USO.

Since this photo was taken there has been a determined attempt by the scientific world to label this object as nothing more than a plant of some sort. A journalist friend and I managed to visit the *Eltanin* during one of its few visits to New Zealand and when we discussed this object with some of the scientists on board, the comment was that it was classed as an artefact. This was before the great hush-up but, regardless of that, I believe that the mathematical proofs will show without doubt that the object is artifical, and most probably an aerial of some sort.

16

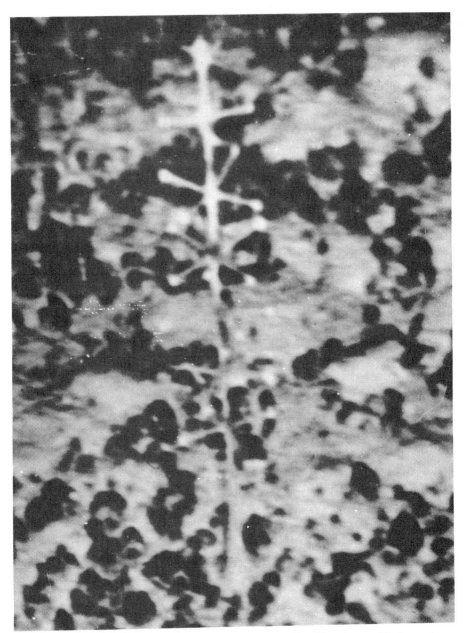

Aerial type object photographed by the survey ship Eltanin on 29 August 1964 while carrying out a sweep of the sea-bed off the coast of South America. Position given was Latitude 59° 08′ south / Longitude 105° 00′ west.

17

DIAGRAM 1

Showing relationship of grid structure to the geographic poles. Each of the two grids has a similar pattern, the interaction of which sets up a third resultant grid. The poles of the three grids are positioned at three different latitudes and longitudes.

C, D, E, F = Corner aerial positions of grid polar square. Similar to aerial discovered by the survey ship *Eltanin*.

J — K = Polar axis.

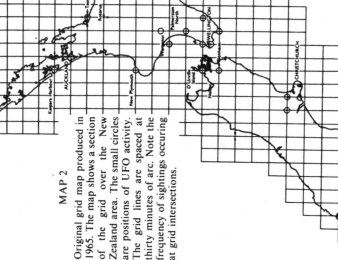

A = Geographic pole
B = Grid pole

Distance C — G — D = 3600 minutes of arc.
Distance C — H — D = 3418.6069 minutes of arc.
Distance C — I — D = 3643.2 minutes of arc

$(3600 - 3418.6069) = 181.39308$

$(181.39308 \times 4) = 725.57233$

$\sqrt{725.57233} = 26.93645 = 2693645$ harmonic.

MAP 2

Original grid map produced in 1965. The map shows a section of the grid over the New Zealand area. The small circles are positions of UFO activity. The grid lines are spaced at thirty minutes of arc. Note the frequency of sightings occuring at grid intersections.

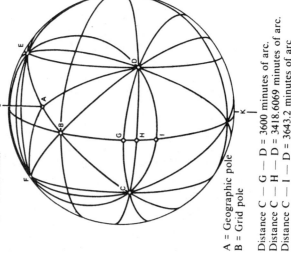
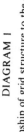
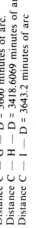

DIAGRAM 3

Showing the relationship of grid polar squares A, B, and C. The polar squares are orientated in reciprocal positions around both the north and south geographic poles.

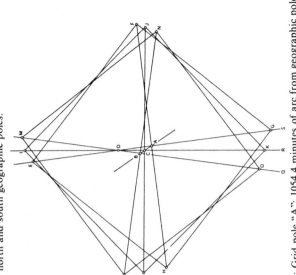

A: Grid pole "A": 1054.4 minutes of arc from geographic pole
B: Grid pole "B": 694.4 minutes of arc from geographic pole
C: Grid pole "C": 864 minutes of arc from geographic pole

D: North geographic pole
E, F, G, H: Polar square "A"
I, J, K, L: Polar square "C"
M, N, O, P: Polar square "B"

Q: Longitude 105 degrees west
R: Longitude 97.5 degrees west
S: Longitude 90 degrees west

DIAGRAM 2

Showing the relationship of a grid polar square to the geographic pole. Each grid has a similar pattern. The pole of each grid is set at a different latitude and longitude.

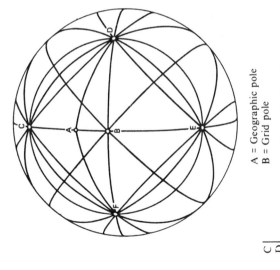

A = Geographic pole
B = Grid pole

$\left.\begin{array}{l} C \\ D \\ E \\ F \end{array}\right|$ = Corner aerial positions of grid polar square

$\left.\begin{array}{l} B{-}C \\ B{-}D \\ B{-}E \\ B{-}F \end{array}\right|$ = 2545.584412 minutes of arc

A—B Grid "A" = 1054.4 minutes of arc
A—B Grid "B" = 694.4 minutes of arc
A—B Grid "C" = 864 minutes of arc (resultant grid)

19

The form of this aerial-like structure also fitted in with the general pattern of the grid as I had envisaged it on the plastic ball. The six main crossbars denoted the radiating points of six or twelve great circles which form the main structure of the grid.

I centred the grid on the position of the object found by the *Eltanin*, and the 180° reciprocal of this in Russian Siberia, lining the whole thing up with the section I had found in New Zealand. I found the system to be lined up very closely with the magnetic field of the earth. The equator of the grid followed very closely the line of zero dip around the world. (That is, the positions on the earth's surface where a magnetic compass needle has only a horizontal and no vertical component).

In my first two books I discussed the methods I used to line up the system and calculate the first estimates of the grid pole positions, and the major focal points of the grid similar to the *Eltanin* "aerial" placement.

The reciprocal position of the *Eltanin* "aerial" is at latitude 59° 08′ north, longitude 75° east, in Siberia. I calculated the length of the diagonal of what I call, for simplicity, the "polar grid square" and found it to be 5091.168825 minutes of arc long. I plotted a track from the Siberian position through the north geographic pole and measured off this distance to locate another corner "aerial" of the polar square. (Square is not technically the right word to use as the four sides are formed by sections of small circles which are in different planes to each other. When the "polar square" areas are transferred from the surface of the earth sphere on to a flat plane such as a map, then a perfect square is formed with sides 3600 minutes long and diagnals of 5091.168825 minutes of arc).

In my first two books I stated, in error, that the sides of the "polar squares" were formed by sections of GREAT circles 3600 minutes of arc long, instead of SMALL circles. The great circle distance between these points is in fact 3418.606915 minutes of arc, which is very confusing to any investigator attempting to reconstruct the grid. I apologise to my readers for this error, which was caused by my lack of access to calculators during my earlier research. In the grid pattern there are actually two small-circle segments, and one great circle segment connecting each of these points which form the polar squares. Each of the segments has a different path over the earth and some tricky calculating is necessary to ascertain the true length. Although I used the wrong term in my earlier publications, the actual calculations derived from the grid system are not altered in any way, and still stand the test of time. Over the last few years I have slightly refined the values I demonstrated previously, derived from a mixture of practical and theoretical studies. I have now set up what I see as a completely theoretical system, discovered by working entirely by calculator. Time will prove how close my calculations are. I have no doubt that I, and others, will continue further to perfect the system as more facts come to light.

Once I had established this first base line I found it quite easy to construct the main skeleton of the grid over the whole surface of the earth.

As my work progressed I found that there were in fact two similar grids, interlocked with each other. The poles of the grids were spaced at different distances from the north geometric pole, and this arrangement set up a series of geometric harmonics which were directly related to the speed of light, mass, and gravity. The interaction of the two grids created a harmonic resonance which, in turn, formed a third resultant grid.

After ten years of work and correlating information I have now calculated

20

theoretical positions for the three grid poles in the northern hemisphere which are very close to my original estimate. Reciprocal positions will give similar values for the southern hemisphere.

Grid pole (A) = Latitude 72.4266° / longitude 90°
west 1054.4 minutes of arc from the north pole.

Grid pole "B" = Latitude 78.4266° / longitude 105°
west 694.4 minutes of arc from the North Pole.

Resultant grid pole "C" = Latitude 75.6° / longitude 97.5°
west 864 minutes of arc from the North Pole.

The diagonal of the "polar square" of 5091.168825 units can be broken down into a series of values:

$$5091.168824 \div 2 = 2545.584412$$
$$2545.584412 \div 7.5 = 3.39411255$$
$$3.39411255^2 = 11.52$$
$$11.52 \div 8 = 1.44 \text{ (speed of light harmonic)}$$
$$2545.584412^2 = 6480000$$
$$\text{Reciprocal of } 2545.584412 = .03928371$$

The harmonic value of 3928371 is of extreme importance as it has a direct relationship with the earth's magnetic field. The harmonic 648 was also shown, in my earlier books, to have many interesting associations. In particular the harmonic table for temperature.

The many other harmonic factors, centred around the "polar square" corner "aerial" positions, form a series of complex mathematical associations, and this can be left for those who wish to carry out their own research. If I can show how to construct the main "bones" of the grid my part of the job will be complete. I have found it impossible, so far, to plot the fine grid structure of lines 7.5 minutes apart, over the whole world, because of the complexity of such an exercise. (A full computer programme would be necessary and I do not have the finance required for such an undertaking).

So far I have confined myself to the New Zealand area, with the small section of finely-spaced grid lines that I originally discovered. Over the years I have been able to plot into this map a great many interesting facts which indicate activity by various scientific groups. This has helped me to gradually build up my own knowledge of the system.

My nosiness has not gone unnoticed — as evidenced by the constant probing of interested parties endeavouring to find out the extent of my discoveries. I hope that in the near future the international combines involved in this advanced research will make known to the public the vast amount of scientific knowledge they have aquired. Possibly this will only happen if and when a world government has been set up to control the scientific wonders which are now within our reach. Enough is known already to make most of our energy and transport systems obsolete — which may explain why the facts are being suppressed?

I have been able to check activity in other parts of the world by applying harmonic calculation to certain positions of latitude and longitude. It is not necessary to use the grid structure, and such, for some types of calculation once the harmonic process is understood. Eventually, when the whole grid has been plotted, the work will be much easier.

In my second book I stated that the first glimmerings of how true space travel might be achieved came to me when I uncovered the clues that led me to the UFO grid which laces about our globe.

I was aware that my calculations were not precisely accurate — in the strict mathematical sense — but I could see that the system was based on space-time geometrics, and at least there was the best possible support for this: none less than the theories of Einstein.

Somewhere, I knew, the system contained a clue to the truth of the unified field which, he had postulated, permeates all of existence. I didn't know at the time that this clue had already been found by scientists who were well ahead of me. I know now that they must have understood something of the grid system years ago. They knew that Einstein's ideas about the unified field were correct. What's more, for many years they had been carrying out full-scale research into the practical applications of the mathematical concepts contained in that theory.

We were told that Einstein died without completing his equations relating to the unified theory. But in more recent times it has been said that he did in fact complete his work but that the concepts were so advanced that the full truth was not released.

The only way to traverse the vast distances of space is to possess the means of manipulating, or altering, the very structure of space itself; altering the space-time geometric matrix, which to us provides the illusion of form and distance. The method of achieving this lies in the alteration of frequencies controlling the matter-antimatter cycles which govern our awareness, or perception, of position in the space-time structure. Time itself is a geometric, just as Einstein postulated; if time can be altered, then the whole universe is waiting for us to come and explore its nook and crannies.

In the blink of an eye we could cross colossal distances: for distance is an illusion. The only thing that keeps places apart in space is time. If it were possible to move from one position to another in space, in an infinitely small amount of time, or "zero time", then both the positions would coexist, according to our awareness. By speeding up the geometric of time we will be able to bring distant places within close proximity. This is the secret of the UFOs – they travel by means of altering the spatial dimensions around them and repositioning in space-time.

I decided to concentrate specifically on three harmonic values which appeared to have a close relationship with each other. Previously I had shown this connection and had truthfully pointed out that I did not know why the relationship was there at all.

The harmonic values which occupied my full attention:

1703 — This was the four-figure harmonic of 170,300,000,000, which is the expression in cubic minutes of arc of the mass, or volume, of the planet earth, and its surrounding atmosphere.

1439 — A four-figure harmonic of 143,900 minutes of arc per grid second, representing the speed of light in grid values.

2640 — This figure expressed in minute of arc values is built into the polar portion of the grid structure, as a geometric coordinate.

I found that when I matched these values harmonically the results were as follows. Zeros to the right-hand side can be ignored in this form of harmonic calculation:

```
 1703
 -264
 1439
```

In other words the difference between the harmonic of mass and the harmonic of light was the harmonic of 264 (or 2640).

It was apparent that if my calculations were more accurately worked out it should be possible to find out just what the 2640 figure referred to.

After more calculation the following terms were found:

```
17025  Earth mass harmonic
-2636  Unknown harmonic
14389  Speed of light harmonic
```

Checking through some five-figure mathematical tables, I found to my surprise that 2.6363 is the square root of 6.95 (from the 1-10 square root tables). In harmonic calculation decimal points as well as zeros to the right or left of a figure can be ignored; so it could be said that the square root of 695 was 2636. I could perceive from this the first steps necessary to solve the elusive equation. I had established that 695 was the harmonic reciprocal of the speed of light, or 1/1439 subject to the accuracy of my calculations at the time. It was now possible to substitute algebraic values — although obviously a computer would be necessary to solve the true values to extreme accuracy.

```
17025 (earth mass)
-2636 square root of speed of light reciprocal
14389 (speed of light)
```

If   C = The speed of light, and
      M = Mass

$$\text{Then } M = C + \sqrt{\frac{1}{C}}$$

23

I had the first part of a unified field equation in harmonic values. To take the next step I first had to go back to Einsteinian theory, particularly the famous equation $E = MC^2$, where E is energy, M is mass and C the speed of light.

Einstein declared that physical matter was nothing more than a concentrated field of force. What we term a physical substance is in reality an intangible concentration of wave-forms. Different combinations of structural patterns of waves unite to form the myriad chemicals and elements which in turn react with one another to form physical substances. Different wave-forms of matter appear to us to be solid because we are constituted of similar wave-forms which resonate within a clearly defined range of frequencies — and which control the physical processes of our limited world.

Einstein believed that M, the value for mass in the equation, could eventually be removed and a value substituted that would express the physical in the form of pure energy. In other words, by substituting for M a unified field equation should result which would express in mathematical terms the whole of existence — including this universe and everything within it.

Einstein maintained that the M in his equation could be replaced by a term denoting wave-form. I had found a substitute for M in terms of wave-forms of light. So the obvious step, to me, was to replace Einstein's M with the values of C found from the grid system . The results are as follows:

Einstein $E = MC^2$

Cathie grid $M = C + \sqrt{1/C}$

Therefore $E = (C + \sqrt{1/C}) \, C^2$ (Harmonic equation 1)

I now had a harmonic unified field equation expressed in terms of light — or pure electromagnetic wave form — the key to the universe, the whole of existence: to the seen and the unseen, to forms, solids, liquids and gases, the stars and the blackness of space itself, all consisting of visible and invisible waves of light. All of creation is light.

It was now necessary to refine my calculations and attempt to discover a way to practically apply this initial equation.

The equation is that from which an atomic bomb is developed. by setting up derivatives of the equation in geometric form, the relative motions of the wave-forms inherent in matter are zeroed, and convert from material substance back into pure energy.

This explained the workings of a nuclear explosive device, but it still did not yield the secret of space-time propulsion. The grid system which I discovered by the study of the movement of unidentified flying objects was harmonically tuned to this basic equation, yet a UFO does not disintegrate when it moves within the resonating fields of the network.

There had to be an extension of the equation which so far I had missed that would produce the necessary harmonics for movement in space-time.

In the polar areas of the grid the geometric values of some of the coordinates appeared to be doubled up. The coordinate of 2545584412 was doubled in the diagonals of the polar squares, with all of its associated harmonics and other factors appeared to be doubled when the pattern was projected onto a flat plain.

I reasoned that a way to check this idea was to increase the values of C in the equation, and observe the changing harmonic of E to see what relative values might emerge. I thought at the time that a direct antigravitational harmonic might become evident, but my recent research has proved this line of thought to be incorrect. In terms of mathematical values I found what I was hunting for in the form of two more equations. In the case of one of the equations I erroneously believed that the derived harmonic value related to the reciprocal of gravity. I know now that what I had hold of was an equation related to the magnetic field of the earth.

The earth being simply a huge magnet, a dynamo, wound with magnetic lines of force as it coils, tenescopically counted to be 1257 TO THE SQUARE CENTIMETRE IN ONE DIRECTION AND 1850 TO THE SQUARE CENTIMETRE IN THE OTHER DIRECTION (EDDY CURRENTS), indicates that natural law has placed these lines as close together as the hairs on one's head.

The spectroscope shows that there is an enormous magnetic field around the sun, and it is the present conclusion of the best minds that magnetic lines of force from the sun envelop this earth and extend to the moon, and THAT EVERYTHING, NO MATTER WHAT ITS FORM ON THIS PLANET, EXISTS BY REASON OF MAGNETIC LINES OF FORCE.

This I agree with, according to my own research. We are taught in our schools and universities that the magnetic field passes through one magnetic pole, then through the body, and out the other magnetic pole. I disagree with this explanation. I believe that the magnetic lines of force enter the body at the poles, then carry out a looped path through the body before passing out the opposite poles.

The flow is not in one pole and out the other, but in both poles, and out both poles, although the field intensity both ways is unbalanced.

If we can visualise one line of force so that we can trace out its path we can form an analogy by imagining it to be similar to a piece of string. First of all we make a loop in the piece of string. Now imagine it being fed through a fixed position with the loop remaining stationary relative to a fixed point. With the length of string as the axis we can now make the loop revolve in a path which is at 90° to the movement of the string. The loop in fact would trace out a spherical-shaped form in space.

The lines of force of the magnetic field would form a lattice, or grid pattern, due to the spin of the planetary body. A good analogy would be an ordinary machine-wound ball of string. The length of string has taken on the form of a ball, and at the same time has formed a crisscross pattern. If we again visualise this as a physical body being formed in space then we can now imagine a small vortex being created at all the trillions of points where the lines of force cross each other in the lattice pattern. Each vortex would manifest as an atomic structure and create within itself what we term a gravitational field. The gravitational field in other words is nothing more than the effect of relative motion in space. Matter is drawn towards a gravitational field, just as a piece of wood floating on water is drawn towards a whirlpool. The gravitational fields created by the vortexual action of every atom would combine to form the field of the completed planetary body.

The world grid that I speak of is the natural grid that is formed by the lattice pattern of the interlocking lines of force.

The unbalanced field of 1257 lines of force per square centimentre in one direction and 1850 in other does not tell us very much in itself. But if we use the information to calculate the field strength over an area which has a harmonic relationship with the unified fields of space, and if the basic information is correct, we should find some mathematical values of great importance.

At the time of writing my last book I was not aware of the extreme importance of the values at that stage of accuracy. I was close enough to see how they fitted into the equations, but a further fine tuning was necessary to reveal the knowledge locked within these two simple numbers.

The basic unit for harmonic calculation is the geodetic inch, or one seventy-two thousandth of a minute of arc; one minute of arc being 6000 geodetic feet. If we take the values 1257 and 1850 lines of force per square centimetre and calculate the field strengths for one square geodetic inch, the field density is 8326.71764 and 12255.08864 lines of force respectively. The fields being in oppostion to each other. The combined field density is equal to 20581.80628.

Allowing for very slight variations in the conversion factors the difference in field strengths (12255.08864 minus 8326.71764) is equal to 3928.371. We could say that the resultant field density one way is equivalent to field 'A' minus field 'B', or 3928.371 lines of force. This value I found to be the harmonic reciprocal of the grid coordinate 2545.584412.

The combined field strength of 20581.80628 lines of force can be harmonically associated with several other interesting facts, to be demonstrated in other sections of this book.

We can now formulate another equation in order to demonstrate the association of the earth's magnetic field with the speed of light.

Harmonic equation 2

$$\text{Field } (A - B) = (2C + \sqrt{1/2C})\,(2C)^2 = 3928.371 \text{ harmonic}$$

$$\text{Where C} \quad = 144000 - 90.9345139$$
$$= 143909.0655$$

The reduction in light speed of 90.9345139 minutes of arc per grid/sec. creates a very interesting factor, because:

$$90.9345139 = \frac{3928371}{432}$$

The reduction in light speed is therefore equal, in harmonic terms, to the resultant field strength divided by the radius of spherical mass. In this case the radius being the distance, in minutes of arc, from the earth's centre to the average height of the atmosphere. (432 being a harmonic of 4320 minutes of arc).

We can now formulate a third equation by inserting the value for the speed of light at the earth's surface. By mathematical conversion this was found to be 143795.77 minutes of arc per grid second, where one grid second was 1/97200 part of the time taken for one revolution of the earth.

Harmonic Equation 3

$$2693645 = \sqrt{(2C + \sqrt{1/2C})\,(2C)^2}$$

Where C
$$= 144000 - 204.23$$
$$= 143795.77$$

The research will be extended until all the answers are in but the results appear to back up my belief that as the harmonic of light is fractionally decreased, the energy which is released is converted to form physical matter.

From this we can get a glimmering of how an unidentified flying object is able to create a series of resonating frequencies which alter the physical properties within and around it, thus causing a change in the space time frames of reference in relation to the earth or other planetary body.

As I have stated in my previous publications, natural law is not erratic. The universe does not rely on chance to manifest within itself the physical substances which we perceive and call reality. A very strict ordered system of mathematical progressions is necessary to create the smallest speck of matter from the primeval matrix of space.

During my years of research into the complexities of the earth grid system I have gradually built up a picture in my mind of the possible geometric combinations necessary to form matter from resonating, interlocking waveforms.

Matter and anti-matter are formed by the same wave motions in space. The waves travel through space in a spiralling motion, and alternately pass through positive and negative stages. Matter is formed through the positive stage, or pulse, and anti-matter through the negative pulse.

Each spiral of 360° forms a single pulse. The circular motion of an electron about the nucleus of an atom is therefore an illusion. The relative motion of the nucleus and electrons through space gives the illusion of circular motion. The period during the formation of anti-matter is completely undetectable, since obviously all physical matter is manifesting at the same pulse rate, including any instruments or detectors used to probe atomic structures.

The period or frequency rate between each pulse of physical matter creates the measurement which we call time, as well as the speed of light, at the particular position in space of which we are aware, at any given moment.

If the frequency rate of positive and negative pulses is either increased or decreased, then time and the speed of light vary in direct proportion.

This concept would explain time as a geometric, as Einstein theorised it to be.

A rough analogy of physical existence can be made by reference to a strip of motion picture film. Each frame or static picture on the film strip may be likened to a single pulse of physical existence. The division between one frame and the next represents a pulse of anti-matter. When viewed as a complete strip, each frame would be seen as a static picture — say one at either end of the strip — then the past and the future can be viewed simultaneously. However, when the film is fed through a projector, we obtain the illusion of motion and the passage of time. The divisions between the static pictures are not detected by our senses because of the frequency, or speed, of each projection on the movie screen. But by speeding up or slowing down the projector, we can alter the apparent time rate of the actions shown by the film.

To continue this analogy: our consciousness is the projector. The conscious 'I am' part of our individuality passes from one pulse of physical matter to the next within the framework of the physical structure which we term our body, thus giving the illusion of constant reality, and the passing of time.

It is logical to assume that we have a twin stream of consciousness on the anti-matter side of the cycle, which in fact creates a mirror-image of our own individual personality. (This postulate has already been put forward by scientists). The frequency of manifestation of both streams of consciousness, that is, the plus and the minus 'I am', would position our awareness of the illusion of reality at a particular point in space and time. In other words, if the frequency of pulse manifestation is altered, even fractionally, our awareness of reality, in the physical sense, will shift from one spatial point to another. In fact, we would travel from one point in space to another without being aware that we had traversed distance in the physical sense. This would be space travel in the truest sense.

Lets's look at another analogy: we can consider a simple spiral spring as representing the wave motion of an electron through space. Every second 360° spiral of the spring represents the path of the electron in physical matter, while the opposite applies to anti-matter.

The theory outlined above explains why light has been described as being caused by both a wave motion and a pulse. Both explanations are correct.

A pulse of light is manifested when the energy level of the atomic structure is altered by outside influences (theory of Max Planck). In the physical plane, the electron of the atomic structure appears to jump from its orbit. According to my belief, the electron *does not jump orbit*. But this is the illusion we obtain, since we are not equipped to perceive the path of the electron during the anti-matter cycle. What actually happens is that the radius of the spiralling motion is increased or decreased in order to absorb or release the energy imparted to, or removed from, the atomic structure. If the energy is imparted, then the electron must extend orbit in order to maintain balance in the system; and vice versa. Light, or any other radiant energy above or below light frequency, is therefore manifested by undetectable changes in the radius of the spiral motion of the electron during the anti-matter cycle.

If this hypothesis is correct, movement from one point in space to another point, regardless of apparent distance — in other words, true space travel — is completely feasible. By manipulating the frequency rate of the matter-anti-matter cycle, the time and speed of light can be varied in direct proportion to any desired value.

All the mathematical evidence amassed so far indicates that the maximum number of individual elements to be found in the universe will be 144. Each of these elements will have, in theory, six isotopes, which will make up a completed table of separate substances numbering 1008. An isotope is an atom of the same element which has a different nuclear mass and atomic weight.

Mathematically, the progression would create 144 octaves of separate substances giving a theoretical value of 1152. The difference between the total number of substances (1008) and the harmonic value in octaves (1152) would be 144, the light harmonic.

Once the precipitation of physical matter has occured, the buildup of substances takes place according to a very well ordered mathematical sequence. Light-waves, guided seemingly by superior intelligence, form intricate interlocking grid patterns which graduate from the simple to the more complex, as the elements from hydrogen at the lower end of the scale, to element 144, come into being.

When we think of reality we must think of mass in relation to any physical manifestation, and the smallest particle of physical matter that we are aware of is the electron. Therefore electron mass must be the starting point in our quest for a feasible theory to explain the structure of matter.

The average radius of action of the electron around the atomic nucleus must also have a constant harmonic value in order to set up a system of expanding spheres which encompass the structure of each element. As the number of protons in the nucleus increases with the buildup of each element, the spherical space which houses the electron shell must expand to accommodate an equal number of electrons. Although the protons and electrons are nothing more than extremely concentrated wave-forms, we consider them as physical particles in order to build up a picture of our model. As each electron cloud, or shell, expands outward from the nucleus, we find that it can accommodate only eight electrons. The shell is then filled up and another expansion must take place in order to form a new shell or harmonic zone, which again builds up to a maximum of eight electrons. As the magnitude of the harmonic resonance intensifies, heavier and heavier elements are produced until we reach a maximum of 144 elements. The light harmonic is then equal and the cycle has been completed. The whole series is a repetition of octaves of wave-forms forming more and more complex structures.

In my earlier work I had assumed that the harmonic radius of the atom was equal to the mass ratio of the proton and electron. I now realize that although I was on the right track, the theoretical model demonstrated was partly in error. This necessitated another search into the physics books and I now feel that the following calculations based on the experimental values are getting close to the truth.

It would be logical to base the harmonic interaction on the geometric structure of the hydrogen atom. If harmonic equivalents can be derived from the basic values established by experimetal physics, and remain within the laid down tolerances, then almost certainly a new theory should be evident. Especially if the harmonic values closely match those found in the unified equations previously demonstrated.

The distance given between the electron and the proton in the hydrogen atom is approximately 5.3×10^{-11} metre. (Physics Part 2, Halliday & Resnick) I have discovered that a value of:
5.297493×10^{-11} metre fits in very neatly with the previously established harmonic terms. If we convert this value into its geometric equivalent, then:
5.297493×10^{-11} metre
$= 17.15150523 \times 10^{-11}$ geodetic feet
$= 205.8180628 \times 10^{-11}$ geodetic inches

The radius of the hydrogen atom is therefore very obviously tuned to the harmonic value of 20581.80628, which is the number of magnetic lines of force per square geodetic inch. The diameter of the hydrogen atom would be, 411.6361256.

If we calculate the circumference of the atom in terms of harmonic geodetic feet then:
$17.15150523 \times 10^{-11}$ geodetic feet radius
$= 34.30301$ harmonic diameter
$= 107.7660$ harmonic circumference.

Now if we allow spacing on this circumference for eight electron positions we have:
107.7660 divided by 8
$= 13.47$ units

But an electron has only half a spin value; the other half taking place during the anti-matter cycle, so:
13.47 x 2 to allow for the double cycle,
$= 26.94$

Allowing for the accuracy of the conversion factors etc. would make the harmonic geometrics of the hydrogen atom comply fairly closely with the geometric energy value derived from the unified equation (2693645). A comupter program set up for curved geometry should, in theory, show a perfect match.

We can now use the hydrogen atom as a base line to form a theory regarding the formation of the complete atomic table of elements. I believe that the harmonic radius of 205.8180628 units would remain constant throughout the whole range of elements. The orbits of electrons in all substances taking up harmonically spaced positions to the power of ten. In other words by shifting the decimal point to the right or left of this basic harmonic, the orbital radius of all electrons can be calculated. (See diagram 5).

This would apply to the whole range of 144 elements and their isotopes. Physical reality, as we perceive it, being manifested by the concentrated interlocking of harmonic wave-forms, which are built up progressively from a foundation of fundamental wave-packets.

The square of the diameter of the hydrogen atom (4116361257) is equal to the harmonic of mass at the centre of a light field, 1694443. This value also shows up in the cycle of element formation due to the introduction of neutrons into the atomic nucleus. It is stated in the physics books that the maximum number of neutrons that can be contained in the atomic nucleus is 1.6 times the number of protons. The theory of harmonic formation agrees with this. If the ratio of protons and neutrons in the basic element is taken as 1:1 then as each isotope is built up due to the introduction of neutrons we have the mathematical progression of 1:1, 1:1.1, 1:1.2, 1:1.3, 1:1.4, 1:1.5, 1:1.6, for the element and the six isotopes; then as the harmonic increases to 1:1.694443, and above, towards 1:1.7, we get the formation of the next higher element. The cycle would then repeat itself.

The rest mass of the proton is given as 1.67252×10^{-27} Kg, and a mass ratio of 1836 is laid down for the proton and electron. I believe that the harmonic values approach those found in the unifed equations when the atomic structure is accelerated towards the speed of light. According to Einstein the mass increases, and I believe the mass of the proton increases towards the 1694443 harmonic. If the energy level is built up above this point a condition would be reached where a change in physical state would occur. That is, the harmonic would be approaching 1.7 to 1.7018, the surface mass harmonic for an atomic structure, and a change would be triggered.

A gravitational connection with mass becomes evident when the normal gravitational acceleration is converted into grid equivalents. The physics books state that gravity acceleration varies according to latitude on the earth's surface, and also with altitude, or distance from the centre of the earth. The variation at sea level from 0° to 90° latitude is equal to 32.087829 feet/sec^2 to 32.257711 feet/sec^2.

I decided to calculate the grid gravity acceleration at latitude 52.8756° which is 37.1244° from the geometric pole. The reciprocal harmonic of this position (371244) is equal to 2693645. The interpolated standard gravity acceleration at this latitude is 32.194417 feet/sec^2.

The grid time factor I discovered has stood up to scrutiny over the years and is based on 27 periods for one revolution of the earth. Normally we use 24

31

periods of one hour each. The 27 periods, I call 27 grid hours. A grid hour is slightly shorter than a normal hour, and is divided into sixty grid minutes, each of which is equal to sixty grid seconds.

Therefore for one revolution of the earth we have a standard time of 86,400 seconds as against a grid time of 97,200 grid seconds. The ratio is 8:9.

So: $32.194417 \quad \times \dfrac{6000 \times 8}{6080 \quad 9} = 28.24071667$

If this factor is multiplied by 6 then:

$28.24071667 \times 6 = 169.4443$

1694443 harmonic $= (C + \sqrt{1/C})$ Where $C = 143000$ minutes of arc per grid/sec.

Later research indicated that gravity acceleration is manifested directly from the harmonics of light itself. This will be demonstrated in my next book.

As my own research has shown me that physical reality is manifested by the harmonic nature of light, it appears logical that a vehicle constructed to the principles of harmonics will be required to set up the space-time fields necessary. If this is so, then the first criterion will be that the vehicle must resonate in perfect harmony with the complete table of elements in our physical universe. If it does not, then it would be more than probable that any element or particle of matter not in harmonic resonance within the vehicle structure, or payload, would be left behind when the space-time field was activated. The results would be embarrassing, to say the least!

It would be impractical to construct a vehicle made from an alloy of the whole range of 144 elements in the theoretical atomic table. Apart from this, such an alloy is no doubt a physical impossibility.

The clue which suggests a method of overcoming this problem is the way matter is built up in octaves of wave-forms. If an octave of elements could be combined, which would set up a resonating field tuned to all the elements in the table, and the unified fields of space then, maybe, we would have a method of crashing the time barrier.

I put forward the following proposal for consideration. If an octave of elements is the answer let us make a selection from the theoretical table of elements of 144. If we divide 144 by 8 we get divisions of 18 units, therefore we will select each of the elements we require, 18 units part, as follows:

Atomic number   18: argon
Atomic number   36: crypton
Atomic number   54: xenon
Atomic number   72: hafnium
Atomic number   90: thorium
Atomic number 108: X
Atomic number 126: Y   UNDISCOVERED ELEMENTS
Atomic number <u>144: Z</u>
Total number   648

It can be seen that the total harmonic value of the atomic numbers of the combined elements is 648. The square root of this number is 25.45584412, the harmonic of which is found in the polar sections of the world grid. Three new elements just recently discovered have atomic numbers of 116,124 and 126. Do the scientists know something, and are they now looking for numbers 108 and 144.

DIAGRAM 4

Showing the harmonic wave formation of a basic element and the six associated isotopes.

WAVE FORM OF ELEMENT

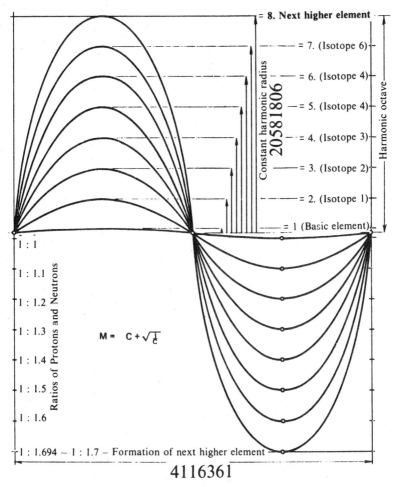

$$M = C + \sqrt{\frac{1}{C}}$$

4116361

DIAGRAM 5

Showing the harmonic wave-form which creates an atom of matter and antimatter, in alternate pulses.

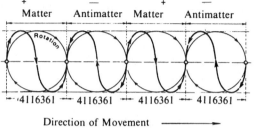

+	—	+	—
Matter	Antimatter	Matter	Antimatter

⸱4116361 — 4116361 — 4116361 — 4116361 —

Direction of Movement ⟶

A point on the surface of the spherical mass would be rotated through the eqivalent of 371.2766511 degrees for each of the matter and anti-matter cycles. (742.5533022 degrees for the double cycle). Spiral Pi in this case would be equal to 3.24.

Electron Orbits

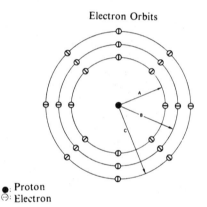

● : Proton
⊖ : Electron

A: Harmonic radius 205.818062
B: Harmonic radius 2058.18062 (In terms of harmonic geodetic inches)
C: Harmonic radius 20581.8062

A: Harmonic radius 17.1515052
B: Harmonic radius 171.515052 (In terms of harmonic geodetic feet)
C: Harmonic radius 1715.15052

The circumference remains a constant harmonic of 107766085 giving an electron spacing harmonic of 1347076. By doubling this harmonic to allow for the matter and anti-matter cycle we have a value of 2694 which closely complies with unified field equation (3) 2693645. A full computer program should make these values match exactly.

Harmonic values based on the Hydrogen Atom.

34

THE HARMONICS OF GREENWICH

Of the 32 boroughs that make up the greater city of London, the most famous would undoubtedly be Greenwich. The area was established in its present boundaries on April 1 1965 by the amalgamation of the former boroughs of Greenwich and Woolich, once known, according to a document dated 918, as Gronwic and Uuluuch.

In 1423 the Duke of Gloucester enclosed Greenwich Park and constructed a watchtower on a hill overlooking the river. This was later to become the Royal Observatory which was founded in 1675, in order to the finding out of the longitude of places for perfecting navigation and astronomy' (Royal warrent, dated 22 June 1675).

In these early days it was very difficult to calculate the longitude position of a ship on the high seas. The arc distance of longitude is measured along a parallel from some starting point. As the earth rotates on an axis which is perpendicular to the planes of the parallel circles, each parallel rotates 360° during each day, or 15° per hour. Because of this the difference in sun time at one place may be calculated by observing the sun at its zenith, but it is difficult to calculate the sun time for two different places simultaneously. The time at one of the places must be known at the other, in order to accurately calculate the longitude. This problem was solved by carrying a chronometer set to the time of a known place. Any great circle from pole to pole, termed a meridian has at all positions along it the same sun time.

All meridians are similar and unfortunately there is no natural starting point from which to begin their numbering, as there is with latitude. There was such confusion over which meridian to choose as the prime starting point for navigation purposes that in 1884 the one that passed through the Royal Astonomical Observatory at Greenwich was internationally agreed upon as the 0°, or prime, meridian. Longitude from that time has been designated as east or west from the Greenwich meridian, to 180°. The length of a degree of longitude varies as the cosine of the latitude.

The main building at Greenwich was designed by Sir Christopher Wren, and has been used as an astronomical museum since 1960. It is said that the brightly lighted area around London made the Greenwich site unsuitable for viewing the stars so the observatory was moved to Herstmonceaux Castle in Hailsham, Sussex. The new site has been operational since 1967, although the old position remains the marker for longitude zero. Greenwich time is adjusted accordingly from the new site.

All the information available on the reasons, and methods, for choosing the site to mark the position of zero longtitude indicated that the choice was a random one, and that the decision of the international body could have placed the zero meridian at any one of an infinite number of positions around the world. I fully believed this to be so until I began to study the mathematical implications of the grid system. I found that many of the geometrical calculations I was experimenting with were only valid when related to the zero position at Greenwich, and the appropriate ninety degree intervals around the world. I was getting what appeared to be valid answers but could not understand the reason why. Many of my critics in the academic circles were quick to point this out, and argued that as the Greenwich meridian was an arbitrary position then all my work was inaccurate, and that the geometric harmonic values discovered must be in major error.

Until recently I had no answer to this and had to accept the derision and disbelief of those not familiar with the main body of my research. When all the evidence I had amassed over the years was studied as a whole it indicated very strongly that the zero position was not random, and that some very positive mathematical process was involved in the choice of this particular line. I fully realised that if my suspicions were correct, the implications were tremendous. If the line was positioned due to purely mathematical considerations, instead of convenience, then it was obvious that the international body concerned was conversant with the associated unified geometric equations just recently discovered in my own research. Who could possibly be aware of this in the year 1884.

The search for the proof I required lasted many years, with the critics snapping at my heels, and deriding my work at every opportunity. I had several verbal battles with so called experts through the media, and TV, and although I could not hope to win such debates, I believe that I was able to hold my own.

Now I believe that I have discovered the necessary proof, which will show the validity of my calculations. The evidence indicates that the Greenwich meridian was meticulously positioned by a group with advanced mathematical knowledge.

Initially I believed that the Great Pyramid in Egypt had a connection in some way with the mathematical puzzle, and my first efforts at solving the problem were centred round this area. I carried out my calculations using the pyramid as a geometric focal point and found that I was able to establish a series of harmonics which were compatible with those found in the main body of my work. One particular set of harmonics was associated with a scientific establishment in Cairo which indicated to me that research was possibly being conducted in the same areas that I was interested in. The positioning of this geometric pattern formed a direct relationship with the Greenwich longitude. this suggested to me that the line was not arbitrary but I felt that more evidence was required to prove the point beyond doubt. In the end I decided to put the whole thing aside and let the matter simmer for a while. I had found in the past that a fresh look at a problem often helped to find the required answers. A year went by before I had another attempt at it.

The key to the geometric problem proved to be centred around the city of Rome. I had spent several weeks feeding coordinates into the computer relating to various religious centres, and places where religious manifestations had occured, in the hope of discovering a connection with the natural laws of mathematics. The results I obtained were quite startling. (See chapter 19).

It slowly became evident that the geometric placing of the Vatican city could be of extreme importance. A careful analysis of the latitude and longitude values within this small area was required to discover some rather interesting harmonics.

The geometric focal point of interest proved to be: Latitude 41° 54′ 22.68″ north / Longitude 12° 27′ 08″ east.

It took some time to solve the significance of the latitude position but eventually I discovered that the difference in displacement of latitude, measured in minutes of arc, from the equator and the north geographic pole created an easily recognised harmonic value, as follows:

Latitude displacement from the north pole	= 2885.622 minutes of arc.
Latitude displacement from the equator	= 2514.378 minutes of arc.
The difference in latitude displacement.	= 371.244 minutes of arc.

The resulting harmonic of 371244 is the reciprocal of the value 2693645 obtained from unified harmonic equation (3).

The great circle displacement of the focal point from Greenwich longitude, calculated at the Vatican latitude was seen to be:
555.5555 minutes of arc.
which is equal to:
69.44444 x 8 (one harmonic octave)

The harmonic 694444 repeating being the reciprocal of the speed of light, in free space; 144000 minutes of arc per grid second, relative to the earth's surface.

The direct great circle distance between the focal point and Greenwich proved to be:
767.6 minutes of arc.
which is equal to
12.7933 degrees.

If this value is subtracted from 360° in order to ascertain the great circle distance between the two points measured the long way round, then we have:
347.2066 degrees
which is half harmonic of:
694.4 (again the reciprocal harmonic of the speed of light)

The area of the cross-sectional segment of the earth bounded by the focal point, the north geographic pole and the earth's centre is equal to:
1377.783014 square degrees, in relation to the earth's surface. The square root of the reciprocal of this figure presents a harmonic of:
2694 (see electron spacing, chapter one)

All of these mathematical relationships will be regarded as pure chance but I would like to add one more just to extend the laws of probability a little further.

The great circle displacement of the focal point in Rome and the longitude passing through the Great Pyramid complex at Cairo, calculated at Vatican latitude, is equal to:
833.3333 minutes of arc.
The square of this number is equal to:
694444.4 (the speed of light reciprocal)

Other interlocking harmonics were found to be associated with several of these points but I believe that those demonstrated will be sufficent to indicate the amazing seeming coincidences which connect them directly with my own research.

It appears that the longitudes passing through both Greenwich and Rome have an important mathematical significance but further research will be necessary to substantiate the theory. Maybe the required answers could be found within the ancient manuscripts held in the Vatican libraries.

The latitude of Greenwich has been listed with slight variations:
In 1776 = 51° 28' 40"
In 1834 = 51° 28' 39"
In 1856 = 51° 28' 38.2"

DIAGRAM 6

Showing the relationship of Greenwich with the Vatican City in Rome and the Great Pyramid in Egypt.

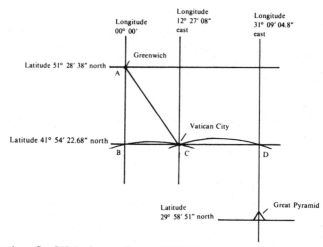

Distance A — C = 767.6 minutes of arc = 12.7933 degrees
360 degrees minus 12.7933 degrees equals 347.2 degrees
This is equal to a half harmonic of 694.4

Distance B — C = 555.555 minutes of arc. This value divided by 8, or one octave is equal to 69.4444.

Distance C — D = 833.333 minutes of arc. The square of this number is equal to 694444.

Not to Scale.

The Harmonic Geometrics of the Earth

The inhabitants of Earth, until comparatively recent times, thought their planet was the most important piece of real estate in the Universe. It was believed that Earth was the only body in space that harboured intelligence, and that, although the Universe consisted of an infinite number of Galaxies and planetary systems, our private God in his wisdom, had left the rest of His vast creation empty of life. The religious organisations generally believed that the Earth was formed for the express purpose of providing a home for man. The scientific organisations had the view that no other planet was capable of supporting life forms, and that the whole thing was an accident. The chances being very remote that the process would be repeated a second time.

Now that we are on the threshold of moving out into deep space, all the old views of our uniqueness are changing, and it is being realised by the new generations that all of creation is a carefully planned process, engineered by some tremendous, omnipresent, super intelligence, and based on the unbreakable laws of mathematics and geometry. We are now slowly beginning to understand these laws, and with the understanding comes the realisation that because of them our uniqueness is no longer a valid concept. The same orderly process that precipitated our planet from the essence of space has no doubt been repeated countless numbers of times to produce systems very similar to ours, which in turn have been populated by beings much the same as ourselves. Hopefully, of course, they exercise more restraint and wisdom than we do in their dealings with each other, and take more care of their immediate environment. Not like some of our sicentists who use the recently discovered knowledge to destroy large chunks of our world by reversing the geometric propositions which govern reality.

Over the last few years there has been a great explosion of scientific curiosity about the structure of the Earth's interior. This is being carried out by physically drilling thousands of feet into the surface in order to closely examine the extracted material; examination of recorded data produced by earthquake and volcanic activity; electronic probing beneath the surface, and electronic and photographic surveillance of the earth's surface, and subsurface, by means of satellite. Thousands of scientists are scattered all over the world, collecting data and probing for new information to feed into the computer banks for analysis. Not much of this great collection of information is made known to the public.

In general terms, we know from readily obtainable publications that the Earth's crust consists of granitic and basaltic layers which have an average thickness of 20 to 25 miles. Below this extends what is called the Mantle, to a depth of around 1,800 miles. At this depth is the boundary of the Outer Core; a suspected shell consisting of sulphides and oxides. The Outer Core is about 1,310 miles thick and is said to consist of heavy metals in molten form. From this inner boundary the Inner Core extends another 850 miles or so to the centre of the Earth. It is believed that the Inner Core consists of the same materials as the Outer Core, but that it is in a solid state due to the tremendous pressure. Some scientists say that at the centre of the earth there is another smaller core which consists of high density atoms.

The crash programme initiated by the world scientific community, in order to probe the geometric structure of the Earth roused my own curiosity, and caused me to pay more attention to the mysteries beneath my feet. Millions of dollars were being diverted into this research by the super-powers, and I felt that something momentous must have triggered it all off. It was possible that the geometric make-up of the Earth had within it the mathematical key to the rest of the Universe. If some definite geometric formula could be found, then it could be applied to other Planets and systems in the regions of space yet to be explored by us. The knowledge derived from the Earth could also add to the information required in order to construct the type of vehicles necessary to safely get us out there.

The scientists were not saying too much about their activities, particularly that going on in the Polar regions, but I had my suspicions that the basic geometric approach that I had applied in my own work was being adapted for many other types of scientific research that I had not even thought of. A check of the geometric positions of some of the scientific bases confirmed my suspicions. Similar harmonic values as those previously published in my books were evident.

This hinted most strongly to me that the key to the inner structure of the Earth was by the application of the universal measurement found on the surface. I had found that this basic measure was the distance subtended by one minute of arc, or what is commonly known as one nautical mile. This measurement is a constant when applied to great circle tracks.

I believed that if it were possible to solve the puzzle of the inner geometrics of the Earth by application of this constant measure, then by implication the same criteria could be applied to the geometric make-up of any other spherical body in the Universe, regardless of size. All that would be required would be the linear measure of one minute of arc on any appropriate spherical surface in order to calculate the other parameters of the body.

This would tend to suggest that Planets of similar size to the Earth, and with similar orbits around a sun of comparative size would have almost the same requirements as regards atmosphere, temperature and gravity etc, in order to support life much the same as ours.

To check the theory it was necessary to convert the known approximate measurements of the inner Earth into minute of arc, or nautical mile equivalents. The best way to tackle the problem, I believed, was to start with the radii of the inner and outer cores. When converted, these measurements would possibly give a rough indication of the presence of universal harmonics, if the respective volumes were calculated. As each core appeared to have an outer shell of highly active material, the outer boundaries were not very clearly defined. The thickness of the shells were not indicated in any of the publications that I could find, so the given measurements could only be taken as approximate.

DIAGRAM 7

Geometric Cross Section Of The Earth

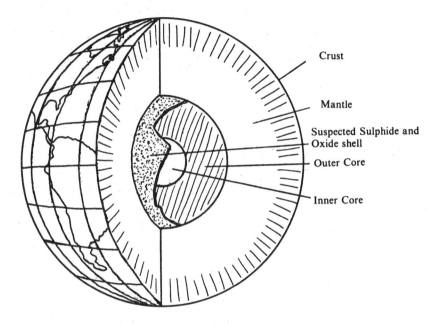

Crust

Mantle

Suspected Sulphide and
Oxide shell

Outer Core

Inner Core

The Earth's crust consists of granitic and basaltic layers which together have an average thickness of between 20 and 25 miles. Below this the Mantle extends to a depth of around 1,800 miles to the boundary of the Outer Core. This area is said to be formed of heavy metals in molten form, and is about 1,310 miles thick. The Inner Core, given as 850 miles thick, is said to consist of the same materials as the Outer Core, but possibly in a solid state due to the tremendous pressure. It is believed by some scientists that at the centre of the Earth there is another much smaller core which consists of high-density atoms.

The given values were converted as follows:

Inner Core radius = 850 statute miles = 738.15789 nautical miles
Outer Core radius = 2160 statute miles = 1875.7894 nautical miles.

DIAGRAM 8

Cross-section, demonstrating the geometry of the Earth's interior. The indications are that all spherical bodies in the Universe are created by the interaction of unified geometric fields. All measurements in minute of arc units (nautical miles) relative to the earth's surface.

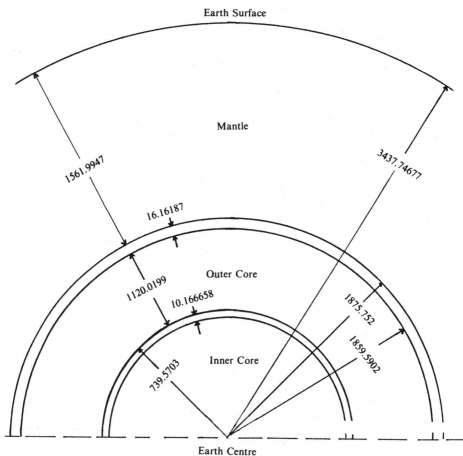

I had formed a rough theory that somewhere in the geometric relationship of the inner and outer core would be found a mathematical key to the unified field. I have stated previously in my work that the harmonic interaction of the unified fields in space cause the precipitation of matter, and the illusion of reality. The initial radii calculated were very close to values which would allow this connection to be made.

A radius of 739.5703 nautical miles to the outer boundary of the inner core would give a volume of 1694443000 cubic nautical miles (or minutes). A radius of 1859.5902 nautical miles to the inner boundary of the outer core would give a volume of 2.693645^{10} cubic nautical miles (or minutes). The shell of the outer core had a calculated thickness of 16.16187 nautical miles, which is equal to 0.2693645 degrees equivalent. The shell of the inner core had a calculated thickness of 10.166658 nautical miles, which is equivalent to 0.1694443 degrees.

The inner core appeared to have a tuned resonance of 1694443, and the inner and outer core combined, that of 2693645 harmonic. Both values much in evidence in my research.

The radius of the surface of the outer core shell equalled 1875.75207 nautical miles. This converted to 2159.9569 statute miles which is extremely close to the given value of 2160 statute miles. The radius to the outer boundary of the inner core shell of 739.5703 nautical miles converted to 851.626 statute miles which is again very close to the given value of 850 statute miles.

I concede that my values will require further refining but I believe that this rough model is not far from the truth. I am merely constructing a theoretical geometric picture for others to examine and evaluate.

It seems that the whole of the earth is structured in such a way that all its parts resonate at a pulsed beat in harmony with the unified field. I find it hard to believe that the formation of our world was some primeval accident, or the whim of some personal God. The whole Universe must be manifested under the same unbreakable mathematical laws. We are but a small infinitesimal mote in the eyes of the intelligent entity that created the Cosmos.

The next breakthrough came when I received a note from a young researcher by the name of Andrew Guthrie. My wife and I had made first contact with Andrew when he was fourteen years old, and keenly delving into the mysteries of electronics. In those days he had an old shed in the back yard stuffed with bits and pieces of radio gear, and wires strung all over the section, plus probes hammered into the ground in various geometric patterns. He was very excited because he had detected electrical effects emanating from the earth, and was sure some sort of power source could be developed from this. He had made a study of my books and wished to help in any way he could. We encouraged his experimentation, although warning him to be very careful that he did not succeed in electrocuting himself, or blowing himself up. Since that time he has admitted to a few frights. He is now in his early twenties and has carried out constant research on his own into the theories of harmonic transmission.

One of my main problems was related to the reduction in the speed of light during the formation of matter. The first indications were that this value was a finite one, and that once matter was manifested, the speed of light remained at a constant reduced value. I was obtaining very good results in my research but could not understand the reasons for the slight variations that showed up in many of my calculations. The hint was there, that the reduction in the speed of light was a variable, depending on position, but until the time I received the note from Andrew I was unable to find an acceptable formula to allow for the discrepancies. My initial calculations had shown that from a value of 144000 minutes of arc a grid second, in free space, the speed of light reduced to around 143830.56 minutes of arc a grid second at the earth's surface, at which point solid matter was manifested to form the planetary body. This was a good working hypothesis and enabled me to discover many startling facts relating to the earth, and calculate values connected with the unified field.

Andrew tackled the problem, and while I was spreading my own research over a wider area, he concentrated his energies in order to help solve it.

His theory was that the speed of light reduced from 144000 minutes of arc per grid second in free space, to a value of 143000 minutes of arc per grid second at the centre of a planetary, or other body.

In other words the speed of light was reduced by 144th of its value at the centre of a light field which manifested matter. The fraction 1/144 is equal to 69444 harmonic, or the speed of light reciprocal.

Andrew further postulated that the reduction from 144000 to 143000, a reduction of 1000 nautical miles per grid second could be again divided into 144 units, each of 6.944 nautical miles per grid second. See diagram 9.

I had a strong feeling that Andrew was correct, but the problem was how to fit this theory into the earth harmonic system. If the reduction could be divided into 144 units of 6.944 what was the ratio of these units above and below the earth's surface. As it was not known at what altitude above the surface that the reduction in light speed commenced it was difficult to calculate how the reduction pattern could be applied.

I eventually discovered that the key was a geometric one and related to the number of degrees in a circle; 360 divided by Pi or 3.1415927, was equal to 114.591559. Further investigation with a calculator revealed that this value could be directly applied to the reduction in light speed from the surface of the earth to the centre. If each unit of reduction was taken as 6.944 nautical miles per grid second then the number of units from the surface to centre equalled 114.591559.

The distance from the earth's surface to the centre is 3437.74677 nautical miles. If we divide this by 114.591559 units we find that a distance of 30 nautical miles is traversed by each drop of 6.944 nautical miles per grid second in light speed. Taking the concept further we could say that for every nautical mile traversed towards the centre of a light field, there is a drop of 0.23148148 nautical miles per grid second of light speed.

There was now a firm basis to work on and it was now possible to make use of the theory to position the whole light field in relation to the earth and check the results from the known facts. The most obvious fact with which to attempt a corelation was the speed of light at the earth's surface. For this calculation it was decided to work backwards from the earth's centre, to the surface.

The given speed of light at the surface is 186,282 statute miles per second which would convert to:
143,796.6316 nautical miles per grid second.
The reduction in light speed from the surface to the centre equals:
114.591559 x 6.944 = 795.724 nautical miles per grid second.
If we add this to the speed of light at the earth's centre:
143,000 + 795.724 = 143,795.724 nautical miles per grid second.
Therefore the theoretical geometric value of the speed of light at the earth's surface is 143,795.724, as against an experimental value of, 143,796.6316; a difference of 0.9076 nautical miles per grid second.

The degree of error is so small that I believe the theory is validated and could now be used to check other scientific facts relating to earth harmonics. The next step was to calculate the altitude at which the reduction commenced above the earth's surface. It was logical to assume that this would be at the outer boundary of the main atmosphere, as this would be the upper limit of the formation of matter due to the vortexual action of the light field. The average height of the atmosphere above the earth is believed to be around 1,000 statute miles. (see Readers Digest World Atlas, page 108). As shown, the reduction in light speed is equal to 1,000 nautical miles per grid second, equal to 144 units of 6.944 nautical miles per grid second. The number of units above the earth's surface is therefore 144 minus 114.592 which equals 29.408 units. As each unit is equal to a movement of 30 nautical miles towards the light field centre, then:
29.408 x 30 = 882.24 nautical miles.
Therefore the theoretical geometric height of the main atmosphere above the surface is 882.24 nautical miles, which converts to 1015.9 statute miles. This conforms fairly closely to the given estimates so once again the theory appears to hold out.

At this point we could look at the geometric altitude of the magnetosphere which is a deep radiation zone consisting of charged particles, extending from the upper limits of the main atmosphere to an estimated distance of 40,000 statute miles. (see Life Nature Library Book, The Earth, page 67). If we convert this estimated value of 40,000 statute miles into nautical miles, or minutes of arc related to the earth's surface, we have a value of : 34,736.842 nautical miles.

According to all other indications I would give a theoretical value for this distance of : 34,722.22 nautical miles.

This would be a half-harmonic of 694444, repeating; the reciprocal harmonic of the speed of light.

A glance at diagram (9) will show how the energy pattern of the light field can be associated with the varying energy harmonic of the unified field. At the outer limit of the spiralling light field the speed of light is 144,000 nautical miles per grid second, giving a geometric energy harmonic of

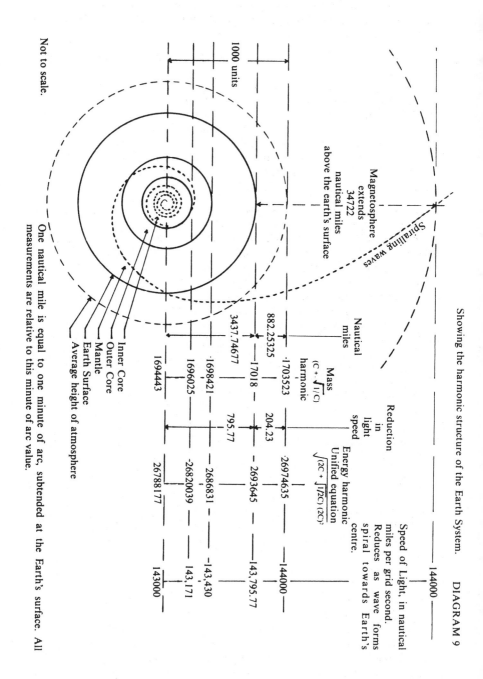

Showing the harmonic structure of the Earth System.   DIAGRAM 9

Not to scale.

One nautical mile is equal to one minute of arc, subtended at the Earth's surface. All measurements are relative to this minute of arc value.

1000 units

Magnetosphere
extends
34722
nautical miles
above the earth's surface

Spiralling waves

Inner Core
Outer Core
Mantle
Earth Surface
Average height of atmosphere

Nautical
miles

Mass
$(C + \sqrt{1/C})$
harmonic

3437.74677
882.25325
·1703523
·1698421
1696025
1694443

17018

Reduction
in
light speed

204.23

795.77

Energy harmonic
Unified equation
$\sqrt{(2C + \sqrt{1/2C})(2C)^2}$

26974635
2693645
·2686831
·26820039
26788177

Speed of Light, in nautical
miles per grid second.
Reduces as wave forms
spiral towards Earth's
centre.

144000
144000
143,795.77
143,430
143,171
143000

26974635. This value reduces to 26936455 at the earth's surface; 26868315 at the boundary of the outer core; 26820039 at the boundary of the inner core and 26788177 at the centre of the field.

Andrew discovered another startling fact when he was carrying out various calculations relating to the centre of the light field. The note he sent me regarding this went partly as follows:

Captain look closely at your mass equation : $M = (C + \sqrt{1/C})$

Substituting 144,000 naut/miles/grid sec. for C: Mass = 170352313 harmonic.
Substituting 143,000 naut/miles/grid sec. for C: Mass = 169444294 harmonic.

It appears that the 1694443 harmonic denotes the central point of a light field.

It was pleasing to find that a member of the next generation was able to grasp the concepts that I had put forth in my earlier publications, and was able to help in extending the knowledge. If my books help to spark off further original research in more young minds I will feel that my efforts have been worthwhile.

If we now look at the surface and cross-sectional areas of the earth in terms of nautical mile, or minute of arc, values in regard to distance on the surface some quite interesting facts emerge.

The cross-sectional area is equal to 37127665.09 square nautical miles. The harmonic reciprocal of this number is 26934093.

The surface area is equal to 148510660.36 square nautical miles. Each quarter of the earth's surface is therefore equal to 37127665.09 square nautical miles. The harmonic reciprocal again being 26934093.

I would have expected the area harmonics to be similar to the energy harmonics derived from the unified equations calculated at the earth's surface (2693645). This would have made all the facts fit together very neatly. In order to make them fit there would have to be a loss of area somewhere.

It is possible that the answer to the puzzle will be discovered in the geographic pole areas. Calculations show that things may not be as they seem in these areas. As both poles are covered with vast caps of snow and ice it is not possible to chart the contours of the land masses beneath by normal methods. Over the years many books have been written, and speculations abound regarding the so-called holes at the poles. Until recently I have dismissed all such stories as figments of the imagination, but work on the calculator has shown evidence in favour of the existence of circular depressions and relatively small holes in the vicinity of the poles. If they do exist the areas would be plugged with thousands of feet of ice and would not be visible from the surface. It is said that the ice at the south pole is around two miles thick.

It has also been speculated, up till now, that if the holes do exist, they would be coincident with the geographic poles. I do not believe this to be necessarily so. It is possible that they are off-set from the geographic axis in much the same way as the earth's magnetic poles, and have some obscure relationship with the earth's magnetic field. All the published diagrams showing the various fields surrounding the earth indicate that they take on a cross-sectional shape in the form of a doughnut. There are definite holes in the poles of the radiation field but the Earth polar areas which lay directly below these clear sections have always been regarded as solid areas. As the Earth was created from the same wave motions that form the surrounding fields, then there is the slight probability that the doughnut pattern is also applicable to the planetary sphere formed at the centre.

A small amount of evidence which could back up this theory was placed in my hands a few months ago by an overseas friend which I will reproduce here, in the hope that a reader will be able to supply more data. The source and date of the following extract are unkown:

"What would happen if Halley's Comet collided with the Earth? Now we may know since new evidence has accumulated indicating that something weighing about 15 billion tons hit Antarctica at 45,000 miles per hour about 700,000 years ago.

That's about the size and speed of an object like Halley's Comet or a rocky asteroid three miles in diameter.

The impact of such a celestial blockbuster would rip open a gigantic crater and toss billions of tones of melted rock and steaming vapours into the atmosphere, to be showered over a large portion of the Earth.

The evidence that such an event actually happened was recently announced by geophisicists John Weihaupt and Franz Vanderhoven of Purdue University. Their measurements of gravity changes over a section of Antarctica called Wilkes Land revealed a depression some 150 miles in diameter under the ice. The feature is interpreted as a crater resulting from the impact of a massive object from space. ..."

My interpretation of the report is that the hidden crater could be a clue to the possible existence of the mysterious so-called holes at the poles. If my speculation is correct then there should be a similar crater of the same dimensions hidden beneath the ice at the geometrically opposite point in Greenland. At the centre of each crater I would expect to find a hole which descended into the bowels of the earth. It would not surprise me if the scientists have already established a base beneath the ice at the spot — suspended in the ice plug, or ice window, over the hole.

The mathematical evidence is as follows:
The diameter of the hidden crater is given as, some 150 miles.
A close approximation of:
150.2189714 miles,
would be equivalent to:
130.4533173 nautical miles (or minutes of arc at the earth's surface)
The square of the diameter would be:
17018.068
which is equal to the 17018068 harmonic of mass at the earth's surface.
The area of the crater would be:
13365.95932 square nautical miles
Which is equal to:
3.712766477 square degrees (equivalent to the earth's surface)
The reciprocal of this value:
0.269340936.

These harmonics are evident in the full cross-sectional area of the earth.

The theoretical diameter of the suspected hole at the centre of the crater would have a value of:

90.9345139 nautical miles (or minutes of arc at the earth's surface)

The area of the hole:

6494.524813 square nautical miles.

Therefore the area of the holes both north and south:

12989.04962 square nautical miles.

Area of the earth's surface equals:

148510660.3 square nautical miles.

Minus the area of the holes equals:

148497671.3 square nautical miles.

This value divided by 4 to allow for each 90 degree sector equals:

37124417.82

The reciprocal of this number equals:

2.693645_{-8} harmonic (unified equation)

The diameter of the hole would be harmonically equivalent to the drop in light speed in the harmonic unified equation (2) demonstrated in chapter one. This is related to the earth's magnetic field.

The position of the crater is given somewhat vaguely as somewhere in Wilkes Land. The exact latitude and longitude at this time is unknown to me. If it does turn out to be a natural depression related to the earth's structure then I would expect the position to be harmonically related to the Greenwich longitude in some way. If this proves to be so, at some future time, then the Greenwich longitude would be mathematically assured, and it would show beyond doubt that the initial calculations were not produced by chance. Any information available from readers would be greatly appreciated.

We move on now to a comment from a Life Nature Library book called, The Earth. On page 13 is the following information.

"The gravitational fields of the sun and the Moon have several different effects on the spacial movements of the Earth because of the constantly changing relative positions of the three bodies. Because the resultant forces are not constant, one effect is a slight nodding of the earth's axis called nutation. The axis moves through one nutational cycle every 18.6 years which coincides with the length of a full cycle of the motions of the moon.

I believe that the movement also hints at a relationship with the forces inherent in the geometry of the unified field. The cycle of 18.6 years is also a geometric one as the earth in this time carries out 18.6 full spirals through space, or full circles around the Sun. The Moon likewise in this time completes 18.6 patterns of movement.

It has been demonstrated time and again in my work that the value of 18595902 (harmonic), or 186 in round figures, has a direct relationship with the energy harmonic of the unified field; 2693645. A sphere with this harmonic radius has a volume of 2693645 units. A very careful computer analysis of the cycle could show that the harmony of the spheres is absolute and that the unity between all things prevails.

While we are at it, let's check the mean orbital velocity of the earth, given as around 18.5 miles per second (66,000 miles per hour) in the Readers Digest, Atlas of the Universe, page 35.

If we assume a very close approximation of 18.51071268 miles per second, the following harmonics are evident:

18.51071268 miles per second

= 14.28897119 Nautical miles per grid second

= 857.3382716 Nautical miles per grid minute

= 51,440.2963 Nautical miles per grid hour

= 1,388,888 Nautical miles per grid day

= (694,444 x 2)

This means that every time the earth completes one half of a revolution, it moves through space a distance of 694,444 nautical miles, or minutes of arc, in relation to its surface. The harmonic 694,444 of course being the harmonic reciprocal of the speed of light, 144,000 minutes of arc a grid second in free space. This would seem logical to me. If the earth is manifested from the depths of space by a unified light field, then its movement through space should have some harmonic affinity to the field. In this instance the relationship is that of the light reciprocal. More computer work for somebody to prove the point?

The most important problem tackled by man in the last 25 years, apart from delving into the mysteries of the atom, has been to find the most efficient way to leave the surface of the earth and move out into the environment of space. The main hurdle that had to be overcome was the restricting force of gravity. Right through our known history, we have been chained to the earth by this so called force, and regardless of the vast amount of scientific knowledge accumulated until the present time, the fundamental reason for the creation of a gravitational field remains unknown. Scientists have made many attempts to devise some sort of instrument to detect gravity waves which they believe to have originated from other parts of the galaxy. But, so far as I am aware, they have been unsuccessful. Could this be because gravity is not a force as we normally understand it, and that gravity waves, as such, do not exist? Could it be that the gravitational effect is manifested by nothing more than the relative motions of the wave forms of two or more bodies in space. The proof of this is visible to us in the motions of the many satellites around the earth. The only thing that keeps them up there is their velocity in space relative to that of earth. If the velocity is reduced below a certain critical factor, then the satellite will spiral in towards the earth's surface. Granted it takes a great deal of energy to get it up there, but once that critical velocity is attained it will circle the earth forever, if need be, as long as it is above the atmosphere, which would cause friction and energy loss.

As all previous evidence suggests that the earth is formed by the vortexual action of a light field, it would seem probable that the harmonics associated with light could have a direct bearing on the gravitational effect. In order to nullify the gravitational effect it would be necessary to set up a geometric proposition which would be in harmonic oppositition to that of the light field. I pondered on this for a while, then came to the conclusion that the harmonic opposition would have to be a geometric energy level contrary to that of the unified field; and the figure derived from the unified field was 2693645, within present accuracy. So I had to search for the reciprocal of this number which in harmonic terms is, 371244169.

The text books say that in order to escape the gravitational attraction of earth, a body must reach a velocity of 25,000 miles per hour. To test the theory we must change this value into geometric terms equivalent to those at the earth's surface. The terms being nautical miles, or minutes of arc, and grid time. A check on the calculator showed that although a body was no longer influenced by the gravitational attraction of the earth at 25,000 miles per hour, the actual transition point was when the body passed through a velocity of 24,960.42634 miles per hour — as follows:

24,960.42634 miles per hour
= 21,676.15973 nautical miles per hour
= 19,267.69755 nautical miles per grid hour
19,267.69755 squared
= 3712441691 harmonic
the reciprocal of which equals
2693645 harmonic.

From this it was possible to formulate an equation in terms of the speed of light and the unified field which would create an anti-gravitational effect:

$$\text{Escape velocity harmonic} = \sqrt{\sqrt{\frac{1}{\sqrt{(2C + \sqrt{1/2C})\,(2C)^2}}}}$$

$$= 19,267.69755 \text{ nautical miles per grid hour.}$$

Where C = the speed of light harmonic at the earth's surface.

A computer programme would be necessary to demonstrate the slight variation in this value due to the changing energy harmonic of the unified equation during the transition from the earth's surface to the level of escape velocity.

I believe there are clues in other sections of this book regarding the means of making practical application of this equation. I have no doubt that there are scientific groups that have already done so.

THE HARMONICS OF THE GREAT PYRAMID

It is obvious that knowledge of vast importance to mankind is locked up in the secrets of the pyramids and the very word *pyramid* should give us the first clue. The literal meaning is "fire in the middle". On page 86 of *The Great Pyramid — Its Divine Message,* by D. Davidson and H. Aldersmith, another derivation of the word is given: *pyramid* is the Grecianised form of the Hebrew *urrim-middin* — "light measures". The Egyptian name for the Great Pyramid is *Khuti* — "the Lights". In the Semitic languages the equivalent name is *urim* — "the Lights". In Phrygian and Greek, the root *ur* (light) became successively *pur* and *pyr* (fire) and *pyra* (plural), "beacon fires".

In Chaldee and Hebrew *middin* equals "measures". hence the chaldee-Hebrew name for the Great Pyramid — in Egyptian *Khuti,* "the Lights", is *Urim-middin (purim-middin)* or "lights-measures".

A little thought will make it obvious that the Cheops pyramid and all similar edifices were not built by normal means. Some of the 70 ton blocks of red granite were transported from quarries which are 600 miles from Giza. The usual explanation that hundreds of slaves carted these across the desert using wooden rollers and raffia ropes is ridiculous. consider: the number of trees necessary to make rollers to transport 2,500,000 blocks; the tons of raffia necessary to twist into miles of rope; the accommodation, housing and feeding problems of the slave labour employed.

There is only one answer to the riddle of such construction methods: antigravity. Only by this means could the large blocks be moved over great distances and placed so accurately. The time factor of the building programme would also have been reduced drastically by diminishing the weight of the blocks during their movement from quarry to pyramid.

Another problem to be overcome was the cutting and dressing of the blocks. Can you imagine hundreds of slaves cutting 70 to 600 ton blocks of solid granite out of deep quarries with primitive tools; then lifting them out without machinery; then squaring and dressing the surfaces to a mirror finish with a hammer and chisel; then loping off across the desert, on occasion for 600 miles, to dump them in a stockpile at the base of the pyramid?

The blocks are so finely dressed that I would suggest that the method of cutting was by use of laser beam. The laser (or amplified light beam) would be harmonically tuned to create a beam of light that was selective to granite only. I believe that a laser can be constructed so that it is harmonically tuned to the frequency rate of any type of matter.

The pyramid builders were not primitive people. The designers were scientists of extremely high intellect and the work was carried out by highly-skilled craftsmen using methods far more advanced than are known today. The reason for construction was also far from the mundane one of providing a tomb for the odd Pharaoh. A Pharaoh would have to be odd to tie up so much manpower resources and wealth in such a project merely to have his remains stored in a gigantic stone box.

My research has led me to believe that the Great Pyramid, particularly, was constructed for a definite scientific purpose. The exact purpose is not yet clear, although the mathematics show that the fundamental measurement throughout the structure is based on the harmonic frequency of light. Calculations also indicate that the passageways and chambers have been engineered in such a way as to form wave guides and cavity resonators which are tuned to light, mass and gravitational frequencies.

I found some interesting facts in a pamphlet written in 1972 by a Mr G. Patrick Flanagan, Ph.D., on the Pyramid and its Relationship to Biocosmic Energy.

Mr Flanagan states that the Great Pyramid of Giza is a powerful source of biocosmic energy. He calls this particular field of science Magnetic Form Resonance and says that his research results confirm that the energy is of a special magnetic nature — the forces that bind the universe together. Energies of microcosmic levels may be tuned in with microcosmic devices such as the pyramid. "The Pyramid generates millimicrowave or nanowave radiation by the simple fact that it has five corners — the four base corners plus the apex. The corners are in effect a type of nanowave radiator. The radiation from the molecules or the atoms of matter in the pyramid combine by the angles of the corners into a beam which besects the angles and transmits a beam of this radiation towards the centre of the pyramid. The molecules or atoms of this area absorb these energies by resonance. As the energy increases, the electron orbits start to expand. As more energy is absorbed more expansion occurs. There would be a point at which, if there were too much energy absorbed, the atoms would disintegrate, and the electrons would fly off, but the energy required for this would be far more than the pyramid could concentrate. As the energy increases there is an increase in circulation and finally there is a highly saturated energy atmosphere in the wave bands around 10 nanometers. The energy would also radiate outwards from the corners of the pyramid."

An article was printed in the 23 August, 1972 issue of the Toronto Star which concerned the theories expounded on the structure of pyramids by Eric McLuhan, son of Marshal McLuhan and an electronics specialist at Sir Michael's College.

McLuhan says that "pyramids do something. They are not just glorified tombstones, as many of the early pyramids show no evidence of burial. A cardboard pyramid of the right dimensions — the same dimension as the Great Pyramid of Cheops — is capable of sharpening a dull razorblade placed inside it, or of dehydrating meat. Researchers in Czechoslovakia, France, the USA and elsewhere have satisfied themselves that the pyramid's shape, in some way that we don't undertand, acts as a device for manipulating forms of energy that modern science hasn't yet defined. But how?"

When McLuhan saw a photograph of the bent pyramid at Danshur, he considered it to be a two-frequency octahedron and the fact that Egyptian priests in ancient times had used the same geometric concept set him thinking. He says "the reason the pyramids have remained an enigma is the separation between disciplines. If an archaeologist knows nothing about electronics, he is not likely to see that the pyramids were tools; a sophisticated piece of technology."

To test his theories he farmed out several experimental pyramids to scientists in Toronto, Hamilton and Ottawa. One is dehydrating food, one is sharpening razorblades, and in a third they're experimenting with semiconductors — the crystalline electronic components that are the basic building-blocks of modern miniaturised electronics. McLuhan speculates that the semiconductors grown inside the pyramid could be the most efficient ever known because they have been grown in a magnetically pure environment.

He theorises that as the transistor manipulates electrons, so the pyramid can focus, or deploy, the forces of magnetism and gravity. The dehydration and edge-sharpening effects are explained in terms of wave mechanics. Oxygen atoms behave differently inside magnetic fields. Magnetism can affect the way they bond with, or dissociate from, other elements. Since the razor's edge is composed of metal oxides, and since oxygen atoms depart during the dehydration process, McLuham suspects that a coherent magnetic field inside the pyramid may be the explanation. "The pyramid is a resonating cavity", he says, "just like a trumpet, a cyclotron or a hi-fi speaker."

Another interesting article which points to the fact that the pyramid shape sets up some type of electromagnetic or gravitational force was published by the London Times on 14 July 1969. The article written by John Tunstall says in part:

"Scientists who have been trying to X-ray the pyramid of Chephren at Giza, near Cairo, are baffled by mysterious influences that are throwing into utter confusion the readings of their space-age electronic equipment. For twenty-four hours a day for more than a year, in the hopes of finding secret chambers thought to exist within the six-million-ton mass of the pyramid, they have been recording on magnetic tape the pattern of cosmic rays reaching the interior.

The idea is that as the rays strike the pyramid uniformly from all directions, they should, if the pyramid is solid, be recorded uniformly by a detector in the chamber at the bottom.

But if there were vaults above the detector, they would let more rays through than the solid areas, thereby revealing their existence. More than one million dollars and thousands of manhours have been spent on the project, which was expected to reach a climax a few months ago when the latest IBM 1120 computer was delivered to Ein Shams university near Cairo.

At Ein Shams, Dr Amr Gohed, in charge of the installation at the pyramid, showed me the new IBM 1120 computer surrounded by hundreds of tins of recordings from the pyramid, stacked up in date order. Though hesitant at first, he told me of the impasse that had been reached.

"It defies all the known laws of science and electronics," he said picking up a tin of recordings. He put the tape through the computer which traced the pattern of cosmic ray particles on paper. He then selected a recording made the next day and put it through the computer. but the recorded pattern was completely different.

"This is scientifically impossible," he told me ...

I asked Dr Gohed, "Has this scientific knowhow been rendered useless by some forces beyond man's comprehension?"

He hesitated before replying, then said: "Either the geometry of the pyramid is in substantial error, which would affect our readings, or there is a mystery which is beyond explanation — call it what you will — occultism, the curse of the Pharaohs, sorcery, or magic — there is some force that defies the laws of science at work in the pyramids!"

This particular research project was sponsored by the US Atomic Energy Commission, the Smithsonian Institute, and the Ein Shams University in Cairo.

Davidson and Aldersmith go to great lengths in their book to refute the idea that the Pyramid was constructed as a tomb and that it was built to serve some other purpose.

The direct proof against a tombic theory is an engineering proof, and a definitely convincing engineering proof. The first ascending passage which leads from the entrance or descending passage into all the inner passages and chambers of the Pyramid was, and is, closed by a tightly fitting granite plug or block at its lower or entering end. According to the exponents of the tombic theory, this plug was retained loose in the Grand Gallery or elsewhere in the Pyramid's upper system, until the death of the king. The mummy case, it is alleged, was then dragged up the ascending passages and deposited in the King's Chamber; after which the granite plug was released and permitted to slide down from the Grand Gallery into the first ascending passage to its lower end. Here according to the theory it came to rest, tightly wedged in, impossible to remove except by quarrying. In this position it effectively sealed access to the upper passages and chambers. There the plug still remains, sealing the access, and entrance to the first ascending passage behind the plug is gained only by means of Al Mamoun's quarried shaft, which was excavated about AD800.

Now the peculiar fact concerning this plug is that it would fit just as tightly the depth of the upper end of the passage as it does the lower. Any engineer, architect or constructional operative knows that it is impossible to slide or push a block of stone, however smoothly dressed and accurately squared, along a passage, after the passage has been completely constructed, if the block fits the passage tightly. It is a matter of experience in such circumstances that the block will jam in the passage unless it has at least three quarters of an inch clearance all round ... it is therefore obvious that the first ascending passage was plugged as soon as the building of it began ... from this it is certain that the first ascending passage and the upper passages and chambers were not intended for any contemporary purpose, that they were not intended for the transit and reception of the royal or any other mummy, and that the Great Pyramid was not built as a tomb.

Another fact pointed out was that of the ventilation shafts provided for the King's and Queen's chambers. The shafts were not needed during construction and fresh air is of no earthly use to a mummy. The shafts to the Queen's chamber were not completely cut through the walls until 1872 by a Mr Wayman Dixon and a Dr Grant. The position of the other shaft was only discovered because of a small crack in the wall and the remaining five inches was cut from the stonework. The position of the other shaft was calculated from the location of the first. They made the statement: "The ventilation shafts were provided for the future, when the Pyramid should be the subject of study by the people of a later civilisation."

I was surprised to find during my delving into all the writings I could find on the Pyramid that the measurements taken by each scientific expedition sent to probe the structure differed to a remarkable degree. The cause of this was mainly due to the fact that most of the outer casing stones have been stripped off over the years in order to construct other buildings around Cairo. Also, the top few feet of the Pyramid are missing, thus making it difficult to ascertain the exact completed dimensions. There is also the sneaking suspicion that some of the measurements were engineered to fit some pet theory. (I acknowledge that I also could be accused of this, but will set forth my theoretical set of measurements and await further scientific analysis in the future by independent groups to either confirm or deny my conclusion).

Some of the various measurements found by others are: Colonel Howard Vyse, son of General Richard Vyse, found a base side length of 764 British feet, and a casing stone angle of 51°51'.

Frenchmen Coutelle and Le Pere found a base side length of 763.62 British feet. By using the casing stone angle of 51° 51' and the French base length of 763.62 feet, a theoretical height of 485.5 feet was calculated, assuming a special base-side to height ratio.

From the book *The Source of Measures* by Skinner, the height as calculated by Professor P. Smyth (see *Our Inheritance in the Great Pyramid)* approximates a value of 486 feet 2 inches. Another calculation in this book gives a height of 486 British feet and a base side of 763.407 feet. In *The Great Pyramid — Its Divine Message* by D. Davidson and H. Aldersmith, various values are given: base 754.916 feet; height 484.416 feet — base 754.916 feet, height 480.833 feet — base 760.916, height 484-416 feet.

At the time of writing my third book, the Pulse of the Universe, Harmonic 288, I believed that I was in possession of enough information to attempt a breakdown of the structure in terms of light, gravity and mass harmonics. Recent research has indicated that although I was getting close to the mark a further refining of the calculations was necessary in order to correlate the measurements with the harmonic wave patterns associated with the formation of matter. I had based my calculations solely on a system of geodetic measure as I was not aware at the time that the so-called pyramid inch and the geodetic inch, or foot, had any direct connection with each other.

The Pyramid inch is given in most publications as being equal to 1.0011 British inches, and is said to be derived from the distance measured between the earth's north and south poles. There has been much argument as to whether this particular standard of measure is valid, or just something dreamed up by various researchers in order to fit some pet theory. Myself included.

I believe I have found a clue to its validity in connection with the so-called stone Boss which is evident on the granite leaf suspended in grooves across the entrance to the Ante-Chamber. The Boss is roughly horse-shoe shaped and measures approximately 5 x 5 pyramid inches on its outer face. Time has taken its toll and the surfaces are no longer smooth, so absolute accuracy in measuring it is no longer possible. It has been said in some publications that one British investigator was caught trying to file down the stone so that it would conform exactly to the British inch. Most embarrassing.

If it can be eventually accepted that the original size of the Boss face was 5 x 5 pyramid inches then the question presents itself — why the odd size of five inches? The Boss itself appears to have no function, other than being a key to the basic measure used in the pyramid construction, so with this in mind I checked with the calculator to see whether this particular dimension had any mathematical connection with geodetic measure.

The following results were obtained:
5 Pyramid inches multiplied by 1.0011
= 5.0055 British inches
= 4.939638157 geodetic inches (ratio = 6080 - 6000)
= 0.411636513 geodetic feet.

Allowing for minute conversion errors I believe that we can safely say that : 5 pyramid inches are equal to 0.411636125 geodetic feet.

The harmonic of 0.411636125 squared is equal to 0.1694443 which in turn is equal to the harmonic of mass at the centre of a light field, as demonstrated in other sections of this book. The structure of the atom is also associated with this number.

After discovering this I could then see that the pyramid was constructed to a dual system of measurment which helped to ensure the secrecy of its true purpose. There was no need to convert the pyramid inch into some other system of measure in order to solve the original dimensions. The geodetic associations are automatically allowed for in the construction.

Taking into account the many slight distortions due to subsidence over the thousands of years since the building's erection, the harmonic measure of 411636125 units is found in several sections of the internal cavaties.
The King's Chamber 411.636125 x 205.8180624 pyramid inches.

The width of the descending passage	= 41.1636125 pyramid inches
The width of the ascending passage	= 41.1636125 pyramid inches
The width of the passage entrance to the Queen's Chamber	= 41.1636125 pyramid inches
The width of the floor in the Grand Gallery	=41.1636125 pyramid inches
The height of the Coffer in the King's Chamber	=41.1636125 pyramid inches

All these clues point us towards a possible solution to all the other dimensions.

In my last book I presented theoretical units of 763.675323 feet for the base side length and 486 feet for the original height. The mathematical evidence now available, which has been gathered from many sources since that time, indicates that a slight modification of the values is necessary to bring them closer to perfection. I do not expect this to be the final result as further refining of the theoretically perfect pyramid will continue as more mathematical correlations are discovered. The most important thing, I believe is to present the findings as they come up so that others can work on the problem and eventually either substantiate, or disprove, the theoretical proposition.

The previous base measure by the Frenchmen, Coutelle and Le Pere of 763.62 British feet, and the height estimated by Professor P. Smyth of 486 feet 2 inches would now appear to be closer to the original.

My recent work on the calculator in connection with the harmonic relationships of the speed of light, mass and gravity have led me to the conclusion that the measurements could have been: 763.6063832 British feet for the base side length, at the corner socket level, and: 486.4 British feet, for the height.

As I now believe that the Pyramid inch is a valid measure and that the secrets of the structure are based on this value, it is necessary to convert all other measurements into these units. So

763.6063832 British feet
=9163.276599 British inches
=9153.208071 Pyramid inches
= 762.7673392 Pyramid feet, for the length of the base side. And:
486.400458 British feet
= 5836.805496 British inches
= 5830.392064 Pyramid inches
= 485.8660053 Pyramid feet.

Now, if we analyse these dimensions a pattern will emerge which will show proportions which have a direct harmonic relationship with mass and gravity. A base side length of:
762.7673392 Pyramid feet gives a diagonal length for the base square of:
1078.715915 Pyramid feet which means that the distance from the centre of the base to each corner equals; 539.3579575 Pyramid feet.

A glance at diagram 10 will show that the base can be constructed on four interlocking circles, each of which has a diameter of 539.3579575 Pyramid feet.

The circumference of each circle is:
1694.443 Pyramid feet, which has the associated harmonic affinity with mass and gravity.

The height of:
485.8660055 Pyramid feet creates a reciprocal harmonic associated with the mass value.

The reciprocal equals:
20581806 harmonic (see the magnetic field — chapter one)
This number doubled:
= 411636125 harmonic.
This number squared
= 1694443 harmonic.

All the interrelated values are evident in the structure of the atom.

The base side length shown has been measured, as stated, at the socket levels into which the Pyramid is keyed. The south east socket depth, from platform level, is given as 41.216 British inches in the book called, *The Great Pyramid, in Fact, and in Theory* by William Kingsland, M.I.E.E. This depth is equal to 41.17 Pyramid inches when converted. (could we say a more accurate figure would possibly be 41.1636125 Pyramid inches? — interesting).

The main body of the Pyramid has been constructed on a level platform which in turn has been constructed on the surface of the natural rock foundation. It has been argued that the true base measurement should be taken at this level, but I think now that the measurements at both levels are valid from a mathematical point of view.

Mr Kingsland states in his book that, "It is now recognised by Sir Flinders Petre and also by the Egyptian Government survey that the proper base line measurement should be taken at platform level at the foot of the casing stones. The measurements made by the two observers are given for all four sides, and I will tabulate them as given in the published report of the Egyptian Government survey.

Side	Length, Petrie 1880	New Determination 1925	Difference
North	9069.4	9065.1	+— 4.3
South	9069.5	9073.0	+— 3.5
East	9067.7	9070.5	+— 2.8
West	9068.6	9069.2	+— 0.6
Mean	9068.8	9069.4	+— 0.6

The agreement is seen to be very remarkable, and it is unlikely that we shall obtain any more accurate figures in the future, or at all events until the three remaining base sides are cleared of rubbish so as to enable a direct measurement to be made. Even then however, we should expect the correction to be very small."

As will be seen from the table the measurements fell within a certain range of tolerance, so I will be bold enough to assume a true base length, at the platform level, of 9070.363465 British inches, which falls within this range. If we now convert this to Pyramid inches we have:
9060.397029 Pyramid inches for the base length, at platform level. If we now compare the two base perimeters, at socket level and platform level we have:
9153.208071 Pyramid inches at socket level.
9060.397029 Pyramid inches at platform level.
92.811042 Pyramid inches difference.
for all four sides the difference in perimeter measure:
= (92.811042 x 4) = 371.244168 Pyramid inches

The reciprocal harmonic of this number:
= 2.693645 -03 (2693645 harmonic — unified equation)

It appears from this that both the perimeter values should be taken into consideration, and would suggest that other researchers follow this line of mathematical analysis in order to verify the theory. I believe this to be the correct approach, but it will take much more verification to prove it. This could only be done by further survey. The two perimeter values at the different levels could explain why previous investigators, myself included, have assumed that the base of the pyramid had a waisted in effect on each of its four sides. It was thought that the two perimeters had been measured at the same level.

The calculated slant height from each corner of the Pyramid, at socket level, to the apex, equals:
725.9289103 Pyramid feet
The square root of this value
= 26.943

Which approximates very closely the unified harmonic of 2694 found in the structure of the Hydrogen Atom. (See Chapter one).

The most important area of the pyramid is the 'Kings Chamber', and it is around this position that all the harmonically tuned forces were focussed. Again, because of subsidence through the years, and possible earthquake damage, it is very difficult to ascertain the original measurements. Many of the joints in the walls have opened up and the floor of the chamber is now buckled and twisted out of shape. The width of the gaps in the vertical joints of the walls are given by Petre as: three joints on the north side 0.19 inch. One joint on the east side 0.14 inch. Five joints on the south side 0.41 inch. Two joints on the west side 0.38 inch. His estimates for the original length and width of the chamber are as follows:

	North Wall	South Wall	East Wall	West Wall
Top	412.14	411.88	206.30	206.04
Mean	412.40	412.11	206.29	205.97
Base	412.78	412.53	206.43	206.16

The height of the chamber was the most difficult to measure because of the buckled floor but the following table was presented by Piazzi Smyth in his book, *The Great Pyramid, Its Secrets and Mysteries Revealed.*

Height of King's Chamber near North-east
angle of room   =230.8
North side   = 229.7
North-west angle   = 229.2
South-west   = 229.9
South side   = 229.5
South-east angle   = 230.8
North-east angle repeated   = 230.8

The mean height here = 230.1, but is certainly smaller than it should be; for so many of the floor stones, from which the heights necessarily had to be measured, were disturbed and to some extent risen up (like the drawing of a tooth), as though in consequence of earthquake disturbance. hence, the true quantity must be much nearer the greater, than the smaller, limit of the measured heights, and should probably be called   =230.70 British Inch.
                                                   = 230.47 Pr. do.
Assumed true "first height" on the whole   = 230.389 Do. do.

The above, "the first height", or that from floor to ceiling, is so called to distinguish it from "the second height", or that of the granite walls themselves. Walls fully measurable now only in the N.W. corner of the room, where three of the floor-blocks are taken out, and show the wall there reaching down 5.0 inches beneath the floor level. This 5.0 inches completes the regularity of height for all the five courses of granite blocks forming the walls of the room; seeing that each of the four upper courses certainly measures 47.2 British inches, nearly, in height; and the first, or lowest of the five, though measuring only 42.1 from the floor, yet measures 47.1, if we add on the 5 inches observed at the only place where we can look at the bases of the walls underneath the floor-level. All this justifies us in announcing as the "second height" of the King's Chamber, or the height of the four walls of it, pure and simple, in themselves (see Plate XVII.) as near to235.30 Brit Inch.
                                                   = 235.25 Pyr. do.
And as certainly lying between   235.20 and 235.30 Do. do.

Several other investigators have published measurements which give a general scattering of values around those listed. The usual method of arriving at an acceptable length, breadth and height for the original is to add up all the various measurements and take an average. This may be a workable method in a general sense, but will not necessarily produce values which are closest to the true ones. In my own previous writings I found that rounded off values of

412 units for the length and 206 units for the width were close enough estimates to show certain correlations, but now, with a far wider mathematical basis to work from, it is obvious that fractional values must be explored in order to arrive at the true purpose of the geometrical construction. Average values will not do, but the truth lies somewhere between the maximum and minimum ones presented.

All the evidence I have amassed to date suggests to me that the most probable set of measurements for the chamber are 412.0889247 British inches for the length, 206.0444623 British inches for the breadth and 230.3647123 British inches for the height.

If we convert these values into pyramid inches by dividing 1.0011 we have:
411.636125 length
205.818062 breadth   Pyramid inches (see diagram 11)
230.111589 height

These units of construction would endow the chamber with a remarkable set of properties. The formation is that of a cavity resonator harmonically tuned to the wave-lengths of atomic structures and the earth's magnetic field. (see chapter one). An imaginary sphere which would completely enclose the chamber would have a diameter of 514.5451567 pyramid inches, and a circumference of 1616.491284 pyramid inches. This would be equal to 134.707607 pyramid feet. the harmonic of 134707607 is that found in the spacing of electrons around the atomic nucleus. If we double this value to allow for the matter/anti-matter cycle then:
(134707607 x 2) = 269415214 = the harmonic derived from the unified equation.

It appears that the width and height of the passageway from the Grand Gallery into the chamber was also engineered to create a wave pattern tuned to universal harmonics. There is much distortion here, also, but all the various measurements given indicate an association with the 41.1636125 value. It is considered that the original cross-sectional area was equivalent to 1694.443 square pyramid inches.

The height of the Kings chamber above the pyramid base can also be considered as harmonically viable in relation to the mass values. In the book, The Great Pyramid, by Davidson and Haldersmith, the measurements are given as, original, 1701.87 and existing, 1692.2 British inches. As several inches of subsidence have occured it is most probable that the original height was either 1701.807 or 1694.443 pyramid inches, which would have a harmonic affinity with either the mass value at the earth's surface, or at the centre of the earth sphere. I would bet on the value of 1694.443 pyramid inches which would conform with all the other dimensions.

In my earlier analysis of the chamber I had assumed that the Coffer had originally been placed in line with the north south axis of the pyramid.

My recent work with a computer indicates that the present position of the Coffer is very close to where it should be for optimum results in harmonic resonance. If the theory proves to be correct, then if any person lay prone in the Coffer with his head towards the north, the head position would be bombarded with a complex interweaving of resonating wave-forms tuned to the infinite. The brain cavity of the occupant would have been positioned 394.549635 pyramid inches from the vertical axis of the pyramid, 64.15887 pyramid inches from the north wall of the chamber and 84.72215 pyramid inches from the west wall of the chamber. The resulting harmonics created would be:
394.549635
Divided by 5 (remember, 5 pyramid inches = 0.411636125 geodetic feet)
= 78.909927 pyramid units
A sphere of this radius would have a volume of:
2058180.625 cubic pyramid units which relates to the earth's magnetic field and mass.

64.15887 squared would equal:
4116.36125 Harmonic.

84.72215 multiplied by 2 would equal:
169.4443 harmonic.

A computer analysis has been carried out on the Coffer itself and all the measurements show that it was constructed very precisely in order to intensify the harmonic resonance of 1694443 units. The height of the Coffer was 41.1636125 pyramid inches in its original state and the cubic capacities were also found to be harmonically related to this value.

The Grand Gallery and the Queen's Chamber were also checked out on the computer and showed the same harmonic properties in their design. The Grand Gallery created a wave guide of tremendous proportions, tuned to the unified equations, from which harmonic resonances were fed into the other chambers.

The so-called displacement factor found by Professor Petrie is worth looking at as well.

The existing displacement of the Passage System, as defined, was measured by Professor Petrie as follows:

	Petrie's stated possible range of error.
Entrance Door on North Face	=287.0 B″ ± 0.8 B″
Entrance Passage End in Natural Rock	=286.4 B″ ± 1.0 B″
Beginning of Ascending Passage	=286.6 B″ ± 0.8 B″
End of Ascending Passage	=287.0 B″ ± 1.5 B″

Within the range of error shown would fall the value of 287.429525 British inches, which would convert to 287.1137 Pyramid inches. The square root of this being: 16.94443. Again I would put my money on it.

I have amassed so much evidence from the computer backing up the harmonic theory that it could be the basis for a book on the pyramid alone.

I will leave it to the reader, who is interested enough, to carry out further investigation into the structure. Many months of work are required but the results are well worth it.

All the evidence points to the fact that the pyramid was built for the living and not for the dead. The purpose was for the expansion of the mind. The reasons are open for speculation. A communications device; a cosmic telephone box; a device for initiation into the mysteries of the Universe? Your guess is as good as mine.

I hope one day to visit the King's Chamber and probe the forces within the structure. If there are scientists in the world who have the vision and curiosity to carry out research along the lines that I have outlined I would urge them to make the necessary approaches to the Egyptian government, and their own governments, for funds to start a full-scale effort to solve the mysteries of the pyramids.

I believe that this one project could be the most important in the history of man.

Note 1:

The displacement of the Great Pyramid from the Resultant Grid Pole in the north, at latitude 75° 36' north/longitude 97° 30' west, is 4172.5842 minutes of arc. (great circle).

This converts to:

69.54307 degrees equivalent.

The reciprocal of the speed of light (143795.77 minutes of arc per grid second, at the earth's surface) is equal to:

$6954307 \,{-}^7$ harmonic

Note 2:

The value of the ancient Egyptian Cubit is given in various publications as around 20.6 British inches. I believe that the true ancient measure was equal to: 20.60444623 British inches, which equals: 20.58180625 pyramid inches. This in turn is equal to: 4.11636125 pyramid units of 0.411636125 geodetic feet, and 1.694443 geodetic feet.

DIAGRAM 10
Showing construction
of Great Pyramid base.

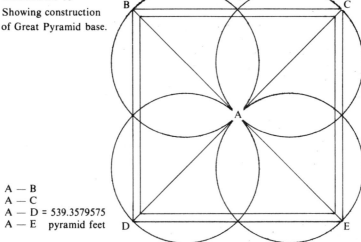

A — B
A — C
A — D = 539.3579575
A — E   pyramid feet

The circumference of each circle = 1694.443 pyramid feet.

Outer base side length
= 9153.208071 pyramid inches
= 762.7673392 pyramid feet
= 763.6063832 british feet
Inner base side length = 9060.397029 pyramid inches
= 755.0330857 pyramid feet
= 755.8636219 british feet

The length of the outside base perimeter minus the length of the inside base perimeter is equal to: 371.244172 pyramid inches. The reciprocal of this value is equal to the 2693645 harmonic (unified equation).

The height of the pyramid = 485.8660055 pyramid feet
The reciprocal = 0.002058180625 harmonic.

64

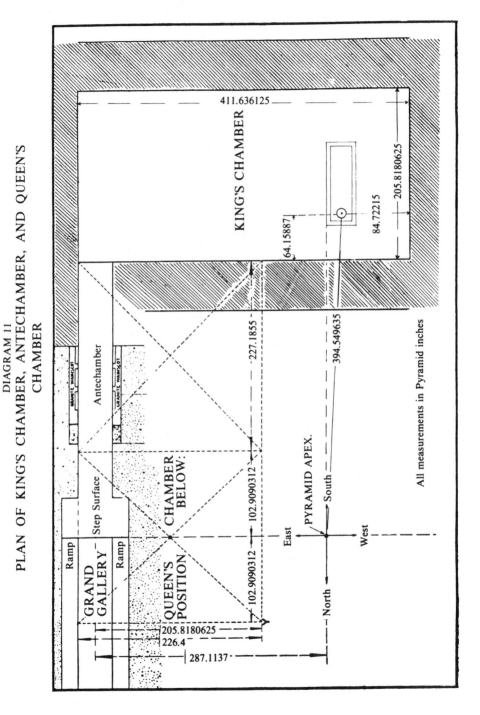

DIAGRAM 11

PLAN OF KING'S CHAMBER, ANTECHAMBER, AND QUEEN'S CHAMBER

65

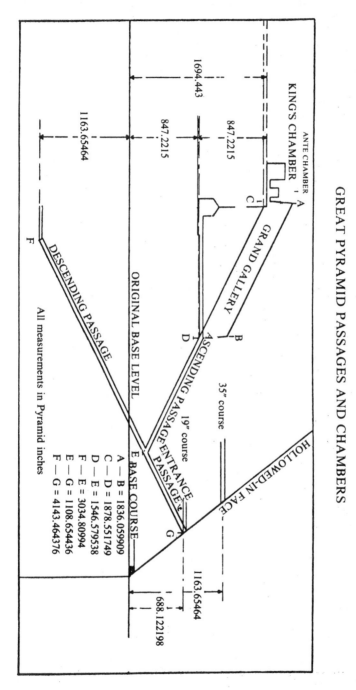

DIAGRAM 12

GREAT PYRAMID PASSAGES AND CHAMBERS

KING'S CHAMBER

ANTE CHAMBER

GRAND GALLERY

ASCENDING PASSAGE

ENTRANCE PASSAGE

DESCENDING PASSAGE

ORIGINAL BASE LEVEL

E BASE COURSE

HOLLOWED-IN FACE

19" course

35" course

1694.443

847.2215

847.2215

1163.65464

1163.65464

688.122198

A — B = 1836.059909
C — D = 1878.551749
D — E = 1546.579538
F — E = 3034.80994
E — G = 1108.654436
F — G = 4143.464376

All measurements in Pyramid inches

66

THE HARMONICS OF WATER, TEMPERATURE AND SOUND

One of the unique chemicals in the world is the odourless, colourless and tasteless substance which we call water. The molecular structure is bonded together so strongly that until recent times it was thought to be an indivisible element rather than a chemical compound. The molecule resists being broken up, more so than does that of many metals. It appears to be repelled from most organic substances, but has an affinity with nearly all the inorganic materials. The characteristics of water are at variance with almost all the rules common to other chemicals. Instead of contracting when it is frozen, it expands; and as a solid, being lighter than the remaining liquid, floats on top of it. As it freezes, each molecule bonds with four other molecules in a continuing process which forms a series of crystals strung together in elongated pyramid shapes. The interiors of the pyramid structures are hollow, thus creating a substance which is lighter per unit volume than the original material.

A particularly odd thing about water is its temperature at the freezing and boiling points. They are completely out of step with normal chemical theory. The temperature range is displaced when compared with that of other substances. Usually, chemicals similar to water in molecular structure descend the scale in regular order; that is, the lower the molecular weight, the lower and narrower the temperature range. As an example, if we compare water with hydrogen telluride, hydrogen selenide and hydrogen sulphide, it should be at the bottom of the scale. Instead, it is at the top.

If water followed the rules it should boil at about-91°C, and freeze at about -100°C. But instead it is commonly known that it boils at 100°C and freezes at 0°C. It is lucky for all life on earth that this is so, otherwise water could not exist in its natural state as a liquid.

The reason for the queer behaviour of water, in the scientific sense, is put down to the geometric structure of the water molecule, which is made up of two hydrogen atoms and one of oxygen. The hydrogen atom consists of a nucleus surrounded by a single "shell", or zone of action. This shell is activated by a single electron, but there is room for two. The oxygen atom has two shells, with the outer shell activated by six electrons, but in this case there is room for eight. An atom with an unfilled outer shell is not stable, and is attracted to other atoms in order to share electrons and complete the shell to regain stability. The oxygen atom does this by combining with two hydrogen atoms, the two electrons from the hydrogen atoms filling the outer shell of the oxygen atom. In turn, two electrons from the oxygen atom combine with those of the hydrogen atoms. This sharing of electrons by the three atoms creates a very strong and extra-ordinary stability within the water molecule.

When the two hydrogen atoms link with the oxygen atom they form a lopsided molecule, the hydrogen atoms forming up on one side of the oxygen atom in a V-shaped configuration. Most textbooks to which I have referred give the angle between the hydrogen atoms as an approximation of 105°. Two technical books on chemistry in my library show experimental values of 104° 30′, and 104° 27′ respectively. It is fairly obvious from all my research that the *exact* angle is not known, although the angle found by experiment and calculation is reasonably close to being correct.

Because of this small doubt regarding the absolute angle I feel that I have a certain justification in setting forth my theories regarding the geometric arrangement of the water molecule. I believe that the molecule is arranged in such a geometric configuration that the system is harmonically tuned to the natural scale of temperature. Water, in other words, is so special that the temperature gradient can be regarded as the fundamental basis on which to build a scale of temperature tuned to all the natural reactions of physical substance.

Temperature has a direct relationship with the energy levels and basic wave-motion within the geometric atomic structure of all physical manifestations.

As water is the most essential chemical for all life, as we know it, I believe that nature has provided it a special place in the scheme of things, which indicates its extreme importance. It does not fit comfortably into our tables because of its uniqueness, and future research, I'm sure, will reveal the many other secrets inherent in its structure.

The temperatures that are of immediate interest to us are the freezing and boiling points. These have been laid down, either by accident or design, as 0° centigrade (or Celcius) and 100° centigrade. This was most fortunate, as a scale based on 100 degrees is a perfect foundation upon which to set up a harmonic series to the base 10. The harmonic temperature gradient between these two points is therefore fairly accurate. The fixed point which was chosen to set the constant for the standard temperature scale was what is termed the "triple point" of water. This is the temperature at which, ice, liquid water, and water vapour coexist. This state can only be achieved at a definite pressure and is unique. The vapour pressure being 4.58 millimetres of mercury, the temperature at this standard fixed point is arbitrarily set at 273.16 degrees Kelvin (273.16° K), adopted in 1954 at the tenth general conference on weights and measures in Paris. The centigrade scale therefore indicates a temperature of 0° C at this point and the Kelvin scale + 273.26° K. The value of -273.16° centigrade, or 0° Kelvin, is the theoretical point at which all energy levels approach zero. *Physics, Part I*, by Robert Resnick and David Halliday, states on page 532 that "the Kelvin scale has an 'absolute zero' of 0° K, and that temperatures below this do not exist. The absolute zero of temperature has defied all attempts to reach it experimentally, although it is possible to come arbitrarily close. The existence of the absolute zero is inferred by extrapolation. The student should not think of absolute zero as a state of zero energy and no motion. The conception that all molecular action would cease at absolute zero is incorrect. This notion assumes that the purely macroscopic concept of temperature is strictly connected to the microscopic concept of molecular motion. When we try to make such a connection, we find in fact that as we approach absolute zero the kinetic energy of the molecules approaches a finite value, the so-called zero-point energy. The molecular energy is a minimum, but not zero, at absolute zero".

An appended note states that "it is possible to prepare systems that have *negative Kelvin temperatures*. Surprisingly enough, such temperatures are not reached by passing through 0° K but by proceeding through infinite temperatures. that is, negative temperatures are *not* colder than absolute zero, but instead are *hotter* than infinite temperatures."

A considerable amount of information is given in regard to the setting up of temperature scales for various branches of scientific research but it appears that it is very difficult to achieve absolute accuracy when measuring temperature in the extreme ranges.

The "International Practical Temperature Scale" was set up for the purpose of standardising temperature values in most countries of the world. A further extract from the *Physics* book states: "An international practical temperature scale (IPTS) was adopted in 1927 (revised in 1948 and again in 1954 and 1960) to provide a scale that can be used easily for practical purposes, such as for the calibration of industrial or scientific instruments. This scale consists of a set of recipes for providing the best possible approximations to the Kelvin scale. A set of fixed points and a set of instruments is specified to be used in extrapolating between these fixed points, and in extrapolating beyond the highest fixed point. Formulas are specified for correcting the basic temperatures according to the barometer reading. The IPTS departs from the k لvin scale at temperatures between the fixed points, but the difference is *usually* negligible. The IPTS has become the legal standard in nearly all countries".

What this all boils down to is the fact that all published temperatures for various physical reactions cannot be regarded as absolute values, when all the provisos and corrections are taken into consideration. The physical processes involved in measuring a temperature have a tendency to alter the temperature being measured.

So we see that all the various temperature scales set up by the different methods of scientific research can never be regarded as absolute in accuracy. The very best laboratories in the world, with the finest equipment available, can produce only very close approximations of absolute values. This is certainly no fault of the scientist as he must, by his very calling, only consider that which his instruments and experiments tell him. He must not *assume*.

On the other hand, the world produces mavericks like myself, who are not bound by the strict rules of science. I am perfectly free to assume and speculate. Possibly wrongly so, but intuition in certain directions sometimes produces results that no amount of scientific instrumentation could attain.

For this reason I set forth my interpretation of an absolute temperature scale based on factors which interconnect all the harmonic relationships found in my previous research. I feel that universal harmonic theory can encompass all things and that definite relationships exist between all physical processes. Time will prove whether I am right or wrong in my assumptions, but I feel that research in this direction could be of value.

I believe that the scale of temperature is a natural harmonic series which has very definite and unchangeable values at the fixed points where changes of state in matter occur. This harmonic series I believe to be constant through the range of matter and antimatter cycles of the physical processes discussed in other sections of this book. I am sure that the fixed point that is termed absolute zero is nothing more than the gateway between physical matter, as we know it, and non-physical or antimatter which exists in the universe. The temperature gradient decreases in our known universe to a fixed point, then increases once more up the harmonic scale within the negative universe, in a pendulum-type interaction.

The basis of the series appears to be tuned to the temperature gradient between absolute zero and the critical point of water. The critical point is defined as the specific temperature above which a substance can exist only in the gaseous state, no matter what pressure may be applied. The value for water is given as 647.29 degrees Kelvin, or 374.13 degrees centigrade.

I suggest that the true value of this point is exactly 648° K above absolute zero, in terms of pure energy.

The square root of 648 is harmonically equal to values found in my original work ($\sqrt{648}$ = 25.455844).

It seems to be so universally intertwined with all the other research that I have carried out that I'm positive it has a place in the scale of temperature.

We can now come back to the geometric structure of the water molecule, and speculate on the true relationships of the oxygen and hydrogen atoms. Something within this structure has made it unique. That something I maintain to be the V-shaped angle made by the hydrogen atoms. According to experiment, the angle appears to be somewhere between 104° 27' and 104° 30'.

In my previous publications I have suggested various intermediate angles which would create resonances with the theoretical harmonic values already established. I now believe that the most likely basic angle set up by the hydrogen atoms is 104° 27.6718165'. This is equivalent to 6267.671816 minutes of arc. The square of this number is 39283710. Similar harmonics are evident throughout this book in relation to the earth's magnetic field. The harmonic reciprocal of this value being 2545584.

In table 1 I have set up a comparison to demonstrate the relationships between the standard scale of temperature and the Cathie theoretical system. I propose that the Cathie system indicates more directly the reason for certain physical manifestations due to termperature, particularly the reaction of helium at extremely low temperature. In the *Life* book I have on the properties of matter, there is a section dealing with substances that have been frozen to supercold temperatures. One of the substances is helium, and the statement is made

"The outlandish antics of liquid helium ... Though named after the hottest spot in the solar system (*helios* is Greek for the sun) helium gas can be turned into the coldest of fluids. It liquefies only at the fantastically low temperature of -269° centigrade. When lowered two more degrees, it deviates so radically from its usual behaviour that scientists renamed it helium 'II'. Among its

TABLE 7

Showing comparison between the Cathie temperature scale and the Celsius temperature scale.

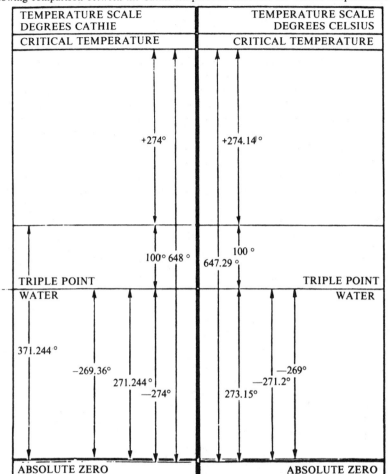

TEMPERATURE SCALE DEGREES CATHIE	TEMPERATURE SCALE DEGREES CELSIUS
CRITICAL TEMPERATURE	CRITICAL TEMPERATURE
+274°	+274.14ɪ°
100° 648 °	100 ° 647.29 °
TRIPLE POINT WATER	TRIPLE POINT WATER
371.244 ° −269.36° 271.244 ° −274°	−269° −271.2° 273.15°
ABSOLUTE ZERO	ABSOLUTE ZERO

Absolute zero:
The temperature at which a body would be wholly deprived of heat, and at which a perfect gas would exert no pressure.

Triple point of water:
The temperature at which ice, water and water vapour are in equilibrium.

Critical temperature:
That temperature above which it is not possible to liquefy a gas by the application of pressure alone. To liquefy a gas it must be cooled below its critical temperature before being compressed.

many weird tricks, it makes metal magnets float in the air, and casts a cold eye on gravity, flowing as if nothing at all were resisting its motion."

A photo shows a small lead disc immersed in a bath of liquid helium. The lead disc becomes a super-conductor, and when a small bar magnet is placed near it, the bar induces a current in the lead. Meeting no resistance, the current turns the lead into a powerful electromagnet that keeps the bar hovering above it.

The temperature points at which the liquefaction of helium "I" and helium "II" occur, are given as -269° and -271°. I believe that allowing for temperature corrections and the slight variation of the standard scale from the Cathie Scale, the absolute temperatures will be found at values of --269.3645° and -271.244°. Helium I would then form at the harmonic of 2693645 and Helium II at the harmonic of 371244 (when the temperature difference is taken from that of 0° centigrade and 100° centigrade respectively, the freezing and boiling points of water; the harmonic intervals being when changes of state occur). The reciprocal of 371244 is 2693645 (harmonically).

The sudden switch to a reciprocal value at -271.244° centigrade would explain the sudden occurrence of superconductivity and magnetic repulsion.

Air becomes a pale blue liquid at a temperature of -194.4° centigrade. If this occurs at the same point on the "harmonic scale" then we have another interesting relationship. (1944 $\div$ 3 =648).

There are many signposts indicating to us that temperature is a critical factor to be reckoned with when attempts are made to bring about certain physical reactions in matter. My research shows me that the modern alchemist would need a thorough knowledge of the harmonic relationships of elements, temperatures, electrical frequencies and sound before he could successfully bring about transformations in matter. The evidence strongly suggests that only very small amounts of energy would be required to transform elements, or carry out any number of wondrous experiments with physical substance, if all the factors necessary to cause the reactions were vibrating in resonance, one with the other.

We shall now have a look at sound in relation to the general theory of harmonic affinities. Throughout our lifetime we are being bombarded by sounds. Even if we stood in a windless desert and thought we were being subjected to absolute silence, we would be engulfed in sounds, even though so minute that we would not be able to perceive them. Even the tumbling of a grain of sand produces a sound.

The varieties of sound are limitless and we, as humans, can be influenced to a remarkable degree by the type of sounds that we are subjected to. Pleasant music to one may be regarded as a discordant noise to another. The conception of music of a Chinese, or Japanese, is quite different, for example, from that of a European. The music of one is no doubt slightly irritating to the ear of another. Although music could be termed noise, or noise could be termed music, according to the taste of the listener, there is nevertheless a subtle distinction between the two. Noise could be regarded as a cacophony of sounds void of regularity, whereas music could be termed the art of combining regular sounds of definite pitch, which are rhythmic and harmonious to each other, in order to please the sensibilities.

When judging what is, and what is not, musical to the ear, it comes down to a matter of convention. The quality or pleasantness of any particular piece of music would be considered to be very different depending on the nationality of the judge, but fundamentally the fact which would influence the choice would be the mathematical relationships of the sounds.

The basis of the mathematical relationship in sounds is the octave, which reveals a very regular and precise periodicity based on the phenomenon of pitch variation. The pitch of a sound is that property that makes it appear to be higher or lower than other sounds.

The pitch of a sound is relative to the frequency of the vibrations from which it is produced, and is measured in the number of complete vibrations in one second. The pitch is raised or lowered by increasing or decreasing the frequency. Each note on a musical scale is recognised by the distinct frequency accorded to it. Once a note has been designated by a certain pitch, all other notes have a definite mathematical relationship to the original. The credit for the discovery of the mathematical ratios must go to our old friend Pythagoras. It is said that he made use of a stretched string divided into twelve equal parts to investigate the mathematical relationships between musical notes. He found that if a particular note or musical sound was produced by a specific string length, a similar note of the next higher octave was produced by halving the string length. A note of the next lower octave was produced by doubling the string length. An interval of eight notes is termed an octave. The interval is the difference in pitch between the first and the eighth note. There are seven individual notes which are designated A to G respectively. The first and eighth notes are designated by the same letter but are distinguished from each other by a small dash beside the letter.

For some obscure reason, octaves have been lettered commencing with the letter C. So a scale of notes would be indicated by the series
CDEFGABC' octave one
C'DEFGABC" octave two, and so on.

Notes which are an octave apart sound similar, rather than as completely different notes, the difference being that of pitch. The pitch is the property by which a note appears to be higher or lower than other notes, and is directly related to the number of vibrations per second, or frequency, from which it is produced.

If a string is divided at the two-thirds mark, the pitch is raised by a fifth, an interval embracing five notes. If divided at the three-quarter mark, the pitch is raised by a fourth, an interval embracing four notes. The ratios are mathematically fixed and with others form the natural or diatonic scale.

If the pitch of any note is known it is possible to calculate the pitch of any other note in an octave by use of the standard mathematical ratios. The international standard for pitch is taken as 440 vibrations a second for treble A. The standard scale is then calculated from this frequency. With musical instruments such as the piano, where the actual number of notes that can be produced is fixed and limited, the natural scale has been extended by the addition of semitones. The scale is mathematically adjusted to produce a chromatic, or tempered, scale of twelve different notes (there being thirteen notes of equal temperament in an octave). The constant ratio between the pitch of the consecutive semitones is given as an approximate figure of 1.05946. This is interesting from the point of view of my own research.

As this figure is given as only an approximate value let us alter it slightly and call the true value 1.059026875. If we now multiply this number by 16 we have a harmonic value of 16.94443, which is equal to the mass value at the centre of a light field, and the mass value for the proton when it is in an excited, or accelerated, state.

This was the first indication that sound could have some harmonic relationship with physical matter, and therefore light harmonics.

By intuition, I felt that the natural scale, should it be tuned to harmonics directly associated with light frequencies, would indicate some positive mathematical relationship with those of physical matter. Accordingly, I decided to calculate the frequency values of an octave of notes based on a C value of 144 vibrations per grid second. I found, much to my satisfaction, that this full octave of sounds showed a remarkable affinity with the atomic structure of matter when the combined frequencies of the full octave were added up. The sum total of all the frequencies was 1692 per grid second (see Table 2). If eight notes were broadcast at these particular frequencies, the resultant sound should theoretically resonate in very close harmony with the proton in the atomic nucleus.

The controlling frequency would be that of the fourth note, F. In the table this has a value of 192. If this note were varied by the value of 2.4 (that is a minimum frequency of 192 and a maximum of 194.4) then complete control of the resonating system could be obtained. When the frequency of this one note reached a value of 194.4 the sum of the eight separate frequencies would be 1694.4. When the eight notes hit this value disruption of physical substance could possibly occur.

This is the first step in the direction that research should take in attempting to discover the importance of sound in the manipulation of physical processes in matter. I feel positive that elements could be constructed by the simple method of bringing together certain combinations of lesser elements in an environment of harmonically tuned sounds and temperature. particular effects could also be produced by similar methods. For instance, the production of pure electricity: a very small input of energy could, in theory, produce a tremendous output of usable power.

This very fact is hinted at rather strongly when we check back through some of the ancient writings. Desmond Leslie points to this in the book *Flying Saucers Have Landed*. He quotes translations from the ancient Sanskrit records and says that the ancient scribes made a definite distinction between myth, which they call *daiva,* and factual records which they called *manusa.*

It seems that flying machines were quite common in days long ago, and that the engineers and scientists of the time had a far better understanding of propulsion systems than they have now. Apparently, the *manusa* writings give a reasonably clear description of how the flying machine, or *vimana,* was constructed.

TABLE 2

Showing comparison of natural and Cathie scales

	Table of Natural and Tempered Scales			Table of Cathie and Tempered Scales				Cathie Scale in Normal Time	
		Frequencies			Frequency in Grid Time			Oscillations per Second	
RATIOS	NOTES	NATURAL	TEMPERED	NOTES	RATIOS	NATURAL	TEMPERED	NATURAL	TEMPERED
1:1 1.0	C'	264	261.6	C'	1:1 1.0	144	143.888	162	161.874
	C#		277.2	C#			152.443		171.498
8:9 1.125	D	297	293.7	D	8:9 1.125	162	161.507	182.25	181.695
	D#		311.1	D#			171.111		192.499
4:5 1.25	E	330	329.6	E	4:5 1.25	180	181.285	202.5	203.945
3:4 1.333	F	352	349.2	F	3:4 1.333	192	192.064	216	216.072
	F#		370	F#			203.484		228.919
2:3 1.5	G	396	392	G	2:3 1.5	216	215.584	243	242.532
	G#		415.3	G#			228.402		256.952
3:5 1.667	A	440	440.0	A	3:5 1.667	240	241.983	270	272.23
	A#		466.2	A#			256.371		288.417
8:15 1.875	B	495	493.9	B	8:15 1.875	270	271.615	303.75	305.566
1:2 2.0	C"	528	523.3	C"	1:2 2.0	288	287.776	324	323.736

Total 1692

According to the *Samarangana Sutradhara,* the machines were made of light metal and were very strong and streamline-shaped. The metals used were iron, copper and lead. They had a considerable operational range and were propelled by jets of air. They could ascend or descend vertically and cruise at high speed for many thousands of miles.

The Sanskrit *Samarangana Sutradhara* informs us that the "manufacturing details of the *vimanas* are withheld for the sake of secrecy, not out of ignorance. The details of construction are not mentioned for it should be known that ... were they publicly disclosed the machines would be wrongly used. Strong and durable must the body be made like a great flying bird, of light material. Inside it one must place the MERCURY ENGINE with its IRON heating apparatus beneath. By means of power latent in the mercuy which sets the driving whirlwind in motion, a man sitting inside may travel a great distance in the sky in a most marvellous manner ... Similarly by using the prescribed processes one can build a *vimana* as large as the temple of the God-in-motion. Four strong mercury containers must be built into the interior structure. When these have been heated by controlled fire from iron containers, the *vimana* develops thunder power through mercury. And at once it becomes a pearl in the sky ... moreover, if this iron engine with properly welded joints be filled with mercury, and the fire be conducted to the upper part, it develops power with the roar of a lion."

Mr Leslie points out that the esoteric books list some forty-nine different types of fire, the majority of these being of the electrical and magnetic variety. The flying machines can be invisible and move in silence. If sound is to be used there must be great flexibility of all the moving parts which must be made of faultless workmanship ... it can be moved by tunes and rhythms ... As an alternative means of propulsion, it can be driven solely by the power of sound, tunes and rhythms.

I had read these transcripts from the ancient Sanskrit writings some years ago in various publications, but had never got around to trying to apply the knowledge gained from my own research to the methods of creating the power source for propelling the machines. If I had taken the trouble to do a little probing I would have discovered some very interesting facts, as pointed out to me by Mr Jeffrey Cook of Derbyshire, England. Mr Cook contacted me by letter on 9 August 1974 and stated the following: "The ancient *vimanas* were flying machines which supposedly made use of an iron engine filled with mercury. I'm sure you may already be familiar with what an interesting partnership mercury and iron make together, especially when sound waves are passed through them, but if you're not, then perhaps you may find the enclosed data of some interest." he states that the acoustical data he used was taken from the *Mathematical Tables* by "Montague-Beart":

Velocity of sound through mercury = 4764 feet/second
86400 seconds = 97200 grid seconds (per revolution of earth).
Therefore 1 second = 1.125 grid seconds.
Dividing 4764 by 1.125 we get 4234.66 feet/grid second.
However 6000 grid (or geodetic) feet = 6080 feet.
Therefore 1 grid foot = 1.013 feet.

Again, since a grid foot is slightly larger, velocity in grid/feet second must be proportionately less.

Dividing 4234.66 by 1.013 we get 4180.32 grid feet/grid second.

One minute of arc = 6000 grid or geodetic feet.

Therefore 4180.32 ÷ 6000 = .69672 minutes arc/grid second.

The velocity of sound through iron is converted in the same way i.e:

16400 feet/second

= 14577.777 feet/grid second.

= 14390.698 grid feet/grid second.

So we see that at the particular temperature of the two metals when the speed of sound values were calculated, the harmonic velocities were very close to those of the speed of light and the reciprocal, when dealing with physical substances. As a check I referred to my *Science Data Book* by R. M. Tennent and the values given there when coverted were:

Mercury = .696461 minutes of arc/grid second: at 20°C

Iron = 14389.64947 grid feet/grid second: at 25°C

If the temperature were closely controlled then it should be possible to create conditions so that the speed of sound through these two substances is harmonically tuned closely to the speed of light and its reciprocal. An electrical reaction would then most certainly occur.

The harmonic affinity of these metals was also further ascertained by checking the mass numbers. If the particular isotopes of mercury and iron with mass numbers of 198 and 54 were used, the difference in mass number would be 144. I believe that we could reproduce an engine, or power pack, of this type today, now that the fundamental theory is available. I can visualise a sonic generator consisting of thin plates of iron immersed in a bath of mercury. Through the thin iron plates would be broadcast eight harmonically tuned sounds as described earlier in this chapter. The combined sounds would cause a resonance within the iron and mercury which would be tuned to the frequency of the protons within the nucleus of all the atoms in the atomic structure of both metals. The system would be strictly controlled as regards temperature. an imbalance of electrical potential should be created between the two substances and a flow of current obtained. The amount of current flow would probably depend upon the intensity of the input of sound. Once the reaction was initiated it should be possible to tap off a small amount of the power output to activate the sonic generator, thus creating a self-sustaining power source.

If this proved to be a workable hypothesis then a completely pollution free power source could be made available within a comparatively short time. This would then solve the problem of the present-day atomic power stations, which leave highly lethal radioactive material on our hands to be disposed of.

A non-lethal, melodious power station would be an asset in any community.

A more mundane method of using sound to help combat the energy crisis would be the application of ultrasonics as dreamed up by a British inventor, Mr Eric Cottell. An article describing his invention was printed in Newsweek of 17 June 1954.

In a normal combustion engine a combination of fuel and air is burnt, resulting in exhaust gases containing carbon monoxide, water vapour and heavy oxides of nitrogen, which cause pollution. Mr Cottell reasoned that if the air were replaced by water to supply the oxygen for combustion, a considerable amount of the noxious nitrogen oxides caused by the air would be eliminated.

He already had a patent taken out twenty-two years ago for an ultrasonic reactor for emulsifying heavy liquids. By converting the reactor, Cottell was able to break water into particles about one fifty-thousandths of an inch in diameter and to disperse them evenly in oil (or gasoline) to create an emulsion that was 70 per cent oil and 30 per cent water. When burnt, it was found that far fewer waste products resulted and the fuel gave off much more heat. The small water droplets expanded on heating, then exploded into steam, which shatterd the oil into very fine particles creating a much more efficient mixture for burning.

Tests have shown that a car with an ultrasonic reactor attached to the carburettor can get almost double the normal miles to the gallon of gasoline with very little exhaust gas.

Here we have a very simple gadget based on a system of harmonic resonance within the atomic structure of liquids. There are probably many different applications of such a device that would save millions of dollars in energy resources.

Note:

I found some interesting values for heat in the physics books.

1. One British Thermal Unit: 252 calories, 1060 joules. Would a more accurate figure be 1059.026875 joules?

2. Heat of vapourisation of water is 539 calorie/gramme at one atmosphere. Work done on the environment by the system is equal to: 169.5 joules. Would a more accurate figure be equal to: 169.4443 joules? *Is this just a coincidence?*

THE HARMONICS OF THE LASER

In 1960 the electronic engineers coined a new word to be entered into the dictionaries of the world: LASER, which is an acronym made up from the first letters of several words describing an electrical process: Light Amplification by Stimulated Emission of Radiation.

This, however, is not an exact definition as a laser does not actually amplify light in the strict sense. It generates a particular kind of light and should in fact be termed an oscillator. It has also been called a quantum device since its action can be explained by the science of quantum mechanics.

The important difference between ordinary light and light radiating from a laser is that the laser light is coherent. Each ray of light is of the same wavelength, or colour, and is completely in phase with its neighbours, whereas the rays of ordinary light are scattered in all directions. The energy of the light rays generated by the device is emitted in a pencil-thin beam which does not spread out, thus allowing it to be concentrated on a sharply defined point. The radiation can be made so intense that it will burn a hole in a steel plate one eighth of an inch thick placed several feet away.

Radiant energy is propagated in the form of electromagnetic waves. A moving wave forms a series of crests and troughs, and the wavelength is defined as the distance between two adjacent crests or troughs. We say a wave has "moved through one cycle" when it has gone from crest to trough and back to crest again. The frequency of a wave is the number of individual cycles which are executed in one second.

All electromagnetic waves, including those of light, travel at the speed of approximately 186,300 miles per second. As the metric system is used in all scientific measurement, this is usually given a value of 300,000,000 metres a second. Classification of all forms of radiant energy is carried out by a comparison of wavelengths, and a table can be set up forming a spectrum of wavelengths. The electromagnetic spectrum is so arranged that the longer wavelengths are at the bottom of the table.

Only a very small fraction of the electromagnetic spectrum is visible to us as light, and the lower region of this section has a wavelength of 0.000,00075 metre. We see radiation at this wavelength as red light. To simplify matters when calculating wavelength, the scientists invented a measure called the angstrom unit, which is equal to $1/10,000,000,000$ of a metre. This is abbreviated to the letter A. The visible spectrum extends from 7,500 A (deep red) to 4,000 A (blue). The energy of radiation is proportional to its frequency, and the energy of each wave packet, or cycle, is called a quantum. This is measured by multiplying the frequency of the radiation by Planck's Constant.

Planck's Constant

The quantum of action (symbol h). A universal constant. For any specified radiation, the magnitude of the energy emitted is given by the product hv, where v is the frequency of the radiation in cycles per second.

The physics books state this constant to be:

6.6256 x 10 $^{-34}$ kg metre^2/sec.

Plus or minus 0.0005

If my own work was valid then I considered that there must be a grid equivalent of this constant that would fit comfortably into the mathematical structure of the theory. I found that if I used the maximum experimental value of 6.6261 I was able to calculate a new constant which would fit neatly into a system based on my unified geometric equations. Allowing for fractional errors in the conversion factors the following equivalent was produced.

5.876107635 x 10^{-34} kg/38.75968776geo in^2/grid sec.

Two very interesting reciprocal harmonics were evident in the above equation.

5.876107635
the reciprocal equals:
1701806812 harmonic

The volume of any size spherical body, in terms of the length of one minute of arc on its surface, is equal to 1.701806812^{11} cubic minutes of arc. In the case of the earth sphere the minute of arc value is equal to one nautical mile. In the case of atomic particles the length of the minute of arc would be measured at the surface of the spherical field of influence.

The area of the radiation surface: 38.75968776 geo/inches, squared.
This is equal to an area of:
1502.313395 square geodetic inches.

As previously established earlier in this book the resultant strength of the earth's magnetic field, at the surface, is equivalent to 3928.371 lines of force per square geodetic inch. As this harmonic would apply to all spherical fields, in a relative sense, then we can apply it to the microcosmic world of atomic particles.

1502.313395 x 3928.371 = 5901644.375 lines of force (resultant field).
The reciprocal of 5901644.375 is equal to:
1694443 harmonic. (mass at the centre of a light field)

The number of quanta that pass a designated point in a given time depends directly on the intensity of the radiation source.

All light is produced when atoms are subjected to energy changes. When an electrical current is caused to flow through the filament of a light bulb, the atomic structure of the tungsten or other material that it consists of is agitated, and some of the energy is radiated as visible light. The energy levels of the atomic structure of a gas can be caused to fluctuate in the same way.

When an atom absorbs, or imparts, energy it does so according to very strict rules, and each atom has an energy level which represents its stable state. Hydrogen in this stable, or ground state, cannot absorb energy in an amount less than 10 electron volts. If a hydrogen atom is struck by an electron which has an energy of less than 10 EV, the particle will disperse without imparting any of its energy to the hydrogen. If the electron had an energy of 10 EV or more, the hydrogen atom could absorb the 10 EV and the electron would continue on its way with a reduced energy and speed. The hydrogen atom would then be at its first excited state, at which level it would stay for a short time, then fall back to the ground state, shedding its 10 EV of energy as a quantum of electromagnic radiation.

It appears that the energy level in a hydrogen atom can be raised to a total of seven higher states than the stable ground state. As the energy is dissipated in a jump from a higher level to a lower one, the loss is manifested as a packet of radiation.

The process called spontaneous emission occurs when an atom in the excited state, say E^2, decays of its own accord to the lower energy level E, and emits a photon of energy $E^2 - E'$.

Albert Einstein proved mathematically that if the atom in its higher energy state is hit by another photon of the same energy, the decay can be stimulated to occur before its natural time. After the collision, two photons of the same energy would leave the scene of the accident, as it were, and would travel in the same direction, exactly in step with each other.

The process of stimulated emission is the basis for a method of amplifying light waves.

The American scientists James P. Gordon, H. T. Zeiger and Charles H. Townes put this general idea to practical use in 1954. They applied the theory to the amplification of microwaves by the fluctuation of the energy levels of molecules. This type of device was called the "maser", which stood for Microwave Amplification by Stimulated Emission of Radiation. One use of a maser is that of an input amplifier of radio telescopes and of space-tracking receivers that magnify weak signals coming in from space.

The theory was first used to generate coherent light, in 1960, by the scientist T. H. Maiman, an employee of the Hughes Aircraft Company in California. The main parts of the device were a xenon flashtube and a cylindrical ruby crystal. The type of ruby used is a synthetic gem-stone made by fusing aluminium and chromium oxides together. The amount of chromium is only five hundredths of one per cent; but this seems to be the catalyst upon which the action of light amplification depends.

The ruby crystal is flattened at both ends and each end polished to a mirror finish. One end is heavily coated with silver. The other end is not so heavily coated, which causes it to reflect only approximately 92 per cent of the light waves which impinge upon it. The crystal is then positioned within a helical-shaped flashtube. The irradiation of the crystal by this method is called optical pumping.

Mr John Carroll, in his book *The Story of the Laser*, states: "When energy is imparted to an atom ... it is said to absorb energy and to have been raised to a higher or more excited energy state, or level. If the electron then returns to its original orbit (I would say position in its orbit) the atom gives up energy. It may now emit light of a certain precise wavelength. The atom is said to relax to a lower or less excited energy state or level. When light wavelets, or photons, at 5600 A from the flashtube irradiate the ruby rod, they raise the energy of some of the chromium ions dissolved in the ruby from the ground state (1) to various levels lying within the absorption band. Then the chromium ions immediately begin to drop from these higher energy levels. Some drop right back to the ground state, level (1), as they do in natural fluorescence. But others drop to an intermediate or so called "metastable" state, (2). If left alone, the latter chromium ions would continue to drop to level (1), and the result would just be natural fluorescence. But these ions dally for a short but measurable time in level (2), and this is what makes laser action possible.

While the chromium ions are trying to get back to level (1) the flashtube keeps on irradiating more chromium ions. In fact, the two-step movement from state (1) to state (3) and down to state (2) is much faster than the movement from state (2) to state (1). Thus there develops a chromium traffic jam at energy level (2).

... As the pile-up of chromium ions in level (2) continues, another situation develops: soon there are more chromium ions in level (2) than in level (1). This is called population inversion and is essential for laser action.

When you have an inversion of the chromium ion population, the laser resembles a spring that has been wound up and cocked. It needs a key to release it. This is what is meant by "stimulated emission" of radiation. The stimulus is the key that releases the cocked spring. The key is a photon of light of exactly the wavelength to be emitted (6943 A). Emission begins when a random chromium ion spontaneously falls from level (2) to level (1) emitting a photon at 6943 A. The photon strikes neighbouring metastable (level 2) ions, causing them to emit additional photons and these in turn trigger other metastable ions.

As this action builds up, millions of photons are released within the ruby crystal. Some are lost by escaping through the sides of the crystal but a great number are reflected back and forth between the mirrored ends. This causes a stream of photons to be built up until the energy is so great that a beam of single frequency, coherent light passes through the partially silvered end in an intense pulse. Laser action now commences and a continuous pulsing action occurs, setting up a very thin beam of light consisting of waves all in step with each other.

The story of the laser is a very exciting one, and many textbooks can now be obtained explaining the general technicalities of its operation. What is of immediate importance to us in the creation of the beam of photons is the quantum of energy necessary to initiate the action: namely, 6943 angstroms.

This value is very close to the harmonic reciprocal of the speed of light at the earth's surface (143795.77 minutes of arc per grid second. The reciprocal is equal to 6954037 harmonic). I would have expected the laser to react closer to this harmonic energy level at the earth's surface in order to maintain symetry. This would be so if the angstrom unit was based on a standard of geodetic inches .instead of metres, as demonstrated in the conversion of Planck's Constant. A metre is equal to 38.85197368 geodetic inches. I would suggest a standard of 38.75968776 geodetic inches which would unify the measures so that they would conform to the overall theory.

Therefore the new basic unit of wavelength would now be:
1/10,000,000,000 of 38.75968776 geodetic inches.

If the Laser commenced to react at an energy level of 6954 of these units then: 38.75968776 x 6954 = 2695.4 to four figure accuracy. I believe that this deomonstrates very clearly that the atomic structure has a very well defined harmonic order.

When the energy level of a laser device is built up until it reaches the harmonic reciprocal of the speed of light, the creation of a photon must occur if symmetry is to be maintained. The energy packet would create an antiphoton, so we must have a normal photon on the physical side to balance it up.

More and more photons are created in an ever-increasing avalanche, as more energy is pumped into the laser, and eventually the stage must be reached when they saturate the device to overflowing, and burst forth to form an energy beam.

Another important factor in the construction of a laser is the type of material used to make the crystal, or the makeup of the gas in certain types of gas laser. To create a harmonic trigger to initiate the formation of photons it would be logical to assume that special materials would have to be found for the construction that would have a physical harmonic affinity with light, or any other type of radiation it was intended to produce.

In the case of the ruby laser, this was found to be so. A combination of aluminium isotopes could be used to form an aluminium oxide with an atomic weight of 26.93645 (harmonic 2693645). The same would apply to chromium, the atomic weight being 51.84. a mixture giving an atomic weight of 51.69305867 would be equal to 7.18978847 squared. (7.18978847 x 2) is equal to 14.379577; the harmonic of the speed of light at the earth's surface. Gallium arsenide is another material that can be used successfully in solid lasers. In this case the most efficient mixture of isotopes to use would be that which give an atomic weight of 69.543.

In all cases, the laser action is seen to be directly related to quantum jumps that give very accurate values in terms of light, or associated harmonics.

John Carroll states in his book: "Frequency-coherent light also lends itself to frequency multiplication, the technique whereby a closely controlled but relatively low radio frequency can be raised to a higher output frequency. The output of a ruby laser at 6943 A, has been doubled to 3472 A. The input was deep red and the output blue-violet, almost ultraviolet. The reason the wavelengths of laser light are given so precisely is that the emission of laser light depends on the shifting of electrons between atomic orbits and each wavelength is characteristic of one particular orbital shift, or so-called quantum jump."

The fact that laser action depends er..irely on the harmonic affinity of energy and physical materials indicates to me some very exciting possibilities for the future. The next step in research is obviously to construct lasers in such a way that the coherent light beam can be selected to particular wavelengths which coincide with that of specific types of physical matter. If, as I presume, the atomic table of elements is a natural harmonic series, then it should be possible to tune a laser to resonate at the exact wavelength of any type of matter that we choose. If this is so then we would have at our disposal the perfect tool for cutting, or manipulating, any type of material. The atomic structure would not be physically torn apart during the cutting process as it is under present methods. The atoms along the line of the cut would be actually disintegrated with a very small amount of effort, leaving a smooth clean surface. An added, and very important, advantage, would be that any other type of material or physical matter touched by the selective laser would remain unharmed, as the physical wave-form would be out of harmony with the beam.

It is more than a probability that the miles of spacious tunnels and caverns snaking through the depths of the mountain ranges in South America, were carved out by the use of laser-type devices. Thousands upon thousands of tons of rock have been removed and the walls in many places are still smooth to the touch, regardless of their immense age. Only highly sophisticated machines, or electronic means, could have been employed to work extremely hard granite to such a high degree of accuracy and finish.

A pointer to this may be found in an article printed in the *Rosicrucian Digest* of March 1961. The story called "A Beam of Light" by Gaston Burridge discussed the possibility of creating an electronic generator to produce a disintegrating beam. He stated that Nicola Tesla had spoken of such an idea in 1933. Tesla envisaged the beam or ray, as tiny in size, but highly destructive. Possibly no more than one hundred-thousandth of a centimetre in diameter. The range would be about 200 miles, due to the curvature of the earth, and the energy would be about 50,000,000 volts. He estimated the cost of the generator to be about 2,000,000 dollars — a great amount of money in the early 1930s. It would be of great interest to know if the information necessary to make the generator was among the records removed from Tesla's safe by the authorities when he died in 1943.

Was it Tesla who paved the way for the production of the laser? More than possible, I would say, because in the same article another startling occurence was described. Evidently in fort Monmouth, New Jersey, not too long ago, a mysterious happening took place:

Fort Monmouth scientists were experimenting with new ideas in radar-beam transmission. Giant electrical apparatus flexing huge mechanical muscles hummed contentedly. Experimental test results however had not been disappointing, and after a brief conference the three participating scientists gave their foreman word to end the experiment.

Turning to his switchboard operator, the foreman swung his hands palm down at waist level, as a signal to cut off the power. The man at the switchboard repeated the signal then turned to his meters and switches. As he lifted his hand toward the handle of the big switch, all eyes followed the motion ... then before his hand could reach the switch a blinding flash of purple fire arced out from the radar transmitter. An angry demonic hiss followed the flash. The brilliance paused a fraction of a second, flattening itself slightly against a two foot thick concrete laboratory wall, then burst through it with a sharp sizzling noise ... the lavender flame had pierced a forty inch diameter hole, its edges vitrified, without one sliver of material which had once filled it remaining. The stone had evidently become gas almost instantly.

Obviously the above description was the portrayal of an experiment that went somewhat haywire. But the results, although accidental, could no doubt be repeated by intention, and under complete control. It is almost certain that the disintegrater ray is already in the hands of the top scientific and military groups in the world.

I have shown how the atomic weights of aluminium and gallium make these metals ideal for the manufacture of lasers due to their harmonic properties. Another use has been found for them in the construction of high-flux solar cells. The use of normal photovoltaic solar cells is prohibited by the high cost of production.

It has been found by experiment that a particular type of gallium arsenide, or gallium aluminium arsenide heterostructure junction semiconductor solar cells can be operated at light intensities of 2000 times that of full sunlight. The output is between 20 and 40W per square centimetre. The maximum efficiency obtained by use of silicone cells is obtained by a concentration of only about 10 times that of normal sunlight.

Obviously gallium and aluminium have very special properties which can be exploited in various types of electrical apparatus. Other elements or combinations of elements will be discovered in the future, which can be utilised for various types of sophisticated electrical gear, due to their particular harmonic wave-pattern. By this I am referring to the wave-pattern of the geometric structure of the atoms making up an element, or a combination of elements.

Science has only just begun to unlock the mysteries of physical substance. an exciting future awaits us in the discoveries yet to come.

RESEARCH INTO THE GEOMETRIC
STRUCTURE OF MATTER

According to all the evidence now available there is not much doubt that the formation, and dissolution, of matter is directly related to the harmonic geometric interaction of the infinitely variable wave-forms of light. Our own reality being a manifestation of wave-forms which are locked into a series of patterns within a clearly defined set of mathematical boundaries. It follows that there are an infinite number of other realities above and below the harmonic level of the one that we are aware of, which again would have their own set of mathematical boundaries set at the appropriate harmonic intervals.

Although the academics, and scientists, have so far publicly ridiculed my attemps to demonstrate proof of this, it is slowly becoming obvious that they have, for many years, been secretly carrying out research in the same areas that I have ventured into. I believe that I now have the circumstantial evidence with which to fight back.

I thought that an interesting excercise to carry out with my calculators would be a probe into the geometric measurements of some of the accelerator laboratories built to enable investigation into the structure of the atom. In order to achieve the maximum results I was sure that these multi-million dollar scientific instruments would have to be constructed to geometric factors related to my theoretical values. It would then be possible to manipulate the numerous harmonic interactions of the atomic nucleus.

With this in mind I wrote to the public relations offices of three of the main, well known accelerator laboratories, informing them that I was carrying out research into the structure of matter, and requesting any publicity material available that could be of help to me in my work. I also indicated that I would possibly want to reproduce some of the material in a book that I was writing. What I required was some reasonably accurate measurements of the particle accelerator rings of each of the laboratories so that I could calculate the equivalent geometric values.

The laboratories contacted were:
Brookhaven National Laboratory
Upton, New York 11973
United States of America

Fermi National Accelerator Laboratory
Batavia, Illinois 60510
United States of America

The European Organization for Nuclear Research (Cern)
Geneva, Switzerland.

Cern is an organization consisting of twelve member States, and the experimental laboratory covers a large area which straddles the Franco-Swiss border to the north west of the city of Geneva. The member states are: Austria, Belgium, Denmark, Federal Republic of Germany, France, Greece, Italy, Netherlands, Norway, Sweden, Switzerland and United Kingdom. Poland, Turkey and Yugoslavia have observer status.

Cern is the main centre for fundamental research into the structure of matter in the European area and over 600 universities and institutes have participated in the advanced programmes being carried out there. Scientists from any country can be invited to the laboratories for a specific work period and there is collaboration with research organizations in both the USA and USSR. The work carried out there is in the pure research field, and has no connection with the development of weapons.

There are four large machines in the complex; three of them being particle accelerators: a Synchro-Cyclotron of 600 MeV (the SC); a Proton Synchrotron of 28 GeV (the PS), and a Proton Synchrotron of 400 GeV (the SPS). Intersecting storage Rings (the ISR) make up a fourth system which allows collisions between two stored beams of high energy Protons from the PS. MeV is a particle expressed in thousands of millions of electron volts, and GeV is particle energy expressed in thousands of millions of electron volts.

According to the publicity material received from Cern the original laboratory site at Meyrin, Switzerland, was selected in 1952, and is approximately 8 km from Geneva.

The site was extended in 1965 (known as laboratory one from 1971 to 1975) and covers an area of around 80ha, of which 40.5ha are in the Swiss Canton of Geneva, and 39.5ha in the French communes of Prevessin and Saint-Genis-Pouilly in the department of Ain.

The adjoining land under which the 400 GeV accelerator (SPS) has been built (known as laboratory two during the first years of the project) covers 480ha of which 412 are in France and 68 in Switzerland. In addition a further 572ha (509 ha in France) are reserved for possible future development.

The efficiency of each accelerator depends on the maximum energy to which a particle beam can be accelerated, the intensity of the pulses of Protons produced, and the rate at which the machines can be pulsed. Other important factors are the energy spread of the beam, the ejection efficiency, and the length of time a beam can be held stable whilst a small portion is continuously extracted.

The PS feeds Intersecting Storage Rings (ISR) which are not primarily accelerators, but a pair of interlaced annular chambers in which particles previously accelerated in the PS are stored, circulating continuously round the rings in opposite directions. The two beam currents collide almost head on at eight intersection points distributed symmetrically round the circumference.

In the Antiproton scheme, Antiprotons are stored in the Antiproton Accumulator (AA), and fed to the PS for initial acceleration before being passed on to the SPS for final acceleration to 270 GeV. In the SPS, Proton and Antiproton beams are accelerated in opposite directions and made to collide together at two points in the ring. Protons and Antiprotons also collide in the ISR.

In the future it is intended that an Electron-Positron Colliding Beam machine be constructed which will have a circumference of 27 km.

A very detailed description of the construction and uses to which the various machines in the complex are applied was given in the publicity material but the description of the Booster Rings, the SO, the IRS, the SPS and the measurements of the systems were of the most interest to me.

The Protons for the experiments are obtained from Hydrogen gas, taken to 750 KeV by an electrostatic generator and then fed into a Linear Accelerator which takes them to 50 MeV. At this energy the Proton beam enters the Booster a Synchrotron comprising of four 50m diameter superimposed rings which accelerates the protons to 800 MeV before injection into the main ring of the PS. The four Booster rings are filled in turn from the Linac; then the beam emergy is raised by radio-frequency cavities of very compact design, with guidance and focussing round the machine being assured by 32 four channel bending, and 48 four channel quadrupole magnets. The four rings are then emptied in turn into the PS.

In the Proton Synchrotron more than 10^{13} Protons in 20 bunches are accelerated around a circular path 200 metres in diameter once every few seconds. The present main tasks of the PS are to supply accelerated particles to the 400 GeV SPS, to the ISR Colliding Beam machine, to provide particle beams for experiments in the 20 GeV range, and to supply a Proton beam to produce the Antiprotons used in the Antiproton Accumulator (AA). The PS also accelerates antiprotons for the SPS and the ISR.

The ISR consists of two interlaced rings of magnets 300 metres in diameter. The magnets guide and focus the Protons through vacuum tubes which intersect at eight positions round the circumference. Proton beams accelerated in the Synchrotron to energies up to 26 GeV are injected into the two rings in such a way that they travel in opposite directions relative to each other. The beams can be further accelerated up to 31.4 GeV and brought into almost head-on collision in the intersecting regions.

The 400 GeV Super Proton Synchrotron, or SPS, was commissioned in 1976 and then became the world's largest accelerator. Protons are injected at 10 GeV from the PS and are accelerated to 400 GeV before being extracted for use in physics experiments in the west and north experimental areas. The machine was shut down during 1980 - 1981 in order to convert it into a Proton-Antiproton collider. It is now possible to inject counter-rotating bunches of Protons and Antiprotons at 36 GeV and accelerate them to 270 GeV where they are held in collision orbits for 24 hours while experiments are carried out in two collision areas.

The whole complex is built underground in an annular tunnel of 2.2 km diameter, and 4 metres internal diameter. Approximately 1/7 of the system is in Switzerland and the rest in France.

The ring is not a perfect circle as it contains six long straight sections; two of which are used as Proton-Antiproton collision points in underground buildings which house all the equipment. There are six of these underground experimental areas; four in France and two in Switzerland.

The pages of data and photographs forwarded to me from Cern described the various laboratories in great detail and explained much more about the experimental research and future aims of the project. My concern at this point was to analyse the measurements given, and examine the possibility of being able to match them with the geometric harmonic values discovered in my own reseach. My work has indicated that the speed of light at the earth's surface had a value of 143,795.77 minutes of arc per grid second (relative to the surface), this being the most accurate measurement to date. By the manipulation of the geometric harmonics of light and other factors I have been able to produce harmonic values for Mass, Gravity and a series of unified equations, as demonstrated in other sections of this book.

Two of the major values being:

1694443 = The harmonic geometric for mass at the centre of a spherical body.

2693645 = The harmonic value derived from the Geometric harmonic unified equation, calculated at the earth's surface.

All values are based on the universal unit of one minute of arc. The standard for the earth's surface being equivalent to one nautical mile, 6080 British feet, or 6000 geodetic feet.

The importance of these two values is stressed repeatedly throughout the pages of this work.

If they could be comfortably fitted into the geometric measurements supplied for the various components of the laboratory then I believed a circumstantial case could be demonstrated which would indicate that extensive research was being carried out by a group of the worlds top scientists into the geometrics of the unified field. It would follow from this that the basic theories published in my earlier works are very close to the truth, if not right on the mark, and that the unified equations have been known to the scientists for many years.

The analysis of the Booster, the PS, ISR and SPS is as follows:

THE BOOSTER: the diameter of each of the four rings is given as :

50 metres

I found that by assuming a diameter of:

49.97534529 metres, the following values could be obtained:

= 1967.52934 British inches

= 163.9607787 British feet

= 161.8034 Geodetic feet diameter. This value is the harmonic equivalent of the mathematical quantity Phi, or golden section 1618.034. The circumference of each ring would therefore be equivalent to:

508.3203728 geodetic feet.

= 0.08472 minutes of arc (nautical mile) equivalent.

If two rings out of the four are paired, then the combined circumference is equivalent to:

0.16944 minutes of arc.

1694443 harmonic.

THE PS: the diameter given as 200 metres.
I found that by assuming a diameter of:
199.9063073 metres: the following values were evident:
7870.311322 British inches
= 655.859276 British feet
= 647.22955 geodetic feet, diameter
= 2033.3316 geodetic feet circumference
= 0.338886 minutes of arc equivalent.

Therefore for each half of the PS circumference the beam would travel the equivalent of:
0.1694443 minutes of arc (equivalent)
= 1694443 harmonic

The PS is used mainly as an injector for the SPS, which has a given RF frequency of 200 MHz. A method of continuous transfer is used in which Protons are peeled off from the beam circulating in the PS during 10, 5 or 3 turns depending on whether the process is repeated once or more times during a multi-batch filling. The PS also has the task of filling the two rings of the ISR with Protons, and supply Protons for Antiproton production.

It is interesting to note that for every five turns the Protons travel the equivalent of 1.6944 minutes of arc relative to the Earth's surface. It appears that the Proton beam is injected into the other accelerator systems at set harmonic intervals according to the nature of the various experiments.

THE ISR: The given diameter of this machine is 300 metres. The theoretical diameter was found to be:
299.8520717 metres
= 11805.17606 British inches
= 983.76472 British feet
= 970.8204 Geodetic feet
= 0.1618034 minutes of arc (equivalent)

Again a harmonic is found that is a harmonic equivalent of 1618.034, the mathematical value PHi, or the golden section.
0.1618034 minutes of arc
= 0.0026967233 degrees equivalent diameter
= 0.008472 degrees equivalent circumference.

Therefore the two interlaced rings of the ISR would have a combined equivalent circumference of
0.016944 degrees
= 1694443 harmonic

THE SPS: The theoretical analysis of this accelerator proved to be a little more difficult than the others as the ring containing the beam has been distorted by the incorporation of six long straight sections, which would diminish the overall length of the path travelled by the injected Protons. By the application of the known harmonic factors discovered in my previous research I was able to construct a mathematical model that appeared to agree with the given facts.

The publicity material states that the SPS is built underground in an annular tunnel of 2.2 km diameter and 4 metres internal diameter. I found

that by assuming the maximum outside diameter of the tunnel to be 2.200000866 km, and with the accelerator beam circulating near its central point, the maximum diameter of the circular path of the beam would be:
2196.000866 metres
= 86456.55408 British inches
= 7204.71284 British feet
= 7109.913987 Geodetic feet diameter
= 22336.45355 Geodetic feet circumference for the full circle.

If the length of the beam path is reduced by 10.30056633 geodetic feet for each straight section, then the complete circle is diminished by:
10.30056633 x 6 = 61.803398 geodetic feet

The similar harmonic of 0.0006180339 is the reciprocal of 1618.034, or Phi. We now have a full circular value of:
222336.45355 Geodetic feet
And a reduced circular value of:
22274.65 Geodetic feet
Which is equal to:
3.712441692 minutes of arc (equivalent)

This introduces a most interesting factor into the theoretical proposition, because this number, as demonstrated in many sections of this book, is the harmonic reciprocal of the geometric derived from the unified equation calculated at the earth's surface:
2693645

The proposed future construction of a large Electron — Positron colliding Beam Machine, with a given circumference of 27 km also appears to conform to the geometric theory. If the machine was constructed with a beam path of 27.0120272 km, which is fractionally larger than the given value, then:
27.0120272 km
= 27012.0272 metres
= 1063463.511 British inches
= 88621.95931 British feet
= 87455.8809 geodetic feet
= 14.57598 minutes of arc (equivalent)
= 0.242933 degree (equivalent)
The reciprocal of which is:
4.116361257 harmonic.
The square of this value:
16.94443
= 1694443 harmonic

A schematic diagram of the geometric layout of the installations at Cern was also supplied by the public relations department, which gave a fairly accurate indication of the various paths followed by the particle beams in relation to true north. If the theory of geometric relationships was to be consistent then I believed that all the paths taken by the particle beams during injection and ejection from the accelerator rings would have some harmonic affinity with the unified values previously discovered, if the angles formed with the true north line were taken into consideration. I could not envisage the designers of the machines allowing the atomic particles to take random paths which would upset the delicate balance of the geometric parameters of the experiments to be undertaken in the laboratory.

I made a photocopy of the installation diagram, then projected the paths of the particle beams to one point in relation to true north. A check of each angle showed that, with a small amount of interpolation, values could be arrived at which were compatible with the harmonic geometrics previously discovered. The harmonics 2693645 — 16944 — 143,795.77 — and its reciprocal of 69543, could be read into the pattern. Is it just chance that such close approximations were evident, or is there a secret geometric language which, as yet, is not known to the uninitiated.

The Fermi National accelerator Laboratory, at Batavia, Illinois, was next on the list for checking. This accelerator was dedicated in May, 1974, and named in honour of Enrico Fermi, a scientist who was well known for his early work in the development of atomic fission.

The publicity material states that, "The policy at the Fermi National Accelerator Laboratory is to pursue its scientific goals with an emphasis on equal employment opportunity and a special dedication to human rights and dignity.

In any conflict between technical expediency and human rights we will stand on the side of human rights. This is because of our dedication to science. The support of human rights in our laboratory and its environs is inextricably intertwined with our goal of making the laboratory a centre of technical and scientific excellence. The latter is not likely to be achieved without the former."

I agree with all of the above whole-heartedly and would commend such high ideals to the extent that I believe we all have the right of access to higher knowledge, and the secrets of the complex interwoven structure of our Universe.

The process of Proton acceleration at the Batavia Laboratory is very similar to that of the Cern establishment. Hydrogen is ionized in a discharge tube to obtain the Protons which then commence their first stage of acceleration in an electric field of 750,000 volts, created by a Cockcroft-Walton Generator: The Protons then enter a Linear Accelerator approximately a metre in diameter and 145 metres long. When they emerge their energy has been increased to 200 million electron volts (MeV). They are then directed into a booster which consists of a ring of electromagnets (given as 150 metres in diameter). The magnetic fields are pulsed at 15 cycles a second. At each revolution of the ring the Protons pass through electrodes between which an oscillating electric field is generated. The frequency of the field is synchronised in such a way with the orbiting frequency that at each turn the Protons gain in energy. After 20,000 successive boosts the energy is raised from 200 MeV to 3,000 MeV, or 8 GeV.

At this stage a magnetic pulse directs the Proton stream down a long vacuum tube to the main accelerator which has a given circumference of 6.3 km. They are then accelerated once more and after 200,000 revolutions have acquired an energy of 400 Gev. They are then led out of the main ring and proceed to the experimental areas where they collide with various targets in order to create a scattering of particles for examination. The theoretical analysis of the given measurements of the Booster and main Accelerator Rings is as follows:

THE BOOSTER: Given as 150 metres in diameter. The theoretical diameter proved to be:

149.9297129 metres
= 5902.732798 British inches
= 491.8944 British feet
= 485.4221052 geodetic feet in diameter
= 1524.99852 geodetic feet in circumference
= 0.25416642 minutes of arc (equivalent)
= 0.004236107 degrees (equivalent)

If this value is treated as a quarter harmonic, then for every 4 revolutions of the Booster the Protons would travel the equivalent distance of:

0.01694443 (degrees relative to the earth's surface)
= 1694443 harmonic

THE MAIN ACCELERATOR RING: Given as 6.3 km in circumference. The theoretical circumference:

6.299330754 km
= 6299.330754 metres
= 248004.6518 British inch
= 20667.05432 British feet
= 20395.1194 geodetic feet, for a complete full circle.

As in the Cern SPS, the Batavia Main Accelerator has six long straight sections and six medium straight sections incorporated in the system, with facilities at each sector for experimental activity. Calculation indicated that if the circular path was reduced by 10.300566 geodetic feet to allow for each pair of long and medium straight sections, then the full circle was reduced by 61.8034 geodetic feet. This number is harmonically equal to the reciprocal of the mathematical expression 1618.034, or Phi, as shown in the analysis of the accelerator complex at Cern.

The reduced annular path would now measure:

20333.316 geodetic feet, allowing for the straight sections.

Each of the 6 sectors in the annular path would therefore measure:

3388.886 geodetic feet

therefore each sector is equal to:

(1694.443 x 2) = 3388.886
= 1694443 harmonic

Besides the straight sections, each of the identical sectors contain 14 cells. Each of the cells have a given length of 195 British feet.

If we assume a theoretical value of:

194.968576 British feet, then:
= 192.4032 geodetic feet

With 14 cells to each sector, the combined length equals:
2693.645 geodetic feet.
= 2693645 Harmonic (see unified equation)
The implications of this, if the theoretical measurements are close to the actual ones, are self evident.

The Brookhaven National Laboratory at Upton, New York was the third accelerator unit that I contacted for information, and it also appeared to conform with the general theory. This laboratory was established in 1946 in order to carry out research into the peaceful aspects of nuclear science. The two main facilities at present on the site are the High Flux Beam Reactor, (HFBR) which was specially designed to produce intense beams of Neutrons, and the Alternating Gradient Synchrotron, (AGS) which produces intense beams of Protons, Mesons and various other particles. A new machine is to be constructed which has a planned completion date in 1986. The large accelerator named Isabelle will consist of a pair of 2.5 mile Intersection Storage Rings. Protons injected at 30 GeV from the AGS, which is said to be 1/2 mile in circumference, will be closely packed into two rings, then accelerated to 400 GeV. Head on collisions of the particles will occur at six experimental areas where the rings intersect.

The theoretical analysis:

THE AGS: The circumference given as 1/2 mile, or 2640 British feet. If we assume an exact measure of:
2646.887891 British feet
= 2612.060419 Geodetic feet
= 0.4353434031 minutes of arc (equivalent)
= 0.0072557233 degrees (equivalent)
If we shift the decimal place to form a harmonic of this number (0.072557233) then the square root would be:
0.2693645
= 2693645 harmonic (unified equation)
The new Isabelle Accelerator of two interesting rings given as 2.5 miles in circumference, could be given new theoretical measurements as follows:
2.506522624 miles
= 13234.43946 British feet
= 13060.302 geodetic feet
= 2.176717016 minutes of arc (equivalent)
= 0.0362786169 degrees (equivalent)

For two rings:

= 0.072557233 degrees (equivalent)
the square root of this number:
= 0.2693645
= 2693645 harmonic (unified equation)

The remaining evidence required to prove more or less conclusively that the particle accelerators were constructed in accordance with a clearly defined series of harmonic geometric factors, in order to probe the intricate framework of the atom, was the geometric placement of each laboratory system on the world's surface. I had discovered that in order to disrupt the atom, as in an atomic bomb, that certain precise geometric laws had to be adherred to, and the positions chosen on the earth's surface were critical, in order to guarantee a successful detonation. A full explanation of this is given in my earlier books. It was probable that the same series of laws were applicable to the successful operation of particle accelerators. The conditions necessary were both related to the relative motions in space of the atomic wave-forms. The relative motions in space of the Sun and the Earth were extremely important factors when it came to probing the secrets of the atom, and the positioning at specific nodal points on the surface of the earth had to be taken into account. The exercise was one of three dimensional geometry, or four dimensional if time were taken into consideration, and positioning was extremely important if spacial movement was to be accurately calculated.

One factor was the base line from which the position of each accelerator had to be calculated in regards to longitude. There would be four of these placed at ninety degree intervals around the world. I had discovered earlier on in my research that longitude on the earth's surface was not calculated from an arbitrary position, as the text books lead us to believe. (chapter 2). The zero longitude at Greenwich had been very accurately positioned. / calculator check revealed that each accelerator laboratory showed close harmonic relationships with the unified values discovered in my work when related to zero, 90°, 180°, or 270° longitudes.

Similarly, the latitude positions should comply with the theory, and harmonic values closely related to my published values were evident when a calculator check was carried out. The results overall were very satisfactory.

This will be considered pure chance of course, and who am I to argue with the scientists of the day. I have all the results on file and will await the day when other researchers venture into the realm of harmonic geometrics and see if their results compliment mine.

If the machines in the advanced accelerator laboratories are not producing the geometric harmonics which match the theoretical values shown on these pages, then they are very close to them. It would take very little structural alteration of the machines to produce the required harmonics — if I am wrong.

The work has progressed to a stage where the basic equation of Einstein $E = MC^2$ is now merely a stepping stone into a complex mathematical future. The way to the stars by means of dimensional travel is becoming available to us. The bridge to infinity is now within our reach.

THE HARMONICS OF THE
PHILADELPHIA EXPERIMENT

What did happen at the Philadelphia Naval Base in 1943? Did the Americans carry out a full scale experiment in order to make a destroyer, the USS Eldridge, invisible, and transfer itself through space time to another place. There have been persistent rumours over the years that the event did actually take place and if there is any truth in the story the Navy must be doing everything possible to keep the facts from the public. If it can ever be proven that the rumours are true then it will be obvious that a new world order is at hand. It will also be obvious that with the scientific progress since that time a comparitively small group of people now hold knowledge so fantastically advanced that they have the power to rule the world.

The whole intriguing mystery would have remained well hidden if it had not been for a book written by an American scientist, Dr Morris K. Jessup, called the Case for the UFO, published in 1955. In the book he discussed levitation and anti-gravity effects, and during subsequent lecture tours insisted that much of the money being expended on rocket research should be channelled into the possibly more lucrative areas of anti-gravity and the unified field concepts of Dr Einstein.

In early 1956 Jessup received a letter from a person calling himself Carl M. Allen (also known as Carlos Allende) in which he claimed that any further research into Einstein's unified field theory was unnecessary because the Navy had already used it in a scientific experiment which resulted in the achievement of complete invisibility of a Naval destroyer. Evidently the experiment was not a great success as many of the crew ended up with their minds scrambled by the side effects of the intense magnetic fields set up around the ship. Many of these men are still said to be confined to hospitals with no hope of recovery. Much has been written about the terrifying results of the experiment on the crew and it is said that the Navy was very reluctant to carry out further research into the unified field concept at this time, because of the dangers imposed on the personnel involved.

Nevertheless, several experiments were said to have taken place before the programme was brought to a halt. Some were supposed to be carried out in the Atlantic ocean and at least one in the naval base at Philadelphia.

The Philadelphia Experiment, as it is now called by the media, is the one which is of most interest to me. According to all the information available it seems that several tons of electronic gear were placed in the hold of a ship in order to create an intense pulsed magnetic field around the structure. Once the giant generators were set in motion and the powerful field extended round the ship, it disappeared from view; but not only did it become invisible, it reappeared a few minutes later in the water adjacent to the naval base in the Norfolk Portsmouth area, almost two hundred miles away. In a short space of time it again vanished and reappeared at the dock in the Philadelphia naval yard.

The whole story at first glance could be brushed off as the ravings of a maniac; that is if there were not more evidence to back up such wild statements.

A fairly extensive investigation into the alleged incident was carried out by Charles Berlitz and William Moore, and the information that they uncovered was published in what I consider to be a very important book called naturally enough, *The Philadelphia Experiment — The True Story Behind Project Invisibility*. Amongst the facts and the theories advanced by the Berlitz team were the following:

During world war two a Dr Franklin Reno was associated with the experiments carried out by the navy to prove the unified field concepts of Dr Einstein. Although the authorities insist that the famous mathematician did not complete the unified theory, Allende says that the theory was in fact perfected around 1925 - 27. It was almost immediately withdrawn because Einstein thought the whole thing was too far advanced for mankind to handle at that time. In the wrong hands the knowledge could be used to cause tremendous harm to humanity. Evidently a Dr B. Russell was in possession of this information.

A destroyer, the DE 173, was fitted out with complex electronic gear and sometime in October 1943 was used for highly technical experiments while at sea, and at a special secret dock at the Philadelphia Naval Yard.

The experiments successfully rendered the ship completely invisible while at sea and at the berth in the Philadelphia yard. During at least one of the tests in the navy yard the ship disappeared from the dockside and only a matter of minutes later reappeared before witnesses in the harbour area adjacent to the naval base at Norfolk, almost two hundred miles away. In a short time it again became invisible and as if by the wave of a magicians wand it reappeared at the Philadelphia dock.

The liberty ship SS Furuseth left the Norfolk area around the time of the tests at sea and Allende claims to have been one of the crew which witnessed some of the experiments from this ship. Some of the others that watched this amazing spectacle were the chief mate Mowsely, Richard Price, a young sailor from Roanoke Virginia, and a man called Connally from New England.

One of the top brass of the Navy who could verify that the experiment took place is alleged to be Rear Admiral Rawson Bennett, Navy Chief of Research.

On April 20, 1959, the scientist who focussed attention on the experiments Dr Jessup, ended his life tragically in his car through carbon-monoxide poisoning. The official verdict was suicide, but many still believe that he was removed from the scene because he knew too much.

Jessup had spent a considerable amount of time investigating the ramifications of the Philadelphia experiment and his friends were sure that he was conversant with many of the details surrounding the mystery. He had been approached by the navy to carry out scientific work on several projects which could have been connected with the experiments. he appeared to be very depressed and worried about the possible adverse spin-offs from experiments of this type.

Very powerful magnetic generators, known as degaussers, were said to be used by the scientists in the early stages of the experiments in order to set up a resonating magnetic field around the target ship. As the work progressed and they probed further into the unknown these generators were no doubt modified and possibly completely replaced by more sophisticated equipment which would help explain the eventual breakthrough which caused the ship to be displaced geometrically in space-time.

Jessup was quoted as saying, "The experiment is very interesting, but awfully dangerous. It is too hard on the people involved. This use of magnetic resonance is tantamount to temporary obliteration in our dimensions, but it tends to get out of control. Actually it is equivalent to transference of matter into another level, or dimension, and could represent a dimensional breakthrough if it were possible to control it".

This quote by Jessup appears to back up a statement made to me by a mathematician during an interview I had several years ago in a government research department. After three hours of discussion I asked if there was such a thing as the fourth dimension. He smiled and replied that it was possible to work in abstract mathematics in as many as fifteen dimensions. If they exist in mathematical concept, then they exist in fact. He inferred that although their work was confined to a total of fifteen, in theory, there were an infinite number of dimensions.

Dr Jessup discussed many of the aspects of the field experiments with his colleague and friend, Dr Manson Valentine. In answer to a question by Mr Charles Berlitz, regarding a simple scientific explanation for the incident, Dr Valentine is quoted as saying, "To my knowledge there is no explanation in terms of the familiar or orthodox. Many scientists now share the opinion that basic atomic structure is essentially electric in nature rather than materially particulate. A vastly complicated interplay of energies is involved. Such a broad concept lends great flexibility to the universe. If multiple phases of matter within such a cosmos did not exist it would be most surprising.

The transition from one phase to another would be equivalent to the passage from one plane of existence to another — a sort of interdimensional metamorphosis. In other words, there could be worlds within worlds. Magnetism has long been suspect as an involvement agent in such potentially drastic changes. To begin with, it happens to be the only inanimate phenomenon for which we have been unable to conceive a mechanistic analogue. We can visualise electrons travelling along a conductor and thus explain electric current. or we can envisage energy waves of different frequencies in the ether and thus explain the heat - light - radio spectrum. But a magnetic field defies a mechanical interpretation. There is something almost mystical about it. Furthermore, whenever we encounter incredible (to us) materialisation and dematerialisation, as in UFO phenomena, they seem to be accompanied by severe magnetic disturbances. It is, therefore, reasonable to suppose that a purposeful genesis of unusual magnetic conditions could effect a change of phase in matter, both physical and vital. If so, it would also distort the time element which is by no means an independent entity, but part-in-parcel of a particular matter-energy-time dimension such as the one we live in".

Much more has been written along these lines, in many books and articles about the goings on in Philadelphia, and when all the information is contemplated as a whole one can't help forming the opinion that something very important occured in that particular navy yard during, and immediately after, the war years.

One of my own contacts, during an eighteen month period of my earlier researches, when questioned about the experiment, stated that it did take place, although many problems were encountered. He did not elaborate too much, but indicated that I was getting very close to the truth. This man, after an extensive study of my work, offered me a position with a scientific group at a proposed very lucrative salary. After two days of thinking about it, I turned the offer down, and advised our own government agencies of my decision. I realized that my knowledge was not of much use to them, but my silence was.

I had been conversant with the general details of the Philadelphia experiment for some years, and I now felt that I had sufficient knowledge of harmonic theory to carry out a series of mathematical checks in order to verify in some way the truth, or otherwise of the story. I surmised that if the harmonic geometric unified equation, that I had discovered from my research, was correct, then some aspects of it would have to be evident in the geometric displacement of the ship, if it had taken place. My equation had been derived from Einstein's, and was an extension of his $E = MC^2$ in geometric terms. If all the known facts were put together, with a little bit of luck, something should show up.

The position of each naval base could be ascertained from local maps, so reasonably accurate latitude and longitude positions could be calculated within the boundaries of each area. If the rough positions were fed into a calculator then it should be possible to zero in on the actual points on the earth's surface between which the displacement took place. Even if the results were not exact, a reasonable possibility of success might be evident.

The first rough measurement on a geographic map of the area indicated that I could be on to something. The distance in minutes of arc, or nautical miles, between the two bases appeared to be within the range of values previously discovered in my research and the calculated values of latitude and longitude which fell within the general area also showed a geometric affinity with grid harmonics.

I eventually had a position within each base area which had satisfactory harmonic connotations with the grid and a calculated distance between the two points which showed a relationship with the unified equations. This inital plot showed three major mathematical values that indicated that the areas in question could have been possible choices for a unified field experiment.

I had carried out this mathematical probe into the possible verification of the experiment approximately October 1978 and decided to contact Mr Charles Berlitz, author of the book, 'Without a Trace', which made reference to the activities of the naval scientists. Mr Berlitz obviously had access to many of the facts relating to the case and I thought it possible that he could supply me with accurate information as to the ship position in the special dock at the naval base. I could then check my theoretical calculations against actual positions, and if necessary correct the hypothesis. I realised that I would have been extremely lucky to hit the jackpot the first time.

I received a very encouraging reply from Mr Berlitz and was informed that he had passed my request to Mr Bill Moore, who at the time was working in partnership with him to produce a book specifically about the Philadelphia experiment. The letter I eventually received from Mr Moore, dated 30 September, 1978, indicated his interest in my theory, but suggested that I send over my initial calculations so that they could be checked by him for accuracy. He refused to pass on to me the ship position during the experiment at this time in order to prevent me from tailoring my calculations in such a way as to match the facts. He said, in part, "If, indeed, these thusly arrived at coordinates match the real ones of the experiment your theory would be certainly advanced in the process. If not, an indication that you were on the wrong track would appear equally valuable in guiding the value of future work". This to me was a fair enough challenge, and as Mr Moore indicated that he was aware of the exact position in question I sent off the data for his assessment.

A further letter from him dated 7 January, 1979, duly arrived within which he said that although he was not certain that he fully understood my theories he felt confident enough to work through the mathematics and try and provide me with some answers. The precise coordinates of the place the ship was allegedly transported to, he said, were not recorded; but on the other hand the exact co-ordinates of the Philadelphia site were known to him (as a result of confidential information) to be either one of two possible locations — both within close proximity to one another. He said that, "while your calculations have been most interesting in several aspects, and show considerable thought, they fail, by statistically significant amounts to predict the necessary results. In fact with respect to your predictions concerning the Philadelphia site (latitude 39.892128° by longitude 75.17586979°) the location turns out to be an on land position in the midst of what was once a parade ground and athletic field."

Well, what to do now? I had no large scale map with which to check Mr Moore's work. I did not believe that my whole theory was wrong, but I needed more information in order to modify my approach to the problem. The general geometric pattern appeared to fit the areas concerned. I was sure that the latitude and longitude positions were important if the experiment was to be completely successful, but there was the possibility that the scientists had to compromise a little because of other factors. It had been said after all that the experiment did not turn out quite as expected. There had been adverse side effects which were hazardous to the crew.

A friend in Los Angeles came to the rescue by providing copies of large scale survey maps of the naval base areas, and sure enough the athletic field where I had originally plotted the ship to be was clearly visible. Certainly not a good place to park a destroyer. It was pretty obvious that my first attempt at a solution was very much in error. I made a second attempt at orientating the pattern but still remained dissatisfied with the results. The latitudes and longitudes were not harmonically tuned and still did not seem right to me. I decided to shelve the whole thing for a while until I could winkle out some more information. It was in fact over two years later when I went back to the problem and studied the maps once again in search for a satisfactory solution.

100

My main aim was to demonstrate that the experiment was feasible and that geometric coordinates could be calculated within the boundaries of both areas. The actual positions used may forever remain a secret, but certain possibilities may be evident which would help to build up the circumstantial evidence. By this time Mr Moore's book was available to me and proved to be very interesting reading. He had informed me that he knew the exact position of the ship when the experiment took place, but I noticed that he did not publish the information. Maybe he was not completely sure of the site either and hoped that I would provide the necessary evidence.

After studying the maps for some time I finally discovered the latitude which would theoretically give the best results, but it did not coincide with the Philadelphia ship yard. Much to my surprise it was about three miles north of the naval base up the Schuylkill River, adjacent to the Philadelphia College of Science. Another position along this latitude to the east was within a dock area near Penn's Landing. This latitude was equivalent to 143795.77 seconds of arc north, which would have a harmonic affinity with the speed of light at the earth's surface, 143795.77 minutes of arc per grid second. It was of extreme interest to me that the College of Science had been established at this latitude. I had a hunch that the centre of learning had not been placed in this position by chance. A later computer check of the longitude passing through the area strengthened the feeling that somebody knew something. Enough in fact, to create an experimental area viable for the investigation into the structure of matter. Computer checks for the dock site position near Penn's Landing on the Delaware River also showed evidence of important geometric harmonics.

I spent several days trying to fit this area into the geometric pattern that I had previously established by use of the unified equations and ended up completely frustrated. If the pattern was projected from either of these points the experimental ship, once it had been displaced in space-time, would have ended up imbedded in dry land just north of Norfolk Harbour. Very embarrassing for the captain and not a pretty sight.

I had no option at this time but to concentrate again on the docks around the Philadelphia Naval Base itself, and find the closest compromise possible to the geometric position necessary for optimum results. It had been stated afterall that the experiments were not fully successful and the positioning within the boundaries of the Naval Base could have been for any number of reasons. All the available information to date stated that the ship was positioned at a Naval dock when the scientists carried out the trial, so I had to make do with what I had.

I repositioned the geometric pattern to coincide with a dock on the western side of the Naval Base at Philadelphia and found that the projected position fell within the confines of the harbour at Norfolk, fairly close to the Naval facilities to the south and east. I completed writing up this chapter and went on with other parts of the book. I even sent a copy of the chapter to a Senator in the United States hoping for some reaction. This resulted in some indirect attention during a later visit to the country, but nothing of value.

I was still not satisfied. Possibly some experimentation was carried out at the base but somehow I felt that the main experiment would have been more successful if the ship had been positioned in the dock a few miles up the river.

I went over all the information I had gathered regarding the experiment and re-read the books by Moore and Berlitz. The clue I was looking for was on page 115 of 'Project Invisibility', published by these two gentlemen.

Moore had questioned a man who, 'had been employed as a scientist in the Navy's radar program during the war, in a capacity which, had such a project as the Philadelphia Experiment ever occured, almost certainly would have put him in contact with it. When asked a question about what the experiment was ultimately hoping to accomplish, he answered in part ... 'As I say, my immediate knowledge of it was largely peripheral. I believe they did succeed in getting a ship out of Philadelphia, or Newark, for a limited time, probably not more than two or three weeks, and I think I heard they did some testing both along the river (the Delaware) and off the coast, especially with regards to the effect of a strong magnetic force field on radar detection apparatus ...'

That was it; along the river could mean either the position close to the Philadelphia College of Science, up the Schuylkill River, or the dock near Penn's Landing, up the Delaware River. The latitude of both positions coincided with harmonics of the speed of light and the longitudes appeared to be correct when checked against other data. What I had to do now was rethink the geometric proposition. Possibly I was wrong in basing the pattern on the values derived from the unified equations as such. Maybe I should look for coordinates that would produce the necessary harmonics indirectly.

In order to create a pattern that would fit either position a few miles to the north it would be necessary to extend the distance through which the ship was allegedly projected, so that it would end up in the water within the harbour area at Norfolk. Preferably close to the naval docks.

The question could be asked, at this point, 'Why not carry out the experiment entirely on land areas if there was any difficulty in placement. Access would be far easier and some remote area should be available. Antarctica perhaps?

My own research could hint at the answer to this. Calculations indicate that the speed of light is not a constant in relation to space and the planetary surface. The speed of light decreases from 144000 minutes of arc per grid second, at just over one thousand miles from the earth's surface, to 143795.77 minutes of arc per grid second, at sea level. In other words altitude has a direct association with the true speed of light harmonic. Logically we could assume from this that an experiment related to the geometric unified fields could be set up far more easily by making use of the sea as a levelling device to ensure constant light values. This is complicating the issue a little, I agree, but those who understand the mathematical concepts of my work will see the point.

After many hours of calculation I finally produced a completely new pattern that would fit the Penn's Landing position and the Schuylkill River position adjacent to the College of Science. If the experimental ship was projected in space-time from either of these points it would end up in the Norfolk Harbour area, clear of obstacles.

I present this pattern as a purely theoretical exercise to establish the fact that a geometric proposition can be applied to this area which will show relationships with the unified values. If my pattern, by chance, coincides with that of the navy then I would say, with certainty, that the experiment did take place, although it would obviously not be admitted.

The latitude of 39° 56' 35.77", north of the Philadelphia Naval Base, which passed through the Delaware and Schuylkill River sites, set up the prime harmonic of the speed of light, which was 143795.77 seconds or arc. It was now necessary to calculate a latitude in the Norfolk area that would set up some sort of harmonic resonance with the unified fields. I eventually found that the latitude of 36° 55' 08" north, which passed through the Naval Dock area at Norfolk, was the most viable base line. This latitude can be processed mathematically as follows:

Displacement of Norfolk position from the north pole = 53.080935 degrees
Displacement of Norfolk position from the equator = 36.919065 degrees
Difference = 16.16187 degrees
Divided by 60 = 0.2693645 harmonic

It can be seen that this particular latitude would have a positive harmonic relationship with the unified equations.

The longitude of the Penn's Landing position proved to be:
75° 08' 55.8" west.
The longitude of the Norfolk position adjacent to the Naval Base was:
76° 19' 45" west.
The direct great circle track between the Penn's Landing position and the position adjacent to the Norfolk Naval Base docks was found to be:
189.7366596 minutes of arc, or nautical miles. Which is equivalent to:
3.16227766 degrees.

This number group, as shown in other parts of this book, is the only one from naught to infinity which has its own mirror image reciprocal. A resonant field based on this harmonic should have dimensional properties. The circular area swept out by a wave-front of this radius would be harmonically equal to Pi, or 3.141592654
The latitude displacement would equal:
181.452266 minutes of arc.
The square root of this number equals 13.47042, which is a harmonic of the electron spacing in the atomic nucleus.
The longitude displacement would equal:
1.1803288 degrees
The reciprocal of this value equals 0.8472215.
Double this value equals:
1.694443 harmonic.

All in all the pattern agrees quite neatly with a series of unified values and if I was required to set up the experiment I think that this would be my first choice of position.

The pattern would fit just as neatly if the whole thing was shifted to coincide with the position adjacent to the Philadelphia College of Science. In this case of course the projected position would fall further to the west in the Norfolk Harbour area; but still clear of obstacles. I would say that both positions are worthy of attention.

Another thought that crosses my mind is that although the ship was said to have been sighted adjacent to the Norfolk Naval docks was it in fact because of its physical presence. could it have been only a three dimensional image, or hologram, caused by the intense pulsating field effects radiating from Philadephia. Somehow I feel that to actually transfer the physical substance of the destroyer from one point to the other, it would require a second transmitting station at the Norfolk end of the geometric vector. A gradual phase-shifting, in real time, of the interlocked pulsating unified fields between the transmitters would then theoretically result in a physical transference in space-time. The true facts may never be known, but one day no doubt a public demonstration of this type of experiment will be carried out. I firmly believe that anything the human brain can envisage can be carried out in practice once the technology involved can be mastered.

I would venture to comment that — if the Navy did not carry out the experiment, then it should have. The results may not have been perfect, but I am sure they would have been spectacular.

Any further information that readers are able to supply would be most welcome in order to help solve the mystery once and for all. My calculations may not be perfect but I am sure that I am close to the truth.

DIAGRAM 13

Theoretical geometric pattern for the Philadelphia Experiment.

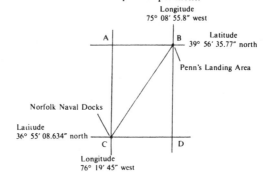

Latitude 39° 56' 35.77" = 143795.77 Seconds of arc north, which is equal to the harmonic of the speed of light at the earth's surface.

Dislplacement of Norfolk position from North Pole	= 53.080935 degrees
Displacement of Norfolk position from Equator	= 36.919065 degrees
Difference	= 16.16187 degrees
Divided by 60	= 0.2693645 harmonic

Distance B — C = 189.7366596 minutes of arc = 3.16227766 degrees. This number group has its own mirror image reciprocal. The circular area swept out by a wave-front of this radius would be harmonically equal to Pi, or 3.141592654.

Latitude displacement A — C = 181.452266 minutes of arc. The square root of this number equals 13.47042 which is a harmonic of electron spacing in the atomic nucleus.

Longitude displacement C — D = 1.1803288 degrees. The reciprocal of this value equals 0.8472215. Double this value equals 1.694443 harmonic.

104

MAP 3

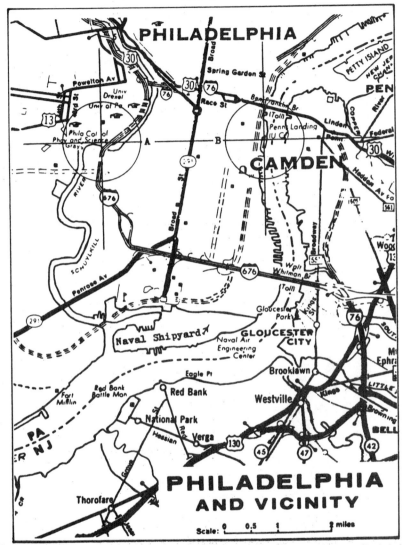

PHILADELPHIA
AND VICINITY

Scale: 0   0.5   1   2 miles

Position A: Theoretical experimental site in the vicinity of the Philadelphia College of Science.

Position B: Theoretical experimental site in the vicinity of Penn's Landing.

Latitude A — B = 143795.77 seconds of arc north. The speed of light harmonic at the earth's surface.

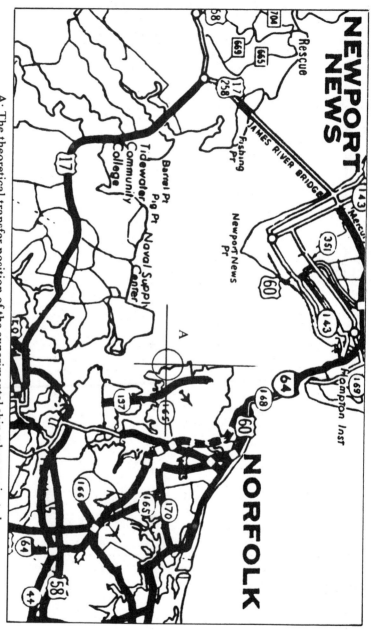

MAP 4

A: The theoretical transfer position of the experimental ship when projected from the Penn's Landing area. The position would be further to the west if projected from the point adjacent to the Philadelphia College of Science.

106

THE HARMONICS OF TUNGUSKA

In my previous books I have described a visitor from space which has caused scientific controversy ever since its arrival at 7.17 am on 30 June 1908. I quote from my last book, Harmonic 288.

The visitor was the so-called Meteorite which caused devastation as far as 65 kilometres away from the area of detonation in the Siberian tundra. Much more evidence is coming to light which proves fairly conclusively that the object was not a meteorite, or anything resembling a natural phenomenon. Recent reports gleaned from the Christchurch Star of 10 August 1976, and National Enquirer 13 May 1975, giving the following information.

The pheomenon was described as a Pillar of flame visible more than 320 kilometres away. The huge fireball changed to a boiling, mushroom-shaped cloud 20 kilometres high. Men 65 kilometres away suffered severe pain and some had their shirts singed on their backs. Trees within a 65 kilometre radius charred and withered. Black rain began to fall. The shock waves from the explosion travelled around the world twice.

The actual path the object traced out creates a mystery on its own. If the phenomenon had been a normal one, that is a meteorite, as has been assumed by most scientists, then the trajectory one would expect would be a parabolic curve. But the thing, whatever it was, exhibited no such regularity. It completely ignored all the ground rules laid down for the entry of objects into the earth's atmosphere; it ignored the laws of physics completely.

First of all, it approached from a southerly direction and, when it reached a latitude of about 58°, it suddenly decided to alter course; it veered off to the east for twenty miles or so, whereupon it changed direction again, executing a sharp turn to west-north-west, just before the impact which wiped out in a flash millions of trees in the surrounding forest area.

A natural object, whether a meteorite or anything else, and performing in accordance with known laws, could not possibly have carried out such a trajectory. That leaves only one conclusion to a logical mind: the object what ever it was, was under the control of some sort of intelligence and the point of impact was not a matter of chance — it was carefully pre-ordained or pre-calculated.

Dr Aleksei Zolotov, a Soviet scientist, states that it was a calling card from a highly advanced civilization in outer space. He has spent fifteen years investigating the mystery and has found evidence of the radioactive isotope cesium-137 in the ring structure of trees at the site. A United States scientist, Bob Ryan, Director of Radiation Safety at the Rensselaer Polytechnic Institute, agreed that the presence of cesium definitely indicated some type of nuclear reaction, as this element is the product of atomic fission. Evidently, fission is the only way you can produce cesium unless you use a nuclear accelerator.

Dr Zolotov was in charge of a Soviet scientific team equipped with the most sophisticated apparatus available in order to investigate the explosion. He said that all the evidence pointed to a nuclear device having caused the fireball, which means it could not have been a meteorite. Only a civilisation from another world would have the technology to do it. Examination of the site with detection equipment proved there was a considerably greater radioactivity in the ashes of the trees in the centre of the explosion than in samples taken on its fringes. All the evidence scientifically recorded at the time of the blast is similar to what is recorded in a nuclear detonation. Dr Zolotov believes it is logical to expect a second demonstration of power in the future.

Since the publication of my earlier books a little more mathematical evidence has come to light which will help prove that the explosion was not a natural event.

The ground zero position of the explosion is generally given as around 60° 55' north / 101° 57' east. As the object detonated at high altitude an exact ground zero point would be difficult to establish but the air position was computed to be in the vicinity of:
60° 55' 47.31" north / 101° 56' 11.22" east.

A small circle of probability could be drawn around this point to allow for computing errors and change of unified values due to altitude. The true position should be within a half mile radius.
The latitude of 60° 55' 47.31" could be processed as follows:
60.92980945 degrees
The square of this number equals:
3712441679 (3712441679 harmonic)
The reciprocal of this number equals:
0.0002693645 (2693645 harmonic)
The Cosecant of the angle can be traced to a close harmonic of 1694443.

A longitude value of 101° 56' 11.22" would place the detonation point at 26.93645 degrees from grid longitude 75° 00' east. Again the unified harmonic of 2693645 becomes evident.

No doubt the speculation will continue as to the reason for this massive explosion in the Siberian wilderness but all the evidence seems to show that the phenomena was not completely accidental. If a marker was placed in this area by some sort of intelligence then it is imperative that some reason be found for the happening. It certainly caught our attention. Obviously the scientists will want to know why.

THE HARMONICS OF KRAKATOA

In my first book, Harmonic 33, I mentioned the devastating explosion of Krakatoa Island, in East India, on August 26 and 27, 1883.

On 26 August a small eruption started, causing earthquakes which gradually grew in intensity; then on 27 August, after a series of gigantic explosions, most of Krakatoa and part of Rakata, another island in the group were blown completely off the face of the earth. Nearly 4½ cubic miles of rock disappeared in this almighty convulsion, leaving a great hole deep in the sea bed, causing massive tidal waves which drowned an estimated 3600 people. The explosions were so great that they were heard in Australia, and as far away as the Indian Ocean. Even the largest atomic bomb could not duplicate the destruction caused by this mighty upheaval. Up to 159 miles away the sky was darkened by the dust in the atmosphere and for months afterwards, brilliant sunsets and sunrises were seen all over the world. The fine dust drifted around the world for years before it finally dispersed.

The computer indicates that the explosion occured at:

6° 11′ 14.65″ south / 105° 25′ 55.5686″ east

The following coordinates from this point are evident:

6° 11′ 14.65″ south

= 371.2441691 minutes of arc south.

The reciprocal of this number:

= 0.002693645 harmonic (unified equation)

The longitudinal displacement from Grid longitude 90° 00′ east would be:

15.432102388 degrees

A theoretical circle of this diameter would have a relative circumference of:

48.48137947 degrees

The reciprocal of this number would be:

0.020626475

Double this value, allowing for the anti-matter cycle:

0.041252951

The square of this value equals:

0.0017018068 (17018068) The mass harmonic at the earth's surface.

The displacement from the resultant grid pole in the south which falls at:

75° 36′ south / 82° 30′ east

= 4236.1075 minutes of arc. (plus or minus 0.13 minutes of arc)

(4236.1075 x 4) = 16944.43 harmonic = mass and gravity.

I believe that the volcanic activity at this point leaves no doubt whatsoever that geometric factors govern the change of state of matter and the unified equations are mathematically valid.

THE PYRAMIDS OF SHENSI

"There are no pyramids in the Province of Shensi", I was told. My informer was a member of the Embassy Of The Peoples Republic of China. While passing through Wellington, on one of my flying duties, I had decided to make a phone-call to the Embassy, to enquire about the existence of several large pyramids discovered in this area of north central China. "There are some mounds of ruins, probably burial mounds, in the area, but no pyramids", continued the Embassy official, "we do not know of any pyramids in China." This was very strange, I thought, because I had in my possession at the time a copy of a United States Airforce survey map, produced from satellite photographs of this very area, which clearly indicated the positions of at least sixteen pyramids. Besides this I had a copy of a photograph of the largest one taken from a U.S. Army DC3 in 1947. Although I informed the official of this, and tried to press the point, he still continued to deny their existence. A few days before, I had mentioned the pyramids during a TV interview, and had been informed that several members of the public had contacted the Embassy, and received the same answer.

Why the denial? Was it conceivable that government officials were not aware of something of such historical importance in their own country. Surely not. In 1937 the long march, lead by Mao Tse-tung, ended in the north Shensi Province, and the Chinese Communists controlled the whole region until 1947. From there they eventually took over all of China. The Shensi pyramids are massive constructions. To remain unaware of them would be like losing an elephant in a city back-yard. The only answer was that the Chinese government did not want the western world to know too much about the gigantic structures until their scientists had completed their own investigations. The secrets to be unravelled, by comparing these pyramids with others around the world, could be so important that the authorities were doing their best to damp down interest in them. Our own governments would no doubt do the same, if they were on our territory, but that did not help me much. Possibly they had already discovered the mathematical relationships that I had. The only way to find out, I realised was to write the Ambassador a letter, explaining why I required the information, and enclosing copies of my maps and photographs. The following is the letter I sent, and the reply from Cultural Office of the Embassy.

The Ambassador
The Chinese Embassy
Wellington
Dear Ambassador,
  Over the last twelve years I have carried out research relating to the geometric structure of the Universe. I have published a certain amount of the information amassed in three of my books, the third of which is called, "The Pulse of the Universe, Harmonic 288'.

In this book I have published three unified equations derived from my research. The equations are in harmonic form.

One of the major values integrated into the equations is that of 16944. My research indicates to me that the value is related to the harmonics of mass. This value, I have found, is also built into the geometric structure of the Great Pyramid of Egypt.

I have enclosed a photocopy of a map of the Shensi Province in China, produced by the United States Airforce, which shows a similar group of pyramids as those in Egypt. The largest of these pyramids is said to be over one thousand feet high. (numbered No. 4 on the map). I have a photograph of this pyramid.

The interesting fact is that the longitudinal displacement of the Shensi Pyramid, and the Great Pyramid, is 16944 minutes of arc. This indicates that both sets of pyramids were built by the same people, with the help of extremely advanced knowledge.

Would it be possible to discuss this with Chinese Scientists, and at some future date travel to the Shensi area to carry out research into the pyramid structures?

I would appreciate any further information which is available on the Shensi Pyramid complex.

I have a great regard for the Chinese, and feel that the sharing of knowledge will help bring peace to the world.

I Remain Yours sincerely etc. etc.
Dated 2nd July 1978

Weeks went by, then I finally received the following reply from the Cultural Office, dated 1st November 1978. See photocopy.

Cap B. L. Cathie,
We have received your letter of 2 July, 1978 addressed to the Ambassador enquiring about the pyramids in the Shensi Province in China.

According to the Chinese experts, the pyramids are tombs of Emperors of the Western Han Dynasty, and the top earth of the tomb is of the shape of trapezium. History records tell different versions about the lives of the buried. As these tombs are not unearthed scientifically and there were no marks on the ground, it is difficult to draw conclusions at the moment.

With kind regards, etc. etc.

Well this was a breakthrough. Now at least the authorities were admitting that the pyramids existed. The pyramids were a fact, but the explanation for their construction appeared to me to be a little shaky. My own research had indicated to me that the reason for their presence was of much more importance than the casing for the bones of some obscure Emperor. I had already demonstrated in my previous book that the Great Pyramid of Egypt held within its structure the mathematical knowledge of an advanced science. What amazes me is the fact that a group of ancient monuments of such

111

enormous size could have remained unknown to the western world for so many thousands of years. Ask 99% of the people you know if they have heard of a pyramid, possibly 1200 feet high, in China, and they will shake their head in bewilderment, as I did a few years ago when I was made aware of it.

It was some time after I knew of its existence before I was able to track down any reliable information regarding Shensi. It was not until I was on a visit to the United States in 1977 that I finally discovered a source of reliable information.

While visiting friends in California, I was introduced to the author, George Hunt Williamson. Several years previous to this I had read two of his books, *'Secret Places of the Lion'*, and *'Road in the Sky'*. We spent a most interesting afternoon discussing various aspects of the search for secret knowledge we were both embarked on, and agreed to exchange information of particular interest. I eventually carried out some calculations for George, and he, through some of his contacts in the United States Airforce, managed to obtain a photo-copy of a survey map of the city of HSI-AN (SIAN) in China, said to be produced from satellite photographs. Clearly marked, in the countryside surrounding the city, are the sites of sixteen pyramids. The maps were sent over to me on October 28, 1977. The following is a quote from George's accompanying letter.

"... I have also enclosed the important article by Schroder on his 1912 trip to Shensi. Read it carefully and follow his description of the trip in the article and I think you will agree with me that he must have first arrived at the pyramid I have numbered (4). If you start there and follow each pyramid to the south west, it fits his description exactly. The two to the east of (4) undoubtedly he did not mention because they were not visible to him, as they must be very small. He says he saw seven pyramids. Actually there are ten in the group. The tenth one is quite some distance from (9), and I don't think he was able to see it. Also it is probably too small. (4) is the Great Pyramid of Shensi (in my opinion) and is approximately 1,000 feet high, while (3) is approximately 500 feet high. In his article he speaks of SIAN-FU; this is the modern HSI-AN (SIAN) on the map. The five pyramids that are S.E. of SIAN-FU could not possibly fit his trip description; neither could the solitary pyramid some distance east of SIAN-FU. The village of Pai-miao-ts'un near (4) must be the village seen in the background of the 1947 photograph ...

Fred Meyer Schroder and his partner Oscar Maman were traders and in 1912 they were running caravans from the Great Wall of China into the interior. Besides dealing in cigarettes, piece goods, candles and tobacco, they traded guns and ammunition to the Mongols. All in all it was a fairly precarious way to make a living, and the pair had many hair-raising and sometimes hilarious adventures. But that is another story.

At one time Schroder, in the company of Bogdo, or Holy One, was on a mission along the Chinese-Mongolian border, when the garrulous old monk said to him, "We'll be passing near the pyramids".

"What pyramids", answered Schroder.

"Why, the great pyramids of Shensi. Haven't I mentioned them to you?"

"You mean burial mounds?"

"Not burial mounds. These are mountains as high as the sky. They are not ordinary earthen burial mounds, though emperors and empresses may be buried in them."

"How many are there?"

"Seven."

"Where are they?"

"In Shensi Province, near our road. I haven't seen them, but I know that they lie near the old city of Sian-Fu".

Sian-Fu is an ancient walled city, which existed long before the city of Peking, and used to be the capital of China.

After several days of hard riding they eventually saw something looming over the horizon that first appeared to be a mountain, until closer scrutiny showed that the sides were regularly sloping, and its top was flat. Schroder was awed at the sight of the largest man-made object he had ever seen. It amazed him that men with the knowledge to construct an ediface such as this, and the ability to carry it out, had disappeared so completely from the earth. As they moved closer they observed seven flat topped pyramids. Quoting from the article by Schroder:

...'We were coming at them at an angle from the east and could see that the northern group comprised three giants, and the rest decreased in size to a small one far in the south. They were spread for six or eight miles across the plain, rising from cultivated land sprinkled with villages. It was more eerie than if we had found them in the wilderness. Here they had been under the nose of the world, but unknown to western countries ...

... The big pyramid is about 1,000 feet high (other descriptions estimate 1,000 to 1,200 feet high) and roughly 1,500 feet at the base, which makes it twice as large as any pyramid in Egypt. The four faces of the structure are orientated with the compass points. At some early period in the history of the country colours were assigned to the four directions. Black was for the north, blue-green for the east, red for the south and white for the west. The flat top was spread with yellow earth.

Once these pyramids had been cased part of the way to the top, but the rock has fallen, or been buried by the debris falling from above. The casing lies exposed at the base, however, and is made of ordinary cut field stone about three feet square. The pyramid itself appears to be made of the pounded earth still commonly used for construction in China. Huge gullies, the size of canyons on a mountain, had opened in the pyramid's side. These had spewed out rock and debris. Trees and undergrowth grew about its sides, obscuring its outlines and giving the added impression that it was a natural mountain. The stupendous dimensions of it almost took my breath away. We rode around it looking for stairways or doors but saw none..."

When Schroder asked Bogdo how old the pyramids were he answered more than 5,000 years. When asked why he thought this he said that their oldest books date from about 5,000 years ago, and they mentioned the pyramids as old then.

Schroder will have been one of the very few people from the western world to have sighted the Chinese pyramid complex, and it's hoped that in the not too distant future the authorities will relax the security screen placed on them so that outside investigators can have a closer look.

The main thing that interested me, of course, was the geographic positions of the pyramids. From the U.S. Airforce map it was possible to plot very accurate coordinates for each pyramid. The general pattern the pyramids made across the plain was also most interesting. It was very similar to the pattern of the pyramids scattered along the banks of the Nile, in Egypt. This hinted at the possibility that the same ancient technicians had a hand in their construction. I had a hunch that each one had a special function, and that a geometric connection could be found between pairs of pyramids in different parts of the world. The obvious way to check this was to calculate the displacements in latitude and longtitude, and great circle distances between individual sites. I spent a very interesting few days feeding the coordinates into my Texas 59 calculator. I could programme this for great circle tracks between points and get read-outs in minutes of arc. As can be seen on map (6) showing the rough positions of the pyramids along the Nile river, a great many combinations of pyramid pairs can be calculated between the Cairo and Shensi areas. Unfortunately the only accurate positions I have of the Egyptian set are those of the three on the Giza Plateau, but this was enough to begin the probe. (If any reader can supply an accurate survey map, or latitude and longitude positions of all the Egyptian pyramids, it would be very much appreciated).

The position of the Great Pyramid in Egypt:
Latitude 29° 58′ 51″ north/Longitude 31° 08′ 57.3″ east.
The positions of the pyramids in the Shensi area:

1.   34° 26′ 42″ N / 108° 56′ 25″ E
2.   34° 26′ 39″ N / 108° 56′ 00″ E
3.   34° 26′ 00″ N / 108° 52′ 36″ E
4.   34° 26′ 05″ N / 108° 52′ 12″ E
5.   34° 25′ 18″ N / 108° 50° 12 E
6.   34° 23′ 25″ N / 108° 44′ 12″ E
7.   34° 24′ 00″ N / 108° 42′ 30″ E
8.   34° 22′ 28″ N / 108° 41′ 35″ E
9.   34° 21′ 40″ N / 108° 38′ 10″ E
10. 34° 20′ 15″ N / 108° 34′ 00″ E
11. 34° 10′ 45″ N / 109° 01′ 12″ E
12. 34° 10′ 41″ N / 109° 01′ 25″ E
13. 34° 10′ 37″ N / 109° 01′ 38″ E
14. 34° 13′ 15″ N / 109° 05′ 42″ E
15. 34° 14′ 05″ N / 109° 07′ 00″ E
16. 34° 23′ 00″ N / 109° 15′ 00″ E

Many different combinations between pairs were calculated using coordinates on the earth's surface where I suspected the ruins of ancient pyramids to be found, as well as the coordinates on the Giza plateau and Shensi. A number of promising harmonic values were indicated which will be used in further research.

Although Mr Williamson had indicated in his letter to me that the Shensi

Pyramid number (4) on the map was the most likely construction to be the one shown on the photograph taken in 1947, and my own rough calculations had indicated a possible connection between it and the Great Pyramid in relation to the 16944 harmonic, an accurate computer check singled out number (6) as the more interesting of the group.

The direct great circle distance between Shensi (6) and the Great Pyramid turned out to be:

3849.5333 minutes of arc, or nautical miles (plus or minus 100 ft or so)

Which is equal to:

64.15888 degrees

This number squared twice is equal to:

16944430 the mass harmonic.

The longitudinal displacement of Shensi Pyramids (4), (5) and (6) respectively from the Great Pyramid, in Egypt (measuring the long way round) came to (4) 16936.755 minutes of arc, (5) 16938.755 minutes of arc, and (6) 16944.755 minutes of arc. (According to the present stage of accuracy).

This initial bit of evidence seems to indicate that the mass harmonic associated with the centre of a light field has a definite relationship with the placement of various pyramid complexes around the world. Different mathematical combinations appear to allow the 1694443 harmonic to be fulfilled. No doubt the larger pyramids have a special function in each group and time will tell which is the larger in the Shensi complex; but each group as a whole has within it all the harmonic combinations necessary to resonate in unison with the unified fields.

What is this trying to tell us? We know that if we set up electronic stations on various parts of the earth's surface, which are in phase with each other geometrically, then we can communicate from point to point through the earth itself. Were these ancient structures built for the same purpose. Did some sort of electronic process have anything to do with the geometric positioning of all the pyramids (and possibly other ancient structures).

There is the possibility that special electronic apparatus was used within the pyramids to create resonance for communication; all signs of which were removed in ancient times. There is also the possibility that no other apparatus was necessary for communication between points, once the pyramids were built. The very design of the buildings may have created the environment to allow direct communication between minds, if the high priests, scientists, or whoever operated within them, placed themselves at specific positions inside the various chambers. Maybe, also, the contact was not confined just to the earth. Under the right set of conditions it may have been possible to communicate interdimensionally, or through millions of miles of space; the earth itself acting as a transmitter. Lots of speculations, but no real answers.

In my last book I made mention of the fact that a Russian electronics specialist, Valery Makarov, and a construction engineer, Vyacheslav Morozov, had published in the science journal, Chemistry and Life, issued by the USSR Academy of Sciences, a theory concerning a massive world grid system. The geometric pattern of the grid was different to mine, but the same mathematical harmonics were inherent in it. Eventually I believe the two

115

systems will be fitted together into one concept. (see Map 5 showing Russian grid). The article was based on studies covering widely separated fields such as archaeology, geo-chemistry, ornithology and meterology. They theorised that the earth projects from within itself a dual geometrically regularised grid. The initial form of the grid being twelve pentagonal slabs over the surface of the sphere. The second part of the grid is formed by twenty equilateral triangles making up an icosahedron. They maintain that by superimposing the two grids over the surface of the earth, a pattern of the earth's energy structure can be perceived.

A look at the diagram will indicate that if the Russians are correct then a pyramid, or some sort of ancient structure, would more than likely be found at a similar latitude as the Great Pyramid in Egypt, and at a longitude of 72 degrees displaced to the east. This would make the position 29° 58' 51" N / 103° 08' 57.3" E, somewhere near the eastern border of Sikang, in China.

There has been reference to a large pyramid being sighted somewhere amongst the mountainous terrain between India and China, although I believe that the more likely position of this particular one to be closer to the Indian border. Nevertheless it is worth presenting the general report in the chance that a reader is able to supply some additional information.

During world war II the United States Airforce flew many missions across the Himalayan mountain ranges between India and China, in order to supply the Chinese armies with food and war materials. During one of these missions across so-called 'dead mans alley' one of the pilots, James Gaussman, had the misfortune to have trouble with his aircraft. One of the engines started cutting out and this could be a terrifying experience in this type of country, where the normal weather conditions were such that if you tried to fly above the mountains you encountered icing conditions, and between the mountains you were met with thick fog and cloud. Gaussman figured that the fuel lines of the aircraft were freezing up and, although it was extremely dangerous, he had no option but to descend to a lower altitude. The engines began to run smoothly again and the aircraft was flown in a hazardous zig-zag fashion through the mountain tops. A rough flight pattern was carried out that would return him to his base in Assam, India. In his report to an intelligence officer he said, I banked to avoid a mountain and we came out over a level valley. Directly below was a gigantic white pyramid. It looked like something out of a fairy tale. It was encased in shimmering white. This could have been metal, or some sort of stone. It was pure white on all sides. The remarkable thing was the capstone, a huge piece of jewel-like material that could have been crystal. There was no way we could have landed, although we wanted to. We were struck by the immensity of the thing".

Gaussman encircled the pyramid three times then continued his hair-raising flight towards Assam. He finally sighted the Brahmaputra river below his plane, from which he was able to ascertain his position, and eventually landed at his home base none the worse from wear. He believes that the world will be amazed if the pyramid is ever found.

'There was nothing around it', he said, 'just a big pyramid sitting out in the wilderness. I figure it was extremely old. Who built it? Why was it built? What's on the inside?'

116

I, too, would like to know the answer to those questions. If there is anything there the scientists have probably already found it from the study of satellite photographs, but are keeping quiet about it.

This whole general area has been shrouded in mystery for centuries, but now that we are able to scan the entire surface of the world by orbiting space cameras, it should not be long before many secrets will be solved. One place, which is of extreme interest, in this part of the world, which may have a connection with the ancient sites is Lhasa, in Tibet. It is said that since historical times the Lamas, and high priests of this mountain town have been guarding the secret knowledge of the ancients. Countless books have been written about the monasteries, and the supposedly vast underground libraries in the area. Lhasa, they say, holds the key to the history of man.

Did the high priests of Lhasa use the geometry of the grid to create a global network for communication, and a means for delving into the laws of nature. If so a calculator programme should indicate possible clues.

I found many interesting geometric coordinates which I will follow up at a later date. I would expect different combinations of harmonic spacing to be used for the many points established on the earth's surface. This would tend to confuse anyone guessing at the truth, and ensure secrecy until the new science was presented to the world.

The small amount of evidence that I have shown here is obviously not enough to prove the point fully, but should help to indicate an area of research which should be very enlightening. If the great circle distances between all the ancient structures were computed I am sure there would be many surprises.

中 华 人 民 共 和 国 驻 新 西 兰 大 使 馆
**EMBASSY OF THE PEOPLE'S REPUBLIC OF CHINA
IN NEW ZEALAND**

1 Nov. 1978.

Captain B.L. Cathie,
158 Shaw Rd.,
Oratio,
Auckland.

Cap. B.L. Cathie,

We have received your letter of 2 July, 1978 addressed to the Ambassador enquiring about the pyramids in the Shansi Province in China.

According to the Chinese experts, the pyramids are tombs of Emperors of the Western Han Dynasty, and the top earth of the tomb is of the shape of trapezium. History records tell different versions about the lives of the buried. As these tombs are not unearthed scientifically and there were no marks on the ground, it is difficult to draw conclusions for the moment.

With kind regards,

Cultural Office,
Chinese Embassy.

The giant Pyramid of Shensi. Photographed by the United States Airforce in 1947 from about 1,000 foot altitude.

World grid system discovered by the Russians

North Pole

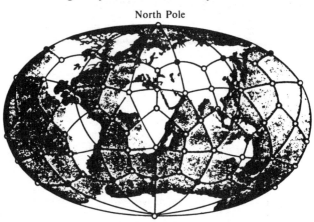

South Pole

As shown in the above diagram twelve pentagram-shaped areas cover the surface of the globe. One pentagram is centred on the north pole and one on the south pole. The other ten are spaced at 72 degree intervals of longitude north and south of the equator.

MAP 5

118

MAP 6

The Pyramids of the Nile Valley : Egypt

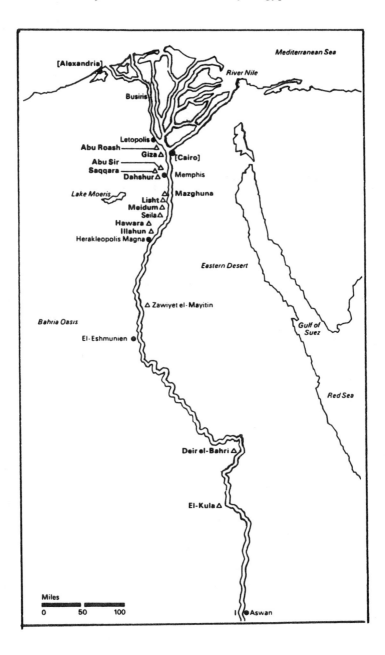

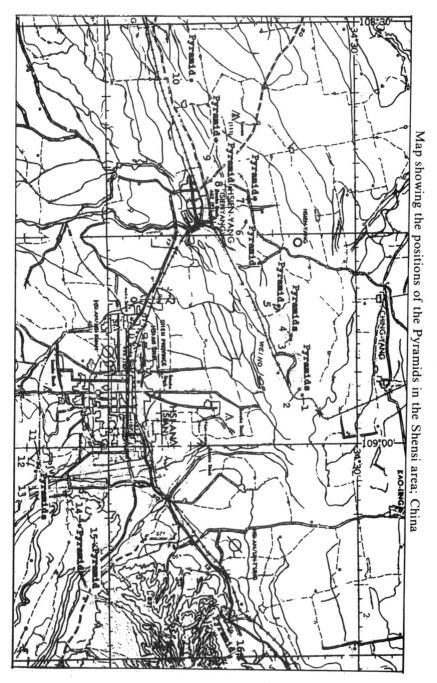

MAP 7

Map showing the positions of the Pyramids in the Shensi area; China

120

THE ENERGY GRID

One of the most important problems facing the world today is the production of sufficent energy to maintain our complex, and constantly changing technological society. The western world is said to be on the verge of economic ruin due to the ever-upward spiralling price of oil, and a desperate search is being carried out in order to find a substitute for fossil fuels. Many different estimates have been given as to when the reserves of oil will be depleted, but all agree that in the not too distant future the tap is going to run dry, and unless some other type of energy source is found, civilisation as we know it will collapse.

The more backward countries, the so called third world, are already in a state of extreme hardship, due to lack of finance and technical skill, and millions of people are starving to death yearly — the cause — basically the lack of cheap, and abundant, energy.

I have expressed in my writings many times that this state of affairs is completely unnecessary, because the scientific knowhow is already available to set up a completely new system of energy production that would free the whole world community from a reliance on oil as a primary fuel.

Atomic energy, using todays methods, is not the answer, as the disposal of highly toxic waste is a very real problem, and the end result could be the radio-active poisoning of the environment. Possibly, some time in the future, a new type of atomic reactor will be designed that will not produce such dangerous waste material, and therefore solve the problem, but this may be so far off that the immediate disasters facing us could not be avoided.

I believe that the only way that civilisation will survive will be to carry out a crash program in the setting up of an energy system based on the world geometric grid. We are literally standing on trillions upon trillions of electron volts of energy, which can be tapped to provide all the power necessary for our technological programmes, and transport facilities. The energy is immediately available, self generating, and in unlimited supply. The knowledge required to tap it is also available, but is being kept from the public for reasons not made known. Nicola Tesla, one of the world's greatest geniuses, proved the practicability of such a system in the 1930s, but no-one would listen and his work was suppressed. It has been said that the financial empires would not allow it. See my third book, The Pulse of the Universe, Harmonic 288.

The earth is a highly charged ball of electrical energy which is in static form. If this charge is brought to a harmonically tuned resonance then it can be drawn off under complete control, and applied in much the same way as power from a hydro-electric station. Theoretically it should also be possible for private consumers to draw off small amounts of power at geometric points scattered all over the earth.

I am not a technologist, and would not be able to design the necessary hardware, but I believe I can understand the basic theory. I am sure that a workable network of stations could be set up within ten years if the public was fully informed, and all the major governments chanelled their efforts and finance into the project. But it will not be allowed. The comparatively small amount of research being carried out in this field in secret will continue, but the financial cartels will maintain their control of world affairs. I do not suggest that anarchy should be the rule, or that chaos and upheaval should be caused by uncoordinated efforts in such a venture, but with an open approach to the problem, and the cooperation of all the worlds scientific groups, we could create a fantastic future for us all. At the present time we are held to ransom by a comparatively small section of society who hold control of the world energy supply.

As suggested the world energy grid is the key to the problem. The system is geometric in nature, so therefore the method of tapping it is also a geometric one. If the earth can be imagined as a ball of pure energy, made up of uncountable millions of interlocking wave forms, pulsating at the speed of light, then possibly the basic methods can be understood.

At certain geometric nodal points in the system there will be extreme concentration of energy because of the perfect harmonic interlocking of the resonating wave forms. It will be at these points where power stations can be set up in order to tune in to the build-up of harmonic resonance and draw off electrical energy. Other similar points would be utilized for the excitation of the world system, so that a continuous supply of power is available. Each station could have a dual purpose, so that power could be drawn off, or fed into the grid, according to supply and demand. Every country in the world would have an unlimited supply of electrical power.

I have been asked many times whether it was possible to set up such a station in New Zealand — particularly near our largest city of Auckland, in the north island. The answer is yes, I believe we could. I am sure, that in theory, such a position is available to us in the southern regions of the Manukau Harbour, which again is in a south western direction from the central city area.

By the study of all the information available to me during all my years of research, and corelating this with other scientific activity — which is not supposed to exist — I would venture to stick my neck out and suggest that a very good place to sink the major energy probe into the earth would be at a latitude and longitude point of: 37° 07′ 27.876″ south / 174° 43′ 12″ east. A secondary probe, which would react harmonically with the first, could be sunk at a latitude and longitude of 37° 08′ 07″ south / 174° 46′ 24″ east. The positions are as close as I can calculate with my meagre facilities, and I would expect a small percentage of error, but the distance of number two probe from number one would be 2.693645 nautical miles, or minutes of arc, and the bearing of number one from number two would be 287.099136 degrees. The distance would be tuned to the unified equation, and the square root of the bearing would give a resonance factor of 16.944 (light field).

The reasons for choosing these two points are that number one is orientated to the grid based on the earth's axis (normal latitude and longitude), and number two is orientated to the earth's energy grid, which is off-set to the normal axis of rotation. In theory, a reaction should be set up between the two points, and a flow of electrical energy produced.

A glance at diagram (14) will indicate the geometric harmonics associated with the two positions. The latitude of position 'A' will create a direct reciprocal reaction to the unified equation:

latitude 37° 07′ 27.9″ is equal to:

37.1244167 degrees

The reciprocal of this value:

0.02693645 (2693645 harmonic)

Mathematical evidence associated with the grid indicates that the position of zero longitude through Greenwich is not an arbitrary one, and that geometric calculations from this base line are valid. It has been found that harmonic resonances can be calculated within each 90 degree sector, and therefore I believe that there should be at least four of each of these major harmonic points (A and B) north and south of the equator.

The displacement of point 'A' from longitude 90° 00′ is:

84.72 degrees (D — A)

this value doubled equals:

169.44 (harmonic 16944, light field)

The hypotenuse of the geometric triangle formed on the earth's surface, (A — E) is equal to:

85.79229 degrees

If this value is considered as the diameter of a circle, on a flat plain, passing through points 'A' and 'E', then the circumference is equal to:

269.5 degrees, harmonic equivalent.

It can be seen from this that the position has a very strong affinity, in geometric terms, with the unified equation, gravitational forces, and the light fields.

As position 'B' is displaced at a distance of 2.693645 minutes of arc, and is directly on the grid, it has similar affinity with the universal forces. The angle of displacement helps to strengthen this due to the evidence of the 16944 harmonic. The vertical displacement of 'B' from 'A' adds to this with a geometric of 0.725572 minutes. The square root of a harmonic to this number 7.25572, is equal to 2.693645.

I discovered in addition to all the obvious harmonics present that the relationship of point 'B' to the resultant grid pole, in the south, and the resultant grid Equator, also produced direct associations with the unified equations.

All in all, I sincerely believe that our future energy requirements could be produced from this small area south of Auckland. It will be interesting to see if the scientific groups have as much faith in the theory as I do.

DIAGRAM 14

Showing the theoretical positions of surface probes for the production of electrical energy from the earth.

A — B = 2.693645 minutes of arc.
B — C = 0.725572 minutes of arc.
C — A = 2.594 minutes of arc.
Circumference of circle = 269.5 degrees equivalent on a flat plain.

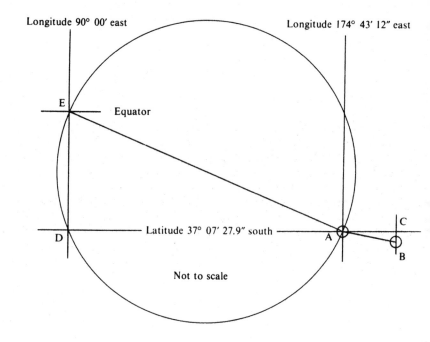

Position A = Probe established at a harmonic point in relation to the earth's axis.
Position B = Probe established at a harmonic point in relation to the earth grid system.

E — D = 37.124416 degrees (reciprocal = 0.02693645)
D — A = 84.72 degrees (84.72 x 2 = 169.44)
A — E = 85.79229 degrees (85.792 x 3.14159 = 269.5)

THE HARMONICS OF STONEHENGE

Who built Stonehenge and why did they build it? What is the true purpose of this geometric pattern of gigantic stones, said to be at least thirty-five centuries old, standing like ghostly sentinels on the Salisbury Plain in the Southern part of England. As the centuries have gone by many different investigators have tried their luck at deciphering the mystery of the complex, and to date I consider that none of them have come close to the truth. So far the reasons given for the construction are far too mundane to explain the immense effort, and meticulous planning, necessary to erect the stones with such precision.

In my second book, Harmonic 695, I suggested the probability that Stonehenge could have been designed as a gigantic crystal set. A massive geometric device constructed in ancient times to serve as a transmitter and receiver of signals from the heavens. This conclusion was reached because many of the known measurements were very close to those found in my own research. Also a peculiar fogging effect was evident on many photographs taken of the stones which indicated that some sort of radiation was emanating from them.

Since that time I have spent many months carrying out a calculator analysis of the geometric pattern and feel that I am now ready to challenge the scientific community, as to the previous interpretations made by them, regarding the basic reason for the construction. Maybe I was partly correct in my initial assumptions, but further probing has revealed that far more interesting secrets are inherent in the structure, which could lead to a much better understanding of the complexities of our immediate universe.

The first known records relating to Stonehenge were those that appeared in the first edition of Historia Anglorum by Henry, who was the archdeacon of Huntington. He did not seem particularly impressed by the structure and was not able to offer any possible reason for it being there. The year 1129 was evidently not a good one for taxing the imagination.

The next effort was written around the year 1135 by Geoffrey of Monmouth, called the Historia regum Britanniae. According to the information available this man was not classed as a very reliable historian but was the first to give a reason for the existence of the stoneworks, even though the whole story was obviously a complete fabrication. He says that the stones were erected to serve as a monument to subjects of Aurelius Ambrosius, King of the Britons, who had been laid to rest by the sword swinging followers of Hengist the Saxon. Merlin the magician was asked how these men should be honoured, and he replied that if an everlasting monument was required then Ambrosius should, ... send for the choria gigantum que est in killaro monte hybernie, the giants Dance which is Kildare, a mountain in Ireland. For there is a stone structure, which no one today could raise without a profound knowledge of the mechanical arts. They are stones of a vast size and wonderful quality, and if they can be brought here they will stand forever.

Merlin convinced the boss that this was the very thing needed to do the job in the grand style and after the Irish were defeated in battle used his knowledge of magic to shift the stones to Salisbury Plain where they were placed in the pattern that has mystified everyone up until modern times. May be there was such a man with the mysterious powers attributed to Merlin in ancient times, because superior scientific knowledge must have been applied to place the stones so accurately, but the story is a bit far fetched. I find it hard to imagine a King in those days spending so much time and money to set up a memorial to his subjects. More likely the poor old subjects were squeezed to the limit to extract more taxes from them. Times haven't changed much.

Quite a time passed by before anyone else showed an interest in probing the mystery of the stone complex. In 1655 John Webb, the son-in-law of Inigo Jones, a famous English architect, published a book called, The Most Notable Antiquity of Great Britain, Vulgarly Called Stone-Henge, standing on Salisbury Plain, Restored, by Inigo Jones, Esquire, Architect General to the Late King. (Charles 1) Jones had actually been commissioned to carry out a survey of the stones because of the curiosity of the then King, James 1, but he must have used a banana as a measuring stick for much of his work because it is now considered highly inaccurate. The large upright stones in the centre of the complex, called the trilithons, were those of which the measurements were most controversial. It is obvious, from the modern day ground plan, that these stones were placed in a horseshoe, or oval shaped pattern. It is said that there were five trilithons in the original group. Jones, in his work, shows six arranged to form a perfect hexagon. He states that the Sarsen stones are fifteen and a half feet high, when in fact they are around thirteen and a half feet, as will be demonstrated.

The next on the list was a Dr Charleton, a Fellow of the Royal Society, who after much deliberation concluded that stonehenge was built by the Danes. His effort, published in 1663 was called, Chorea Gigantum or, The Most Famous Antiquity of Great Britain, Vulgarly called Stone-Heng, Standing on Salisbury Plain, Restored to the Danes. According to Charleton a metal plate was discovered at the Stonehenge site, during the reign of Henry VIII, upon which there was inscribed writing in a strange language, which could not be deciphered by the learned men at that time. He theorized that as the message was not spelled out in Latin, then the Romans were not the builders then by a process of elimination finally settled on the Danes. (The finding of the metal plate has not been authenticated, and I would be most interested to hear from any reader who is able to provide any information regarding this). My own investigations hint at the probability that some sort of key to the mystery of the stones could have been left behind to enable a future race to decipher the problem. Possibly the key is still buried somewhere on the site waiting to be found.

It was 1740 before the next publication saw the light of day, called, Stonehenge, A Temple Restor'd to the British Druids, compiled by William Stukeley. His work was influenced greatly by John Aubrey who had completed a manuscript, Monumenta Britannica, some years before this. The ring of chalk filled holes at the outer rim of Stonehenge are today called the Aubrey Holes after this researcher. Stukeley maintained that British architects designed and built the structure round 460BC.

We now come to the computer age and one of the most complex analyses yet carried out on the stone circle. Gerald Hawkins, an astronomer at the Smithsonian Astrophysical Observatory in Cambridge, Massachusetts, Chairman of the Department of Astronomy at Boston University; and a research associate at the Harvard College Observatory, remeasured all the stone alignments, fed all the results into a modern computer, and came to the conclusion, according to his book, that Stonehenge was a sophisticated and brilliantly conceived astronomical observatory, used by three different groups of people over a 400 year period beginning around 1900 BC. He ascertains that the Aubrey holes were probably used as an eclipse predictor.

I have no wish to denigrate Mr Hawkins monumental effort, but with all due respect, I intend to challenge his interpretation, and present a calculator based analysis of my own, in accordance with the harmonic unified equations, demonstrated in my earlier works. Stonehenge is a more profound edifice than a mere eclipse predictor. My earlier work had hinted at the fact that elements of the unified equation, discovered from the world grid system, were inherent in the geometric structure of the stones. I was sure there was much more to be discovered if I spent the time with a calculator and seriously analysed the full pattern. The next thing was to obtain the most accurate measurements available in order to transpose them into the geometric equivalents to see if anything became evident. It so happened that friends of ours had recently returned from a trip to England, and they had brought back with them a copy of The Official Handbook of the Department of the Environment, which gave a complete description and very accurate measurements of the whole complex. This was just the information that I required as I realized that my calculations would be questioned very thoroughly, and it would be much harder to disprove the values if the basic figures had been produced by a government department.

For the purpose of analysis the measurements must now be converted into geodetic feet and inches, the ratio being 6080 British feet to 6000 geodetic feet in one minute of arc, at the earth's surface. (All measurements are converted in this ratio).

Obviously it is now impossible to obtain perfect measurements of the original plan as the stones have been weathered and mishapen over the centuries. Assuming that the government survey provided the most accurate average measurements available I considered that if I could correlate the whole of the structure into one mathematical concept and still remain fractionally close to the given averages I could present for examination a new theory for the basis of construction.

The harmonic values to look for would be those derived from the unified equations, discovered in my earlier works:

2693645	= Energy harmonic derived from the unified equation.
13468225	= Half harmonic of 2693645
37124416	= The reciprocal of harmonic 2693645.
14379577	= The harmonic of the speed of light at the earth's surface.
69543074	= The reciprocal harmonic of the speed of light.
34771537	= Half harmonic of 69543074.
972	= The harmonic of time (97200 grid seconds in one earth day)
324	= Earth resonant harmonic.
648	= (324 x 2) Harmonic temperature scale.
254558	= Harmonic square root of 648. (length of polar diagonals, gri
3928371	= Reciprocal harmonic of 254558. (earth's magnetic field)

Any other value found should be harmonically derived from the above.

The place to start the quest was to analyse the Sarsen Circle, or main ring of large standing stones. There were 30 of these, with 30 lintels each cut to a curve to fit the circle. The standing stones measured on an average of seven feet wide by three and one half feet thick and thirteen feet six inches above the ground. The inside faces of the stones were co-incidental with a circle 97 feet in diameter. The bases of the stones are set into the ground to depths of four and one half, to six feet.

There are two possible solutions when we consider the harmonic dimensions of the Sarsens. The first, and most likely, assumption is that the original conception of the pattern was for a mathematically perfect structure. This would mean that the stones, in the ideal concept, would have been gently curved to accurately fit the circular formation. This is the way I have shown them in the theoretical diagrams. The second assumption is that the stones were square cut and positioned tangently to the Sarsen Circle. Which ever solution is the correct one, I believe that the average measurements given are close enough to enable us to calculate the designed cubic capacity of each stone with reasonable accuracy.

First, the width of the stones; given as an average of seven feet. A fractionally larger value of 7.0027247 feet would convert to 6.9105836 geodetic feet. This is slightly smaller than the harmonic reciprocal of the speed of light at the earth's surface, 6.9543, but can be explained by the alignment of the end faces towards the centre of the circle. The length would be 6.9543 geodetic feet towards the outer periphery, as shown.

The thickness of the stones, given as an average of 3.5 feet. A fractionally large value of 3.523516 feet would convert to 3.4771537 geodetic feet. this is half the reciprocal harmonic of the speed of light, 69543.

The height of the stones, given as 13.5 feet. A slightly higher value of 13.663398 feet would convert to 13.4836166 geodetic feet, which is equal to 161.8034 geodetic inches (harmonically equivalent to $\emptyset$, or 1618.034). The very small discrepancy of height can be easily explained by a change in ground level with time.

The cubic content of each stone, of the section visible about the ground, would therefore be 6.9105836 x 3.4771537 x 13.4836166 = 324 cubic geo/feet.

128

If we pair the stones we get the value 648, and the derivatives 254558 and 3928371. If we multiply 324 by 30 to find the cubic content of all the stones within the circle above the ground, we get 9720, a direct harmonic of the grid time value of 97200.

The next step was to position the Sarsen stones extremely accurately on an inner circle which would set up a base line to solve the rest of the complex. All the rest of the calculations would be dependent on this line. The given diameter of this circle was 97 feet. A short calculator program indicated that the most likely original value was 96.95393616 feet, which is so close that it almost matches that of the government survey. The conversion value would now be 95.67822642 geodetic feet diameter, with a radius of 47.83911321 geo/feet. The area enclosed by this circle was 7189.788478 square geodetic feet, which is a half harmonic of the speed of light at the earth's surface, 14379.577 (143795.77). A more than satisfactory result.

I then found that I could form another base line by calculating the circumference of a circle passing through the Sarsen stones which could be evenly cut into 30 segments with a length of 6.9543 geodetic feet and 30 segments with a length of 3.71244 geodetic feet. This created geometric harmonics which were reciprocal to the speed of light and the unified equation. The circumference measured 320.0024724 geodetic feet and the radius 50.92997495 geodetic feet.

Working back from this base line towards the centre I found that if I used a distance of 13.468225 geodetic feet (half the harmonic of 2693645) I could position the circumference of the Bluestone circle. A glance at diagram (17) at this stage will demonstrate the harmonic relationships being built up. The given diameter for the Bluestone circle was 76 British feet. The calculated diameter came to 74.9291729 geodetic feet which converted nicely to 75.928235 British feet; again within a minute fraction of the government survey figure. The plan was working out very accurately and after a few weeks I had solved enough of the puzzle to form a general idea on how to tackle the rest of it.

The next step was to study the geometric relationship of the Aubrey Circle.

At this stage I found that I had two different values to deal with. The government survey handbook stated that the Aubrey holes were, "so carefully placed on the circumference of a circle 284 ft 6 inches in diameter, that the centre of none of them is more than 1 ft 7 inches from this circle".

Gerald Hawkins, in his book, Stonehenge Decoded, states, "They formed a very accurately measured circle 288 feet in diameter".

If both of these statements are correct then it is obvious that the average measurements were taken between different points. The government survey was to the centre of the Aubrey Holes, and Hawkins measurement, to the outside perimeter of the holes. At the present time, due to distortion over the centuries, the holes now vary from 2.5 to almost 6 feet in width, so both measurements must be only very good averages.

It took some time with the calculator to fit both diameters into the harmonic pattern, but eventually I found a solution that conformed with the two different values.

By a cross check of all the data my calculator indicated a diameter between the centres of the holes which was very close to the government one. This was 285.1965664 British feet, which converted to 281.44398 geodetic feet. A variation of 8.358 inches from that of the government average. Well within the tolerance of one foot seven inches.

This now gave a good indication of the original width of the holes; 2.824 geodetic feet. The radius being 16.944 geodetic inches. Both harmonics 2824 and 16944 are related to gravity acceleration and mass, as demonstrated.

When converted to British feet 2.824 geodetic feet is equal to 2.8616533. If we now add 2.8616533 to 285.1965664 the resulting diameter should be close to that found by Hawkins, which encompasses the outside perimeter of the holes. The value proved to be 288.0582 British feet which is only 582 ten thousandths of a foot in variance.

The spacing of the holes — that is their distances apart — was given by the government as just on 16 feet. According to the circumference found in my calculations the spacing worked out to be 15.999 British feet, which converted to 15.78897 geodetic feet. Again an extremely close proximation to the survey.

Now to the relationship between the Bluestone circle and the Aubrey circle. I discovered that if I projected lines from the centre of the complex which intersected every second Aubrey hole, A — B — C in diagram (17), then this formed a pie-shaped segment which in turn overlapped a smaller segment created by projecting lines through every second Bluestone, D — E — F — G. When the areas of these two segments were calculated the harmonic interaction was found to be very interesting.

Area of Aubrey segment A — B — C = 2221.85533 Square geo/ft.
Area of Bluestone segment D — E — F — G = 1926.76975 Square geo/ft.
= 295.08558 difference

(295.08558 x 2) = 590.171152
The reciprocal = 0.0016944 (1694443, mass harmonic)
Also: 1926.76975 squared = 3712441.669
The reciprocal = 2693645 harmonic; unified equation.

Piece by piece the puzzle was fitting together and I could visualize a complete structure with each of its parts finely tuned harmonically with the other.

There was another relationship between the 56 and 60 spacing of the Aubrey holes and Bluestones which was not evident unless looked at in three dimensions. Up until this point I had only analysed the pattern looking down from above, but now imagine a half sphere enclosing the whole complex, and coincident with the Aubrey circle. The diameter being 281.44398 geo/ft. The cubic content of the half sphere would be:

5836392.855 cubic geo/ft.
5836392.855 divided by 56 = 104221.3
5836392.855 divided by 60 = 97273.2
6948.1 difference

I would expect this value to move towards 6954.3 (the reciprocal harmonic of the speed of light) when further accuracy has been accomplished.

A look now at the ground plan of Stonehenge, will show that there are two circles of evenly spaced holes positioned between the Sarsen stones and the Aubrey circle, and also a horseshoe shaped array of large standing stones within the Bluestone circle. It was not my intention to try and solve the harmonic geometric placement of these sections of the complex for the purpose of this book as I felt I had gone far enough to prove the point I wished to make, but curiosity got the better of me and I managed to break some of it down in time for its inclusion.

The two rings of holes are termed Y and Z holes and according to the government survey the Z holes are just outside the Sarsen circle from 5 to 15 feet away. The Y holes are about 35 feet away. On the average they were 6 feet long and 3.5 feet wide, and 35 — 40 inches deep. Considering all the other evidence I would bet the original measurements were 5.901644 geo/ft long and 3.477 geo/ft wide. As yet I am unable to solve the Z hole circle, but the Y hole circle worked out to be as follows:

Given distance outside Sarsen circle	= 35 British feet.
Calculated distance outside circle	= 34.88411797 British feet.
Converts to	= 34.42511642 geo/ft.
Distance from centre of complex	= 34.42511642 + 51.3162669
	= 85.74138332
Circle with this diameter	= 269.3645 (2693645 harmonic)

The central area of the large standing stones was the most significant portion to solve geometrically, as no plan measurements have been given in any publication so far sighted. The government survey plan was the only source of information, but, as it was very accurately drawn, and had a scale in British feet attached, it was possible to obtain a fairly precise approximation of the original dimensions of the geometric ovals involved.

There are two patterns in the shape of a horseshoe. The outer is made up of five trilithons (three stones; two standing with one across the top). The inner originally consisted of 19 bluestones. All were evenly spaced. The trilithons were graduated in height, the smallest being at the open end of the horseshoe; 16.5 feet high, or with lintels 20 feet. The next pair on each side; 17.75 feet, or with lintels 21.25 feet. The central trilithon at the base of the horseshoe, if it was complete, would have stood 22 feet, or with its lintel 25.5 feet. The width of the openings between the uprights is given as somewhere between twelve to thirteen inches.

If I had attempted to solve this section earlier I probably would have failed, as I would not have had much information to draw on. Now I was armed with the geometric key to the structure. The main value for which to search was the harmonic of 2693645; the basis for the unified equation.

There is not much left of the inner horseshoe of 19 bluestones. Originally they were said to consist of slender stones, the tallest about 8 feet high, and the end ones only about 6 feet. They are the same type of stone as that forming the second circle; spotted dolerite. According to the survey map it does not appear as if these stones were originally laid out in the form of a true oval. The stones in the hollow of the horseshoe coincide with a half-circle, the diameter of which is given in the government survey as 39 feet. According to my calculations the original diameter of this circle would have been 39.0492003 British feet, which is extremely close.

39.0492003 British feet equals 38.535395 geo/ft.

$$= 19.267697 \text{ geo/ft radius.}$$
$$\text{squared} = 371.244169$$
$$\text{Harmonic reciprocal} = 2693645$$

The next most interesting measurements were those of the Trilithon oval and a series of values were obtained from the large survey plan I now possessed. After a thorough check the average measurements for the major and minor axis were found to be between 54 and 55 British feet for the major axis and between 45 and 46 British feet for the minor. It did not take me long to realise that the true measurements were more likely to be 54.591205 and 45.492671 British feet accordingly.

When converted, these values came to:

53.872899 geodetic feet: major axis: = radius of 26.93645 geo/ft.
44.894083 geodetic feet: minor axis: = radius of 22.44704 geo/ft.

$$= \text{radius of } 269.3645 \text{ geo/inches}$$

In appears that both the axis of the oval are in harmony with the unified equation; 2693645.

There was another important section of Stonehenge left to tackle but this would be difficult as no accurate measurements were available. The 30 Sarsen stones were bridged by 30 Lintel, each of which were cut to a curve to fit the circle. Each one was anchored to the upright stones by a knob, or tenon which fitted into a hole, or mortise, cut at each end of the under side of the Lintel. It seems from the photographs and drawings that the cross section of these stones is roughly (3.4771 x 2.3533) square geodetic feet, which would fit into the rest of the pattern. I would venture to suggest, from evidence of initial calculations that the original full circle was engineered to have a volumetric capacity of 2545.5844 cubic geometric feet. The derivatives of these values are already well explained.

Further interesting facts were revealed when I checked the surface area of the spherical fields which were coincident with the Sarsen and Aubrey circles. The field set up by the Sarsen stones would enclose the whole of the central section and would have a surface area of 28759.1539 square geodetic. feet. This would be equal to twice the speed of light harmonic at the earth's surface, 14379.577, (143795.77). Anything within the boundaries of this field would therefore remain locked into the three dimensional reality frame of reference which governs our normal concept of space and time.

The surface area of the spherical fields coincident with the circles passing through the centre of the Aubrey holes, and the outer periphery of these holes, could be varied between a minimum of 0.0069444 square nautical miles, or minutes of arc, and 0.006993 square nautical miles, or minutes of arc. Harmonics of this nature would set up opposition to the light fields at the earth's surface or those that would prevail in space. In other words space-time could be altered by the manipulation of the outer, all enclosing field.

Overall, I considered the results quite fantastic, taking into account that this was a first attempt to interelate the full pattern into one concept. The initial values used in the base lines were only fractionally different to those published by the government.

When I had finalised my analysis I was elated. The central oval was tuned to the unified equation, as was all the parts of the whole edifice. I now knew that if I could be proven correct in the mathematical implications of the overall pattern, then I had discovered something which could be of profound importance to the human race. This was the key to the heavens.

I could now visualise the layout of Stonehenge as the plan of a gigantic and wondrous machine. A machine that would not be confined by the barriers of time and distance. A machine that would allow us to travel amongst the stars.

The very pattern of Stonehenge is suggestive of the disc shaped vehicles traversing our skies, and with a little imagination it is possible to analyse roughly what the geometric arrangement is trying to tell us.

The Sarsen stones, and central Trilithons, could be likened to enormous electromagnets which would set up interlocking force fields around the vehicle. The Trilithon section remaining stationary in relation to the Sarsen section which would spin around it. The Trilithon section, because of the fact that the oval arrangement is open at one end, would act as a form of magnetic jet, and give directional control to the craft. The interaction of the Sarsen and Trilithon fields would possibly create the spinning motion.

The Bluestone circle, and Aubrey circle, could possibly represent wound field coils, much like those in the armature of an ordinary electric motor. That is suggested by the coupling of every second position in either circle. If these field coils were then rotated, in either direction, in relation to the large electromagnets, then spherical fields would be produced which would encompass the whole disc-shaped vehicle.

The Y and Z holes, and the inner horseshoe, could represent some sort of controlling field arrangements, to give stability and fine tuning to the craft.

All the electromagnetic fields, thus created, would, as demonstrated in the previous set of calculations, be in perfect resonance with the unified equation, and therefore that of light itself. By manipulating the fields throuh the infinite range of harmonics available, an interdimensional effect could be manifested which would allow travel in space time.

Is there something buried at the centre of Stonehenge which will give us the key to all this? Is the pattern the basic plan for a vehicle that would take us to the stars? Is it worth a million dollars to investigate?

The evidence has been available to us for centuries — but will anyone believe it? — I think not.

Before the critics start tearing me to pieces I ask them to consider the following question very carefully:

Would it be possible for me to make use of government survey charts in order to construct such a harmonically related geometric model, which is not only two dimensional, but three dimensional in concept, if it did not have a basis in fact. Again — I think not.

DIAGRAM 15

Stonehenge

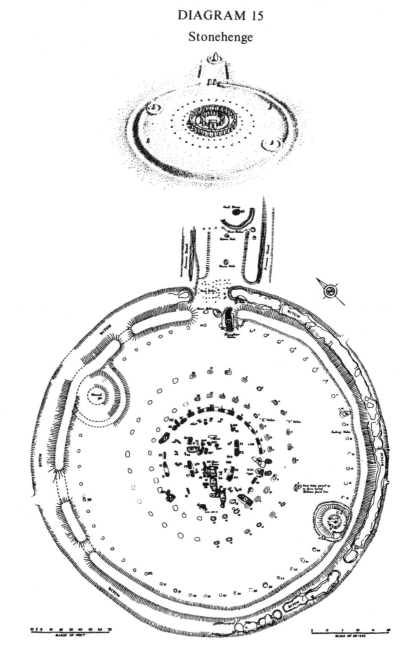

DIAGRAM 16

Offical groundplan of Stonehenge courtesy Department of Environment

DIAGRAM 17

Showing the harmonic relationship of the Sarsen and Bluestone circles with the Aubrey Hole circle.

Diameter of Aubrey circle = 281.44398 geo/ft = 285.1965 British/ft
Diameter of Sarsen circle = 95.678226 geo/ft = 96.9539 British/ft
Diameter of Bluestone circle = 74.9235 geo/ft = 75.9224 British/ft

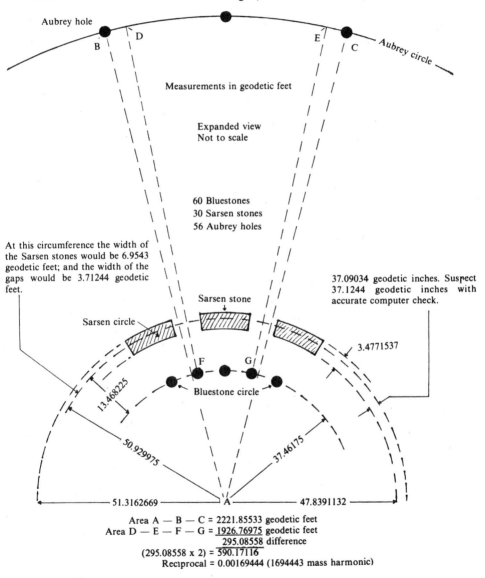

Aubrey hole

B   D   E   C   Aubrey circle

Measurements in geodetic feet

Expanded view
Not to scale

60 Bluestones
30 Sarsen stones
56 Aubrey holes

At this circumference the width of the Sarsen stones would be 6.9543 geodetic feet; and the width of the gaps would be 3.71244 geodetic feet.

37.09034 geodetic inches. Suspect 37.1244 geodetic inches with accurate computer check.

Sarsen stone

Sarsen circle

3.4771537

13.468225

F   G

Bluestone circle

50.929975   37.46175

51.3162669 — A — 47.8391132

Area A — B — C = 2221.85533 geodetic feet
Area D — E — F — G = 1926.76975 geodetic feet
295.08558 difference
(295.08558 x 2) = 590.17116
Reciprocal = 0.00169444 (1694443 mass harmonic)

135

DIAGRAM 18
Plan view of Stonehenge complex

A = Bluestone Circle
B = Sarsen circle
C = Z Hole Circle
D = Y Hole Circle
E = Aubrey Hole Circle
Diameter of the circle F — G = 85.7413833 geo/ft.
Circumference = 269.3645 geo/ft.

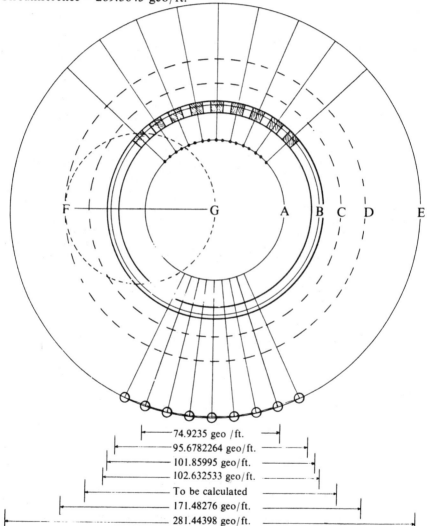

DIAGRAM 19

Showing theoretical geometric pattern of Trithilons

not to scale

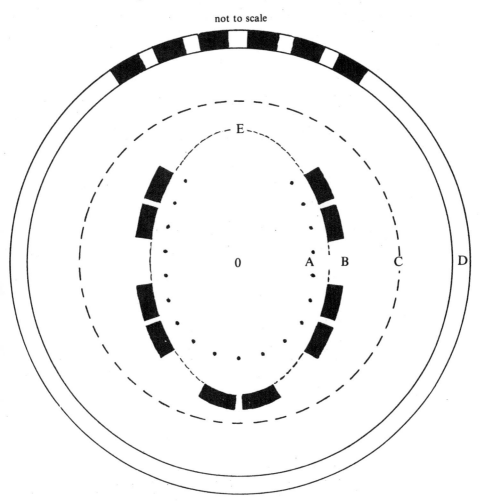

A: Bluestone horseshoe
B: Trithilon horseshoe
C: Bluestone circle
D: Sarsen circle

0 — A = 231.21237 geo/inches = 19.267697 geo/ft. (squared = 371.24416)
0 — B = Minor radius of Trithilon Oval = 269.3645 geo/inches.
0 — E = Major radius of Trithilon Oval = 26.93645 geo/feet.

DIAGRAM 20

Showing the vertical cross section of a theoretical disc-shaped space-craft based on the harmonic relationships of the concentric circles in the Stonehenge complex. The bottom of the craft is shown as a mirror image of the top. Harmonically tuned spherical fields would be coincident with the Aubrey and Sarsen positions, and an allipsoidal field with that of the Trithilons. the Blueston, and X and Y hole patterns could possibly indicate the relationship of other secondary fields set up to control the craft.

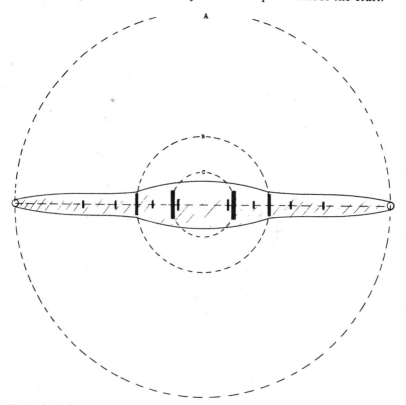

A: Spherical field boundary coincident with Aubrey circle.
B: Spherical field boundary coincident with Sarsen circle.
C: Allipsoidal field boundary coincident with Trithilon oval. In this particular cross-section the field appears circular.

THE SECRETS OF LEVITATION

A New Zealand scientist recently gave me an intriguing extract from an article published in a German magazine, relating to a demonstration of levitation in Tibet. After obtaining a translation by a German journalist, in English, I was amazed at the information contained in the story, and was surprised that the article had slipped through the suppression net which tends to keep such knowledge from leaking out to the public. All the similar types of stories that I had read up until now were generally devoid of specific information necessary to prove the veracity of the account. In this case a full set of geometric measurements were taken, and I discovered, to my great delight, that when they were converted into their equivalent geodetic measures, relating to grid harmonics the values gave a direct association with those in the unified harmonic equations published in my earlier works.

The following extracts are translations taken from the German article: 'We know from the priests of the far east that they were able to lift heavy boulders up high mountains with the help of groups of various sounds ... the knowledge of the various vibrations in the audio range demonstrates to a scientist of physics that a vibrating and condensed sound field can nullify the power of gravitation. Swedish engineer Olaf Alexanderson wrote about this phenomenon in the publication, Implosion No. 13.

The following report is based on observations which were made only 20 years ago in Tibet. I have this report from civil engineer and flight manager, Henry Kjelson, a friend of mine. He later on included this report in his book, The Lost Techniques. This is his report:

A Swedish doctor, Dr Jarl, a friend of Kjelsons, studied at Oxford. During those times he became friends with a young Tibetan student. A couple of years later, it was 1939, Dr Jarl made a journey to Egypt for the English Scientific Society. There he was seen by a messenger of his Tibetan friend, and urgently requested to come to Tibet to treat a high Lama.

After Dr Jarl got the leave he followed the messenger and arrived after a long journey by plane and Yak caravans, at the monastery, where the old Lama and his friend who was now holding a high position were now living.

Dr Jarl stayed there for some time, and because of his friendship with the Tibetans he learned a lot of things that other foreigners had no chance to hear about, or observe.

One day his friend took him to a place in the neighbourhood of the monastery and showed him a sloping meadow which was surrounded in the north west by high cliffs. In one of the rock walls, at a height of about 250 metres was a big hole which looked like the entrance to a cave. In front of this hole there was a platform on which the monks were building a rock wall. The only access to this platform was from the top of the cliff and the monks lowered themselves down with the help of ropes.

In the middle of the meadow, about 250 metres from the cliff, was a polished slab of rock with a bowl like cavity in the centre. The bowl had a diameter of one metre and a depth of 15 centimetres. A block of stone was manoeuvred into this cavity by Yak oxen. The block was one metre wide and one and one-half metres long. Then 19 musical instruments were set in an arc of 90 degrees at a distance of 63 metres from the stone slab. The radius of 63 metres was measured out accurately. The musical instruments consisted of 13 drums and six trumpets. (Ragdons).

Eight drums had a cross-section of one metre, and a length of one and one-half metres. Four drums were medium size with a cross-secion of 0.7 metre and a length of one metre. The only small drum had a cross-section of 0.2 metres and a length of 0.3 metres. All the trumpets were the same size. They had a length of 3.12 metres and an opening of 0.3 metres. The big drums and all the trumpets were fixed on mounts which could be adjusted with staffs in the direction of the slab of stone. The big drums were made of 3mm thick sheet iron, and had a weight of 150 kg. They were built in five sections. All the drums were open at one end, while the other end had a bottom of metal, on which the monks beat with big leather clubs. Behind each instrument was a row of monks. The situation is demonstrated in the following diagram:

DIAGRAM 21

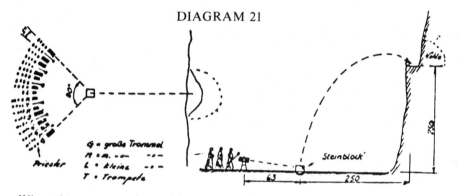

When the stone was in position the monk behind the small drum gave a signal to start the concert. The small drum had a very sharp sound, and could be heard even with the other instruments making a terrible din. All the monks were singing and chanting a prayer, slowly increasing the tempo of this unbelievable noise. During the first four minutes nothing happened, then as the speed of the drumming, and the noise, increased, the big stone block started to rock and sway, and suddenly it took off into the air with an increasing speed in the direction of the platform in front of the cave hole 250 metres high. After three minutes of ascent it landed on the platform.

Continuously they brought new blocks to the meadow, and the monks using this method, transported 5 to 6 blocks per hour on a parabolic flight track approximately 500 metres long and 250 metres high. From time to time a stone split, and the monks moved the split stones away. Quite an unbelievable task.

Dr Jarl knew about the hurling of the stones. Tibetan experts like Linaver, Spalding and Huc had spoken about it, but they had never seen it. So Dr Jarl was the first foreigner who had the opportunity to see this remarkable spectacle. Because he had the opinion in the beginning that he was the victim

140

of mass-psychosis he made two films of the incident. The films showed exactly the same things that he had witnessed.

The English Society for which Dr Jarl was working confiscated the two films and declared them classified. They will not be released until 1990. This action is rather hard to explain, or understand. : End of trans.'

The fact that the films were immediately classified is not very hard to understand once the given measurements are transposed into their geometric equivalents. It then becomes evident that the monks in Tibet are fully conversant with the laws governing the structure of matter, which the scientists in the modern day western world are now frantically exploring. It appears, from the calculations, that the prayers being chanted by the monks did not have any direct bearing on the fact that the stones were levitated from the ground. The reaction was not initiated by the religious fervour of the group, but by the superior scientific knowledge held by the high priests. The secret is in the geometric placement of the musical instruments in relation to the stones to be levitated, and the harmonic tuning of the drums and trumpets. The combined loud chanting of the priests, using their voices at a certain pitch and rhythm most probably adds to the combined effect, but the subject matter of the chant, I believe, would be of no consequence.

The sound waves being generated by the combination were directed in such a way that an anti-gravitational effect was created at the centre of focus (position of the stones) and around the periphery, or the arc, of a third of a circle through which the stones moved.

If we analyse the diagram published with the original article, then compare it with the modified diagram, we become aware of the following coordinates, and the implications, when compared with my previously published works.

The distance between the stone block and the central pivot of the drum supports is shown as 63 metres. The large drums were said to be one and one half metres long, so the distance from the block to the rear face of each drum could be close to 63.75 metres considering that the pivot point would be near the centre of balance. My theoretical analysis, by calculator, indicates that the exact distance would be 63.7079 metres for the optimum harmonic reaction. By mathematical conversion we find that this value is equal to 206.2648062 geodetic feet, which is harmonically equal to the length of the earth's radius in seconds of arc (relative to the earth's surface) 206264.8062. This also leads us to the following associations:

(206.2648062 x 2)

= 412.5296124

This number squared:

= 170180.68 which is the theoretical harmonic of mass at the earth's surface. The four rows of monks standing behind the instruments in a quarter circle added to the production of sound by their loud chanting and must be taken in to account in regards to the geometric pattern. If we assume that they were standing approximately two feet apart, we can add a calculated value of 8.08865 geodetic feet to the radius of the complete group. This gives a maximum radius of:

214.3534583 geodetic feet.

The circumference of a complete circle with this radius would be:
1346.822499 geodetic feet.
Which is a half harmonic of:
2693.645 (unified field)
The distance from the stone block to a calculated point within the cliff face and the height of the ledge on the cliff face from ground level is given as 250 metres. If we can now imagine that the raised stone blocks pass through a quarter arc of a circle during their flight from ground level to the hole in the cliff face, then the pivot point of the radius would be coincident with this position. See diagram.
The theoretical radius was found to be:
249.8767262 metres which very closely approximates the estimate.
This converts to:
809.016999 geodetic feet.
The diameter of the full circle would therefore be:
1618.034 geodetic feet.

A circle with this diameter has a circumference of 5083.203728 units, which can be divided into three even lengths of 1694.4. It therefore appears that the levitated blocks, once resonated to a certain frequency, would tend to carry out a flight path that is coincident to one third of a circle. The spacial distance being equivalent to the mass harmonic at the centre of a light field, 1694443.

The instruments used by the group, in theory, would also have been tuned to produce harmonic wave forms associated with the unified fields. The given measurements are in rounded off parts of a metre but in practice some slight variations from these measurements would be expected in order to create the appropriate resonating cavities within the instruments. The geometric arrangement, and the number of instruments in the group would also be a most important factor.

If the given measurement for each type of drum is modified fractionally and converted to its geometric equivalent an interesting value for the cubic capacity is evident.
The large drums:
1.517201563 metres long, 1.000721361 metres wide
= 58.94627524 geodetic inches long, 38.88 geodetic inches wide.
= 69984 cubic geodetic inches capacity
= 40.5 cubic geodetic feet capacity.
Therefore the cubic capacity for eight drums:
= 324 cubic geodetic feet.
This harmonic value is built into the world grid and is equal to half the harmonic 648.
The medium sized drums:
1.000721361 metres long, 0.695189635 metres wide
= 38.88 geodetic inches long, 27.00948944 geodetic inches wide
= 22276.59899 cubic geodetic inches capacity
= 12.89155034 cubic geodetic feet capacity.
Therefore the cubic capacity for four drums:
= 51.56620136 cubic geodetic feet.

If we multiply this value by 8 to allow for the interference pattern at the focal point caused by the eight larger drums we have:
412.5296108
This number squared:
= 17018068 the mass harmonic at the earth's surface.
The small drum:
0.303440311 metres long, 0.200144272 metres wide
= 11.78925501 geodetic inches long, 3.888 geodetic inches wide
= 559.8719984 cubic geodetic inches capacity.
= 0.324 cubic geodetic feet capacity.
The harmonic produced from the small drum is therefore the same as that produced from the large drums but at a much higher pitch.
The trumpets:
The length of each trumpet, slightly modified, would be:
3.112550314 metres
= 120.928723 geometric inches.
The length of six trumpets combined would be:
725.572338 geodetic inches.
The square root of this number:
26.93645 (the harmonic 2693645, unified equation).
The width of the bell mouth of each trumpet:
0.303440311 metres
= 11.789255 geodetic inches, which is equal to the length of the small drum.

The blocks of stone which were levitated were said to have the same basic dimensions as the large drums, although the drums were cylindrical in shape and the stones square cut. If we use the same modified measurements, then:
The blocks of stone:
= 1.517201563 metres long, 1.000721361 metres wide
= 58.94627524 geodetic inches long, 38.88 geodetic inches wide
= 89106.39633 cubic geodetic inches capacity
= 51.56620157 cubic geodetic feet capacity
If we multiply this value by 8 and square it as we did with the medium sized drums then the resultant harmonic:
= 170180.68 again the mass harmonic at the earth's surface.

Finally in our theoretical exercise we come to the polished slab of rock with the bowl shaped cavity at the centre, upon which the cut stones were placed in order to be levitated. Obviously the polished cavity had a purpose, and helped to create a frequency vortex within which the cut stones were raised. A full analysis cannot be given at this time as the radius of the cavity has not been calculated, but the given measurements are interesting in themselves. The cavity width of one metre would be similar, when modified slightly, to the stone blocks:
1.000721361 metres
= 38.88 geodetic inches
= 3.24 geodetic feet (half the harmonic of 648)
The depth of the cavity, given as 15 centimetres would have a revised calculated value of:

14.97414932 centimetres
= 5.895334377 inches
= 5.817764187 geodetic inches
= 0.484813682 geodetic feet.

As the dish-shape was focussed upwards towards the stone block to be levitated it would be expected that some type of reaction would take place which had an effect on the mass. The geometric shape of the cavity does seem to be engineered in such a way that the projected frequency vortex causes a reciprocal reaction to the mass harmonic of each block.
The reciprocal of:
0.484813682
= 2.062648055
Twice this value:
= 4.12529611
The square of this value:
= 17.018068 (the harmonic of mass at the earth's surface, 17018068)

I believe that there is not much doubt that the Tibetans had possession of the secrets relating to the geometric structure of matter, and the methods of manipulating the harmonic values, but if we can grasp the mathematical theory behind the incident, and extend the application, then an even more fascinating idea presents itself.

In my last book I mentioned the flying machines described in ancient records, that flew through the air with a melodious sound, and theorised that the sonic apparatus was tuned to the harmonic unified equations.

Now the Tibetans have given us a direct indication of how to construct a sonically propelled anti-gravitational flying machine. All that is necessary is to complete the circle of sonic generators, indicated by the drums, trumpets, etc., and we have a disc which creates an anti-gravitational lifting force at the centre. (see diagram 23).

To create this diagram I made four photo-copies of the original illustration showing the arrangement of drums, trumpets etc. and then cut out the 90 degree segments and fitted them together into a circular pattern. This was then photo-copied a second time in the relationship with a disc-shaped vehicle. When the circular pattern was formed it became evident that the Tibetans had placed the drums and trumpets on the arc of a quarter circle, but the placement of the Priests behind the drums tended to form a spiral. This conforms with the concept of the formation of matter due to the spiralling, vortexual, wave motions in space, discussed in my earlier works. Similar wave motions would have to be created in order to manipulate matter.

The inner diameter of the sonic generators in the theoretical vehicle would be 412.5296 geodetic feet, with the previously described harmonic associations. The outer diameter, estimated from the placement of the Tibetan priests, would be 428.7069166 geodetic feet. If we square the inner diameter we have the harmonic of mass 17018068 relative to the earth's surface, and the outer diameter would give a circumference tuned to the unified equation. The lift vectors through the centre would resonate at

144

harmonic frequencies in opposition to the mass value at the centre of a unified, or light, field = 1694443.

From this it would appear that a vehicle could be constructed that would resonate at frequencies in sympathy with the unified fields demonstrated throughout this work.

It is my opinion that our own scientific establishments are far ahead in this type of research, and that many experimental vehicles have already been constructed. High frequency generators have probably taken the place of the low frequency sonic methods, and electronic systems produced which would allow complete control of movement.

With this type of research going on, I would say that the days of the conventional aeroplane are numbered.

DIAGRAM 22

Showing relationship of Priests, drums and stone blocks, to the hole in the cliff face.

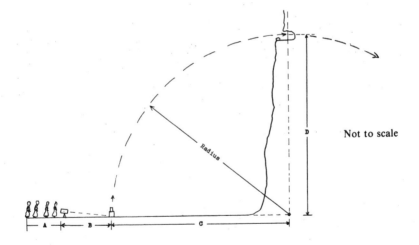

Not to scale

Distance
A = 8.08865 geo/ft.
B = 206.2648062 geo/ft.
C = 809.016999 geo/ft. .
D = 809.016999 geo/ft.

DIAGRAM 23

Diagram showing how the geometric pattern of sonic generators created by the Tibetan Monks can be combined in a circular, or disc, shape. the resultant forces of the harmonic fields set up would combine into a doughnut shaped anti-gravitational field which would levitate the disc, or vehicle.

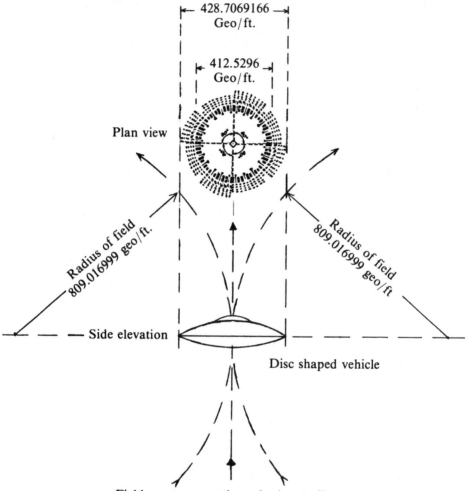

|← 428.7069166 →|
Geo/ft.

|← 412.5296 →|
Geo/ft.

Plan view

Radius of field
809.016999 geo/ft.

Radius of field
809.016999 geo/ft

Side elevation

Disc shaped vehicle

Field creates an anti-gravitational effect.

412.5296 squared = 170180.68 = mass harmonic
428.7069166 diameter = circumference of 1346.822499
= half harmonic of 2693.645 (unified equation)

THE HARMONICS OF THE IRISH
ROUND TOWERS

Amongst all the small bits of interesting information brought to my attention was an article by a Mr Philip S. Callahan published in a news letter put out by the Planetary Association for Clean Energy. It was headed Celtic Low Energy Electromagnetic Round Towers, and dealt with the possible original function of a series of obelisk-like round towers found in Ireland. I must confess that I have never heard of these towers before, but will try and track down information on them. If any reader can supply information on their precise locations and dimensions it would be most welcome.

Evidently the towers were constructed by Monks in ancient times for some mysterious reason, but according to the article they are now thought to be massive electronic collectors of cosmic microwave energy — in other words, tuned magnetic antenna. Because the towers are constructed of sandstone blocks it is thought that they are similar to silicon semiconductors, and that they have the properties of a DC rectifier. Because of their dielectric properties they could have the ability to detect and store cosmic electromagnetic, and magnetic energy — much like a massive crystal set. It is thought that they act as tubular wave-guides for meter-long radio wavelengths.

One of these towers is on Devenish Island in County Fermanagh, Ireland, and is 25 metres high. One of the most intriguing things about the towers is that the access door built into them is quite some way above ground level, which appears to be most inconvenient. It is now the theory that the reason for the high placement was an electromagnetic one. Evidently it is very difficult to tune an antenna system by mathematical means alone. To create sharp resonance it is generally found that the antenna has to be lengthened or shortened, by practical methods once it has been constructed in order to obtain a clear signal. As the article says, it would be very difficult to do this with a 25 metre high tower.

This problem was evidently overcome by filling the space between the door and the ground with dirt in order to set up conditions tuned to certain wavelengths. In some towers the cavity is completely empty, while in others it is filled to various heights up to door level. Mr Callahan says, "the monk Round Tower builders could easily tune the towers to night sky radiation by going inside and filling the base with dirt until they received the right message. The question is, what is the right message from the cosmic sky?"

There is maybe a clue to this if the problem is tackled by the application of universal harmonics discovered in my research. The height of the Devinish tower is given as:

25 metres.
which is equal to:
984.25 inches
which is equal to:
82.020833 feet
which is equal to:
0.0134902686 minutes of arc, at the earth's surface.

If we now apply a slight correction, or fine tuning — in other words; chuck a bit of dirt in — then:
0.013468225 minutes of arc, at the earth's surface, equals:
81.886808 feet
which is equal to:
982.641696 inches
which is equal to:
24.959149 metres

The harmonic of 0.013468225 being of course a half wavelength of 0.02693645. Harmonic 2693645 is derived from the unified equation, with a speed of light value of 143,795.77 minutes of arc a grid second, at the earth's surface.

Were the monks communicating with intelligence from space?

DIAGRAM 24

Shows a cross-section of the Kilmachdaugh Tower in the Republic of Ireland.

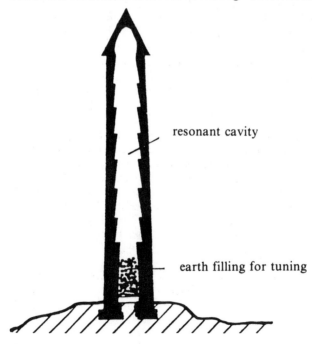

resonant cavity

earth filling for tuning

THE MAGNETIC MOTOR — AND
STONEHENGE

United States patent No. 4,151,431 could provide the description of a device that will be the prime method of motive power for all manner of vehicles in the future. The six pages of data describe how it is possible to generate motive power, as in a motor, using only the energy contained in the atoms of permanent magnets. On his initial approach to the Patent Office the inventor, Howard Johnson, was informed, "We don't grant patents on perpetual motion machines." Various physicists stated emphatically, "It won't work because it violates the law of the conservation of energy." But Johnson refused to accept that the laws of science are unbreakable. He resisted the persistent opposition, and states that, "Physics is a measurement science, and physicists are especially determined to protect the law of conservation of energy. Thus the physicists become game wardens who tell us what laws we can't violate. In this case they don't even know what the game is. But they are so scared that I, and my associates, are going to violate some of these laws that they have to get to the pass to head us off".

Mr Johnson has said repeatedly that he has never suggested that his invention provides something for nothing. He makes the point that no one talks about getting something for nothing when discussing extraction of enormous amounts of atomic power by means of nuclear reactors and atomic bombs. He regards the methods as similar. He postulates that the energy may be associated with spinning electrons, perhaps in the form of a, "Presently unnamed atomic particle". Most scientists violently disagree with this although a few of the converted, including some who are associated with large and prestigious research laboratories, are intrigued enough to suggest that there should be a hunt for the answer, be it a particle or some other as yet unsuspected characteristic of the atomic structure.

I was informed of Howard Johnson's work by Col. J.J. Pruente, a researcher and inventor from Tucson, Arizona who had read my earlier books. He had, himself, been working on a similar type of motor and hoped to have a working model in action soon. I was greatly intrigued by the information supplied on the Johnson motor, and impressed by the simplicity of the design. I believed it possible that my harmonic theory could in some way be connected with Mr Johnson's work, and with the kind help of Col. Pruente I was able to obtain copies of the patent application, and finally, after a year of tracking him down, communication directly with the inventor who lives in Blacksburg, Virginia. He kindly gave permission to quote from his patent application and a magazine article describing his basic work.

But what of Howard Johnson himself? The magazine article states that, his credentials appear to be impeccable. Following seven years of college and university training, Johnson worked on atomic energy projects at Oak Ridge; did magnetic research for Buroughs Company, and served as scientific consultant to Lukens Steel. He has participated in development of medical electrical products, including injection devices. For the military he invented a ceramic muffler that makes a portable motor generator silent at 50 feet; this has been in production for the past eighteen years. His contributions to the motor industry include; a hysteresis brake, non locking brake materials for anti-skid application, and new methods of curing brake-linings; and a method for dissolving asbestos fibres; plus many more ingenious devices. He is connected with more than 30 patents in the fields of chemistry and physics.

Mr Johnson does not waste time building fancy, or elaborate, equipment when he can get the same result with simple assemblies. He jokes about this and calls himself, "the sticky tape scientist." His prototype devices were assembled with sticky tape and aluminium foil.

The first consists of more than a dozen foil-wrapped magnets formed into the shape of a broad arc. Each magnet is extended upward slightly at each end to form a low U-shape, in order to concentrate the magnetic fields where they are needed. The overall curvature of the mass of magnets apparently has no particular significance, except to show that the distance between these stator magnets and the moving vehicle is not critical. A transparent plastic sheet atop this magnet assembly supports a length of plastic model railroad track. The vehicle, basically a model railroad flat-car, supports a foil-wrapped pair of curved magnets, plus some sort of weight in some cases merely a rock. The weight is needed to keep the vehicle down on the track, against the powerful magnetic forces that would otherwise push it askew.

The device is a rough representation of a linear motor, and when the small vehicle is placed on one end of the track it accelerates and literally zips from one end of the track to the other. By reversing the vehicle it works just as well from the other end.

The second assembly consists of a tunnel constructed of rubber magnetic material that can be easily bent to form rings. This was one of the demonstration models Mr Johnson took to the U.S. Patent Office during his appeal proceedings. It took him nearly six years of legal negotiations to obtain his patent.

A third device, and the one that I was most interested in, has the U-shaped magnets standing on end in a rough circular arrangement, oddly reminiscent of England's Stonehenge. This assembly is mounted on a transparent plastic sheet, supported on a plywood panel, pivoted underneath on a free turning wheel obtained from a skate-board. If an 8-ounce Focusing magnet is placed in the centre of the ring and kept about four inches away from the outer circle. the 40-pound magnet assembly will immediately begin to turn and accelerate to a very respectable rotating speed, which is maintained for as long as the focusing magnet is positioned in the magnetic field. If the focusing magnet is reversed the large assembly will turn in the opposite direction. Although the demonstration device is very crudely made it shows without doubt that it is possible to construct a motor powered solely by permanent magnets.

When I read this I was elated. The model constructed by Mr Johnson proved in a very practical way the mathematical and theoretical work I had carried out previously on the harmonic geometrics incorporated in the design of the Stonehenge complex. (Chapter 13) The combined evidence made it almost certain now that the Stonehenge pattern was a blueprint for a machine of some sort. The circle of large stones representing a powerful array of magnets, and the stone Horseshoe at the centre representing the focusing magnet. I have complete confidence in suggesting that Howard Johnson would have an almost perfect machine if he constructed his magnetic motor in an exact duplicate of the geometric proportions as that of Stonehenge. I would like to see, at some future date, my theoretical calculations and Mr Johnson's practical application married together into one project in order to prove the concept.

The motor based on Johnson's findings is of extremely simple design. As the diagrams indicate, the stator/base unit would contain a ring of spaced magnets backed by a high magnetic permeability sleeve. Three arcuate armature magnets would be mounted in the armature which has a belt groove for power transmission. The armature is supported on ball bearings on a shaft that either screws or slides into the stator unit. Speed control, and start stop action would be achieved by the simple means of moving the armature toward and away from the stator section.

There is a noticeable pulsing action in the simple prototype units that may be undesirable in a practical motor. The movement can be smoothed, the inventor believes, by using two or more staggered armature magnets.

In the table supplied by Mr Johnson, showing the magnetic field strengths taken at various positions in the experimental motor (table 3) I have marked the section that indicates the Zero air gap values A, B, C and D. I considered that it would be in this position that any associations with harmonic theory would be found — if indeed there was any at all. I had previously discovered that matter was manifested from the pure energy field by the complex interlocking of the magnetic lines of force which constitute the energy grid, and it was possible that the imbalance of magnetic forces in the Johnson motor would show a connection with these basic harmonic values in some way.

After studying the data I decided to add the field strength values of the repulsion forces (A + D) together, and the same for the attraction forces (B + C), then see what the mathematical relationship was, one to the other.

(A + D) = 6,950 + 19,375 = 26,325 Gauss Repulsion
(B + C) = 26,775 + 11,325 = 38,100 Gauss Attraction
$$38,100/26,325 = 1.447293$$

The value 1.447293 hinted at a possible relationship with the speed of light geometric harmonic of 1.4379577 (at sea level) and as the values were only derived by a rough experimental method I felt that a close approximation could be calculated which would enable the mathematical relationship to be expressed as an equation. This in turn would indicate how to construct a motor with a maximum efficiency.

The theoretical values proved to be:

(A + D) = 6,954.3 + 19,416.70681 = 26,371.00681
(B + C) = 26,371.00681 + 11,549.38548 = 37,920.39229

$26,371.00681 = \sqrt{1/C}$ Harmonic

$37,920.39229 = 1/\sqrt{1/C}$ Harmonic

$$1 / \sqrt{1/C} \Big/ \sqrt{1/C} = C = 1.4379577 = \text{(speed of light geometric harmonic)}$$

The experimental air gap of 3/8 inch was worth looking at as well. It seems that the operation of the motor was smoother and more efficient at this gap value:

3/8 inches = 0.375 inches (British)

= 0.3700657 inches (Geodetic)

I would suggest that in theory the most efficient gap value would be:

0.371244169 (Geodetic inch)

= 0.376194091 (British inch)

= 3.0095527 eighths of an inch (British)

The reciprocal value of 0.371244169

= 2.693645 harmonic

= Unified equation harmonic at sea level.

DIAGRAM 25

Showing construction of demonstration model magnetic motor. Copied from U.S. Patent Document 4,151,431.

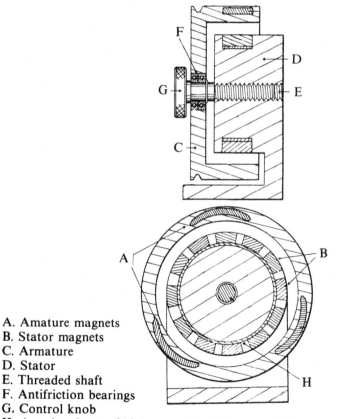

A. Amature magnets
B. Stator magnets
C. Armature
D. Stator
E. Threaded shaft
F. Antifriction bearings
G. Control knob
H. Annular sleeve of high magnetic field permeability.

TABLE 3

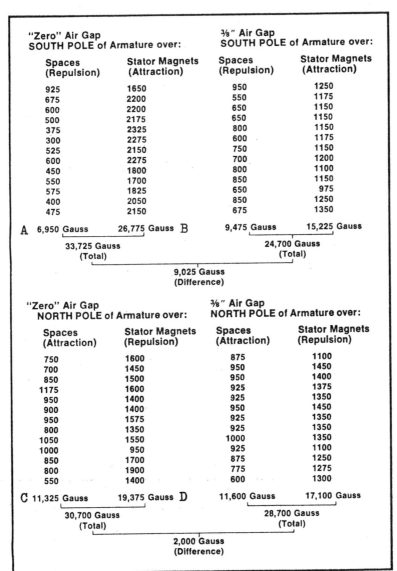

"Zero" Air Gap SOUTH POLE of Armature over:		⅜" Air Gap SOUTH POLE of Armature over:	
Spaces (Repulsion)	Stator Magnets (Attraction)	Spaces (Repulsion)	Stator Magnets (Attraction)
925	1650	950	1250
675	2200	550	1175
600	2200	650	1150
500	2175	650	1150
375	2325	800	1150
300	2275	600	1175
525	2150	750	1150
600	2275	700	1200
450	1800	800	1100
550	1700	850	1150
575	1825	650	975
400	2050	850	1250
475	2150	675	1350

A 6,950 Gauss   26,775 Gauss B   9,475 Gauss   15,225 Gauss

33,725 Gauss (Total)   24,700 Gauss (Total)

9,025 Gauss (Difference)

"Zero" Air Gap NORTH POLE of Armature over:		⅜" Air Gap NORTH POLE of Armature over:	
Spaces (Attraction)	Stator Magnets (Repulsion)	Spaces (Attraction)	Stator Magnets (Repulsion)
750	1600	875	1100
700	1450	950	1450
850	1500	950	1400
1175	1600	925	1375
950	1400	925	1350
900	1400	950	1450
950	1575	925	1350
800	1350	925	1350
1050	1550	1000	1350
1000	950	925	1100
850	1700	875	1250
800	1900	775	1275
550	1400	600	1300

C 11,325 Gauss   19,375 Gauss D   11,600 Gauss   17,100 Gauss

30,700 Gauss (Total)   28,700 Gauss (Total)

2,000 Gauss (Difference)

Readings taken at the north and south pole of the armature magnet indicate there is constant off balance situation. Note in one case the total difference is 2000 Gauss while in the other the total is 9,025 Gauss. The force conditions are far from identical.

THE GEORGE ADAMSKI STORY
FACT OR FICTION?

George Adamski; A man revered by many, hated by a few, an enigma to some, ridiculed by the majority. The first man in modern times to claim contact with a being from another world — a space-man.

George described himself as a philosopher, student, teacher and saucer researcher. He lived on the southern slopes of Mount Palomar, in California, where he spent much of his time searching the skies with his two reflector telescopes. One was a fifteen inch, housed within a small dome, and the other a six inch which could be used on a special stationary mounting, or attached to a portable tripod.

For most of his life he believed that there was other intelligence in the Universe much like our own, but until 1946 thought that interplanetary travel was not feasible because of the vast distances involved. On 9th October 1946 he, and some friends, were watching a meteoric shower to the south of Palomar when suddenly, as he recounts in his book, 'After the most intense part of the shower was over, and we were about to go indoors, we all noticed high in the sky a large black object, similar in shape to a large dirigible, and apparently motionless. I noticed no cabin compartment, or external appendages were visible ... while we were still watching it pointed it's nose upward and quickly shot up into space, leaving a fiery trail behind it, which remained visible for a good five minutes.'

Shortly after, a San Diego radio station broadcast a report that during the meteor shower a large cigar-shaped space ship had been observed by hundreds of people over San Diego.

From that time on Adamski spent hours searching the skies hoping to see more of the craft, and in August 1947, with four friends, he sighted a further 184 objects passing across the sky in squadron-like formations of thirty-two. Then late in 1949 he claimed that he was visited at the cafe in Palomar Gardens, by two men named, J. P. Maxfield and G. L. Bloom who worked at the Point Loma Navy Electronics Laboratory, near San Diego.

They asked him if he would help them to get some good photographs of the unidentified objects by using his small manoeuvrable telescopes. It was decided that the moon would be a good focal point for a routine search. From this time on he forwarded photos of what he believed to be space-craft to the authorities, but no confirmation was ever passed back to him.

He now knew beyond doubt that there were alien ships moving about within our airspace, and he said in his book:

Since then, winter and summer, day and night, through heat and cold, winds, rain, and fog, I have spent every moment possible out doors, watching the skies for space craft and hoping without end that for some reason, some time, one of them would come in close, and even land. I have always felt that if the pilot within one of these ships would come out and we could meet, there would be a way for us to understand one another, even though our words might be different. And I have thought, too, that it would be interesting to take a ride in one of these craft. It would not matter too much where they took me nor even whether they brought me back to Earth. I have become very much interested in learning more about them and their ways of living'.

As it became known that Adamski was watching the skies for UFO activity he began to receive reports of landings of strange craft in the desert areas within driving distance of Mount Palomar. With the hopes of making contact with the occupants of the craft he made a number of trips into isolated areas of the desert and waited, but to no avail. Then in late 1952 he was contacted by a Mr and Mrs A. C Bailey, and Dr and Mrs George H. Williamson, with a request to advise them when he next planned a trip into the desert. They were also extremely interested in the UFO activity, and had carried out their own sorties into the desert in the remote chance that contact could be made. They reasoned that by combining their efforts their chances would be greater.

Adamski agreed, and a trip was arranged for a meeting near a small town called Blythe, California, on 20th November 1952. After some minor mishaps, Adamski, accompanied by Mrs Alice K. Wells, the owner of Palomar Gardens and the proprietor of the cafe there, and Mrs Lucy McKinnis, his secretary, met up with the others on the road a few miles from Blythe. After breakfasting in the town they all had a discussion as to the best location to set up a watch and it was eventually agreed that they would make towards Desert Centre, some way back to the west, then turn right up the highway which leads to Parker Arizona. They did this, and at approximately 11 am they parked on the side of the road about eleven miles up from Desert Centre.

A short distance from where they were parked a shallow dry wash bed crossed the highway in a dip. This seemed to originate from the base of a mountain ridge which ended about 2 city blocks distance from the road. George Adamski and Al Bailey spent about half an hour exploring the area, then they all grouped together beside the road to have a picnic lunch, and scan the clear skies around them.

A light twin engined plane caught their attention as it crossed the mountain ridge to the west, then shortly after it had passed overhead, as Adamski states in his book: 'Suddenly, and simultaneously, we all turned as one, looking again towards the closest mountain ridge, where just a few moments before the first plane had crossed. Riding high, and without a sound, there was a gigantic cigar-shaped silvery ship, without wings or appendages of any kind. Slowly, almost as if it was drifting, it came in our direction; then seemed to stop, hovering motionless'.

There was great excitement amongst the party and many suggestions about what to do, but Adamski kept his cool, as he was sure that although a possible contact would eventuate, the area that they were in was too exposed to view from other passing cars. He shouted for someone to take him back down the road, and Lucy and Al Bailey jumped into the car; the three of them then raced about a half mile along the highway, then along a track in towards the ridge. They stopped the car not quite a half mile in, to the west of the highway and after telling the others to return to the rest of the party and watch all that went on, Adamski collected his camera and telescope equipment and made for the base of a low flat-topped hill formation, about 200 feet further in towards the ridge. The whole time this was going on the huge ship had slowly followed the car and was then almost directly overhead.

While Lucy and Al Bailey were returning in the car the huge UFO turned in the sky and silently crossed over the top of the mountain ridge, and was lost from sight just before a number of aircraft arrived overhead, possibly sent in to intercept it.

Adamski spent the next five minutes or so setting up his telescope and camera attachment, hoping all the time that the large craft would return after the conventional aircraft had left the area.

Suddenly, a short distance away, Adamski saw a man standing at the entrace of a ravine.

What eventuated from this point on turned out to be the first claimed meeting with a man from another world. All the fantastic, if true, details were given in a book published in September 1953 by Adamski, called 'Flying Saucers Have Landed.' The book caused great controversy and George found himself the centre of world-wide attention. A world lecture tour followed and thousands of people flocked to his meetings hoping to hear, or see, evidence which would prove the existence of intelligent, thinking, beings like ourselves in other parts of the Galaxy. Unfortunately, this was not to be so, because George could not back up his statements with hard evidence. His quiet approach, and basic honesty, was not enough. Very few people believed him. Some were unsure, but the great majority looked on him as a charlatan and crank; and I must admit that at the time I was one of the many who were not quite sure of this man. He came across as a person who was honest and truthful, but without the evidence there was no hope of convincing many of those attending his lectures that the encounter was factual.

Some years later while on a holiday tour of the United States I happened to meet, quite by chance, Dr George Hunt Williamson at the home of a mutual friend, and naturally the episode with Adamski out in the desert was brought into the conversation. Dr Williamson insisted that Adamski had been telling the truth and that every detail given in the book was just as it happened. Adamski had in fact published photostat copies of affidavits, sworn by all the witnesses before notaries public, in his book. I was more inclined to believe that the meeting had taken place after discussing it with Dr Williamson, as he himself appeared to be honest and forthright — but the doubt was still there. Such a momentous happening required much more proof. We agreed to keep in contact, and two years later, in March 1979, my wife Wendy, our two boys and I were again on a holiday trip to the States and we arranged to meet Dr Williamson in Los Angeles. After touring around for several weeks we finally met up with him again on 22nd April.

At this time Dr Williamson was staying at the home of Dame Thelma Dunlap who was a researcher and archaeologist. We were invited to stay also for a few days and we gladly accepted. Dame Thelma is a remarkable person and has packed many adventures into her 78 years. In her younger days she had been an assistant to the District Attorney, and had worked with Scotland Yard; carried out work as a detective, and had been a long time friend of Howard Hughes. We thoroughly enjoyed the time spent in her home.

By this time George Adamski had passed on, but the story of his desert meeting was still very much alive and during our first evening at Dame Thelma's we discussed it at great length. A friend of Dr Williamson, Mr John Griffin, arrived and we all checked over maps of the Palomar and desert areas where Adamski claimed he had observed and photographed UFO activity. It was decided that we would all take a trip to Palomar the next day and stay over for the next two nights at the restaurant and camp site where Adamski had his telescopes, on the southern slopes of the mountain. I did not expect very much to eventuate from the trip but I wanted to get the feel of the place and see for myself where the historical happenings had occured — if true.

The next morning I hired a station wagon and we set off on a two car convoy for Palomar. The trip turned out to be an adventure in itself as this was my first time driving on the Los Angeles freeway. In a very short time I found that playing Russian Roulette was a far safer occupation than driving on these freeways at 60 miles per hour during the peak hour. Never-the-less we made it, more I think by good luck than good driving, and arrived at Palomar Gardens late in the afternoon.

The place had a run down look about it, and we were surprised to find that all that remained of the cafe mentioned in Adamski's book was the brick chimney of the fireplace. All other traces of his stay there had been removed. There was now only a small building not far off the main road where a caretaker lived and sold a small line of groceries and cigarettes etc. A small ablution block was further up the slope amongst the trees, surrounded by several rough camping sites. The area appeared abandoned, which was a pity because it could have been developed into quite a nice tourist attraction. Our family group chose to book into a motel we had passed a few miles back down the road, and the others in the mean time set up camping gear on one of the sites up amongst the trees. We returned later in the evening and had a most enjoyable gathering around a blazing camp fire until late into the night.

The next day was spent exploring the general area and visiting the Mount Palomar Observatory to see the much publicised 200 inch telescope. Another camp fire discussion was held that night, then back to Los Angeles next morning, playing Russian Roulette again on the freeway.

I am not sure what we hoped to achieve by this, but I had actually stood on the site where George Adamski had mounted his telescopes and took his photos, and somehow felt an affinity with this man. I, too, had met with villification and frustration, because I had dared to inform the public of things that vested interests preferred to remain hidden away. I felt that I had stood in Adamski's shoes, and wanted to help him prove his case; but could find nothing there that would indicate he was telling the truth. A few streaks of light had passed through the clear skies late on the second night, but there was not enough evidence to prove they were other than conventional aircraft. A man from another world did not pop in for a chat and a share of our picnic lunch — a very enjoyable experience, but nothing more.

Another two years went by, then around mid 1981 I finally discovered a method by which a circumstantial case could be established in favour of Adamski. The approach, as I had now found in the main body of my work, had to be a mathematical one. I was now in possession of a great deal of knowledge regarding spherical geometric harmonics, backed up by the geometric unified equations developed from my research.

It was obvious to me now that true space travel could not be accomplished by the use of rocket type vehicles, and brute force. The only way possible to traverse the vast distance between planetary systems was by manipulation of the space-time geometrics of the universe itself. The problem was one of relativity. The geometric unified equations I had discovered indicated to me that it was possible to set up a series of resonating electromagnetic fields which would alter the space-time matrix which governed the physical processes. By the use of an intense field of this type it would be possible to create a shift in space-time. In other words, a mass enclosed in such a field could be displaced from one spacial point to another in an incredibly short amount of time. Under these conditions, a trip between two planetary systems could be accomplished in a matter of hours, instead of years.

The type of machine required to do this would have to be constructed in such a way that all its components were harmonically tuned to the unified equations; and the very material, or elements, of its construction, would have to be combined in such a way that they, too, resonated in harmony with the enclosed fields.

I had all the information necessary, in my now bulging files, to check the veracity of Adamski's statements, and the major bit of evidence available was the clear photo taken through his telescope on the slopes of Mount Palomar. This photo has been published world wide, but what the public is not generally aware of is that a photo was taken of a similar object in England, on the morning of 15th February, 1954.

Stephen Darbishire, a thirteen year old boy at the time, lived in a small town called Coniston, Lancashire. During this particular morning he and his cousin, eight year old Adrian Myer, decided to climb the small steep hill behind his home. He took with him his small kodak camera, hoping to get some good pictures of birds; this being one of his favourite pastimes. Just beyond the hill rose the summit of Coniston Old Man (2,575 feet).

I quote from a book published by Leonard G. Cramp (1954). 'At eleven a.m. Adrian was looking towards the mountains; Stephen was looking away in the opposite direction. Suddenly Adrian thumped him on the back and shouted: "Look at that thing".

Down from the direction of the sun a strange silvery round object was descending. It came to earth about a hundred yards away and disappeared behind a bit of rising ground. A few seconds later it came into view again. Suddenly, it tipped up on its side and shot up into the sky with a deep swishing sound, but until then it had been completely silent. In a few seconds it had disappeared in the clouds.

Just before it went down behind the rise, Stephen succeeded in obtaining a photo. As the object came into view again he took another. Unfortunately, he had not set his camera properly, so the picture was blurred, but enough appeared on the plate for us to make several very important observations.

According to Stephen, the object had a silvery glassy appearance, like metal or plastic which light goes through but which you can't see through. (the word he was searching for was translucent). At first it was directly in the sun's rays and very bright. But as it began to rise, clouds cut off the direct sunlight so the boys were able to see it more distinctly. It was a solid metal-like thing, with a dome, portholes, and three bumps or landing domes underneath. In the centre the underneath was darker and pointed like a cone. At first three portholes were visible but then it turned slightly and we saw four. There was what looked like a hatch on top of the cabin dome.'

The film was taken to a Mr Pattison who had a photographic studio in Coniston village and after they were processed he contacted the Darbishire home and informed them, "there's something on it and it looks like a flying saucer".

'Sure enough there was a definite saucer-shaped object on the negative which, although a bit blurred, was clear enough for the three balls or landing domes to be distinguished; also a suggestion of dark portholes, while the dark cone beneath was clearly visible ...'

'Stephen stated, and it was confirmed by his parents, that he had never read the book, Flying Saucers Have Landed, or even an abridged account of Adamski's experience, but he admitted that he had seen a photograph of the Adamski saucer as published in the Illustrated on 30th September 1953. He said that although this saucer picture had shown a saucer with three portholes in a row, the one he had seen had four in a row. In his drawing he had only shown three, but as the saucer went away it turned slightly so that a fourth porthole had come into view. His guess was that it was a different type of saucer.

But in one of the unpublished Adamski photos, four portholes in a row are clearly shown.

He did not know this.

This on top of the other evidence was enough to convince all the investigators at the time that Stephen was not only telling the truth, but also that he had seen the same saucer, or an identical model, as Adamski.'

Leonard Cramp believed that he could prove beyond doubt that the two sightings were of a similar machine by the method of geometric projection. His aim was to show that .. 'Just as one can produce a true perspective or photographic representation of an object from a general arrangement or engineering drawing of that object, so it is also possible, by a reversal of the procedure, to reproduce an orthographic arrangement from a photograph, especially a photograph of an object which is truly circular, such as a flying saucer.

If we can produce an orthographic view from Adamski's photograph and reproduce another from the Coniston photograph, to the same scale, we can show quite clearly any similarity. Further, if we can show by superimposing one over the other, that they are identical, where is the man who is going to proclaim the result to be a coincidence ...'

A brief description of the method is given as follows: (see diagram 29) showing projections of the Adamski and Coniston UFOs).

A — B represent the unforshortened diameters.

C — E represent the foreshortened diameters.

If we make two marks, distance A — B apart, on the edge of a piece of paper and turn the paper, so that the marks lie one on each of the two lines C — D and E — F, at A1 and B1, this will represent the disc at the photographed angle, but viewed from one side, that is, it will be shown as a straight line. By bisecting this and drawing a right angle G — H, we now have the vertical axis of the ship, on to which the true height H — K can be projected. The angle X can be measured off and that will be the angle which the ship made with the camera when photographed. From this it will be seen that the rest is simply repetition of the above, though it will be necessary to establish the vertical axis and one or two horizontal axes on the photograph first. When the various points are connected up, as in the diagrams, we have then a fairly accurate orthographic view of a real space ship ...'

In his book Leonard Cramp stated that Adamski had estimated the diameter of the ship he photographed as thirty-two to thirty-five feet, and based his detailed orthographic drawing on the maximum of 35 feet. This was a fortunate decision, as will be seen, when his work is checked against the present analysis. Adamski's actual estimate was closer to this figure, as he said in his book, Flying Saucers Have Landed, page 218: ... 'While changing the position of the camera on the eyepiece, I took careful note of the size of this saucer by making mental calculations and comparisons with known distances. Instead of being 20 feet in diameter, as I had guessed it to be while on the desert, I found it was approximately 35 to 36 feet in diameter. And as far as I could judge, it was between 15 to 20 feet in height'...

By using his scale of 35 feet in diameter Cramp was able, by geometric proportion, to calculate the measurements of various important parts of the photographed vehicles. His estimates are shown below:

Overall diameter of ship	35' 0"
Overall height of ship	15' 1"
Diameter of cabin	15' 9"
Height of cabin	8' 3"
Diameter of portholes	1'6"
Diameter of spheres	4' 10"
Diameter of outer ring	29' 2"
Diameter of inner ring	23' 2"
Diameter of central cone	12' 6"

Now, nearly thirty years later, I can see that Leonard Cramp was getting very close to the truth, but he was unable to decipher the meaning of the measurements that he so meticulously produced.

By checking all the information that was now at my disposal, and basing my own analysis on harmonic proportion, and the unified geometric equations, I was able to calculate the following values: (see diagram 28)

British measure
6080 British feet to
one minute of arc.

Geodetic measure
6000 Geodetic feet to
one minute of arc.

British measure feet	Geodetic measure feet
A: 34.9514863 British feet	34.49159833 geodetic feet
B: 29.06013986 ″	28.6777696 ″
C: 23.3972696 ″	23.0894108 ″
D: 12.49052028 ″	12.3261713 ″
E: 4.894899776 ″	4.8304932 ″
F: 4.894899776 ″	4.8304932 ″
G: 2.2746335 ″	2.244704166 ″
H: 8.4444 ″	8.3333 ″
I: 15.86332588 ″	15.6545979 ″
J: 15.31763824 ″	15.11609038 ″

Close examination of the above will show that all of the measurements are very close to those produced by Leonard Cramp — but the true secret is revealed when the British measurements in feet are converted into their equivalent geodetic values. The values searched for had to be in close proportion to those of the original projection, and also in particular harmonic proportions which were related to the geometric unified equations. The machine had to be constructed in such a way that all its parts were able to interact in harmony with the geometrics of the physical environment around it. The average values incorporated in the design had to be derivatives of 2693645 and 1694443, or their reciprocals, if I was correct in my theoretical approach to the problem. Then, by expansion, or contraction, of the resonating electromagnetic fields surrounding it, such a vehicle could position itself relative to space and time.

We will analyse each measurement separately:

A: The major diameter of the disc — 34.49159833 geodetic feet.
This when converted into geodetic inches would equal:
413.89918 geodetic inches.
If we can now imagine that when the machine is in operation it would create a spherical resonating electromagnetic field around itself, then the radius of the sphere would be:
206.94959 geodetic inches.
And the volume of the spherical field would be:
37124418 cubic geodetic inches
The reciprocal of this value in round figures is:
0.00000002693645
So we see that the primary controlling field of the vehicle has a reaction which is in opposition to the normal harmonic equivalent of the unified field in physical space — 2693645
B: The diameter of the first inner disc, or ring, of the vehicle:
28.6777696 geodetic feet.
The radius of the ring would be:
14.3388848 geodetic feet.

The volume of the enclosed spherical field would be:
12349.08377 cubic geodetic feet.

This value baffled me for a while until I realised that the resultant field most probably reacted in conjunction with the three interlocking fields set up by the three ball-like protuberances beneath the craft. The larger field would therefore be modified within three different sectors, which would enable complete directional control, if the intensity of each of the three superimposed fields was varied to any degree.

The spherical field could be divided into three sections each of:
4116.361257 cubic geodetic feet.
The square of this number equals:
16944430
The harmonic of 1694443 has a direct relationship with the mass at the centre of a light field, and is also equal harmonically to six times gravity acceleration. (demonstrated in other sections of this book)
C: The diameter of the second inner disc, or ring, of the vehicle:
23.0894108 geodetic feet.
This is equivalent to:
277.07293 geodetic inches.
The radius equals:
138.536465 geodetic inches.
And the resultant volume of the surrounding spherical field:
11137325.4 cubic geodetic inches.

This field again apparently reacted in conjunction with the interlocking fields of the three balls, and when divided into three sectors gave the following values for each sector:
3712441.8 cubic geodetic inches.
The harmonic reciprocal of this value in round figures is:
2693645
Again we have a reaction in opposition to the unified field.
D: The diameter of the central cone:
12.32617133 geodetic feet.
If we imagine a coil around the periphery of this cone which would create a spherical field, then, the diameter would be equal to:
147.914056 geodetic inches.
The radius:
73.957028 geodetic inches.
And the volume of the spherical field:
1694443 cubic geodetic inches.
Again a reaction with mass and gravity.
E and F: The diameter of the ball-shaped appendages and the central hub.
4.8304932 geodetic feet.
The physical volume of each of these spheres was calculated as:
59.01644532 cubic geodetic feet.
The reciprocal of this value:
0.01694443 — the 1694443 harmonic again.
The central hub could be treated in the same manner.

162

The radius of the circle upon which the three balls were positioned equidistantly was also checked and proved to be:

8.631453 geodetic feet.

The volume of the spherical field which would be coincident with their centres would be:

2693.645 cubic geodetic feet — unified equation harmonic.

: The distance the hub projects below the outer disc:

2.244704166 geodetic feet

Which is equivalent to:

26.93645 geodetic inches — harmonic 2693645 — unified field.

H: Height of the cabin above the base of the main disc:

8.3333 geodetic feet.

The square of this figure:

69.444 repeating.

Which is harmonically equal to the reciprocal of the speed of light (69444)

I: The diameter of the cabin area:

15.6545979 geodetic feet.

which is equal to:

187.8551749 geodetic inches.

Which would give a circumference of:

590.1644375 geodetic inches.

The reciprocal of this figure:

0.001694443 (1694443 harmonic).

The volume of the cylindrical cabin was then calculated, the height of which was estimated to be just on seven feet by geometric proportion.

The radius of the cabin:

7.82729895 geodetic feet.

The floor area:

192.4747283 square geodetic feet.

The estimated height of the cabin:

6.997399 geodetic feet.

The volume of the cabin:

1346.8225 cubic geodetic feet.

This number is a half-harmonic of the unified field value of:

2693.645 (2693645 harmonic)

J: The height of the central axis of the craft:

15.11609038 geodetic feet.

Which is equal to:

181.3930846 geodetic inches.

The square root of this value:

13.468225

Which is a half-harmonic of:

26.93645 (2693645 harmonic) unified field.

Further geometric analysis was carried out on the craft with excellent results, but I believe the evidence so far demonstrated is more than sufficient to prove beyond reasonable doubt that the machine is a true space vehicle, capable of dimensional travel in space-time.

Adamski was telling the truth — the machine does exist.

I believe that we now have the technology to build one. Maybe not so perfect but a copy good enough to make a start on this new and exciting technology.

If the geometric construction of the space-craft is compared with that of the earth (as demonstrated in chapter 3 The Harmonic Geometrics of the Earth) then a general idea of the geometric, electromagnetic field reactions can be visualised. According to theory, the numerical harmonic value of the unified field remains constant at 26974635 in free space, where the speed of light has a maximum of 144,000 minutes of arc a grid second (relative). During the creation, and in order to sustain, the physical existence of a planetary body, this light value diminishes as the wave-forms spiral in towards the centre of the energy system. The harmonic numerical value of the unified field is therefore diminished in direct proportion, so that at the surface of the spherical mass the harmonic has a constant value of 2693645. Therefore, from the surface of a planet to the threshold of true space the unified field would vary harmonically from the lower value of 2693645 to the maximum of 26974635. It will be seen from this that any altitude above a planetary surface which falls between these two mathematical boundaries will have a unified field harmonic coincident with that level. Any change in altitude, to a theoretical height of 882.25 nautical miles, be it fractional or otherwise, would instantly alter the harmonic of the unified field.

It follows from this that any fractional change in the unified fields surrounding the vehicle would automatically position it, in a vertical sense, at a level above the earth where the equilibrium of the fields would be restored. The horizontal movement would be accomplished tangentially to the earth's surface by the manipulation of the three interlocking harmonic fields tuned to 1694443. Calculation has shown that the reciprocal of the 2693645 harmonic (371244169) has a link with that of 1694443 when associated with the tangent of a spherical surface.

As shown by the calculations the reciprocal harmonic values of the unified field are built into the vehicle to create a reaction with the physical environment. By manipulation of the fields surrounding the ship harmonic imbalances can be caused which will automatically shift the vehicle in space-time to a position of equilibrium.

An interesting fact shown in the analysis is that the overall dimensions of the cabin ensure that the electromagnetic fields surrounding this portion of the vehicle maintain a constant physical environment for the occupants. The harmonic 2693645 is a positive resonant factor that would keep the central spherical field of the ship stable during transition from one space-time reference frame to another.

After completing the analysis of the space craft I decided to concentrate on the positions at Mount Palomar and the desert area where the sightings occured, to check whether there were points on the earth's surface, in the vicinity, which were mathematically significant. Again, I discovered positive mathematical clues which built up the circumstantial evidence in favour of Adamski. The desert area was the most important so I searched around this position on a survey map first, making use of all the information in Adamski's book. He had retraced the movements of the party at a later date and found that the distance up the main road from Desert Centre where he had followed the rough track into the foothills was 10.2 miles. A measurement on the survey map verified that the end of the mountain range was opposite this point on the road to the north west. As the large mother ship had appeared from behind this first outcrop in the range adjacent to the highway I concentrated on the latitude and longitude coordinates in this small area. It did not take long to discover that directly behind the range in a small cove, at the base of the outcrop, the mathematical coordinates were of startling significance.

The latitude proved to be:

33° 53' 19.896" north.

Which equals:

33.88886 degrees.

If we divide the latitude by 2, we have:

16.94443 (1694443 harmonic)

So the latitude occurs at twice the harmonic of 1694443.

The significance of the longitude value was at first a little obscure, but by applying the theoretical evidence that indicates the Greenwich meridian is not an arbitrary longitudinal base-line, but a positive zero marker on the earth's surface, (chapter 2) I found what I was looking for; a connection with the 2693645 harmonic.

The calculated longitude passing through the cove was:

115° 20' 56.2" or 115.348944 degrees west.

In checking the harmonic properties of longitudinal values it is necessary to calculate the displacement of the position in question, east or west, of the longitudes which are at 90 degree intervals from Greenwich. The calculator proved that in this case the 180 degree meridian was the prime base-line. The displacement along a great circle track, at latitude 33.88886 degrees, between longitude 115.348944 degrees west and 180 degrees was:

3162.2775 minutes of arc.

Now this value has a property which is quite unique in itself. It has a reciprocal which is a mirror image of itself. If we divide one by this number we get:

0.0003162277 (a possible doorway between the physical and non-physical)

But to take our probe further:

3162.277 minutes of arc is equal to:

52.7046166 degrees.

The square root:

7.25979

The square root:

2.6944

The harmonic 26944, which would occur at altitude, and 1694443 are undoubtedly present at the position where the mother ship materialised.

I then drew up a spherical triangle on the survey map representing the earth's surface, and connected up the three points of the desert contact site, the Adamski research position on Mount Palomar, and the 180 degree longitude calculated point. (see diagram 26)

The results showed that Adamski was carrying out his search in the most appropriate areas, from a mathematical point of view. Whether by accident or design we will never know. The position of significance on the southern slopes of Mount Palomar, near the Adamski telescopes was:

33.308333 degrees north latitude/116.929444 degrees west longitude.

The calculated great circle track distance from this point to the 180 degree position was:

3099.317166 minutes of arc. (plus or minus 100 geo/feet)

And to the contact site in the desert:

86.31453 minutes of arc. (plus or minus 100 geo/feet)

If we consider these two coordinates as radii, then the spheres of influence encompassed by them would have a certain volume, as follows:

3099.317166 minutes of arc equals:

185959.03 seconds of arc.

The volume of a sphere with this radius equals:

2.693645^{16} cubic seconds.

2693645 harmonic.

The volume of a sphere with a radius of 86.31453 minutes of arc equals:

2693645 cubic minutes.

2693645 harmonic.

The pattern complies with the previous criteria found in my research, and I am confident now that the evidence is strong enough to support Adamski as far as his photographs and the desert contact are concerned. I have found no evidence as yet to support his stories of alleged trips in UFO type vehicles. I doubt if anyone could set up such a mathematical series of coincidences to perpetrate a hoax. I certainly could not.

It is almost as if the space people have deliberately left behind a set of precise mathematical clues for us to follow. They covered the area with a clear set of mathematical finger prints, knowing full well that, in time, someone would stumble on to them.

If those space machines are still watching — what about a contact? — the picnic lunch will be ready.

DIAGRAM 26

Showing the geometric relationships of the Palomar and desert area contact points.

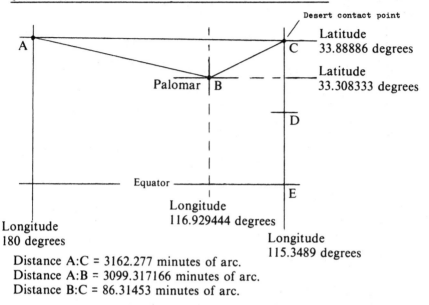

Desert contact point

A   C   Latitude 33.88886 degrees

Latitude 33.308333 degrees

Palomar | B

D

Equator

E

Longitude 180 degrees

Longitude 116.929444 degrees

Longitude 115.3489 degrees

Distance A:C = 3162.277 minutes of arc.
Distance A:B = 3099.317166 minutes of arc.
Distance B:C = 86.31453 minutes of arc.

$\left.\begin{array}{l} C:D \\ D:E \end{array}\right|$ = 16.94443 degrees

DIAGRAM 27

Mathematical analysis carried out by Leonard G. Cramp. 1954

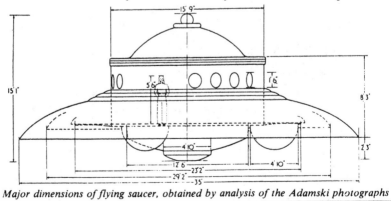

Major dimensions of flying saucer, obtained by analysis of the Adamski photographs

DIAGRAM 28

Mathematical analysis carried out by Cpt. B. L. Cathie, 1981, in accordance with the geometric unified equations.

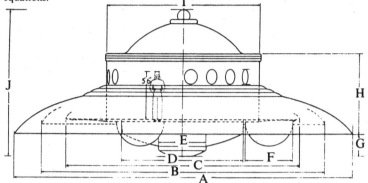

Major dimensions of flying saucer, obtained by analysis of the Adamski photographs.

A: 34.9514863 British feet	34.49159833 geodetic feet
B: 29.06013986 "	28.6777696 "
C: 23.3972696 "	23.0894108 "
D: 12.49052028 "	12.3261713 "
E: 4.894899776 "	4.8304932 "
F: 4.894899776 "	4.8304932 "
G: 2.2746335 "	2.244704166 "
H: 8.4444 "	8.3333 "
I: 15.86332588 "	15.6545979 "
J: 15.31763824 "	15.11609038 "

DIAGRAM 29

Adamski U.F.O.

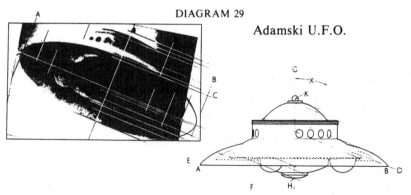

comparison by orthographic projection of the Adamski (top) and Coniston (lower) photographs

See Coniston UFO over page.

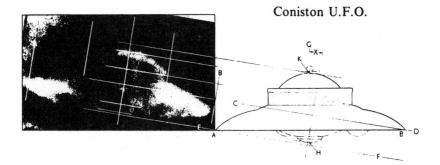

Coniston U.F.O.

DIAGRAM 30

Showing the various geometric interlocking fields of the **Adamski U.F.O.**

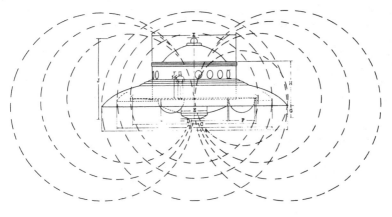

THE HARMONICS OF DESTRUCTION

In my earlier books I have demonstrated the geometric nature of the Atom Bomb and the method of detonation in relation to the harmonic structure of physical mass. I had discovered during my research that an atom bomb was an intricate geometric device which could only be detonated by placing it below, on, or above, a calculated geometric position in relation to the Earth's surface. The geometric trigger that caused the disruption of matter within the bomb was the spacial relationship between the Earth and the Sun at a given instant of time. This knowledge made it obvious to me that an all out atomic war would be impossible as each bomb would have to be detonated at a certain place at a certain time which could be precalculated years in advance by any proposed enemy. The whole process would be completely illogical.

By checking the latitude and longtitude of the Sun position at the time of atomic detonations I was able to discover some of the harmonic geometric coordinates set up between the bomb site and the Sun position at the instant of detonation. Once the secret was known I then found that in some cases I was able to calculate a bomb test ahead of time.

As most of the mathematical combinations are unknown to me I found that the best way to prove the point was to analyse previous bomb tests when the times of detonation were publicised and check the Earth Sun coordinates. As could be expected, once it became known that I had discovered the geometric nature of the bomb, I was contacted by personnel from various agencies and scientific establishments from around the world who tried their best to persuade me to keep quiet about it. I refused, as I believe the public have a right to know the truth about the geometric process involved.

As pointed out previously, the latitude of 11.5905116 degrees is coincident with the islands of Bikini and Eniwetok. This is equal to 695.4307 minutes north latitude. The harmonic 6954307 is the reciprocal of the speed of light at the earth's surface, 143,795.77 minutes of arc per grid second. Both these islands were used for some of the early atom tests. The latitude 37.1244 degrees passes through the atomic test ground in the United States. This harmonic has been demonstrated many times as being the reciprocal of 2693645, derived from the unified equation. The latitude of Mururoa Island in the South Pacific, used for atom tests by the French, creates a half-harmonic of 2637102, which is the square root of 6.954307 to the twelfth place.

Also in my previous work I have indicated that many earthquakes, which seem to be occuring with increasing frequency, are caused by geometric effects associated with atomic tests. We appear to be doing our best to destroy our own planet. It is because of these earthquakes that I decided once again to demonstrate the circumstantial evidence which connects bomb tests with some of the destructive upheavals which occur a short time after. I believe a recent case would be a classic example of this.

On May 27 1983 the Auckland 'Herald' published two news items concerning incidents that occurred approximately ten hours apart. Seemingly there was no correlation between the two happenings but a series of calculations convinced me, beyond doubt, that the first incident was the trigger that caused the second.

The first news item was headlined, "France's N-Blast Decried". It went on to say that the explosion was one of the largest nuclear test bombs to be detonated on Mururoa Atoll. The Australian Foreign Minister was not too happy about the event and said that the explosion was estimated at 70 kilotonnes and that it put relations between France and Australia "under very serious strain indeed". The New Zealand Foreign Minister said, "It is another nuisance really because one of these tests is one too many".

The test was the 54th since France started testing underground in 1975. The time of the explosion was given as, about 5.13 am New Zealand time, on 26th May 1983. (The Auckland "Star" recorded the time as 5.31 am)

The second news item was headlined, "Severe Quake Rocks Japan". The information given indicated that the quake occured at 3 pm New Zealand time, on 26 May 1983. It effected a 300 kilometre stretch of the western coastline killing at least eight people. (more deaths were reported later). A huge tidal wave resulted which caused extensive damage and the Prime Minister declared an emergency and appointed a State Minister to organise relief efforts. The tremor was said to have been centred in the sea off the coastal prefecture of Akita and was calculated at 7.7 on the Richter scale.

I had kept the reports for my own records but had not bothered to check the coordinates as I was busy with other things at the time but a query from Australia, by a reader of my other books who felt there was a connection between the two events, caused me to hunt out the file and get to work on the calculator. The results are demonstrated in diagram (31) and the series of coordinates linking the two points appear to substantiate the theory regarding the triggering of earthquakes.

I accepted the Auckland "Star" time of 5.31 am as the correct one for calculation purposes and found that within a minute of that time the sun was in a relative position equal to 69.44444 degrees from Mururoa Island. This created a reciprocal harmonic to the speed of light at the surface of the atoms in the bomb structure at the instant of detonation. All the geometric coordinates necessary in order to unlock the atomic structure were fulfilled which culminated in the explosion.

The 54th underground test was completed and, theoretically, many other harmonic points around the world received a massive jolt, and loss of mass due to disruption of the earth's magnetic field. According to my research mass is created from the magnetic field itself, and disruption of any of these field force lines will cause destruction of matter. I believe that test after test eventually weakened the earth's crust, just off the coast of Japan, to the extent that the last explosion caused a general collapse. This could be likened to the fatigue effect in metals caused by harmonic resonance.

The coordinates linking the atomic test site and the calculated epi-centre of the earthquake of the coast near Akita were as follows:

The direct great circle distance between Mururoa and the epi-centre:

171

5876.1076 minutes of arc, or nautical miles.
The harmonic reciprocal of this value equals:
0.00017018068 (the mass harmonic at the earth's surface).
The creation of the reciprocal would cause destruction of mass.
The displacement in latitude between the two points was equal to:
3712.4482 minutes of arc, or nautical miles.
The harmonic reciprocal of this value is equal to:
0.0002693645 (the energy harmonic derivied from the unified equation).
This, too, would cause disruption of matter.

The great circle displacement in longitude, at the latitude of the earthquake epi-centre was equal to: 3615.8547 minutes of arc, which created a harmonic associated with the value 1694443. As demonstrated many times, this number relates to the mass harmonic at the centre of a light field.

The geometric pattern appears to be quite precise and tends to substantiate the theory that atom tests do in fact cause major earthquakes. A computer program covering all atomic tests and earthquakes occuring within a short time after detonation could possibly bring to light some quite startling facts.

DIAGRAM 31

Showing the relative positions of the atomic test site at Mururoa Island and the calculated epi-centre of the earthquake off the coast near Akita, Japan.

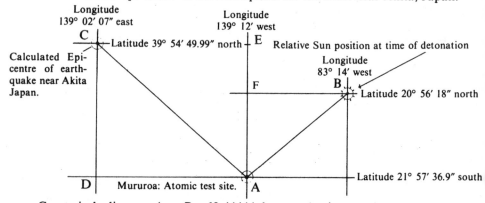

Great circle distance A — B = 69.44444 degrees. (reciprocal light harmonic)
Great circle distance A — C = 5876.1076 minutes. (reciprocal mass harmonic)
Great circle distance C — D = 3712.4482 minutes. (reciprocal unified harmonic)
Great circle distance C — E = 3615.8547 minutes
(3615.8547 x 60 x 60) = 13017076.9
Squared = 1694430000000 harmonic
Angle A — B — F = 34.815937 degrees (Tangent = 0.6954307)

Not to scale

HARMONICS FROM HEAVEN

In my first and second books, Harmonic 33 and Harmonic 695, I made reference to the relationships of various religious writings to the natural harmonic laws. In particular I discussed the journey of the Israelites from Egypt to Sinai via the Red, or Reed Sea, and the scientific clues that were evident at several points along the way. In recent weeks I have extended my research in this area and have discovered such a startling series of mathematical facts that I am not quite certain just what the reaction to them will be. If I am eventually proven correct then the world may not be quite the same again. If nothing else, the information should cause the various churches to seriously consider the joining together of all religious groups into one world wide united christian body. The evidence I have before me shows, with very little doubt, that there should be absolute unity of all religions, particularly the Christians and the Moslems, and that, idealistically, further research should lead to the unification of all the other religious orders.

It all started when I found that the Vatican, in Rome, had been placed, either by divine guidance, or deliberate design, on a geometric position which had direct mathematical relationships with the harmonic unified equations discovered in my earlier works.

Many religious manifestations have occured in places around the world, particularly in the northern hemisphere, during recent historical times and I considered the possibility that these happenings would have to conform with the natural laws of the Universe. Our physical reality is manifested due to the mathematical order of the universe and logically all happenings within the universe would have to conform to some type of unified mathematical process, whether religious or otherwise. As Einstein said. "The Creator does not play dice with the Universe". Nothing would be left to chance.

I thought it would be an interesting exercise to find out what the relationship of several of the recorded religious happenings would be when compared geometrically with the position of the Vatican. Could this position be one of the focal points through which the power of the Creator is able to function.

Let us follow again the journey of the Israelites from Egypt to Sinai and see what the computers can tell us when programmed with the latest geometric information.

The Bible narrates that when the Pharaoh let the people go ... God led the people round by way of the wilderness towards the Red Sea, Exodus 13:17:18 The Lord went before them (the Israelites) by day in a pillar of cloud to lead them along the way; and by night in a pillar of fire to give them light, that they might travel by day and by night; the pillar of cloud by day and the pillar of fire by night did not depart from before the people. Exodus 13:21:22.

The Israelites were deliberately led to the Red sea, which seemed like a very foolish thing to do, because with the Egyptian army coming up from behind the Hebrews were literally caught between the Pharaoh and the deep blue sea. The Bible says Pharaoh thought the Israelites were entangled in the land; the wilderness has shut them in. Pharaoh and his army moved in for the kill with the pillar seemingly having proved a poor guide; that is unless the future events were known to the intelligence controlling the object in the sky. The text suggests that some sort of celestial object totally under its own control, led the Israelites out of Egypt to the Red Sea and then as Pharaoh's army closed in the object moved from the front to the rear of the army of Israel, and kept the two camps separated during the night. Phase one of the operation involved leading Israel to the sea; phase two requires the object to keep the camps separated until darkness falls. Now began phase three; Then Moses stretched out his hand over the sea; and the Lord drove the sea back by a stong east wind all night, and made the sea dry land, and the waters were divided.

I checked the traditional route of the Israelites shown on a modern map of the area and the thing which struck me as unusual was the course followed by them considering that the Pharaoh's army was in close pursuit. First they headed south, south east from Raamses to Succoth, then for some unaccountable reason they turned back and headed north to the crossing point at the Red, or Reed sea. It seemed odd that the Lord should lead the Israelites into a possible trap of this nature when a free route could have been taken to the south east over land, which would eventually have led down to the eastern side of the Gulf of Suez. This route would also have been much shorter, unless of course it was known ahead of time what would happen at the Reed Sea. I believe that this was the case and that a guiding intelligence led the Israelites to the one place in the area where an unforgettable miracle could occur, and the Pharaoh's army destroyed. A geographic position conforming with natural law had to be selected so that all the necessary harmonic coordinates were available.

In my second book I showed that the crossing point was around 31 degrees north latitude, but recent research with a computer has placed the position more accurately at:
Latitude 30° 52′ 46.7099″ north/ Longitude 32° 11′ 22.68″ east.
The vatican focal point is:
Latitude 41° 54′ 22.68″ north/ Longitude 12° 27′ 08″ east.
The direct great circle distance between the two points is equal to:
1156.147 minutes of arc, or nautical miles.
Which is equal to:
19.26769315 degrees.
The square of this number:
371.244
The reciprocal:
2693645 Harmonic.
The great circle distance between the two longitudes at the latitude of the Reed sea crossing is equal to:
1015.4968 minutes of arc, or nautical miles.
Which is equal to:
6092.98072 seconds of arc.
The square of this number:
37124415.9

The reciprocal;
2693645 Harmonic
The displacement in latitude between the two points:
661.599 minutes of arc, or nautical miles.
The area of a circle with this harmonic diameter would be 343774677 square minutes. This number is harmonically equal to the radius of the earth in nautical miles, or minutes of arc relative to the earth's surface.
The latitude of the Vatican creates the following harmonic:

Latitude displacement from the North Pole	= 2885.622	minutes of arc.
Latitude displacement from the equator	= 2514.378	minutes of arc.
Difference	= 371.244	minutes of arc.
The reciprocal of this number	= 2693645	harmonic.

The latitude of the Reed Sea crossing creates the following harmonic:

Latitude displacement from the North Pole	= 3547.221	minutes of arc.
Latitude displacement from the equator	= 1852.778	minutes of arc.
Difference	= 1694.443	Harmonic.

(see diagram 32)

There is no doubt in my mind that the position of the crossing was a very well chosen one because of the geometrics involved, and that it was meant to be recorded in the history books so that we of the future generations could analyse the mathematical importance behind the manipulation of the natural forces involved. Given time, we should be able to duplicate the miracle, if the clues left for us to decipher are followed.

After the successful crossing of the Reed Sea, and the gruesome demise of the Pharaoh's army, the Israelites no doubt gave a huge sigh of relief and made ready to continue their trek southwards again towards Sinai. During this part of the journey other miracles were performed for the pilgrims in order to prevent them from starving in the barren desert. In the third month after their departure from Egypt they arrived at the lower slopes of mount Sinai where the Lord commanded Moses, the leader of the Israelites, to pass on his instructions to the gathered multitudes;

"And be ready against the third day; for the third day the Lord will come down in the sight of all the people upon Mount Sinai. And thou shalt set bounds unto the people round about, saying, take heed to yourselves, that ye not go up into the mount or touch the border of it; whatsoever toucheth the mount shall be surely put to death. There shall not a hand touch it, but he shall surely be stoned, or shot through; whether it be beast or man, it shall not live; when the trumpet soundeth long, they shall come up to the mount. And it came to pass on the third day in the morning and there were thunders and lightnings, and a thick cloud upon the mount, and the voice of the trumpet exceedingly loud, so that all the people that was in the camp trembled. And the Lord came down upon Mount Sinai, on the top of the Mount; And the Lord called Moses up to the top of the Mount, and Moses went up.

And the Lord said unto Moses, go down, charge the people lest they break through unto the Lord to gaze, and many of them perish.

This is the message as taught in the book of Exodus.

The Lord had descended from heaven and come amongst his people. He had come to show the people the power of the Lord, and send them warnings lest they went too close to gaze upon Him. If so they would perish. he came so that He might leave a message with the people, telling them that He was to be obeyed, and that they were to lead a righteous life.

If we check back 1400 years from today we will find that the Emperor Justinian, in the sixth century, ordered the construction of one of the world's first monasteries. The fortress-like building, called St. Catherine's lies at the foot of Mount Sinai on the Sinai Peninsular, and was meant to serve as an outpost of Byzantine Orthodoxy. Christians from all parts of the known world at the time could make a pilgrimage to this monastery in order to worship at the place where Moses spoke to God. The walls of the original building stand to this day. At first I believed that this building had been constructed on the only site of major importance on the mountainside. A series of computer programmes indicated that there were in fact two mathematically interlocked points to be considered.

What started as a simple exercise for me to find a position on Mount Sinai which would show evidence of the descent upon the mountain top developed into a full research effort into the history books. I had to know more about this particular time in history and the origin of the Byzantine religion. Who were the Byzantines, and were they in possession of secret knowledge when the monastery was constructed?

After several days of research and reading through a pile of books relating to the Roman Empire I managed to ferret out the following facts.

During the second half of the third century the collapse of the Roman Empire was imminent, scarcely 300 years after it was founded by Augustus. This was brought about by a combination of factors given in the historical writings as misuse of authority, bureaucratic bumbling, a foundering economy, civil wars, barbarian raids, and private scheming of ambitious men. Round about A.D. 235 the military held sway in the land and during the following fifty years a long line of twenty or so legitimate Emperors and ursurpers took over sections of the Empire.

After these years of turmoil a strong willed Dalmation soldier by the name of Diocletion appeared on the scene. He forced the concept of autocratic power and the divine right of the Emperor, and then went about restoring order to the disintegrating Empire. This indirectly set things up for the rise of Byzantium. By the act of saving the Empire Diocletion brought new life into it and bolsted up the importance of the territories in the east. The resulting Roman state eventually became the foundation for the Byzantium Empire. In the year 305 Diocletion abdicated the throne and the Empire was once more subject to inner turmoil. By 311 there was a power struggle between four different heads of state; each claiming the title of Emperor. the dominating personality, Constantine, was the ruler of the western districts and was born in the Roman province of Moesia. His father, Constantius, was one of the western governors, and his mother was Helena (later St. Helena) who was said to have discovered, and unearthed, the true cross of Christ in Palestine.

After Diocletion removed himself from office, Constantine, who was then a general in the Roman army, became his father's successor and was pronounced Augustus by his followers after his father's death in 306. Six years later Constantine embarked on a series of military battles in order to wrest power from his rival eastern and western Emperors, and by the year 323 he was left the sole Emperor of Rome. During one of his early battles he was said to have seen a vision and to have declared his preference for Christianity.

For the safety of the Empire Constantine decided to move the capital from Rome. He considered that the provincial Capitals to the north and west were far too remote and uncivilised to serve as places in which to centralise the power of the state, so he looked towards the eastern provinces which were more settled and civilised in their ways. He considered, amongst other places, the cities of Jerusalem, Naissus, Nicomedia, Sophia and Thessalonica for his new imperial city, but ultimately rejected them all.

Eventually he chose Troy, the ancient site of the battle between the Greeks and the Trojans, as the best location but while construction work was in progress it is said that God appeared to him and commanded that he move to a more suitable place to establish the new Rome.

The final choice which was acceptable to the Lord was a small town named Byzantium on a tract of land adjacent to the sea of Marmara. What developed from this point in history was the first Christian nation. Thence commenced a long period in history where the Byzantines remained faithful to their Christian heritage. They established a senate and based their system of law and order on the old Roman ideals and at the same time gave support to many monasteries and asked the political advice of mystics.

From here we move on to the sixth century when the Emperor Justinian appears on the scene. He could be called the law maker. It was he who appointed a commission of ten men, in A.D. 528, to classify the constitutions handed down by the Roman Emperors into a single code of 4,652 laws. This code was so explicit that most of the emerging nations of Europe used it as a model for their own legal systems. Justinian was the last of the great Roman Emperors and it was during his reign that the Byzantine Empire became a distinct entity of its own, in contrast to that of Rome. This new and vibrant Empire lasted for a period of 1,123 years, from A.D. 330 — 1453, and its far boundaries were in a state of constant flux. During the time of Justinian the borders extended from Spain in the west, to Mesopotamia in the east; and from the Black Sea in the north, to the coastal areas of Africa in the south.

The history of the Byzantines in an exciting and intriguing period in the emergence of the modern world, and I would recommend that any student of my work study it very carefully. What caught my attention during all the reading I did on this society, based on Christianity, was the mysticism woven like gossamer threads throughout the history of these people.

Mysterious forces seemed to be apparent whenever it was necessary to establish places connected with the religious and political affairs of the Empire. At particular times visions were seen which swayed the decisions made by the heads of state, or God made his presence known by descending from the sky and forcing His will upon the people.

My interest had its beginning at the Reed Sea where God had demonstrated His awe-inspiring powers, then to Mount Sinai where God, again, had commanded His people; from there to Byzantium, the site of the new capital of Rome, founded by Constantine because of visions and commandments from God. From there the Empire had expanded it seemed with the guidance and consultation of the mystic or religious orders. The overlords were always present in the background to mould and direct the proceedings.

Because of my inquisitive nature I carried out a computer check of the various places where mystic happenings had taken place and where religious communitites had made their headquarters. The results were quite devastating.

I had discovered that the guiding intelligence behind all the activity had knowledge far in advance of anything ever imagined to exist in those early times. The concept of the unified equation and the unity of all things was known and many places of major importance could be mathematically related to the harmonics of the light fields.

My studies covered a wide field but for the purpose of this book I will show the results derived from the computer in relation to the ancient sites of Byzantium (now Istanbul), the descent point on Mount Sinai, and St. Catherine's Monastery on the slopes of Mount Sinai. Then we will have a look at Bethlehem, the birth-place of Jesus, Mecca, the birth-place of Mohammet, and several positions around the world where religious manifestations have occured; Lourdes, in France; Fatima and Oporto in Portugal; El Zeitun in Egypt; Campbells Creek in Australia and the most startling of them all, San Sebastian de Garabandal, in Spain.

I had a hunch that the commandment given to the Emperor Constantine to establish the new centre of government at Byzantium had some geometric relationship with the religious headquarters in Rome. If intelligence from outside was guiding the proceedings then this would seem logical. Preliminary checks by computer had indicated that the selection of the new capital had not been mere chance, but I did not expect to end up with the intriguing results that finally eventuated. It did not take long to zero in on a focal position near the centre of the city.

Latitude 41° 01′ 09.7309″ north/longitude 28° 56′ 55″ east.

The great circle track between this point and Vatican City in Rome was found to be:

742.48833 minutes of arc, or nautical miles long.

If we divide this distance by 2 we have:

371.244169

Which happens to be the reciprocal of:

2693645 harmonic.

It was obvious that the two main religious sites had a geometric, harmonic relationship with each other — but why? Why did the heavenly commander require the centres to be so precisely positioned. Was it because communication by the manipulation of natural law could be carried out more efficiently through these points? Do the harmonics of light allow direct communication between the heavenly hosts and their spokesmen on earth when it is necessary to pass on certain directives to the people?

The next step in following this line of thought was to check the positions of Mount Sinai, where the Lord had descended in order to pass on instructions to his people, and St. Catherine's Monastery where the angel of the Lord spoke to Moses.

It is said that people descendant from the early Bedouin servants, in the time of Justinian, still help the monks in the monastery of St. Catherine. Manuscripts that were presented to the monastery centuries ago are now accessible to modern scholars. What secrets are hidden away within the monastic libraries? Is the information still there amongst the recorded data available for research. Startling facts may be within the reach of someone who knows where to look. St. Catherine's is built on the traditional site of the burning bush. (Exodus 3:2-5)

1. Now Moses kept the flock of Jethro, his father in law, the priest of Midian: and he led the flock to the backside of the desert, and came to the mountain of God, even to Horeb. (Mount Sinai)

2. And the Angel of the Lord appeared unto him in a flame of fire out of the midst of a bush; and he looked, and behold, the bush burned with fire, and the bush was not consumed.

3. And Moses said I will now turn aside, and see this great sight, why the bush is not burnt.

4. And when the Lord saw that he turned aside, God called unto him out of the midst of the bush, and said, Moses, Moses. And he said, Here I am.

5. And He said, draw not nigh hither: put off thy shoes from off thy feet, for the place whereon thou standest is Holy Ground.

Before I was able to solve a geometric relationship for St. Catherine's it was necessary to compute a position near the summit of Mount Sinai (or Gebal Musa as it is now called) where the Lord descended in order to command the people.

The most probable position was found to be:
Latitude 28° 32′ 55.6476″ north/ Longitude 33° 58′ 51″ east.

The focal point fell just east of St. Catherine's Monastery and the latitude produced a very interesting harmonic. If the circumference of the parallel of latitude is calculated in minutes of arc, or nautical miles, relative to the equator then we have a value of:

18973.66596 minutes of arc, or nautical miles.
Which is equal to:
316.227766 degrees, relative.

This group of numbers is the only one, to my knowledge, between 0 and infinity which has its own mirror image reciprocal, and could possibly create a harmonic doorway to other dimensions.

The next step was to check the relative position of the landing point with the religious centres of the Vatican, in Rome, and the ancient city of Byzantium. The great circle distances were found to be:

1318.551 minutes of arc = distance Sinai to Vatican.

787.8735 minutes of arc = distance Sinai to Byzantium.

748.2347 minutes of arc = latitude displacement — Sinai to Byzantium.

If the distance to the Vatican is doubled, then squared, we have:

179

(1318.551 x 2) = 2637.102
squared:
6954307 which is the harmonic reciprocal of the speed of light at the earth's surface. (143795.77 minutes of arc per grid second).
If the distance to Byzantium is multiplied progressively by 60, then:
787.8735 x 60 x 60 x 60 = 17018068 = the harmonic of mass at the earth's surface.
If the latitude displacement between Sinai and Byzantium is multiplied progressively by 60, we have: (see Garabandal/Vatican/Bethlehem)
748.2347 x 60 x 60 = 269364.5 = unified harmonic.
The great circle displacement in longitude, calculated at the latitude of the Sinai landing, was found to be:
265.2582367 minutes of arc.
If a circle is constructed through the points using this diameter, then the circumference measures:
138.888 minutes of arc, relative
The half circle would measure:
69.4444 minutes of arc, relative. This being the speed of light reciprocal in free space. (see diagram 33)

The three major positions are as accurate as I can plot them from the computer and I believe that the margin of error is very small compared with the distances involved. Is it possible that the electro-magnetic effects associated with the descent on the mountain top would have produced radiation harmful enough to kill any living thing instantly if it were to approach the area. As the Israelites had no knowledge of these things at the time then the emotion of fear was used to make them obey the commands.

Could it be that proof of the visitation was left behind for future generations to discover when mankind had developed sufficent technical knowledge to scientifically probe the area. A set of instructions perhaps, buried on the site, waiting for someone in our time to find them. An interesting proposition.

The focal point upon which the descent was carried out, according to the computer, created a very strong harmonic relationship with the position of St. Catherine's Monastery. My copy of the Times Index gives this as:
Latitude 28° 33' north/33° 58'east.

After a constant series of calculations I zeroed in to a point within a few feet of the listed values, which should fall within the Monastery walls.
Latitude 28° 32' 59.78" north/33° 58' 00.045" east.
The direct great circle distance between the two points turned out to be:
0.74910827 minutes of arc.
which is equal to:
44.9464962 seconds of arc.
If a circle of this radius was produced with the centre at the Sinai descent point, then the circumference would equal:
282.4071645 seconds of arc, relative
This is a direct harmonic of gravity acceleration:
28.24071645 geodetic feet per grid second/second.

And one sixth of the mass harmonic:
1694443
The angle of displacement of St. Catherine's from the Sinai focal point was calculated to be:
84.72215 degrees.
Which is a half harmonic of:
169.4443

The fact that this harmonic value keeps popping up in the geometric patterns could be very significant. I wondered if this could have some connection with some information I had published in my last book, The Pulse of the Universe, Harmonic 288. On 11th October 1928 Carl Stoiner, with Halls, helped by Van der Pol, transmitting from Einhoven, picked up 3 second echoes on 31.4 metres, which changed to echoes varying from 3 to 15 seconds.

Signal pulses were transmitted at 20 second intervals. Echoes were received in the following delay sequence: 8.11-15, 8,13,3,8,8,8-12,15,13,8,8. In two cases 2 echoes were heard 4 seconds apart. A Mr D.A. Lunan, a graduate of Glasgow University, carried out an analysis of the echoes and concluded that they were being broadcast from a space probe in orbit somewhere in the vicinity of the moon. It was certainly not possible for our own scientists to transmit from space in 1928.

The mystery becomes even deeper when we convert the wave-length of 31.4 metres into minute of arc values:
The value proved to be: 0.016944 minutes
(31.40120934 metres would convert to 0.01694443 minutes exactly)

Is this particular harmonic the one most suitable for communication through space and from point to point on earth? Were the religious groups made aware of this in ancient times? And did they build their Monasteries and religious centres accordingly?

If this is so then the most important place on earth on which to carry out a computer check in relation to the Christian religion would be Bethlehem, the birth place of Jesus, the greatest communicator of them all.
The Times index listed Bethlehem as:
Latitude 31° 42' north/Longitude 35° 12' east.
The computer established a focal point within the town at:
Latitude 31° 41' 45.8857" north/Longitude 35° 11' 48" east
The latitude would be equivalent to:
31.69607936 degrees.
The latitude displacement from the north pole would therefore be:
58.30392064
This value, curiously enough, is harmonically equal to the height of the Great Pyramid in Egypt, in pyramid inches, 5830.392064, and could be processed mathematically in a similar way. This would strengthen the theory that the pyramid complex is in itself some sort of communication device.
58.30392064
divided by twelve would equal:
4.858660053

The reciprocal harmonic would be equivalent to:

0.205818062

Double this value:

0.411636125

Square this result:

0.1694443 harmonic.

If the birth place of Jesus was significant in regard to geometric positioning, for reasons which are yet to be determined, then could the Vatican also have a relationship with this most reverred position? It seemed logical to me that this would be the case as it was becoming more evident with each calculation that the natural law of harmonic geometrics was applicable in relation to all the major religious centres.

The direct great circle distance from the focal point in Bethlehem to the Vatican was found to be:

1247.05787 minutes of arc, or nautical miles.

If this value is multiplied by progressive values of 60, then:

1247.05787 x 60 x 60 x 60 = 26936450 = Unified harmonic.

The great circle displacement in longitude, at the latitude of Bethlehem, proved to be:

69543.07 seconds of arc. (the reciprocal harmonic of the speed of light at the earth's surface: 143795.77) (see diagram 39)

Once I had progressed this far I wondered if the Islamic religions would show similar results if put to the same test. Mahommedism as a religion is almost parallel to the Christian beliefs and apart from the fact that the Arab world do not regard Jesus as anything more than a prophet, just as they do Mahommet, the two faiths could be joined into one all embracing religious body with very little change in belief from either side.

The Holy Well, Zamzam, at Mecca, was regarded as an important religious centre long before the birth of the Prophet. This city was a strong centre of Arab worship and from the tribe of Koleish, who held the most power in the area, came the family of Mahommet.

Mahommet was born in A.D. 570 and His name in its original form means, The Praised. He spent some of his early life as a shepherd and at the age of 25 he took charge of a trading caravan belonging to a wealthy Koreishite widow named Khadijah. Although the widow was fifteen years older than Mahommet they eventually married and lived happily together. They had two sons, who died at a young age, and four daughters, the most famous of whom was Fatima.

It is said that "Mahommet was possessed by an ideal of truth and righteousness and a stern reprobation of evil, injustice, and lying, and their certain punishment; together with visions of his own people as designated by providence to overthrow evil and to preserve true worship at Mecca".

Round about his fortieth year he frequently went into valleys near Mecca to meditate and one of his favourite places was a cave at the foot of Mount Hira, just north of Mecca. It was here, one night, when he was engaged in his pious exercises that the Angel Gabriel came to him as he slept and held a silken scroll before him, and compelled him to recite what was written on it.

Another time while he was resting the Angel Gabriel again appeared to him and said:

"'Oh thou that art covered, arise and preach and magnify thy Lord; and purify thy garments, and depart from uncleanliness; and grant not favour to gain increase; and wait for thy Lord".

He then frequently began to receive revelations. He began to be disturbed by the visitations and at one time was contemplating suicide, and it is said he was "suddenly arrested by a voice from Heaven, and saw the Angel on a throne between the heavens and the earth, who said, "Oh Mahommet, thou art in truth the Prophet of Allah, and I am Gabriel".

Many of the revelations given to Mahommet were alleged to be confirmed by the Jewish scriptures. He repeatedly referred to his own revelation as confirming and attesting the Book of Moses, or the Jewish Scriptures, and claimed that "the learned men of the children of Israel recognised this". The Jews were expecting another Prophet and it is thought that many of them identified Mahommet as this man.

There were so many similarities between the two religions that I believed there must be some sort of geometric tie-up. What applied to one must apply to the other, if the theory was correct.

The Times index lists the position of Mecca as:

Latitude 21° 26′ north/ Longitude 39° 49′ east.

The computer indicated a focal point within the city area of:

Latitude 21° 23′ 38.32458″ north/ 39° 49′ 37″ east

The latitude of the focal point was therefore equal to:

1283.638743 minutes of arc north.

The displacement from the north pole, in minutes of arc, was therefore:

4116.361257 minutes of arc.

The square of this number:

16944430 harmonic.

These results left no doubt in my mind that Mahommedism had a sound religious base and was parallel in some way with the Christian beliefs.

Even allowing for all the minor errors which must be present in my calculations, the overall mathematical evidence was indicating to me that the Heavenly Hosts were communicating to mankind by the use of the natural laws of the Universe, and that by the study of these laws we should eventually understand the meaning behind it all. We were being presented with clues which would help to guide us towards our final destiny.

I now shifted my attention to places in the world where religious manifestations have occured and discovered that the mathematical theory still held.

LOURDES:

February, 11 1858 was a momentous day for a poor fourteen year old french girl, Bernadette Soubirous. While out gathering wood with her sister and friend on the outskirts of the town of Lourdes she had an experience that changed her life, and caught the attention of the world. She suffered from continuous ill health and she found it difficult to keep up with the other two girls who had raced on ahead. She was about to cross a small mill stream when she was startled by a loud roaring noise like a strong wind. There was a grotto on the other side of the stream and from within this she saw a golden cloud emerge, then a beautiful woman appeared.

She looked at Bernadette and smiled, and beckoned her to move forward. She felt completely unafraid and later said, I seemed to know no longer where I was. I rubbed my eyes; I shut them; I opened them. But the Lady was still there, continuing to smile at me and making me understand that I was not mistaken. Without thinking of what I was doing I took my Rosary in my hands and went to my knees. The Lady made a sign of approval with her head and took into her hands her own Rosary, which hung on her right arm. Bernadette recited the Rosary and the lady joined her in reciting the Gloria at the end of each mystery.

The Lady and the golden cloud then returned to the grotto and vanished. Eighteen more appearances were to follow this initial manifestation and large crowds were attracted to the grotto as news of the occurences spread around the district. The vision was only visible to Bernadette, but the majority of the people believed in the visitations as they watched the child talking estatically to her Lady.

On her ninth appearance the Lady revealed a spring of water which is now world famous because of the miraculous cures which take place there. Three churches and a hospital for the sick have been built on the site, and each year a million and a half pilgrims travel to the shrine.

Bernadette's story was thoroughly investigated by a commission set up by the Bishop of Tarbes and on January 18, 1862, he gave his approval for the site to be used as a devotion centre. Bernadette spent most of her life in a convent where she died on April 16, 1879, and was canonized on Dec. 8, 1933.

Although Lourdes is one of the most well known areas where the Virgin has appeared in apparitional form it has proved to be the hardest position to analyse mathematically. I spent several hours checking different combinations of coordinates which fell within half a mile or so from the centre of the township and none of them seemed satisfactory when compared with the Vatican or Mecca. I eventually calculated a position to the west of the town that appeared to be valid, and actually wrote it up for publication, but each time I re-read the text I had a feeling that the whole thing was wrong. I finally decided to recalculate the problem from the beginning and although the results did not place the focal point as far west as I expected, I believe at this time that it is the true position. The frequency rates of this position are based on harmonic octaves, or multiples of 8, as found in other positions around the world.

The Times Index lists the position of Lourdes as:
Latitude 43° 06′ north/ Longitude 00° 02′ west.
The calculated focal point was found to be:
Latitude 43° 05′ 53.952″ north/Longitude 00° 01′ 57.1″ west.
The direct great circle distance from the Vatican equalled:
556.34456 minutes of arc, or nautical miles.
This value divided by 8 equals:
69.54307 which is equal to the harmonic of the speed of light reciprocal at the earth's surface.

The latitude of Lourdes focal point equals:
43.09832 degrees.
This value divided by 16 equals:
2.693645 unified harmonic. (see diagram 34)

OPORTO:
The Portuguese city of Oporto is another area where a strange miracle appears to be taking place. A 17 year old girl, Maria Rosalina Vieira claims that she had a visitation from Jesus Christ on November 28, 1975 and that he told her to fast for the rest of her life. This would be a penance for the sinners of the world.

To the bafflement of medical experts who have given her a thorough medical examination she has not had any food or drink since that time. If she attempts to eat any food she immediately becomes ill. She is now confined to her bed and says that her body is paralysed from the waist down. Most of her time is spent praying and she says that, God has made me content to live like this.

Thousands of pilgrims travel to see her and a Vatican spokesman said there have been other similar mysterious cases.

The geometric analysis of this position turned out to be a very interesting exercise because there appeared to be two possible answers, depending on whether the pattern was centred on the Vatican or Mecca.

The position of Oporto is listed in the Times index as:
Latitude 41° 09′ north/Longitude 8° 37′ west.
In relation to the Vatican the computed focal point was:
Latitude 41° 09′ 49.005″ north/Longitude 8° 36′ 05.5 west. (case one)
In relation to Mecca the computed focal point was:
Latitude 41° 09′ 49.005″ north/Longitude 8° 38′ 45.8″ west. (case two)
The latitude of both cases would be equal to:
41.16361257 degrees
The square of which equals:
1694.443 harmonic
The great circle distance from the Vatican (case one):
944.2631 minutes of arc.
This value divided by 16 equals:
59.01644375
The reciprocal of which is:
0.01694443 harmonic.
The great circle distance from Mecca (case two):
2711.1088 minutes of arc.
This value divided by 16 equals:
169.4443 harmonic (see diagram 35)

I have found in other calculations, in regard to my research into harmonic mathematics, that values can be divisible by multiples of eight in some particular cases. This could be multiples of harmonic octaves in wave-form. In this work I only wish to show the mathematical facts and leave it to others to reason why. The main point that I wish to bring to notice is that by repetition it can be demonstrated that certain values can be derived when calculating between specific points of interest on the earth's surface.

The Oporto case is a puzzle to me as I do not know which focal position is the valid one. The city area where Maria Rosalina has her home is not known to me, but I would assume that the focal point nearest to her would be the most active.

A possible clue to the right answer may be the happenings at the town of Fatima, also in Portugal.

FATIMA: 1917

In the surrounding country-side of Fatima, in a natural depression in the hills called Cova da Iria, three children, ten-year-old Lucia dos Santos and her two cousins Francisco and Jacinta Marto, were making a stone playhouse while tending to the sheep.

Suddenly from a cloudless sky a brilliant shaft of light lit up the area. Frightened they decided to return home and were on the way down the hill with the sheep when another shaft of light filled the air. They were now really scared as they could not see any reason for the phenomena. Then to their amazement they beheld a beautiful Lady standing above a small Oak tree.

Lucia later said, "It was a lady dressed all in white, more brilliant than the sun; shedding rays of light clearer and stronger than a crystal glass filled with the most sparkling water, pierced by the burning rays of the sun.

"Do not be afraid", the Lady said, "I will not harm you".

"Where are you from", asked Lucia.

"I am from Heaven"

"What do you wish of me?"

"I come to ask you to meet me here six months in succession at this same hour, on the thirteenth of each month. In October I will tell you who I am and what I want."

More questions were asked and answers given then the Lady began to slowly ascend in the direction of the east until she disappeared. Every month the Lady returned as she had promised and the children suffered much persecution because of the visitations. Lucias mother was sure she was lying and the civil administrator of the area arrested the children and kept them in jail which caused them to miss the meeting arranged for August 13. During this month the Lady appeared on the 19th.

During the visitation of July 13 between four to five thousand people were present as word of the apparitions were beginning to circulate and they observed that the Sun became dimmer and that a small cloud hovered over the Oak tree.

During one of the visitations Lucia asked the Lady to perform a miracle, "So that everyone will believe that you really appear to us".

"Continue to come here every month. In October I will tell you who I am and what I desire, and I shall perform a miracle so that everyone will have to believe you," was the answer.

More information was given to the children in the following months and the promise of a miracle was repeated in August and September. News of the coming event spread rapidly throughout Portugal and many ridiculed the idea and were sure that the whole thing was some elaborate hoax. Others were extremely excited about the possible miracle and eagerly awaited the day of October 13. As the day approached thousands of people made their way towards Fatima causing chaos and overcrowding on the roads. The 13th turned out to be a cold, miserable and rainy day but this did not dampen the enthusiasm of the pilgrims. They spent the time saying prayers and singing hymns.

By 11.30 over 70,000 people were gathered at the Cova and at two o'clock noon sun time there was a flash of light, and Lucia shouted out, silence, silence, our Lady is coming. The vision again approached from the east and remained suspended in the sky above the oak tree.

Lucia asked, "Who are you madam, and what do you want of me?"

"I am the Lady of the Rosary, and I desire a Chapel built in my honour in this place".

"People must continue to say the Rosary every day. The war will end soon and the soldiers will return to their homes".

"I have so many things to ask you" said Lucy.

"I will grant some of them, the others no. Men must offend our Lord no more, and they must ask pardon for their sins, for He is already much offended".

At the end of the visitation the Lady stretched out her hands and light projected from her palms. She pointed towards the sun, then she slowly disappeared in the brilliant radiance.

Lucia continued to see a series of visions of the Lord and the Holy Family. These were not seen by the mass of pilgrims, but something spectacular occured.

Lucia cried, "Look at the Sun".

The clouds had parted suddenly and the Sun appeared as a phosphorescent disc. Everyone was able to look at it without harm to the eyes. There are varied accounts as to what happened next but the general story is as follows:

The sun appeared to spin, throwing off rays of light like a gigantic pinwheel. The light rays changed successively to yellow, red, green, blue and violet, then the disc suddenly left its place in the sky and plunged towards the earth.

The mass of people were terrified and dropped to their knees in fervent prayer. When it seemed that all would be destroyed the sun stopped its downward plunge and returned to its normal position in the heavens. The longest estimate of the duration of the display was around twelve minutes.

Because of the thousands of witnesses the miraculous event could not be denied and the newspapers throughout Portugal splashed the story across their pages. The event had been announced three months in advance by ten year old Lucia, and the people had witnessed the sign from the heavens.

The Cova at Fatima is now a place of religious devotion and thousands of people travel there every year for healing, and to offer up prayer to their Lady.

In this account of the appearance of "The Lady" she was said to have slowly ascended in the direction of the east at the end of the visitation, and I would accept this clue as a guide in the search for the focal point for the manifestation in relation to the centre of the township.

The position of Fatima as listed in the Times index is:
Latitude 39° 37' north/Longitude 8° 39' west.

A computer check of the Fatima area in relation to the Vatican showed no apparent connections with the harmonic coordinates evident in the other places of interest, and for a while I was unable to find a reason why this should be so. As this visitation is now recognised by the Catholic Church I felt sure that the natural laws of geometrics would show evidence of a Christian influence. After carrying out many calculations without result I considered the possibility that this particular manifestation could have had direct connections with the Moslem faith.

A copy of an article in a Catholic magazine called 'Soul', that was passed on to me, indicated that some Christian groups were also thinking along those lines.

"The centuries long occupation of Portugal (and almost all of Iberia) by the Moors left its mark. Indeed the southern part of Portugal is more reminiscent of Morroco across the Strait of Cadiz. The people there are similar to those of Morroco in their facial characteristics. The survival of many Moorish influences after centuries of freedom shows why Mahommedan religion may be the most difficult to convert to Christianity ..."

The article goes on to say in another section:
"Beginning on April 2,1968, and continuing in 1969 (according to the source published at the time) Our Lady appeared as the Virgin of Light near one of the corner domes of the Coptic Orthodox Church of Our Lady of Zeitoun, near Cairo. The many reported apparitions of Our Lady at this church have been officially pronounced "authentic" by the Coptic Orthodox church and recognised as such by the catholic community in Egypt. **Over seven hundred thousand people saw these apparitions,** including spokesmen for all the Protestant Churches in Egypt. And what is even more important, many proven miracles occured while the apparitions of Our Lady were reportedly in progress — proving that Our Lady was indeed appearing to Her Arab children.

Fr. Jerome Palmer, O.S.B. who made a study of the phenomena at Zeitoun, stated that these apparitions seemed, "from the effects so far, that it would be safe to suppose that the apparitions are meant to heal the divisions that exist between the orthodox and uniate christians and between the Moslems and the Christians in Egypt."

With this in mind I again set forth with a computer program to find the relationship of Fatima with Mecca, the centre of the Moslem faith.
The calculated focal point in Fatima was found to be:
Latitude 39° 37' 54.45" north/Longitude 8° 36' 40.5" west.

The position would be in an easterly direction from the centre of the town, which would confirm the direction of ascension of Our Lady at the completion of the visitation.

The direct great circle distance from Mecca was calculated to be:
2693.645 minutes of arc, or nautical miles.

This was quite a fantastic result as the unified equation is immediately associated here in harmonic form, 2693645. This would create a slight dilemma. The Fatima apparitions have been recognised by the Catholic Church, but the fact that they occured in a Moslem dominated area appears to suggest that the message has been directed at both faiths, and to the world. The great circle displacement in longitude, measured at the latitude of Mecca, was found to be:

2694.617 minutes of arc, or nautical miles.

The displacement in latitude between the two points equalled:
65656.12668 seconds of arc.

A circle of this diameter would have a circumference of:
206264.8052 seconds of arc, relative.

This value doubled equals:
412529.6104

This value squared:
17018068 = the harmonic of mass at the earth's surface (see diagram 36)

Fatima — the daughter of Mahommet.

The appearance of Our Lady at the Zeitoun Coptic Church in Egypt also indicated geometric associations with Mecca.

The Times index gives the position of El Zeitun as:
Latitude 30° 06' north/Longitude 31° 18' east.

The computed focal point in this small area equalled:
Latitude 30° 05' 27.52" north/Longitude 31° 18' 20.3" east.

The direct great circle distance between the focal point and Mecca was:
695.4307 minutes of arc, or nautical miles. This value is the reciprocal harmonic of the speed of light at the earth's surface.

The displacement in latitude was equal to:
31309.1958 seconds of arc.

This value multiplied by 60 equals:
1878551.748 harmonic.

A theoretical circle with this diameter would have a circumference of:
5901644.371 units.

Which is the reciprocal harmonic of:
1.694443-7 (see diagram 37)

Until a short time ago I had not heard of any religious manifestation occuring in the southern hemisphere. All the activity had been confined to the north, and the news media has not reported any supernatural occurances below the equator to my knowledge. This situation changed when I picked up an Australian Post magazine to help pass the time while in the waiting room of the local dentist. The May 1982 edition ran a story about some strange happenings on a small farm at Campbells Creek, a town some 150 km north-west of Melbourne.

Mr and Mrs Christoforos Pavlou, who are co-owners of the 10 hectare property, say the story started approximately two and a half years ago during the time they spent on the farm at week-ends. Their home was at Burwood, in Melbourne.

First of all Mrs Pavlou began to hear church bells which apparently were not audible to other people. Then one day, because of a drought, the sheep had no

189

water and were dying of thirst. In desperation Mrs Pavlou prayed to the Virgin Mary and said, "Panagitsa, please send me some water for my sheep". She explained, "Immediately there was-how do you say it-a willy-willy. The Whirlwind blew around the farm and stopped over there. I felt that we would find water at this spot. My husband called in drilling contractors and in that place they found plenty of pure, sweet, drinkable water. Later, at home in Burwood, I had a vision of the Virgin Mary looking exactly as she does in a picture I have on my shrine at home".

In a later vision the Virgin Mary appeared to her again with Jesus Christ, and said that She wanted Mrs Pavlou to build Her a home on the land between the chicken houses and that it was to have a water tank and taps at six corners. The water from the taps was to be used to heal sick people who came to visit the shrine.

Since that time many strange things have happened, and several people have had miraculous cures when visiting the farm.

If I was correct in my findings regarding the sites in the northern hemisphere then I was certain that the same geometrical relationships would show up in the area around Campbells Creek. That is, of course, if the manifestations were genuine. This could possibly be the first indication of a powerful Christian centre within a southern country.

Out came the maps and I was off on another computer hunt. Not surprisingly the focal point at Campbells Creek turned out to be:
Latitude 37° 07' 27.9" south/Longitude 144° 09' 56.2" east.
The latitude position converted to:
37.124416 degrees.
Obviously the reciprocal of:
2693645 harmonic (unified)

The longitudinal displacement was a little more difficult to solve until I realised that the position, although in the southern hemisphere, would also be coincident with a great circle track from the Vatican, and that harmonic coordinates could be checked at 90 degree intervals along this line. The direct great circle track was found to be:
8576.204671 minutes of arc, or nautical miles.

No immediate harmonics could be found in this number that were associated with the unified values, but when 90 degrees, or 5400 minutes of arc were subtracted in order to check the displacement in the next sector, then a factor did show up.

Direct great circle distance to Vatican	= 8576.204671	minutes
Minus the first 90 degree sector	= 5400	minutes
Displacement in second 90 degree sector	= 3176.204671	minutes

3176.204671 minutes
Is equal to:
190572.2802 seconds of arc.
If this number is multiplied by progressive multiples of 60 we have:
190572.2802 x 60 x 60 x 60 equals:
4116361257

The square of this number:

1.694443[19] harmonic (see diagram 38)

Although I have carried out the same mathematical exercise with coordinates from other positions I believe that what is actually occuring is a progressive increase in the harmonic frequency rates. For practical purposes we divide a circle, or great circle, up into degrees, minutes and seconds by multiplying each value by 60. There appear to be even smaller units below the interval of one second of arc, which seem to increase the frequency rate by each harmonic multiple of 60.

As the Vatican does appear, on circumstantial evidence, to be assoicated with the visions of Our Lady in the Campbells Creek area, and that miraculous cures do occur there, then I believe that the stories, as reported, could be genuine. It is possible that a powerful place of healing has been made available to the needy in the southern hemisphere.

Last but not least we come to what I believe will become one of the most sacred spots on the surface of the earth. San Sebastian de Garabandal.

Garabandal is a small village tucked away in quiet isolation in the Cantabrian Mountains in northern Spain. Approximately 80 cut stone houses protect the community of some 300 people from the cold and misty climate in this little known part of the world.

On Sunday June 18, 1961, at 8.30 in the evening a series of events commenced which brought the village to the notice of the world, and will, in the not too distant future, make it the centre of pilgrimage for possibly millions of people.

Four young girls were playing in a lane on the southern side of the village when suddenly a sound like thunder was heard, then an 'Angel' momentarily appeared in brilliant light. This occured again several more times then on July 1, 1961, the apparition spoke for the first time. "Do you know why I have come? It is to announce to you that tomorrow, Sunday, the Virgin Mary will appear to you as Our Lady of Mount Carmel.

Next day he appeared again with the Virgin Mary, and this was to become the first of approximately 2000 visions between then and November 13, 1965.

The four girls, Conchita Gonzalez, Mari Mazon, Jacinta Gonzalez and Mari Gonzalez talked unselfconciously with the Virgin about simple everyday things and the Lady is said to have often smiled at their childish remarks. At times the Virgin appeared with the infant Jesus in Her arms and on some occasions let the children hold him.

On July 4, 1961 the first message was given with a request that it be made public, on October 18th.

"We must make many sacrifices, perform much penance and visit the Blessed Sacrament frequently. But first we must lead good lives. If we do not, a chastisement will befall us. The cup is already filling up and if we do not change, a very great chastisement will come upon us.

Just before the visitations ceased a second message was given in Her name by the archangel St. Michael.

"As my message of October 18 has not been complied with and has not been made known to the world, I am advising you that this is the last one. Before the cup was filling up. Now it is flowing over. Many Cardinals, many Bishops and many Priests are on the road to perdition and are taking many souls with them. Less and less importance is being given to the Eucharist. You should turn the wrath of God away from yourselves by your efforts. If you ask His forgiveness with sincere hearts, He will pardon you. I, your mother, through the intercession of St. Michael the archangel, ask you to amend your lives. You are receiving the last warning. I love you very much and do not want your condemnation. Pray to Us with sincerity and We will grant your requests. You should make more sacrifices. Think about the passion of Jesus."

Conchita Gonzalez was also told that at some future time a great miracle will occur at Garabandal, but before this, within one year, a very stern warning will be given.

She says, "The Blessed Virgin told me on the first of January (1965) that a warning would be given before the Miracle so that the world might amend itself. This Warning, like the Chastisement, is a very fearful thing for the good as well as the wicked. It will draw the good closer to God and will warn the wicked that the end of time is coming and that these are the last warnings. No one can stop it from happening. It is certain ...

The warning is something that comes directly from God and will be visible throughout the entire world, in whatever place anyone might be. The warning will be a revelation of our sins and it will be seen and experienced equally by believers and nonbelievers and people of any religion whatsoever.

... The warning is something supernatural and will not be explained by science. It will be seen and felt. For those who do not know Christ (non-Christians) they will believe it is a warning from God ...

... I am the only one to whom the Blessed virgin spoke of the miracle.. She forbade me to say what it will consist of. I can't announce the date either until eight days before it is due to occur. What I can reveal is that it will coincide with an event in the Church and with the feast of a saint, martyr of the Eucharist; that it will take place at 8.30 on a Thursday evening; that it will be visible to all those who are in the village and surrounding mountains; that the sick who are present will be cured and the incredulous will believe. It will be the greatest miracle that Jesus has performed for the world. There won't be the slightest doubt that it comes from God and that it is for the good of mankind. A sign of the Miracle, which it will be possible to film or televise, will remain forever at the pines. (A small group of trees to the south of the village).

Conchita made another quite startling statement at the time of the death of Pope John XXIII. She was in the kitchen of her home with her mother when the bells in the church tower in Garabandal tolled for his death. She exclaimed,

"Listen, they are ringing the bells".

"It's for the Pope", replied her mother.

"Certainly ... now only three remain".

"What are you saying?"

"What I heard. That only three Popes remain".

"Where did you pick that up?"

"I didn't pick it up; the Virgin told me".

Conchita has repeated this message at other times; that after Pope John XXIII there remain only three, and afterwards the end of times.

She was asked, "Do you mean the end of the world is coming?"

She replied, "The end of times".

"That isn't the same?"

"I don't know", said Conchita.

John Paul II is now the third Pope since this prophecy so there could be some interesting times ahead for us all.

It seems strange to many people that the small village of Garabandal has been singled out for such a momentous event, but few are aware of the fact that to the south, in the region of Liebana, there is a very ancient monastery called San Toribio that has been restored and is now run by the Franciscans.

Here, in this monastery, is kept the largest remaining single fragment of the true cross; the wood of the cross of Jesus.

It therefore came as no surprise to me when I discovered that a latitude of 43° 08' 37.6" north passed through this area. This would be equal to 43.14377916 degrees.

If we process this latitude in the same way as we did with the Vatican, then:

Latitude displacement from the north pole = 46.8562222 degrees

Latitude displacement from the equator = 43.1437777

Difference = 3.712444

The reciprocal = 0.2693645 harmonic

The latitude displacement between the latitude passing through the region of Liebana and the latitude of the Vatican would be equal to:

74.24866 minutes of arc.

which is equal to twice:

37.124433

which is the reciprocal harmonic of:

2693645

It appears that the last fragment of the True Cross' has been placed in a very special position in relation to the Vatican.

The focal point at Garabandal was computed to be:

Latitude 43° 12' 00" north/ Longitude 4° 24' 52" west.

The direct great circle distance between Garabandal and the Vatican was calculated to be:

748.2347221 minutes of arc, or nautical miles.

If this value is multiplied progressively by 60, then:

748.2347221

multiplied by 60 equals:

44894.08333

multiplied by 60 equals

2693645 harmonic.

The fact that the apparition of the Virgin Mary appeared in this area with the infant Jesus in her arms is of great significance when the great circle distance of Garabandal to the Vatican is analysed.

The great circle distance of Bethlehem, the birth-place of Jesus, to the Vatican, is an exact multiple of the Garabandal value, and in a harmonic sense, connects the two places.

Bethlehem to Vatican
1247.05787 minutes of arc
multiplied by 60 equals:
74823.47221
multiplied by 60 equals:
4489408.333
multiplied by 60 equals:
269364500 harmonic

Garabandal to the Vatican

748.2347221 minutes of arc
multiplied by 60 equals:
44894.08333
multiplied by 60 equals:
2693645 harmonic

(see diagram 39)

There are other harmonic associations which tie Garabandal, the Vatican, and Bethlehem together, but rather than confuse the reader with a mass of calculations I will leave these for another time and place. I believe that the mathematical evidence presented here is more than enough to show that this area of northern Spain will become the most important place in the affairs of mankind.

The promised miracle will happen, I am certain, and my wife, Wendy and I, and our two sons, Stephen and Mark, intend to be present when it occurs.

I will leave the last word in this book to Conchita, and leave you to believe, or not believe. She said this to a Catholic Priest in 1965.

"As the people were talking about trips to space, I asked the Virgin if there were persons living out there, and She told me: "yes", but She didn't add anything more".

DIAGRAM 33

Showing the relationship of Mount Sinai, Byzantium and the Vatican

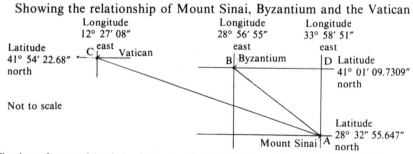

The circumference of the circle of latitude at 28° 32′ 55.647″ north is equal to 316.227766 degrees, relative to the equator. This number has a mirror image reciprocal of 0.00316227766.

Great circle distance A — B = 787.8735 nautical miles
(787.8735 x 60 x 60 x 60) = 170180680 = harmonic of mass
Great circle distance A — C = 1318.551 nautical miles
(1318.551 x 2) = 2637.102
squared = 6954307 = speed of light reciprocal at the earth's surface
Great circle distance A — D = 748.234722 nautical miles
(748.234722 x 60 x 60) = 2693645 unified harmonic

194

DIAGRAM 32

Showing the relationship of the Vatican and the Reed Sea

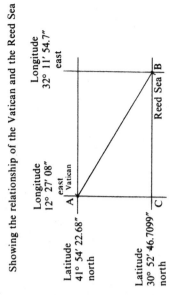

Displacement of Reed Sea from the North Pole	= 3547.221503 minutes	
Displacement of Reed Sea from the Equator	= 1852.778497 minutes	
Difference	= 1694.443	Harmonic
Displacement of Vatican from the North Pole	= 2885.662	minutes
Displacement of Vatican from the Equator	= 2514.378	minutes
Difference	= 371.244	
The reciprocal	= 2693645	harmonic

Great circle distance A — B	= 1156.0616 nautical miles
	= 19.267693 degrees
Squared	= 371.244
Reciprocal	0.002693645 Harmonic
Great circle distance B — C	= 1015.4968 nautical miles (minutes of arc)
	= 6092.9807 seconds of arc
Squared	= 37124405
Reciprocal	= 26936450 Harmonic

Not to scale

DIAGRAM 34

Showing the relationship of the Vatican and Lourdes

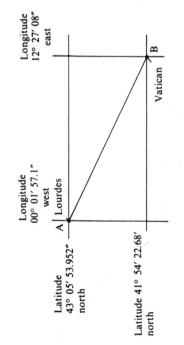

Latitude of Lourdes = 43.09832 degrees
Divided by 16 = 2.693645 harmonic

Great circle distance A — B = 556.34456 nautical miles
Divided by 8 = 69.54307 = harmonic reciprocal of the
speed of light at the earth's
surface

Not to scale

DIAGRAM 35

Showing the relationship of Oporto with the Vatican and Mecca

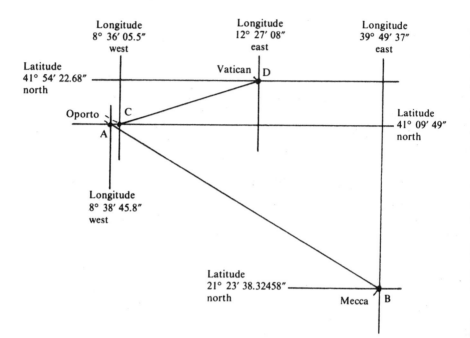

Oporto latitude = 41° 09′ 49″ north = 41.1636125 degrees
The square of this number = 1694.443 harmonic
Great circle distance A — B =2711.1088 nautical miles
Great circle distance C — D =944.2631 nautical miles
2711.1088 divided by 16   =169.4443
944.2631 divided by 16   = 59.01644375
The harmonic reciprocal   = 0.01694443

Not to scale

DIAGRAM 36

Showing the relationship of Mecca and Fatima

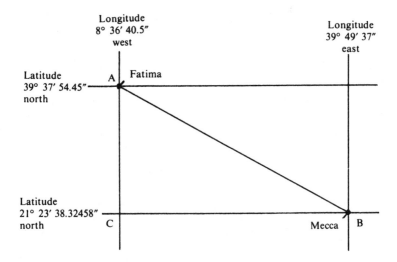

Great circle distance A — B = <u>2693.645</u> nautical miles. Unified harmonic.
Great circle distance A — C = 65656.12668 seconds of arc. A circle of this diameter would have a circumference of: 206264.8052 seconds, relative.
206264.8052 x 2 = 412529.6104
squared = <u>17018068</u> = Mass

Great circle distance B — C = 2694.6 nautical miles. See electron spacing, Chapter one.

Not to scale.

DIAGRAM 37

Showing relationship of Mecca and the Coptic Church at Zeitoun, Egypt

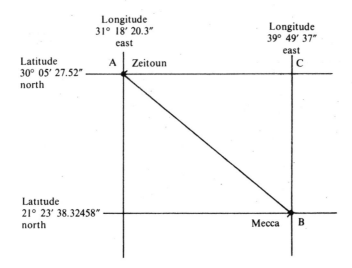

Great circle distance A — B = 695.4307 nautical miles, which is equal to the reciprocal harmonic of the speed of light at the earth's surface.

Great Circle distance C — B = 521.81993 nautical miles. A circle of this diameter would have a circumference of: 1639.345656 nautical miles.

(1639.345656 x 60 x 60)   5901644.36
The reciprocal harmonic   =<u>1694443</u>

Not to scale.

DIAGRAM 38

Showing the relationship of the Vatican and Campbells Creek

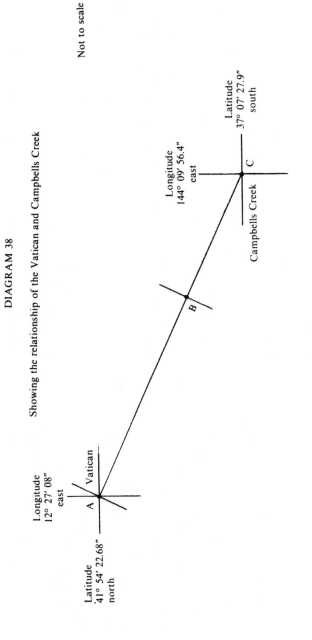

Not to scale

$37°\ 07'\ 27.9'' = 37.1244166$ degrees.
The reciprocal of this number is equal to the 2693645 harmonic.

Great circle distance A — B = 5400 nautical miles (90 degrees)
Great circle distance B — C = 3176.204671 nautical miles.
$3176.204671 \times 60 \times 60 \times 60 = 4.1163612^{7\,10}$
This number squared = $\underline{1.694443^{2\,1}}$

DIAGRAM 39

Showing the relationship of Garabandal, The Vatican and Bethlehem

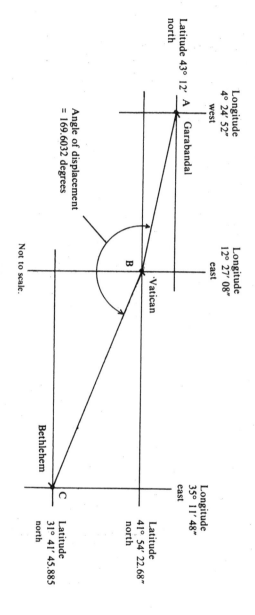

Latitude 43° 12' north

Longitude 4° 24' 52" west

A Garabandal

Angle of displacement = 169.6032 degrees

Not to scale.

Longitude 12° 27' 08" east

B Vatican

Longitude 35° 11' 48" east

Latitude 41° 54' 22.68" north

Bethlehem

C

Latitude 31° 41' 45.885 north

Distance A — B = 748.2347221 nautical miles
Distance B — C = 1247.05787 nautical miles

If the focal position at Garabandal was moved slightly south and to the west then the distance from the Vatican would be 748.2347221 and the angle of displacement between Garabandal, the Vatican and Bethlehem 169.4443 degrees. This could possibly be the focal position for the miracle.

INDEX

ABOUT THE AUTHOR

Captain Bruce Cathie was born in 1930 in Auckland, New Zealand and was educated at Otahuhu Technical College. On leaving school he became an engineering apprentice, then joined the Royal New Zealand Air Force to train as a pilot. After completing his flying training, he spent three years in agricultural aviation, then in 1955 joined New Zealand's National Airways Corporation. It was during this time, in 1952, that an event occured which led up to the publication of this book . . . with a group of friends, Captain Cathie made a prolonged evening sighting of a UFO at Mangere, Auckland.

Since then, he has published three books about his research. In his first book, HARMONIC 33, he presented the theory that the whole world was criss-crossed by an electromagnetic grid system which could be directly related to UFO activity. His second book, HARMONIC 695, carried the research further and presented mathematical evidence which indicated that the grid system was known to our scientists and was being used for secret experimentation; particularly by the nations involved in atomic bomb testing. His third book, THE PULSE OF THE UNIVERSE — HARMONIC 288, took another leap forward and probed into space-time, Dr. Einstein's $E = MC^2$, and the formulation of a series of unified equations. All of the above books are now out of print. His fourth book presented here, THE BRIDGE TO INFINITY — HARMONIC 371244, which summarizes and updates his previous three books, was first printed in New Zealand in 1983. It has now been updated and revised in this trade paperback edition.

Cathie started a new career flying Douglas DC3's after he left the Royal New Zealand Air Force. In March 1977, after the company merged with the overseas airline, Air New Zealand, he was cleared for command on Boeing 737 airliners. He retired from flying in 1981, and now manages a small computer sales and publishing company. He is married and has two sons.

THE ADVENTURES UNLIMITED CATALOG

The Energy Grid

Bruce Cathie

Gypsies reading the ley lines that crisscross England; Taoist priests interperting feng shui charts; Midwestern rainmakers dowsing the parched fields of the American prairie—what do they all have in common? Each of these activities uses the world energy grid to advance health, knowledge and personal fortune. Though it goes by different names, almost every culture has developed an instinctive method of using the energy grid that surrounds and underlies the earth.

What kind of energy does the grid emanate? Where is it to be found? How does it affect daily life? Can we harness it? Our planet's grid of energy is thoroughly examined in this new book by the author of Harmonic 33, Bruce Cathie. Chapters include information on:

- UFO navigation and mysterious aerials
- Nikola Tesla's inventions
- Pythagoras and the Grid
- Atomic detonations and energy vortexes
- Native American power spots and the Australian Stonehenge

Bruce Cathie is a former airline pilot who lives in Auckland, New Zealand. His first book, *Harmoni 33*, was published in 1968.

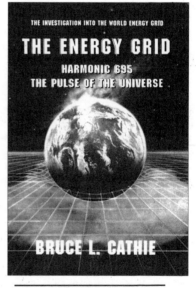

THE INVESTIGATION INTO THE WORLD ENERGY GRID

THE ENERGY GRID

HARMONIC 695
THE PULSE OF THE UNIVERSE

BRUCE L. CATHIE

ISBN: 0-932813-44-5
255 pages, 6x9
Photos, maps and drawings
Index/Bibliography
Science/New Technology/UFOs
$15.95/paper

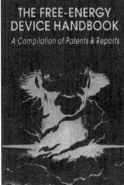

UFOs and ANTI-GRAVITY
Piece For A Jig-Saw
by Leonard G. Cramp

Cramp's 1966 classic book on flying saucer propulsion and suppressed technology is available again. This book is a highly technical look at the UFO phenomena by a trained scientist. Cramp first introduces the idea of 'anti-gravity' and introduces us to the various theories of gravitation. He then examines the technology necessary to build a flying saucer and examines in great detail the technical aspects of such a craft. Cramp's book is a wealth of material and diagrams on flying saucers, anti-gravity, suppressed technology, G-fields and UFOs. Chapters include Crossroads of Aerodynamics, Aerodynamic Saucers, Limitations of Rocketry, Gravitation and the Ether, Gravitational Spaceships, G. Field Lift Effects, The Bi-Field Theory, VTOL and Hovercraft, Analysis of UFO photos and claims, more.
388 pages, 6x9 paperback. Heavily Illustrated. $16.95.
code: UAG

NASA, NAZIS & JFK:
The Torbitt Document & the JFK Assassination
Introduction by Kenn Thomas

This first published edition of the Torbitt Document emphasizes what the manuscript says about the link between Operation Paper Clip Nazi scientists working for NASA, the assassination of JFK, and the secret Nevada air base Area 51. The Torbitt Document talks about the roles in the assassination played by Division Five of the FBI, Defense Industrial Security Command (DISC), the Las Vegas mob, and the shadow corporate entities Permindex and Centro-Mondiale Commerciale. Also claims that the same people planned the 1962 failed assassination of Charles de Gaul, who traced the "Assassination Cabal" to Permindex in Switzerland and to NATO headquarters in Brussels. The Torbitt document paints a dark picture of NASA, the Military Industrial Complex, and the connections to Mercury, Nevada and the Area 51 complex which headquarters the "secret space program."
242 pages, 5x8 paperback. Illustrated. $16.00
code: NNJ

THE FREE-ENERGY DEVICE HANDBOOK
A Compilation of Patents & Reports by David Hatcher Childress

Large format compilation of various patents, papers, descriptions, and diagrams concerning free-energy devices and systems. A visual tool for experimenters and researchers into magnetic motors and other "over-unity" devices with chapters on the Adams Motor, the Hans Coler Generator, cold fusion, superconductors, "N" machines, space-energy generators, Nikola Tesla, T. Townsend Brown, and the latest in free-energy devices. Packed with photos, technical diagrams, patents, and fascinating information, this book belongs on every science shelf. With energy and profit a major political issue for fighting various wars, free-energy devices, if ever allowed to be mass-distributed to consumers, could change the world. Get your copy now before the Department of Energy bans this book!
306 pp. ♦ 7x10 paperback ♦ Profusely illustrated ♦ Bibliography & appendix ♦ $16.95 ♦
code: FEH

EXTRATERRESTRIAL ARCHAEOLOGY
by David Hatcher Childress

With hundreds of photos and illustrations, Extraterrestrial Archaeology takes the reader to the strange and fascinating worlds of Mars, the Moon, Mercury, Venus, Saturn, and other planets for a look at the alien structures that appear there. Whether skeptic or believer, this book allows you to view for yourself the amazing pyramids, domes, spaceports, obelisks, and other anomalies that are profiled in photograph after photograph. Using official NASA and Soviet photos, as well as other photos taken via telescope, this book seeks to prove that many of the planets (and moons) of our solar system are in some way inhabited by intelligent life.
224 pp. ♦ 8½/2x11 paperback ♦ Highly illustrated with photos, diagrams & maps! ♦ Bibliography, index, appendix ♦ $18.95
code: ETA

MAN-MADE UFOS: 1944-1994
50 Years of Suppression
by Renato Vesco & David Hatcher Childress

A comprehensive and in-depth look at the early "flying saucer technology" of Nazi Germany and the genesis of early man-made UFOs. From captured German scientists, escaped battalions of German soldiers, secret factories in Antarctica to today's state-of-the-art "Dream-land" flying machines, this astonishing book blows the lid off the "Government UFO Conspiracy." Examined in detail are secret underground airfields and factories; German secret weapons; "suction" aircraft; the origin of NASA; gyroscopic stabilizers and engines; the secret Marconi aircraft factory in South America, and other secret societies, both ancient and modern, that have kept this craft a secret, and much more. Not to be missed by students of technology suppression, UFOs, anti-gravity, free-energy conspiracy, and World War II. Intro-duction by W.A. Harbinson, author of the Dell novels Genesis and Revelation.
440 pp. ♦ 6x9 paperback ♦ Heavily Illustrated. $18.95
code: MMU

THE FANTASTIC INVENTIONS OF NIKOLA TESLA
by Nikola Tesla
with additional material by David Hatcher Childress

This book is a virtual compendium of patents, diagrams, photos, and explanations of the many incredible inventions of the originator of the modern era of electrification. The book is a readable and affordable collection of his patents, inventions, and thoughts on free energy, anti-gravity, and other futuristic inventions. Covered in depth, often in Tesla's own words, are such topics as: His Plan to Transmit Free Electricity into the Atmosphere; How Anti-Gravity Airships could Draw Power from the Towers he was Building; Tesla's Death Rays, Ozone Generators, and more...
342 pp. ♦ 6x9 paperback ♦ Highly illustrated ♦ $16.95
code: FINT

Man-Made UFOs 1944-1994
50 Years of Suppression

Renato Vesco
David Hatcher Childress

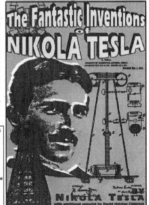

ANTI-GRAVITY

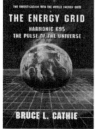

THE ENERGY GRID
Harmonic 695, The Pulse of the Universe
by Captain Bruce Cathie.
This is the breakthrough book that explores the incredible potential of the Energy Grid and the Earth's Unified Field all around us. Bruce Cathie's first book *Harmonic 33*, was published in 1968 when he was a commercial pilot in New Zealand. Since then Captain Bruce Cathie has been the premier investigator into the amazing potential of the infinite energy that surrounds our planet every microsecond. Cathie investigates the Harmonics of Light and how the Energy Grid is created. In this amazing book are chapters on UFO propulsion, Nikola Tesla, Unified Equations, the Mysterious Aerials, Pythagoras & the Grid, Nuclear detonation and the Grid, maps of the ancients, an Australian Stonehenge examined, more.
255 PAGES. 6X9 TRADEPAPER. ILLUSTRATED. $15.95. CODE: TEG

THE BRIDGE TO INFINITY
Harmonic 371244
by Captain Bruce Cathie
Cathie has popularized the concept that the earth is criss–crossed by an electromagnetic grid system that can be used for anti-gravity, free energy, levitation and more. The book includes a new analysis of the harmonic nature of reality, acoustic levitation, pyramid power, harmonic receiver towers and UFO propulsion. It concludes that today's scientists have at their command a fantastic store of knowledge with which to advance the welfare of the human race.
204 PAGES. 6X9 TRADEPAPER. ILLUSTRATED. $14.95. CODE: BTF

THE HARMONIC CONQUEST OF SPACE
by Captain Bruce Cathie
Chapters in this book include: Mathematics of the World Grid; the Harmonics of Hiroshima and Nagasaki; Harmonic Transmission and Receiving; the Link Between Human Brain-Waves; the Cavity Resonance between the Earth; the ionosphere and Gravity; Edgar Cayce-the Harmonics of the subconscious; Stonehenge; the Harmonics of the Moon; the Pyramids of Mars; Nikola Tesla's Electric Car; The Robert Adams Pulsed Electric Motor Generator; Harmonic Clues to the Unified Fields; and more. Also included in the book are tables showing the harmonic relations between the Earth's magnetic field, the 'speed of light,' and anti-gravity/gravity acceleration at different points on the Earth's surface.
260 PAGES. 6X9. TRADEPAPER. ILLUSTRATED. BIBLIOGRAPHY. $16.95. CODE: HCS

FIELD EFFECT
...The Pi Phase of Physics & The Unified Field
by Leigh Richmond-Donahue
Leigh Richmond-Donahue's brief book is an analysis of the structure of the electron which brings to light the anatomy of black holes, superstrings, and the techniques of evolution. Leigh shows how the "field" is complete around the universe and all living things. Our galaxy, ourselves, and the electrons of which we are built function on a logical pattern and operative system. Once you find that pattern, the rest falls into place, including free energy, anti-gravity and human enlightenment.
77 PAGES. 6X9 TRADEPAPER. ILLUSTRATED. $11.95. CODE: FEF

TAPPING THE ZERO POINT ENERGY
Free Energy & Anti-Gravity in Today's Physics
by Moray B. King
The author, a well-known researcher, explains how free energy and anti-gravity are possible with today's physics. The theories of the zero point energy maintain there are tremendous fluctuations of electrical field energy imbedded within the fabric of space. This book shows how in the 1930s inventor T. Henry Moray could produce a fifty kilowatt "free energy" machine; how an electrified vortex plasma creates anti-gravity; how the Pons/Fleischmann "cold fusion" experiment could produce tremendous heat without fusion; and how certain experiments might produce a gravitational anomaly.
170 PAGES. 5X8 TRADEPAPER. ILLUSTRATED. $9.95. CODE: TAP

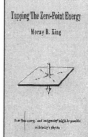

ANTIGRAVITY: THE DREAM MADE REALITY
The Story of John R.R. Searl
by John Thomas, Jr.
A large format book on the anti-gravity work of British scientist John Searl. Seven chapters tell the story of Searl's invention, his troubles with the British authorities, and his determination to continue his research. With photos and diagrams of Searl's flying disc; and technical information on Searl's "Law of Squares," the SEG electric generator, his anti-gravity theories, more.
110 PAGES. 8X11 PAPERBACK. ILLUSTRATED. $25.00. CODE: AGD

ANTI-GRAVITY

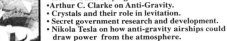

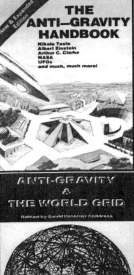

THE
ANTI—GRAVITY
HANDBOOK
Nikola Tesla
Albert Einstein
Arthur C. Clarke
NASA
UFOs
and much, much more!

THE ANTI-GRAVITY HANDBOOK
Edited by David Hatcher Childress, With Arthur C. Clarke, Nikola Tesla, T.B. Paulicki, Bruce Cathie, Leonard G. Cramp and Albert Einstein

The new expanded compilation of material on Anti-Gravity, Free Energy, Flying Saucer Propulsion, UFOs, Suppressed Technology, NASA Cover-ups and more. Highly illustrated with patents, technical illustrationsand photos. This revised and expanded edition has more material, including photos of Area 51, Nevada, the government's secret testing facility. This classic on weird science is back in a 90s format!
• How to build a flying saucer.
•Arthur C. Clarke on Anti-Gravity.
• Crystals and their role in levitation.
• Secret government research and development.
• Nikola Tesla on how anti-gravity airships could
   draw power from the atmosphere.
• Bruce Cathie's Anti-Gravity Equation.
• NASA, the Moon and Anti-Gravity.
230 PAGES, 7x10 TRADEPAPER, BIBLIOGRAPHY/INDEX/APPENDIX. HIGHLY ILLUSTRATED WITH 100'S OF PATENTS ILLUSTRATIONS AND PHOTOS, $14.95. CODE: AGH

ANTI-GRAVITY & THE WORLD GRID
edited by David Hatcher Childress
Is the earth surrounded by an intricate network of electromagnetic grid network offering free energy? This compilation of material on ley lines and world power points contains chapters on the geography, mathematics, and light harmonics the earth grid. Learn the purpose of ley lines and ancient megalithic structures located on the grid. Discover how the grid made the Philadelphia Experiment possible. Explore the Coral Castle and many other mysteries; Including acoustic levitation, Tesla Shields and scalar wave weaponry. Browse through the section on anti-gravity patents, and research resources.
274 PAGES, 150 RARE PHOTOGRAPHS, DIAGRAMS AND DRAWINGS, 7x10 PAPERBACK, $14.95. CODE: AGW

ANTI-GRAVITY
& THE UNIFIED FIELD
Edited by David Hatcher Childress
Is Einstein's Unified Field Theory the answer to all of our energy problems? Explored in this compilation of material is how gravity, electricity and magnetism manifest from a unified field around us. Why artificial gravity is possible; secrets of UFO propulsion; free energy; Nikola Tesla and anti-gravity airships of the 20's and 30's; flying saucers as super-conducting whirls of plasma; anti-mass generators; vortex propulsion; suppressed technology; government cover-ups; gravitational pulse drive, spacecraft & more.
240 PAGES. 7x10 PAPERBACK.HEAVILY ILLUSTRATED.
$14.95. CODE: AGU

ANTI-GRAVITY
AND THE UNIFIED FIELD
Edited by David Hatcher Childress
Albert Einstein
Nikola Tesla
T. Townsend Brown
Gravity Control
UFOs
Vortex Technology
Electro-Gravitic Propulsion
& Much, much more

ETHER TECHNOLOGY
A Rational Approach to Gravity Control
Rho Sigma
This classic book on anti-gravity & free energy is back in print and back in stock. Written by a well-known American scientist under the pseudonym of "Rho Sigma," this book delves into international efforts at gravity control and discoid craft propulsion. Before the Quantum Field, there was "Ether." This small, but informative book has chapters on John Searle and "Searle discs;" T. Townsend Brown and his work on anti-gravity and ether-vortex-turbines. Includes a forward by former NASA astronaut Edgar Mitchell. Don't miss this classic book!
108 PAGES, 6x9 TRADEPAPER, ILLUSTRATED WITH PHOTOS & DIAGRAMS. $12.95. CODE: ETT

Forward by astronaut Capt. Edgar D. Mitchell, Ph. D.

ETHER-
TECHNOLOGY
A Rational Approach to Gravity Control

by Rho Sigma
THE UNDERGROUND CLASSIC IS BACK IN PRINT!

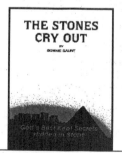

MYSTIC TRAVELLER SERIES

MYSTERY CITIES OF THE MAYA
Exploration and Adventure in Lubaantun & Belize
by Thomas Gann
First published in 1925, Mystery Cities of the Maya is a classic in Central American archaeology-adventure. Gann was close friends with Mike Mitchell-Hedges, the British adventurer who discovered the famous crystal skull with his adopted daughter Sammy and Lady Richmond Brown, their benefactress. Gann battles pirates along Belize's coast and goes upriver with Mitchell-Hedges to the lost city of Lubaantun where they excavate a strange lost city where the crystal skull was discovered. Lubaantun is a unique city in the Mayan world as it is built out of precisely carved blocks of stone without the usual plaster-cement facing. Lubaantun contained several large pyramids partially destroyed by earthquakes and a large amount of artifacts. Gann was a keen archaeologist, a member of the Mayan society, and shared Michell-Hedges belief in Atlantis and lost civilizations, pre-Mayan, in Central America and the Caribbean. Lots of good photos, maps and diagrams from the 20s.
252 PAGES. 6x9 PAPERBACK. ILLUSTRATED. $16.95. CODE: MCOM

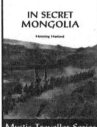

DANGER MY ALLY
The Amazing Life Story of the Discoverer of the Crystal Skull
by "Mike" Michell-Hedges

The incredible life story of "Mike" Mitchell-Hedges, the British adventurer who discovered the Crystal Skull in the lost Mayan city of Lubaantun in Belize. Mitchell-Hedges has lived an exciting life: gambling everything on a trip to the Americas as a young man, riding with Pancho Villa, his personal quest for Atlantis, fighting bandits in the Caribbean and discovering the famous Crystal Skull.
374 PAGES. 6x9 PAPERBACK. ILLUSTRATED WITH MAPS, PHOTOS AND DIAGRAMS. BIBLIOGRAPHY & INDEX. $16.95. CODE: DMA

IN SECRET MONGOLIA
Sequel to Men & Gods In Mongolia
by Henning Haslund
Danish-Swedish explorer Haslund's first book on his exciting explorations in Mongolia and Central Asia. Haslund takes us via camel caravan to the medieval world of Mongolia, a country still barely known today. First published by Kegan Paul of London in 1934, this rare travel adventure back in print after 50 years. Haslund and his camel caravan journey across the Gobi Desert. He meets with renegade generals and warlords, god-kings and shamans. Haslund is captured, held for ransom, thrown into prison, battles black magic and portrays in vivid detail the birth of new nation. Haslund's second book *Men & Gods In Mongolia* is also available from Adventures Unlimited Press.
374 PAGES. 6x9 PAPERBACK. ILLUSTRATED WITH MAPS, PHOTOS AND DIAGRAMS. BIBLIOGRAPHY & INDEX. $16.95. CODE: ISM

MEN & GODS IN MONGOLIA
by Henning Haslund
First published in 1935 by Kegan Paul of London, Haslund takes us to the lost city of Karakota in the Gobi desert. We meet the Bodgo Gegen, a God-king in Mongolia similar to the Dalai Lama of Tibet. We meet Dambin Jansang, the dreaded warlord of the "Black Gobi." There is even material in this incredible book on the Hi-mori, an "airhorse" that flies through the air (similar to a Vimana) and carries with it the sacred stone of Chintamani. Aside from the esoteric and mystical material, there is plenty of just plain adventure: caravans across the Gobi desert, kidnapped and held for ransom, initiation into Shamanic societies, warlords, and the violent birth of a new nation.
358 PAGES. 6x9 PAPERBACK. 57 PHOTOS, ILLUSTRATIONS AND MAPS. $15.95. CODE: MGM

IN SECRET TIBET
by Theodore Illion.
Reprint of a rare 30's travel book. Illion was a German traveller who not only spoke fluent Tibetan, but travelled in disguise through forbidden Tibet when it was off-limits to all outsiders. His incredible adventures make this one of the most exciting travel books ever published. Includes illustrations of Tibetan monks levitating stones by acoustics.
210 PAGES. 6x9 PAPERBACK. ILLUSTRATED. $15.95. CODE: IST

DARKNESS OVER TIBET
by Theodore Illion.
In this second reprint of the rare 30's travel books by Illion, the German traveller continues his travels through Tibet and is given the directions to a strange underground city. As the original publisher's remarks said, this is a rare account of an underground city in Tibet by the only Westerner ever to enter it and escape alive!
210 PAGES. 6x9 PAPERBACK. ILLUSTRATED. $15.95. CODE: DOT

24 HOUR CREDIT CARD ORDERS—CALL: 815-253-6390 FAX: 815-253-6300
EMAIL: AUP@AZSTARNET.COM HTTP://WWW.AZSTARNET.COM/~AUP

ATLANTIS REPRINT SERIES

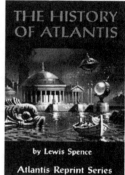

THE SHADOW OF ATLANTIS

ALEXANDER BRAGHINE

THIS 1940 CLASSIC ON ATLANTIS, MEXICO AND ANCIENT EGYPT IS BACK IN PRINT

ATLANTIS REPRINT SERIES

The Shadow of Atlantis

The Echoes of Atlantean Civilization Tracked through Space & Time
by Colonel Alexander Braghine
First published in 1940, The Shadow of Atlantis is one of the great classics of Atlantis research. The Shadow of Atlantis amasses a great deal of archaeological, anthropological, historical and scientific evidence in support of a lost continent in the Atlantic Ocean. Braghine covers such diverse topics as Egyptians in Central America, the myth of Quetzalcoatl, the Basque language and its connection with Atlantis, the connections with the ancient pyramids of Mexico, Egypt and Atlantis, the sudden demise of mammoths, legends of giants and much more. Braghine was linguist and spends part of the book tracing ancient languages to Atlantis and studying little-known inscriptions in Brazil, deluge myths and the connections between ancient languages.
288 pages, 6x9 paperback. Illustrated. $16.95.
code: **SOA**

Maps of the Ancient Sea Kings

Evidence of Advanced Civilization in the Ice Age
by Charles H. Hapgood
Charles Hapgood's classic 1966 book on ancient maps is back in print after 20 years. Hapgood produces concrete evidence of an advanced world-wide civilization existing many thousands of years before ancient Egypt. He has found the evidence in many beautiful maps long known to scholars, the Piri Reis Map that shows Antarctica, the Hadji Ahmed map, the Oronteus Finaeus and other amazing maps. Hapgood concluded that these maps were made from more ancient maps from the various ancient archives around the world, now lost. Hapgood also concluded that the ancient mapmakers were in some ways much more advanced scientifically than Europe in the 16th century, or than the ancient civilizations of Greece, Egypt, and Babylonian. Not only were these unknown people more advanced in mapmaking than any people prior to the 18th century, it appears they mapped all the continents.
316 pages, 7x10 paperback. Heavily Illustrated. Bibliography & Index. $19.95.
code: **MASK**

THE HISTORY OF THE KNIGHTS TEMPLARS

by
Charles G. Addison

Introduction by David Hatcher Childress

The History of the Knights Templar

The Temple Church and the Temple
by Charles G. Addison. Introduction by David Hatcher Childress
The history of the mysterious Knights Templars as told in 1842 by "a member of the Inner Temple." Includes chapters on the Origin of the Templars, their popularity in Europe and their rivalry with the Knights of St. John, later to be known as the Knights of Malta. Detailed information on the activities of the Templars in the Holy Land, the 1312 A.D. suppression of the Templars in France and other countries of Europe, culminating in the execution of Jacques de Molay. Also includes information on the continuation of the Knights Templars in England and Scotland and the formation of the society of Knights Templars in London and the rebuilding of the Temple in 1816. plenty more. Includes a lengthy introduction on the Templars, the lost Templar Fleet and their connections to the ancient North American searoutes by Lost Cities author David Hatcher Childress.
395 pages, 6x9 paperback. Illustrated. $16.95.
code: **HKT**

ANCIENT TONGA & the Lost City of Mu'a

by David Hatcher Childress
In this new paperback series, with color photo inserts, Childress takes into the fascinating world of the ancient seafarers that Pacific. Chapters in this book are on the Lost City of Mu'A and its many megalithic pyramids, the Ha'amonga Trilithon and ancient Polynesian astronomy, Samoa and the search for the lost land of Havaiiki, Fiji and its wars with Tonga, Rarotonga's megalithic road, Polynesian cosmology, and a chapter on the predicted reemergence of the ancient land of Mu. May publication.
218 pages, 6x9 paperback. Heavily illustrated. $15.95.
code: **TONG**

Lost Cities of Atlantis, Ancient Europe & the Mediterranean

by David Hatcher Childress
Atlantis! The legendary lost continent comes under the close scrutiny of maverick archaeologist David Hatcher Childress in this sixth book in the internationally popular Lost Cities series ta it takes him on his quest for the lost continent of Atlantis. Childress takes the reader in search of sunken cities in the Mediterranean; across the Atlas Mountains in search of Atlantean ruins; to remote islands in search of megalithic ruins; living legends and secret societies. From Ireland to Turkey, Morocco to Eastern Europe, or remote islands of the Mediterranean and Atlantic Childress takes the reader on an astonishing quest for mankind's past. Ancient technology, cataclysms, megalithic construction, lost civilizations and devastating wars of the past are all explored in this astonishing book. Childress challenges the skeptics and proves that great civilizations not only existed in the past, but the modern world and its problems are reflections of the ancient world of Atlantis. Join David on an unforgettable tale in search of the solutions to the astonishing past.
524 pages, 6x9 paperback. Illustrated. $16.95.
code: **MED**

Mystery Cities of the Maya

Exploration and Adventure in Lubaantun & Belize
by Thomas Gann
First published in 1925, Gann battles pirates along Belize's coast and goes upriver with Mitchell-Hedges to the lost city of Lubaantun where they excavate a strange lost city where the crystal skull was discovered. Lubaantun is a unique city in the Mayan world as it is built out of precisely carved blocks of stone. Gann shared Mitchell-Hedges belief in Atlantis and lost civilizations, pre-Mayan, in Central America and the Caribbean. Lots of good photos, maps and diagrams from the 20s.
252 pages, 6x9 paperback. Illustrated. $16.95.
code: **MCOM**

ANCIENT TONGA
& THE LOST CITY OF MU'A
by David Hatcher Childress

INCLUDING SAMOA, FIJI AND RAROTONGA

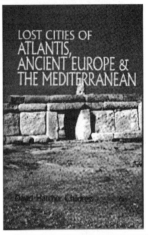

LOST CITIES OF ATLANTIS, ANCIENT EUROPE & THE MEDITERRANEAN

David Hatcher Childress

MYSTERY CITIES OF THE MAYA
by Thomas Gann

Archaeology and Adventure in Central America!
Mystic Travellers Series

Adventures Unlimited Press
One Adventure Place
Kempton, Illinois
60946

24 Hour Telephone
Order Line
815 253 6390
24 Hour Fax Order Line
815 253 6300
EMail orders
adventures_unlimited
@mcimail.com

One Adventure Place
P.O. Box 74
Kempton, Illinois 60946
United States of America
Tel.: 815-253-6390 • Fax: 815-253-6300
Email: aup@azstarnet.com
http://www.azstarnet.com/~aup

ORDERING INSTRUCTIONS

➤ Remit by USD$ Check or Money Order
➤ Credit Cards: Visa, MasterCard, Discovery, &
American Express Accepted
➤ Call ♦ Fax ♦ Email Any Time

SHIPPING CHARGES

United States

➤ Postal Book Rate { **$2.00 First Item** **50¢ Each Additional Item** }
➤ Priority Mail { **$3.50 First Item** **$1.50 Each Additional Item** }
➤ UPS { **$3.50 First Item** **$1.00 Each Additional Item** }
  NOTE: UPS Delivery Available to Mainland USA Only

Canada

➤ Postal Book Rate { **$3.00 First Item** **$1.00 Each Additional Item** }
➤ Postal Air Mail { **$4.00 First Item** **$2.00 Each Additional Item** }
➤ Personal Checks or Bank Drafts MUST BE
USD$ and Drawn on a US Bank
➤ Canadian Postal Money Orders OK
➤ Payment MUST BE USD$

All Other Countries

➤ Surface Delivery { **$5.00 First Item** **$2.00 Each Additional Item** }
➤ Postal Air Mail { **$10.00 First Item** **$8.00 Each Additional Item** }
➤ Payment MUST BE USD$
➤ Checks MUST BE USD$ and
Drawn on a US Bank
➤ Add $5.00 for Air Mail Subscription to
Future *Adventures Unlimited* Catalogs

SPECIAL NOTES

➤ RETAILERS: Standard Discounts Available
➤ BACKORDERS: We Backorder all Out-of-
Stock Items Unless Otherwise Requested
➤ PRO FORMA INVOICES: Available on Request
➤ VIDEOS: NTSC Mode Only
  PAL & SECAM Mode Videos Are Not Available

European Office:
Adventures Unlimited, PO Box 372,
Dronten, 8250 AJ, The Netherlands
South Pacific Office
Adventures Unlimited NZ
221 Symonds Sreet Box 8199
Auckland, New Zealnd

Please check: ☑

☐ This is my first order   ☐ I have ordered before   ☐ This is a new address

Name			
Address			
City			
State/Province		Postal Code	
Country			
Phone day	Evening		
Fax			

Item Code	Item Description	Price	Qty	Total

Please check: ☑

☐ Postal-Surface
☐ Postal-Air Mail
   (Priority in USA)
☐ UPS
   (Mainland USA only)

Subtotal ➤	
Less Discount-10% for 3 or more items ➤	
Balance ➤	
Illinois Residents 7% Sales Tax ➤	
Previous Credit ➤	
Shipping ➤	
Total (check/MO in USD$ only) ➤	

☐ Visa/MasterCard/Discover/Amex

Card Number

Expiration Date

10% Discount When You Order 3 or More Items!

Comments & Suggestions	Share Our Catalog with a Friend